The SWORD'S CHOICE III

The Citrine Earthquake

The SWORD'S CHOICE III

— The Citrine Earthquake —

I.M. REDWRIGHT

To mom and dad.

And, as always, thanks to those of you who read my stories.

Content

Where were we? 15

Prologue 17

1. Border 25

2. Home, bitter home 35

3. A stupid clause 41

4. A classical man 47

5. Tradition 53

6. Battle front 63

7. Empty nest 73

8. A complicated step 83

9. A not so golden tower 87

10. Palace affairs 93

11. Remnants of war 99

12. A second chance 103

13. Unexpected Course 107

14. The best unexpected visit 113

15. Views to the past 121

16. Sword in the mud 127

17. Family duty 139

18. Proof 143

19. Faith above all else 151

20. Making sense 159

21. Eternal glory 165

22. Comrades 171

23. A death request 177

24. Secrets 185

25. A change of plans 191

26. In the name of Aqua Deus 193

27. Wedding.. 197

28. Promise to a traitor 209

29. In the hands of fortune 215

30. Crucial disclosure 221

31. Family reunion.. 225

32. Harsh reality 231

33. An unexpected gift... 239

34. No alternative 245

35. Conflict of interest 249

36. A slight suspicion 257

37. Treacherous rat 263

38. A dream put to the test 267

39. Fidelity.. 275

40. Tirhan Territory 281

41. Witnesses to a gift... 287

42. Redemption.. 295

43. For Gelegen 301

44. Living in the moment... 307

45. As soon as possible 313

46. Another route 319

47. Challenge 325

48. Straight to her jaws.. 333

49. Awakening the storm 337

50. Unforgivable rudeness 343

51. Fire and Scales... 349

52. Decisive battle.. 357

53. An eye for an eye 367

54. Unthinkable.. 373

55. An impossible scenario...................................... 375

56. Royal Favor.. 381

57. Lacrima... 393

58. Legend 397

Thank you for reading the third book of The Sword's Choice!................... 405

The Sword's Choice Characters 407

The Aertians, shrewd and indecisive, ruled by those able to hear things others can't.

The Fireos, passionate and violent, ruled by the chosen phoenix when the sky turns red.

The Aquos, smart and reflective, a queendom controlled by the royal Dajalam family.

The Tirhans, calm and kind-hearted, when the mighty flower blossoms a new ruler rises.

Four nations. Living in a perpetual state known as *Equilibrium*. A perfect harmony. A supposed one.

Where were we?

It may have been some time since you read *The Emerald Storm* (the second book of *The Sword's Choice* series), so here's a little reminder of how things turned out. Also, **at the end of the book, you will find a summary of the most relevant characters we have met so far,** broken down by kingdoms.

Noakh had to scour the entire realm of Tir Torrent in search of his fellow travelers. The Kingdom of Earth promised to be a peaceful territory, but it turned out to be a place plagued by people blinded by the fanatical words of the White Raven, a sage who blamed the Aquos for all the hardships befalling the Tirhan. Because of this, the young Fireo had to hurry and make an alliance with a group of apparent vigilantes in order to find his friends as soon as possible and make sure that they did not die in one of the many torture settlements for unickeys. His quest could not have been more eventful: he was betrayed by his new allies, he freed the Dragon Queen Gurandel, who swore revenge on those who imprisoned her, confronted Princess Vienne; and, to top it off, entered into combat against the Daikan Tirhan to unleash the power of his fire sword and give a well-deserved rest to Burum Babar, now succeeded by his granddaughter, Arbilla.

Things were not easy for Vienne either. She had the mission of hunting down the fearsome enemy capable of defeating Gant and, to do so, she had to learn to invoke the powers of her sword Crystaline. Fulfilling this task would not have been possible without the unconditional help of Alvia, Gelegen and, of course, the little dog Zyrah, with whom she has developed a special bond. On her way, she realized how complicated the world could be, discovered the truth of the reason for the war against the Fireos, and formed a friendship with Noakh, whom she had been tasked to kill. Her journey ended with the

15

revelation of a group of mermaids, creatures she believed to be mythological, who urged her to release the storm.

The stability of Alomenta hangs in the balance. The Aquo troops, led by Queen Graglia, are camped in the west, ready to face King Wulkan and his Fireo army.

On the other side of the world, the Tower of Concord, where the sacred Aertian sword, Tizai, was kept, was destroyed by the Sons of the Church as a result of a plan hatched by Princess Aienne. Now the legendary weapon that protects Aere Tine is unaccounted for...

Prologue

There is an expression often used by Aertian troubadours: music knows no walls, no cells, no borders. And it is said that both the wisest, and the most foolish of Aere Tine know that music is the best way for a message to penetrate deep into the people.

The royal hall of celebration was spacious; a circular, unfurnished room whose grayish walls were covered with scores of the most beautiful and epic compositions, replicas of the originals that were archived in the Cloister, where the representatives of this organization would make sure that the music would live forever. Although fewer in number, that peculiar decoration was accompanied by multiple instruments; lutes and other instruments that had once belonged to some of the most famous troubadours of Aere Tine and that would be priceless to the most ambitious collectors. One of the highlights was a lute belonging to Yurula, the most acclaimed singer-songwriter ever known in Aere Tine, a living legend who flooded the streets of this kingdom, now divided in two, with music.

That night, on the other hand, that hall that had hosted such magnificent parties full of marvelous songs was in absolute silence. It was no time for celebrations. Aere Tine was in pure chaos.

Queen Zarta was lying on numerous yellow cushions whose borders were adorned with vivid vermilion-red details. She felt the light swaying of the wind, the result of the hard work of one of her servants fanning her, a second servant ran a silver comb with extreme care through her unruly long curly scarlet hair, while a third one took great care to offer her juicy black grapes, already duly peeled and seedless, with a calculated cadence.

It was a ritual of rest, feeling the wind on her face as her mind focused on finding a solution to the only issue that mattered at that

17

moment: the sacred sword Tizai had disappeared as a consequence of the destruction of the Tower of Concord.

Whole platoons had been tirelessly searching for it, day and night. However, in vain, no trace of the sword, it was as if it had vanished completely.

At the time, The Tower of Concord had sounded like an ideal solution. To place the sword in neutral territory, a symbol of the unity of Aere Tine despite having split the kingdom in two, Aere Tine South, run by her, Queen Zarta; Aere Tine North, led by her twin brother, King Lieri. Now, after the incident in the tower, Zarta could not help but wonder if they could have avoided it, had they guarded the sacred sword in a less vulnerable place. Unfortunately, in the winds of the past those worries were of no use; she had to focus on the present.

Just at that moment, the large cream-colored door of the royal hall opened, and behind it appeared a young woman in lavish yellowish robes, a wide purple belt and a reddish hat with a thin pink feather. A troubadour. She carried a lute in one hand and a rolled parchment in the other. The door closed behind her. She did not move an inch, waiting for the queen, or one of her maids, to make any gesture that would authorize her to approach.

Zarta watched the slender young woman, reveling in her restlessness. From a distance, she could perceive how extremely nervous she was, trying not to move from her place. First, she glanced in all directions, and then lowered her gaze, as if she was reminding herself to be calm if she wanted her singing to flow with the appropriate tone. The monarch felt some sympathy for the young woman, wasn't it understandable for the troubadour to experience such excitement? After all, she was standing before a queen, just moments away from having the great honor of playing for royalty itself.

She made a graceful gesture with her hand, a motion sufficient to get the troubadour to nod twice and then move toward where Zarta rested. The young woman's enthusiastic steps in her high boots echoed through the room as she advanced through the room at a more frantic pace than protocol would approve of. She stopped in her tracks, maintaining a prudent distance from where the queen and her maids were standing.

The troubadour brought one hand to her face: her index finger placed on her thick lower lip, her thumb caressing her earlobe adorned with two bluish metal rings. She then extended her hand forward, performing the proper Aertian salute.

18

"Your majesty," she began, with a hint of hesitation in her voice, "your brother, King Lieri, sends you this composition," she indicated, slightly raising the hand in which she carried the scroll, "it will be my honor to perform it for you." She added, now raising the arm with which she held her lute.

"Your name?" Queen Zarta requested.

"Josia of Uriven."

Zarta merely nodded. Then her dandelion eyes fell on the maid responsible for serving her the grapes. She quickly got the message, surreptitiously moving around the room, then offered a lectern and a stool to the troubadour.

The artist nodded in thanks to the servant. Then, she sat down on the wooden seat and unwrapped the score slowly, resting it on the music stand with great care. She then placed the lute on her legs, placing her long fingers on the strings as she took a deep breath before beginning her performance.

The silence of the room was interrupted by a beautiful melody.

The queen closed her eyes as the young woman began to play. The first two notes were enough to appreciate that the artist played the stringed instrument with great grace. It was a beautiful, jovial melody, evoking images of a sunny meadow where dewdrops sparkle as they toast in the first rays of sunlight.

Soon the sweet composition was accompanied by a candid voice. Powerful, full of feeling and passion. Voice and music became one, a combination so harmonious and magical that the queen was captivated by the performance.

The lyrics were equally moving. That song spoke of how the goddess Shiana had put the kingdom of Aere Tine to the test. And how Aertians had to fight together, as a united people, to find the sword Tizai.

Undoubtedly, the loss of the sacred sword had inspired the countless artists that populated the Kingdom of Air. However, for Queen Zarta, such repetitive subject matter was certainly beginning to annoy her.

The troubadour was reaching the second part of the composition. Zarta tuned her ear, it was crucial to capture precisely the note that was about to take center stage in the musical piece.

The young artist continued to offer her art, immersed in an ecstasy of musicality. Suddenly, her lute offered a most dissonant sound,

19

completely ruining the song, shattering the magical moment in which she had immersed the room with her delightful interpretation.

The queen's maids let out an almost unison shout of surprise, ceasing outright in their respective tasks of fanning and combing her hair. At that moment, Zarta opened her eyes. The now terrified troubadour's gaze darted between the queen and the sheet music with her mouth open, showing utter dread in her teary honey-colored eyes.

She had ruined that piece of music, and any musician knew the cost of such a dreadful act.

"Mercy, my queen! The sheet music is wrong!" She managed to say between sobs, standing up so abruptly that her lute fell to the floor. "I have played the composition your brother sent you accurately!" she pointed to the sheet music, still sitting on the music stand, "see for yourself." She added, in the form of a prayer.

The monarch did not answer. She simply rose from her cushions and approached her. The queen's arms gently and firmly encircled the troubadour, she was slow to respond, as if she could not believe the great act of compassion she was being a part of. Zarta could feel the young woman's body shaking, the troubadour's tears soaking the fragile fabric of her precious white dress.

"Truly you are most kind, my queen," she thanked between sobs, "your generosity knows no bounds..."

Her words were cut off by a muffled sound. Her eyes widened as she fell to her knees on the ground. Watching as the dagger that had pierced her stomach soaked her yellowish clothes in blood.

She tried desperately to appeal for help to the maidservants with her eyes, then to the queen herself, as if begging for mercy. However, all those present there remained motionless, as if they were simply witnessing a performance in a play.

Queen Zarta's gaze shifted to the walls of the room, ignoring the young woman who was bleeding to death at her feet. One of the maids stepped forward, took the score from the music stand and bent down to pick up the lute from the floor.

The maid responsible for combing her hair hurried to take a quill, dip it in a pot of ink and write the troubadour's name at the bottom of the score. *Josia of Uriven*, read Queen Zarta as the maid sprinkled some powder to dry the ink. She found a strange pleasure in watching her maid write the names of the troubadours in her clear and stylish handwriting.

"In that corner, it will fit perfectly," the queen indicated pointing to a part of the wall, moments later she walked towards the doors of the room, trying to remember the musical note that had ruined the beautiful song.

* * *

Zarta dismounted from her prized silver-backed mare, dressed in a discreet dark maroon hood. It had been a short ride and, in spite of this, her lower back ached terribly, an ailment that had plagued her ever since she had first ridden a horse so long ago.

She remembered the troubadour and the song she had played. *A gift from your brother*, she had said moments before playing it. The troubadour had had the audacity to point out that it had not been her mistake, but that it was the sheet music that was wrong. And she was absolutely right.

She glanced ahead. The moon was shining so brightly that night that she could see with great clarity. The place was quiet and deserted. She mentally reviewed the song, focusing on the note that ruined the piece of music, an *A minor*. She was not in the wrong place.

It was a coded message, one that she and her brother had crafted when they were just kids, and that no one but them knew about. A secure and unique method of communication for which they only had to pay with the lives of an enthusiastic troubadour. A more than fair price to guarantee the safety and privacy of both.

Their method of secret communication was certainly simple: in each musical composition they sent to each other, they always included a note that did not fit in the second part of the composition, thus completely ruining the song. This out-of-place note corresponded to a specific meeting place they had predetermined. Additionally, the degree of the wrong note, major or minor, indicated the timing of the meeting: the same night for minor, or dawn the day after receiving the piece for major.

With that coded message with an *A minor*, her brother had indicated that they were to meet in the black swamp at dusk. Her nose wrinkled as her brand-new leather boots sank slightly into a muddy patch she hadn't seen. The place smelled like rotten eggs.

21

She tied her mare to a tree with gray bark, and took two steps. She then whistled four times, her sounds short and repetitive.

"At last!" Her brother Lieri said, appearing from behind a tree, "what took you so long?"

Lieri walked up to her, giving her two affectionate kisses on the right cheek, the way Aertians greeted each other warmly.

The resemblance between the two was extraordinary; beyond the fact that Zarta's hair was long and Lieri's was limited to a rebellious fringe, the only noticeable difference was a small notch on his lower lip, a consequence of having fallen from the top of a cupboard while both were coordinating to try to get some cookies when they were children. For added similarity, they both had an identical scar in the middle of their already slightly wrinkled foreheads.

"Calm down, brother; if you wanted me to arrive sooner, you wouldn't have arranged the meeting in this stinking, remote place..."

"Any news?" He said anxiously, "have your soldiers found the sword?"

Zarta shook her head. "No sign of Tizai..."

"Mine don't manage to find it either. Oh, Zarta, what are we going to do? Without the sword, Aere Tine is as unprotected as you and I are!"

"First of all, you're going to calm down."

"Calm down? Don't you realize the situation? The sword is gone! Our kingdoms couldn't be more vulnerable right now!"

"And, despite that, we have neither been attacked nor received a declaration of war," Zarta reminded him, "that means we are not in danger."

"But it could be the beginning of a plan of attack," he said, exalted. "If it were I who had concocted such a ruse, right now I would be directing my troops to..."

Zarta approached her brother, brushed aside his long locks, and gently rested her forehead on Lieri's in such a way that both scars joined. This posture conveyed immense peace to both, probably because they had lain joined at the head during gestation. Many Aertian theologians believed that precisely this unique union was the reason why both had been chosen by Tizai to rule, thus dividing the Kingdom of Air in two.

The queen remained in that posture, rocking slightly. She began to sing, the same song her late father used to sing to them when they were lying down and ready to sleep.

"Run... run like the wind..."

22

The sweet song began. With each verse she could notice how her brother was gradually calming down.

"Well," she continued once the song ended, "don't worry about the sword, brother, we'll find Tizai sooner or later. The important thing is to be prepared in the face of whoever the enemy is that attacked us."

Lieri frowned. "Some brainless courtier suggested that it had been you, that you had orchestrated the fall of the Tower of Concord to get your hands on the sword... but don't worry, sister, I've made sure that idiot won't try to convince me with such crude nonsense again." He nodded as he brought his index finger to one end of his neck and moved it quickly to the other side.

"I don't suspect you in the least either, brother." She answered him with a smile.

And it was true, if there was someone she could trust in that ruthless and selfish world in which they had to live was Lieri. He wasn't just her twin brother, but he also shared a special bond with her: they were born conjoined at the head. A miracle they had survived and that, in addition to an identical scar, had caused them to always feel a special connection, a unique fraternal love that could withstand anything, and the incident in the Tower of Concord was not going to change that.

"Brother, let's not lose our cool; we have to get Tizai back as soon as possible. That's why we have to call on all our strength..." Zarta urged him, trying to think. "The sword could be anywhere; we would need to combine the forces of our armies day and night to find it."

"Yes, but it could take years. There must be another way." Lieri replied frustrated. "Some way that won't put us at risk by devoting our armies in the search for Tizai..."

Zarta sighed. That trait was the only one she didn't like about her brother, he overthought things too much. He was always looking for the most ingenious way to proceed before any action, excessive reflections that delayed what for her was the most obvious and practical solution, to look for the sword in every hidden place of Aere Tine day and night.

"Not to mention that employing all our military force in the work of finding Tizai would mean leaving our borders defenseless." Lieri continued his reflection, "something unthinkable as long as we do not know who caused that attack on the Tower of Concord."

"It has to be the Fireos, who else?" Zarta indicated, shaking her head.

Lieri nodded. "Of course, I had also thought that they would be the culprits. My investigators have concluded that the destruction of the tower was caused by using vulcanite, the reddish mineral that abounds

23

in Fireo lands. Such a detail no doubt leads us to believe that they are the prime suspects, but why on earth attack us just at this time?" He considered, shrugging. "My spies have informed me that Fireo troops are moving toward their borders with the Queendom of Water, yet another war between the two kingdoms. And if war against the Aquos is imminent, why would Firia provoke our ire and thus risk being attacked from a second flank? It makes no sense at all."

"Don't give it so much thought, brother," Zarta tried to stop him in his musings, "the Fireos are as stupid as they are violent. There's no further explanation."

Just then, she could feel her brother's eyes light up. Some idea had sprouted in his mind.

"What if we didn't have to employ our armies to find the sword?" He proposed. "Why not turn to our people for such a task?"

Zarta pondered such an option for a moment, then shook her head. "It's a good idea, but I don't think it would work. The citizens wouldn't carry out the search with the same intensity as a trained and paid army would." She decided.

"It seems to me that you underestimate our people, dear sister, we need only offer in return a sufficiently succulent reward that there is not a single man or woman who would not be captivated to join the quest." He said raising an eyebrow and smiling mischievously at her.

Zarta looked at him, puzzled, "gold and land?" She tried to guess.

Lieri shook his head.

"A much, much better reward, something they have never seen but will undoubtedly desire," Lieri paused for effect, "a Royal Favor."

Zarta's eyes widened. "You really are a genius, brother."

1. Border

The silvery fish swam peacefully, trying to find food in the reeds that inhabited the shallow waters of the crystal-clear stream. Suddenly, a face with brown eyes and black hair appeared reflected on the surface; it was time to swim for life.

The Fireo observed his reflection, first sliding his hands over his eyebrows, and then through his now notably long hair. He looked from one profile, then another, as if contemplating his face for the first time.

A resounding *splash* erased his image, something had disturbed the surface of the waters completely. Hilzen stood in the middle of the stream, head down, legs and arms drenched and the pendant that housed the drawing of his daughter swaying from side to side. The devout Aquo sighed deeply.

"You know, Noakh, if instead of admiring yourself so much you would cooperate a little, we would have had a delicious fish dinner today."

"I still look incredibly weird," he replied, turning to look at himself in the now once again calm waters. His hair and eyebrows had returned to their natural black color—a shade he oddly never sported. He'd always dyed his hair blonde, ever since he could remember, to avoid drawing undue attention in the Aquadom. He continued to observe himself, his hand now bent on straightening his bangs, "besides, I told Halftal to keep my hair as short as possible, why does it look so patchy?"

"You look like a Fireo," Hilzen replied, standing up and emerging from the waters, "horrible, that is." He punctuated.

Noakh smiled. He glanced back at his friend, his hair and beard now the same blond color as the day they had met.

"You looked good with brown hair; I don't understand why you went back to your original shade."

The devout Aquo grimaced. "If I'm going to be judged anyway, at least let it be by my real hair color." He said, nodding proudly.

"Quite right," Noakh nodded, understanding his friend's motives. Hilzen had been mistaken for a unickey after dyeing his hair brown and, as a result, had been sold into slavery. It was understandable that he would be hesitant to resort to the same ploy to wander into Aertian territory. "Besides, reddish hair would look horrible on you." He added, letting out a chuckle as he imagined his friend with a cherry-red hair and beard.

Noakh glanced at the water again, leaned a little closer and extended his arm, reaching his hand into the cold water so he could take a drink. He felt really good, full of vitality, and without any pain in his body. He had spent several weeks unconscious after his fight with Burum Babar. His body had finally rested as much as it had not been able to while he was urgently trying to find his friends alive throughout the Tirhan kingdom.

They had recently entered Aere Tine, the Kingdom of Air, and were on their way to the border town of Tuens Laya to reunite with Dabayl. Their yellow-eyed friend had left weeks before, accompanying Halftal, who wanted to visit the city of Stirrup, renowned as the cradle of music.

Cold droplets began to fall on his face; a light, almost imperceptible rain had started. For some reason, those droplets led him to think of her. "Do you think we'll ever see her again?"

"Who?"

"Vienne, of course."

Hilzen shook his head disapprovingly.

"What?" Noakh said defensively, "I'd just like to know how she's doing."

"Are you ready to resume our path?" Hilzen asked, ignoring his concerns.

Rising to his feet, Noakh couldn't grasp his friend's irritation over his interest in the princess. She was a nice and pleasant young woman he had connected with, was it so wrong to want to know about her whereabouts? In any case, it seemed he had no way of knowing how she would fare, so he could only wish that their paths would cross sooner or later.

26

He glanced at his belt. His steel sword and Distra hung from it, "ready."

They began their march. The welcoming Aertian landscape was nothing short of captivating. Trees with off-white bark had crowns full of russet-colored leaves. Playful squirrels, boasting mahogany fur and unusually large tails, jumped energetically from one branch to another —a sight Noakh had never witnessed before. A strong breeze filled his lungs with the smell of damp moss as the sun broke through thick clouds.

Something told him they were going to be lucky. His intuition dictated that their passage through the Kingdom of Air was going to be much smoother than their bumpy ride on Tir Torrent and the Aquadom.

They turned down a path and came face to face with a guardhouse. A palisade blocked part of the path, allowing access only from two sides, each guarded by a soldier, next to which were low tables. A third soldier was positioned right in the middle, in front of the palisade. The latter was making a gesture with his finger, urging them to approach.

Chest protected by plate, longbow in hand and uniform half in dark yellow tone half in purple, Noakh observed, *it must be the uniform of the Southern Kingdom*, he assumed.

Having grown up in the Queendom of Water, he knew very little about Aere Tine being such a remote territory. However, he did know one thing. Aere Tine was ruled by twin siblings, consequently, that domain had been split in half.

Noakh and Hilzen, following the instructions of the apparent platoon captain, began to walk resignedly toward the captain of that platoon. Judging by Hilzen's pale and barely blinking face, he seemed as anxious as him.

It was a strange feeling. They had nothing to hide, or rather, nothing to hide that had anything to do with the Aertians. Nor had they committed any act they regretted. And all this did not prevent them from feeling absurdly nervous in the presence of authority.

Finally, the captain motioned for them to stop with his hand. His gait was peculiar, to say the least. He swung his left arm with every step as any person would, but his right arm remained fixed, glued to his body.

"Good morning, gentlemen," he said, greeting them as he stood before them, his steady voice breaking through an incredibly dense and manicured square beard as reddish as his hair.

Noakh was ready for the obvious question: why are an Aquo and a Fireo traveling together? It was an understandable concern, given the well-known fact that both peoples harbored a mutual and ancestral bitter hatred. This was compounded by the recent revelation from Vienne that both kingdoms were once again at war.

Without another word, the captain stood a short distance from Hilzen. He inspected him closely. "Come in with my comrade," he said finally, pointing with a gloved thumb at one of the two soldiers at his back.

As Hilzen obeyed his instructions, the captain moved laterally, taking a wide step, now standing in front of Noakh. The young Fireo felt his piercing yellow eyes boring into him, as if they were trying to read his mind. He was so close that he could smell a sour odor of sweat. The man's gaze swept up and down his face, lingering first on his hair, then on his brown eyes, before finally lowering his gaze and focusing on his swords.

I wonder what disturbed him the most, he said to himself.

"Come in with my other companion," he instructed, stepping aside. Noakh did not overlook the fact that, with him, he had taken more time in his inspection than with Hilzen. He heeded the orders and walked until he approached the Aertian soldier assigned to him by the captain.

"Deposit all your belongings on the table if you would be so kind, sir." The soldier said.

Noakh obeyed. He took off his belt, leaving it and his swords on the table. Then he reached into his pockets and took out a couple of white strawberries he had picked from a tree not long ago and kept as a snack. Just as he was about to say that was all he had; he remembered the pendant. He pulled out the holy water pendant from his neck. Hilzen had told him it was a gift from Gelegen, an apology for killing Cervan and his horse. After laying the pendant on the table, he nodded to the soldier.

"I will now proceed to inspect you." He informed Noakh, standing behind him, "extend your arms and legs, if you would be so kind."

As if I have a choice, Noakh thought, complying with the request. The soldier's hands started with his boots, then moved to his pants, and then to his lower back and buttocks.

As the man's hands methodically searched him, he glanced over at Hilzen, who was in the same process of inspection. He spotted the objects on his table, a crossbow, the pendant he so adored that

28

contained his daughter's drawing of his family, a sachet of coins that Gond had kindly given them and... a sapphire. Noakh frowned, where had Hilzen gotten a sapphire and why hadn't he told him about it? Then he noticed a detail, emeralds produced light, it stood to reason that sapphires were good for something, but for what?

"Clean, you may collect your things, sir."

Noakh nodded, starting to put on his belt. Ready to go.

"Name and reason for your journey, sir?" The soldier asked before Noakh could even make a feint of taking a step. The soldier had picked up a piece of parchment that he rested on a piece of wood as a stand and an orange quill.

Noakh opened his mouth, instinctively ready to tell any lie. However, his eyes shifted back to Hilzen.

If our testimony is too different from each other we will arouse suspicion and be arrested, he concluded. He glanced at his friend, he was also being interrogated, and could not hear what he was saying. Those soldiers had been intrepid enough to place them both at a safe distance, so that they could not know each other's answers to their questions.

An ingenious tactic on their part, yet terribly problematic for us, Noakh thought.

"Noakh Lumiorel," he revealed to the soldier. His last name was his father's name ending in *rel*, the word in Flumio meaning *son of* according to what little he knew of the Aquo language. "We just came to see the kingdom and visit our friend Dabayl, I don't think you know her." As he finished speaking, he realized the absurdity of his answer, of course he wasn't going to know her. Why was he so nervous if he had done absolutely nothing?

The soldier nodded, jotting on his parchment.

"Do you plan to undermine the integrity of the Kingdom of Aere Tine South?"

Noakh frowned at such an unexpected question. "Of course not," he replied.

He was about to ask him the purpose of such a question, being obvious that no one with such intentions was going to be honest in his answer, however, he decided it was better to limit himself to answering.

"Do you intend to make an attempt on Queen Zarta's life?"

"No." He replied, unable to help squinting.

"Is your stay in Aere Tine South governed according to the codes of conduct stipulated by the Wind Council and will you allow the Maiden of the Bell to guide you in your death?"

Noakh had to summon all his restraint to prevent himself from grimacing. He had no idea who this maiden was, just as he had no knowledge of such an institution.

"It is," he confirmed, assuming it was the answer that was going to cause him the least trouble.

"All right," the soldier replied, looking away from the document, "in the name of Queen Zarta, we welcome you to the Kingdom of Aere Tine South, enjoy your stay and may the Maiden of the Bell guide you with her music on your darkest nights."

"That's very kind of you." Noakh replied picking up his stuff and continuing on his way.

He still couldn't believe those questions; did they expect someone who was going to commit a crime to confess on the spot?

Hilzen, ended up just a moment later, joining him.

"You don't intend to attempt against Aere Tine either, do you?" Hilzen said, elbowing him jocularly, as they resumed their march. "I wonder how they would react if they knew they had just allowed to pass the soon to be king of the Fireos." He added, amused.

* * *

Both of them panted heavily. The ascent to the village of Tuens Laya was both steep and treacherously slippery. The terrain now was flattening out, the giant blades of a mill stood out against the endless wheat field in the distance and the many houses with triangular-shaped roofs that scattered until they disappeared into the horizon.

Not far in the distance rose a dark gray stone wall from which only one building protruded, an elongated, slender, circular stone tower that, at least from a distance, looked incredibly narrow.

"Are... you... sure... we're in Tuens Laya?" Noakh questioned, speaking haltingly from shortness of breath. His feet ached after all that walking, he lay down on the ground and pulled off his boots and socks. "Much better." He said breathing in relief as he felt the breeze on his bruised toes.

Hilzen surveyed the ramparts, one hand on his belt, while his chest heaved with each breath. He looked towards the building. "The

30

regional grain tower is tall and slender, there is no other like it, so it will especially catch your eye, you can't miss it unless you go blind," Hilzen said, mimicking Dabayl's aggressive tone, "it is here." He then pointed towards a path that wound its way through the grass, leading to an arch in the wall.

Hilzen frowned, "what's that?"

They both looked at the strange figure. He walked slowly, each step producing a *clunk* as the metal of his attire caught and reflected the intense rays of sunlight.

A knight wearing his radiant armor, Noakh thought at first, then leaned forward, still sitting on the ground. On closer inspection, that was not armor at all.

His head was covered by a small pot, on his chest and back were strapped what looked like cooking trays; his thighs, on the other hand, were protected by rows of shiny objects that, given the distance, Noakh guessed must be knives and forks.

Hilzen grimaced in puzzlement and Noakh shrugged his shoulders; both looked at each other dumbfounded. Both were silent, as if hypnotized, just watching the slow but steady pace of the man and his peculiar dress.

"Looks like he's heading towards town," Noakh finally said once that abnormal armored man was moving away. He got up and started walking toward the road.

Hilzen mimicked him, dusting his pants, then shook his head, "no matter the realm, this boy just won't stop meddling." He scoffed, following him.

They arrived at the entrance to the village, guarded by two soldiers carrying halberds, a man and a woman with very curly hair, both located under the arch that led to the village. When they saw them, they stood up, one of them ordered them to stop.

"Names?"

Noakh and Hilzen introduced themselves. The woman jotted down some information on a list. *Surely the awkward and absurd questions will start again*, he guessed.

Instead, the man nodded to them that they could pass. In the background they heard some clapping, were they celebrating something in that village?

At the end of that long street, they saw the metal-clad man again. Perhaps it was his impression from afar, but were those people not

31

clapping their hands for that man armed with such peculiar armor? Hilzen and Noakh exchanged a fleeting look of confusion.

On the sides of that road were white stone houses adorned with large windows. In all of them hung various utensils that swayed in the gentle wind, and on these utensils rested several birds of various colors. Although Noakh did not know the reason for those utensils, he was sure that it must have some religious or cultural reason, for what little he knew, in Aere Tine the goddess of the wind was worshiped, he raised his eyebrows, of all the gods of the four kingdoms she was the only one whose name he did not know.

In front of the doorways of these houses were several families seated on esparto grass chairs. They ceased their clapping as they passed by; the reddish hair of those Aertian villagers shining in the strong sunlight. Their eyes in various shades of yellow seemed to look at them with such stupefaction that it was evident that the smiles on their lips were not entirely sincere.

"What on earth is going on in this place?" He said quietly to Hilzen, who was walking beside him. "Why are they applauding that tin man, is he part of some strange ritual?"

"I'm almost more surprised that we haven't had any problems with any of the guards we've come across."

Noakh nodded, *absolutely right*. He looked in both directions, no sign of the tin man. Then he heard the ruckus.

In front of a building larger than the houses they had come across, several men and women sat at a long table, raising their glasses, uttered a word Noakh did not understand, and then clinked them together so vigorously that beer splashed in every possible direction, soaking their sandwiches, which were so large that his mouth watered.

"You know, Hilzen," Noakh began, smiling. "Maybe we should go into the tavern to find out how things work around here."

"At last, you speak wisely," replied his friend, fixing his eyes equally on those appetizing morsels.

They approached the door to enter the establishment, but Noakh stopped in confusion at the entrance. There was no door, but a curtain of bluish cloth that he could easily push aside with his hand.

"I wonder what measures they will take to ensure there are no break-ins at night."

The smell of the establishment was strong, the light came in through the dirty windows. The truth was that the interior of the tavern was not much different from those he had visited in the rest of the kingdoms.

32

Several tables were occupied by jovial customers who were enjoying some huge, succulent sandwiches, accompanied by generous salads in the middle, and plenty to drink.

Behind the bar stood a titanic-looking man, his shoulders and trapezius were such that he appeared to have no neck.

"Beer?" Asked Hilzen, tilting his head comically, unsure if it was customary to consume such a drink in that realm, or perhaps it was known by a different name entirely? He hastily pulled out five silver coins, making it clear that they had money to spare for their consumption.

The tavern keeper nodded, quickly grabbing all the coins, to the surprise of Noakh and Hilzen, who were shocked at the high cost. Such an amount could have paid for an entire afternoon of drinking in the Queendom of Water.

"You're coming for the anniversary, aren't you? Or are you going in search of the Royal Favor?" He asked them in a powerful voice as he opened an almost black wooden barrel and poured the beer into the most generous wooden tankards Noakh had ever seen.

Hilzen and Noakh exchanged glances again, obviously they weren't there for either, although, thinking about it, maybe it was better to say they were?

"Oh, yes," Hilzen replied in a tone that sounded the least bit convincing to Noakh. "Because of the anniversary thing."

The tavern keeper nodded again, placed the two jugs on the dark wooden bar, then placed two small glass cups with two fingers of a reddish drink next to each of them.

Noakh watched his glass cup, puzzled, grasped it between his index finger and thumb, and tilted it slightly. He brought it to his nose and began to sniff it.

"Isn't it blood?" He asked, grimacing in confusion at the tavern keeper.

"Good blood," he pointed out, resting his giant hands on the bar. "The best in the whole county." He added proudly. "Come on, drink up." He then reached out for the small glass Noakh was holding, snatching it from him and then placing it on the beer nearest to the Fireo and dropping it.

The glass disappeared into the beer after a quick *blop*. The foam then turned an orange hue.

Hilzen shrugged, grabbed the other cup and likewise condemned it to drown in that brown sea. Then he grabbed both jugs and handed

33

one to Noakh, who accepted it, not without some reluctance at having such a peculiar and unpleasant garnish.

The tavern keeper filled a small glass with a blackish drink and raised it toward them. "Grimm Jala."

"Grimm Jala," Noakh and Hilzen repeated.

"No!" The tavern keeper said, gruffly, yet kindly, "Grimm Jo Ne, Grimm Jo Ne... enjoy it, enjoy it yourself." He translated for them.

"Grin yo me." Noakh tried to imitate him, though with a terrible accent.

They took a gulp. Noakh's drink made its way down his throat, burning, bitter and leaving an aftertaste in his mouth so harsh that he had to muster all his strength to avoid grimacing, for fear of offending the tavern keeper.

"Well, and what's being celebrated?" Hilzen asked, aware that there was no point in continuing to pretend.

"The anniversary, of course!" Said a woman with a dark complexion and bulging eyes at the table closest to the bar, turning around, "for the last ten years we have always celebrated this special day, the day of that brutal and bloody confrontation between the two factions of young men. Since then, this day is celebrated with applause and that epic combat is repeated."

"Two groups of young men who had a fierce fight? Is that what is being celebrated?" Noakh tried to understand.

"In a way, yes." Replied the tavern keeper, seemingly unconvinced at such a description. "Only that one of those sides is made up of a growing group year after year and... the other is always made up of just one stubby young man."

Hilzen whistled, impressed. "That youngster must be incredibly strong if he alone is able to stand up to a crowd."

The tavern keeper gave an intense laugh, "Strong? Far from it, he'll end up unconscious in the middle of the square like every year."

"What!" Noakh exclaimed in alarm. Suddenly all those insults he had received as a child for the color of his eyes, for being different, began to rekindle intensely. "You damned scum of a people!"

Noakh, filled with anger, suddenly lunged at one of the tables, extending an arm and knocking all the jugs to the floor with a loud clatter. He then stormed towards the door.

"And you guys are no better if you just celebrate and clap like idiots!" He chided them as he disappeared out the door.

2. Home, bitter home

The wood mermaid sang, equally bathed by the drops from the sea and the sky. The Merrybelle was forging ahead through the light rain, undeterred, in what seemed like a battle against the waters to prove that there was no ocean it could not conquer.

Vienne stood with her arms outstretched, trying not to lose her balance as she walked barefoot on the wet wood of the gunwale. She was staring blankly at the horizon, having a fixed point to look at helped her to stabilize herself and, incidentally, to reflect. On her outward journey to Tirhan territory, she had been dressed in light armor and comfortable clothing that would allow her to fight with ease; on her return, however, her attire was again a nice white linen dress whose cut, luckily for her training, only reached her knees. From her drastic change of attire, it might seem that the fight was over, but that was far from being the case. However, that fight was not going to be waged with a sword, but with words and power. And that was a battle for which Vienne was as unprepared as she was unwilling.

Perhaps that was the reason she was trying to distract her mind with these exercises, as if she was hoping that, regardless of how far the Merrybelle sailed, it would never reach port? Vienne knew she should be immensely happy to be home, but happiness was not exactly what she was feeling at the moment.

Her experience in the Kingdom of Earth was unforgettable; she had seen the world firsthand, experiencing both its endearing and cruel moments. Was that what life was all about—learning from hardship and smiling at the memory of the beautiful?

A feeling of sadness came over her—would there be any memorable moments from now on? It might seem a somewhat pessimistic view, however, Vienne had no doubt that her older sister had not been wasting her time. Katienne would have spread her ambitious claws

35

across the entire queendom, trying to grab as much influence as possible. As Vienne's feet touched solid ground everything would revolve around proving that she was not the weak young girl that practically the entire reign believed her to be. A power struggle against her ambitious older sister.

She glanced at her sash, where Crystaline rested—always at her side, just as her mother had taught her. *Perhaps showing my powers will be enough to make Katienne lose favor with the Church*, she felt a glimmer of hope, *yes, surely demonstrating my control over the sword's powers will be enough to make her step aside.*

It was the only thing she could hold on to.

Her sister enjoyed the support of the Congregation of the Church and, as if that were not enough, her courtship with the heir to the powerful and wealthy Delorange heir seemed to foresee that all the nobility would sooner or later be on her side, if they were not already.

So much support for her sister... Vienne, on the other hand, was alone.

She heard a light tread on the deck. The princess smiled, leaping up to land on the damp wood to greet her visitor.

"Not quite alone, right, Zyrah?" She said, bending down and nuzzling her head. A gesture the canine returned with a vigorous lick on her cheek. "Give me a paw," she commanded, Zyrah obeyed instantly, "roll across the deck," the animal ran her body along the damp wood, "very good!" she rewarded her, gently patting her back.

During the boat trip, she had practiced giving various instructions to the little dog, she was a most intelligent animal, though also somewhat stubborn. The absence of her master had been hard for the dog, but his absence had also served to bring her even closer to Vienne, who found Zyrah a pleasant companion.

It was true, she was not going to face her sister alone. Besides Zyrah, she also had the support of Gelegen, her Aunt Alvia and, of course, there was Aienne; how much he wanted to see her, hug her, ask her what she had been doing all that time and tell her about her adventures in Tir Torrent! She had to tell her so many things... especially about Noakh, the boy she had been entrusted to eliminate, and yet...

Noakh, will you be fine? Will you at least be alive?

Since the young Fireo had fought Burum Babar his whereabouts were a mystery to her; yet the little she knew of Noakh was enough for her to believe that he would have been able to survive such fierce combat. She had asked Gelegen for the favor of finding him, but she had yet to hear from the veteran.

She spotted a point in the distance, which, before even she could feel desolate about it, transformed into a harbor. The Merrybelle was unmoved by Vienne's anguish, continuing to ride the waves swiftly and steadily. Soon, the ship approached the Royal Harbor: white stone and gilded decorations—as pristine as one would expect the entrance to the sea, home of the Aqua Deus, to be.

The Merrybelle stopped gently. It had been tied to the dock. The princess felt a knot in her stomach, as if tied by that very rope.

"Are you ready, Vienne?" said her aunt, positioning herself behind her back.

No.

"Yes." She ended up saying, standing up and turning to her.

Alvia held out her arm, offering her a long juniper green cloak with a hood. The princess gladly accepted the garment, put it on, shading her face under the hood. *The fewer surprises on my arrival, the better*, she decided.

Her Aunt Alvia seemed to be in a better mood. She spoke to her more kindly and, even Vienne would say, with a certain respect. That did not detract from the fact that she seemed to have not quite forgiven her for leaving Gelegen behind because of her request. It would be some time before they heard from the veteran.

A tingle went through her stomach. She had asked Gelegen to give Noakh her sapphire, Vienne's sapphire, for communication. It had been a risky act. The sapphire linked to the one he had given Noakh was in her mother's hands, and what if Noakh had already spoken to her? It would be her mother who would hear the message, giving rise to countless uncomfortable questions. In any case, it all seemed to lead to the same conclusion, she was going to earn a reprimand for her actions. At least she hoped such a lecture would be worth it.

They began to descend the gangway. The princess was deeply grateful to the Aqua Deus that her voyage was unannounced, no one in the port was waiting for her. However, that did not detract from the fact that she did not feel thousands of eyes watching her on her descent, after all, the Merrybelle was probably the most popular vessel in the entire queendom. Likewise, her Aunt Alvia was a Knight of Water. She certainly wasn't the best company to go unnoticed....

"I'll see to it that we arrange for transportation." Her aunt told her.

The princess nodded. She followed the Knight of Water's path with her eyes, watching her as she walked away. On her way she noticed that her aunt stopped at a humble stall where a wooden figure of a mermaid was holding two scales. Vienne raised her eyebrows in surprise recognizing such a symbol, the place where Alvia had stopped belonged to a Gifter. It was an Aquo custom, many sailors liked to try their luck, they left their goods on land, in the hands of a Gifter, and signed a simple agreement: if they returned, they were to be returned the amount of money they had deposited in double, if they did not return, the Gifter kept the deposit. She was surprised that her aunt would participate in such a custom, however, she was happy for her, the Aqua Deus had blessed them with a prosperous return home and, as payment, she would receive double the amount she had deposited.

She glanced down at the white marble floor, noting with astonishment that she was alone.

"Zyrah?" She said quizzically.

She felt her heart skip a beat. Had the dog run away? Or, even worse, had she been kidnapped? She began to look from one side to the other. Sailors efficiently carrying nets, barrels piled up on the side near the ship they were to be loaded onto, people lining up to get on a nice sailboat whose sails looked silvery... no sign of the dog.

Suddenly, she heard a high-pitched, annoying bark that she recognized instantly. She turned in the direction from which it came.

She breathed a sigh of relief, there it was!

Zyrah was running and barking around a man and a woman holding a baby in her arms wrapped in countless blue fabrics. He was tall and with a hat covering his head, she shorter and with a face as pale as it was beautiful covered in golden curls. A beautiful couple, Vienne appreciated. The princess walked towards them, stopping some distance away, observing the scene sitting on a barrel. The couple smiled at Zyrah's enthusiasm, just as Zyrah seemed to enjoy their company. At such extenuation she assumed that Zyrah must know them, perhaps they were friends of Gelegen? Or, simply, she had taken a liking to them.

Now, closer, she noticed a detail that caught her attention. Their eyes. Green hers, brown his... the princess smiled at the dilemma that baby would have presented before the gods. She had heard about the Crossbreed Curse, according to which a baby born from the relationship of an Aquo with a citizen of one of the other kingdoms would be born with blond hair, but its eyes would never be blue.

However, what would happen if, like that couple, neither of the ascendants had blue eyes? Would their offspring be born with eyes like the sea according to this belief?

The man helped his wife crouch down, she pulled the clothes away from the baby's face, pulling the little creature closer to Zyrah. The little dog greeted the baby by wagging its tail vigorously, then proceeded to lavish the baby's face with countless licks, to which the baby responded with what looked like a smile. They glanced towards Vienne, nodded, and bid the dog farewell—she with a kiss on Zyrah's head and he with gentle pats on her side. Then, they let her go.

Zyrah darted towards Vienne, wagging her tail from side to side with intense agitation. She seemed elated.

"Have you made any little friends, Zyrah?"

"Woof!" Confirmed the canine.

3. A stupid clause

Pom, pom, pom.

Rough knocking on the door awakened Aienne. She had fallen asleep in her armchair the night before, reading a gripping story about a young witch. She sat up with a jolt, the book, which she had forgotten she was holding on her belly, fell to the floor.

Stretching herself awake, she bent down to retrieve the book, placing it on the couch. Who could it be, this early? The rooster hadn't even crowed, it was still somewhat dark. She walked over to the basin and washed her face; conscientiously rubbing her eyes, she always had large eye crusts when she got up in the morning.

She felt a shiver. She had not expected any visitors in fact. Since her mother the queen had urged all the princesses to decide what their future would be, they had all been gradually leaving the palace and that included her. Aienne considered herself fortunate; her new role as a researcher came with the perk of residing in a simple home near the research facility. It was a very modest house, it had essential furniture; lacking good finishes or quality wood and, of course, no servants. However, the youngest of the Dajalam family had quickly become accustomed to her new simple way of life, away from the abundance and comforts of the palace.

Pom, pom, pom. It sounded again.

Few people knew that she lived in that place; she had lost the already scarce contact with most of her sisters. The truth was that she did not know the whereabouts of practically any of them. She thought she heard Lorienne propose to Dambalarienne that they both join the army, but she didn't pay much attention to what her other sister's response was. Her only concern was Vienne, and unfortunately, she still knew nothing about her whereabouts.

She turned on a light, leaning out of the window overlooking the entrance.

Two soldiers, she observed. Her heart skipped a beat, recognizing the orange uniform. Soldiers of the Delorange family. One of them turned toward the window, Aienne crouched down. *They must have seen me, or maybe they saw the candlelight.*

She began to breathe heavily when she realized that they were Delorange soldiers. *Have they found out that it was me who freed Dornias and the rest of the nobles? Not only that, I also set fire to part of their home... if they know it was me, we are in serious trouble.*

She had to run. No, they had seen her, it would be stupid to run. Confronting them was not an option either, for some stupid reason she did not keep any weapon in her dwelling. She had no choice; she had to open the door and try to control the situation. She would deny any accusation and evade the situation as best she could.

"Princess Aienne, we bring an invitation for you." It was heard from the other side of the door.

She raised an eyebrow; *did he say an invitation? It might be a trap,* she pondered. Regardless, she decided to open the door. She stumbled in front of the soldiers and bowed her head slightly by way of greeting, her lips incredibly pressed tight in an effort to appear normal.

Seeing her, the two soldiers displayed the Aquo reverence. One of them extended his arm, offering her a parchment sealed with an orange seal. The princess took the document with alacrity, broke the seal and unrolled it, then began to read it with extreme curiosity.

Katienne Dajalam and Filier Delorange would like to invite you to their engagement ceremony to be held...

She did not need to read any further. She tore that parchment in half with fury, before the astonished gaze of both soldiers.

"Excuse me, Princess, we need confirmation as to whether you will be attending the ceremo...."

Blam! The princess's response was reflected in the form of a slamming door. She turned red with anger; how could that idiot Katienne even think of inviting her to her stupid engagement ceremony?

* * *

The corridors of the research facility were more deserted than usual. *Where is everyone?* She wondered. Aienne couldn't care less about the lack of investigators, she was simply irritated by everything that morning. Ever since those soldiers had knocked on her door, she had been deeply irascible; and to that had been added uneasiness. Katienne was going to perform a proposal ceremony, she would definitely seize such an opportunity to gather additional allies to her despicable cause, to usurp the throne.

Meanwhile, she still had no news of her favorite sister. *Oh, Vienne, will you be all right?*

She noticed someone, gently grabbing her arm.

"Sorry to interrupt your thoughts, Aienne, some soldiers were looking for you." A sparse-haired young man politely indicated to her.

Aienne gritted her teeth, *those stupid Delorange soldiers again? Haven't I made it clear to them that I have no intention of attending such a farce of a ceremony?*

She headed for the entrance. Quick as an arrow, chin high, fists clenched and brow furrowed. It seemed she had to make it even clearer to them that she didn't plan to go, that she wanted nothing to do with Katienne, nor with the poor wretched idiot who was intending to marry her.

She stopped dead in her tracks. Standing in the doorway was Lampen, his hand raised, preventing access to the workshop. Aienne stepped aside, positioning herself near a window from which she could both hear her mentor and see everything with her own eyes.

Surely Lampen is covering my back, she thought relieved. She leaned out of the window, just enough to see; she wanted to witness the frustrated faces of those soldiers. Her face changed completely when she saw their uniforms, those were not the colors of the Delorange soldiers, a mermaid on the chest with a three-pointed crown on top, the insignia of the Royal Guard, what were the palace soldiers doing there? Had her mother given orders to force her to attend the engagement of her older sister? It sounded as absurd, as it was feasible.

Lampen finished speaking with the guards, dismissed them formally, and closed the door. In his hand he held a parchment.

"What did the guards want, Lampen?" Stormed Aienne as soon as he turned around.

The Research Counselor gave a slight gasp. Then he looked at her, concerned.

"Come with me to my office, right now." He said gravely. Then he began to walk.

"Is something wrong, Lampen?" said Aienne haltingly after running to stand just behind him. "What did those guards want, did you tell them I'm here? I'm in grave danger, aren't I?"

The counselor did not answer her, simply stopped in front of his office door. He grabbed the knob, turned it and opened the door, then he pointed inside with the parchment, urging her to enter. Not a single word.

"Lampen, you're scaring me." Aienne replied, taking a seat in the chair across the table from the counselor. Her throat was dry; her eyes fixed on the counselor as he moved around the room before settling into the chair across the table.

Their gazes met for a second. The counselor cleared his voice.

"The Royal Guard has come asking for you, they wanted to..."

Aienne didn't need to hear any more. "Oh, no, Lampen, they're going to force me to attend that farce of a ceremony, aren't they?" Seeing Lampen frown, the princess seemed to understand everything. "They know, don't they? They know I helped the nobles escape and they're going to punish me for it! I won't be able to help Vienne if I'm imprisoned!" Realizing that her arrest might be imminent, she began to breathe heavily.

Before she continued to jump to conclusions, Lampen raised his hand, urging her to calm down.

"They wanted to deliver this to you," the counselor leaned slightly, offering her a small scroll. "And no, it's nothing related to your sister's ceremony or the nobles you freed." He anticipated, guessing Aienne's next intervention.

The princess made a quizzical grimace, then inspected the document before opening it. The blue wax seal with the drawing of a mermaid surrounded by a circular frame with crowns was untouched. The Royal Seal.

She broke the seal roughly and tried to unroll the parchment quickly, but her hands were shaking with nervousness.

She began to read, skipping the usual flourishes with which she knew all too well court-related documents began, turning her attention to the document's core content.

In times of war, such as the one we currently face, certain measures are required to ensure that the Dajalam dynasty will endure regardless of the outcome of the conflict. It is the absolute priority of the

Queendom to ensure that the bloodline chosen by the Aqua Deus does not become extinct, which is why, as the youngest descendant of the Royal House, you enjoy the privilege of having been selected to embark on a journey to a confidential location, where you will be kept in custody and kept safe from harm.

Such a concession is both an honor and a duty. For, should the course of the war be unfavorable, the Aqua Deus forbid, you will be the hope that in the event of the greatest of tragedies, one day the Dajalam blood will once again reign with honor, rigor and justice.

That is why you are urged, as soon as possible, to go to Royal Harbor. The place from which the pertinent departure will commence, and from there, you will be directed to your safe destination.

Signed:

Meredian, Crown's Favourite.

Aienne frowned, confused at the pomposity of such a speech. She understood perfectly well that Meredian, the Tribute Counselor, had been appointed Crown's Favourite of the queen and, therefore, acted on behalf of the queen while she was absent. However, the true intent of the document eluded her.

"They want me to sail to a secret location so that my family does not become extinct?" She assumed perplexedly, raising her gaze to Lampen, who was still watching her seriously. She certainly hadn't expected the guards' visit to pertain to such a request, but that being the case, what was causing Lampen's obvious discomfort?

"That bastard Meredian has invoked that stupid clause..."

Aienne raised her eyebrows; it was the first time she had heard the Research Counselor curse.

Lampen sighed, pausing to look up at the ceiling momentarily, then shook his head and continued, "*Culua ne conservio prosapia electica,*" he uttered, in perfect Flumio, "also known as the *Chosen Lineage Preservation Clause,*" Lampen clarified, looking straight ahead, "it is customary that, in the face of a war of this magnitude, certain precautionary measures are taken to ensure that the royal family is not completely annihilated.

A defeatist, antiquated, and stupid move if you ask me." He added, visibly annoyed.

"So, you knew this was going to happen?"

Lampen sighed. "At my last meeting at the palace, such a stupid clause came up. Of course, I knew of its existence too, but obviously it was not among my plans to mention it. However, Meredian brought it

45

up. Once he did, there was no doubt in my mind that you, being the youngest of the princesses, would be the one chosen to make such a journey and so it has been."

The princess stared in shock. *They intend to lock me up on an island... far from the Aquadom. I won't be able to do anything, I won't be able to help Vienne.* She felt a shudder, moments before reading that message she had languished at the thought of being forced to attend a mere ceremony, now, she would even be willing to lead the celebration itself compared to the ostracism that seemed to be her fate.

She looked at Lampen, hopeful. Surely he had already devised some plan to avoid such an annoying assignment.

The counselor seemed to read her thoughts, shaking his head. "I can't help you this time, Aienne," he said regretfully, "as much as it irritates me, once such a clause is invoked there is nothing that can be done."

"Is there really no alternative?" She said, crestfallen. She imagined herself. Alone, with no word from anyone, unable to do anything but wait for the war to unfold. Could there be any worse fate than to sit idly by and do nothing?

"I'm afraid there is no other option..."

"What if I refuse?" She proposed, "I can pretend I never read that document and go about my business as if nothing had happened."

Lampen shook his head. "Think a little, young lady. What good would it do to evade your responsibility like that? True, you can disregard this message, but I assure you that Meredian will spare no effort to find you and make sure you sail to safety. This is a very serious matter, Aienne, as much as I dislike Meredian's choice, I can understand his decision to invoke the *Chosen Lineage Preservation Clause.* Being in his position is not easy. The Aqua Deus knows well that I was glad to learn that the queen had placed her trust in him and not in me to be in charge of the queendom in her absence!"

"But Meredian has no right to dictate my future!" The princes complained, "Vienne needs help and I'm not going anywhere. If they want me to get on that ship, they'll have to put me in chains first. And now, if you'll excuse me, I have work to do."

4. A classical man

Filier Delorange nodded proudly as he gazed around the large and busy courtyard. He was standing in an elevated area, from which he had a privileged view of the festive bustle his grounds had become. The stream had been cleared that very morning, the bushes had been duly trimmed into the shapes of mermaids and fish while purple lilies lined the thick black walnut wooden structures that stretched around the courtyard. According to what one of the soldiers in charge of security had informed him, six hundred and eighty-six guests were in his domain, all of them wearing their best clothes.

His servants could not have been busier, running back and forth with trays laden with glasses of the best vintage wine he could offer. It could not be otherwise on such a unique occasion. Filier himself had overseen the selection of the vintage: a wine with a clear and translucent blue hue, a velvety texture, and a ripe berry aroma that left a delightful fruity flavor on the palate. Such a pleasure for the senses whetted the appetite, which is why trays of the most exquisite culinary succulences of the time were also constant. In particular, the dish that the chef had titled *Tender venison delights with rainbow caramel and nutmeg* seemed to be particularly acclaimed.

Such a display was necessary. For within its decorated grounds were prominent members of the Congregation of the Church, Father Ovilier himself had honored them with his presence. Likewise, the most prestigious noble families had accepted his invitation. No one wanted to miss such an event.

With such a crowd and such select guests he had taken care of every detail within his power. His father had taught him in his teenage years that a nobleman should not only be a nobleman, but also behave like one. Following such wise advice, he had spared nothing, and was even proud to have been able to hire for the occasion a first-rate cook, the

47

famous Arneguius, whose dishes were so revered that some said that only his culinary art could satisfy the appetite of Aqua Deus himself. Filier could not give his opinion on the matter, he was too nervous to try a bite. However, judging from the satisfied faces and the subsequent chatter after the meal, everything seemed to be to his diners' liking.

He had no doubt that it was the proposal ceremony with the largest number of guests ever witnessed. It was an act as simple as it was moving, the bride was to ask for the groom's mother's hand, a cordiality through which they displayed their satisfaction with an upcoming marriage. To many Aquos it was a custom as old-fashioned as it was unnecessary, but Filier always found it a beautiful act, and what was to become of traditions if families as respectable as his were to cast them aside? In a way, it bothered him that customs were being lost. He considered himself a classical man and proud of it. The Aquo traditions were beautiful in his eyes and he was not ashamed to follow them as closely as he could. Before the act he was about to perform, it was customary for the whole family of both parties to be present. However, fate, or perhaps circumstances, had prevented some relevant members of both lineages from attending. Despite the fact that Katienne's mother was not present, which was a more than important absence since she was also the queen and, if that were not enough, High Priestess; and that two princesses were also absent, for Filier such absences were not comparable to the absence of his brother. Dornias had not even been able to be invited, his location was unknown, just like that of the other nobles who had managed to escape from the cellars with him.

A realization suddenly struck him. *My mother-in-law is going to be the queen*, he thought, swallowing his breath. He knew from his relatives and close friends that relationships with the couple's families were not always straightforward, so why did the confrontations his friends could have had all suddenly seem like mere child's play compared to the rifts he anticipated were going to take place in the royal Dajalam family?

However, these were all concerns that he would have to deal with when the time came. Now he had to make sure that the proposal ceremony went perfectly. He reached into the inside right pocket of his elegant dark silk jacket to confirm that everything was in order. He felt the lump, *everything is in place*, he reassured himself.

His attention was focused on a certain select corner. There were several young girls dressed in the most avant-garde dresses, surrounded

48

by various noble suitors who, Filier guessed, were trying to catch their attention. There was good reason for that, that group consisted of none other than the Dajalam princesses.

They were a lovely bunch. Polite, eating and drinking with an excellent protocol taste. They chatted animatedly, always maintaining their composure and good manners. He knew that at any moment they would all come to greet him and he had to make sure he remembered their names to address each one with the respect they deserved. He sighed, there were so many... however, they would soon be his sisters-in-law, so he tried to remember each and every one of their names.

Lorienne, Candenne, Urulenne, Dalienne, Mimienne, Zurienne, Dambalarienne, - with the name of this princess Filier could not help wondering if the queen had run out of ideas for naming her daughters, - *Sendarienne, Pondarienne, is that all?* He mused, mentally reviewing, *no, one is missing,* he glanced over, *Bolenne,* he added, spotting the plump young princess sitting in a chair. *Ten,* he concluded, satisfied with his feat. Of course, Princess Vienne had not been invited for obvious reasons, while Aienne had declined the invitation, according to the messenger, in very bad form.

All of them, plus Katienne of course, made up the thirteen Dajalam princesses.

Ironically, the two absent princesses were the ones he was most curious about. The rest of Katienne's sisters were pleasant and polite with him, something to be expected when you have been educated in the palace, and even more understandable when he was heir to the noblest and wealthiest family in the whole queendom. Perhaps for that reason, so much formality and politeness, whether feigned or not, made them unfascinating companions.

Speaking of the Dajalams, he tilted his head, trying to find his favorite princess in the crowd.

There she was. Radiant, in a white dress with bluish details that accentuated her excellent figure but was at the same time an appropriate attire for a family gathering. Katienne was talking casually with Father Ovilier and a group of nobles that, from a distance, he did not recognize.

He felt a goofy smile creep across his face. Had he ever dreamed that he would marry such a beautiful and incredible woman? Probably not even a dream could have led him to consider such a portentous destiny.

Their eyes met. She smiled at him in such a way that Filier's heart melted completely. He nodded, took a deep breath and walked towards her with a firm, calm step. It was time to start the act.

He continued to move in her direction, cordially greeting the many guests who approached him to thank him for inviting them.

"If I may," he said bowing his head to the guests with whom his fiancée was speaking. They gave the Aquo reverence to both of them.

Filier gently took Katienne by the elbow, and Katienne followed suit. Then they began to walk side by side, the people crowding on either flank so as not to miss anything, forming a path that would allow them to continue the ritual.

"You look ravishing, my beloved," he whispered softly, before the expectant eyes of the onlookers. Katienne merely smiled at him with her eyes, a slight gesture before blowing kisses to her sisters, who had positioned themselves in the front row to enjoy the most privileged views.

They reached the small pond, stepping into it after removing their shoes and socks. It was a shallow pool, the water reaching slightly above their calves. Filier felt the cold water work its way between his toes, sending a shiver up his spine.

They held hands and looked into each other's eyes before the attentive gaze of everyone present. It was Katienne who knelt down, as tradition dictated, without letting go of his hands.

"My dear, these are difficult times," Katienne began, loudly enough for all to hear. Filier did not notice even a hint of nervousness in her voice, he admired her poise and confidence, "many would say that this is not the time for such a celebration, but I think just the opposite, whatever the outcome of the war, I want to make sure that everything that is to come, good or bad, will be with you. That is why I want to ask you, in front of all these family and friends, would you do me the honor of standing by my side forever, so that our remains may one day rest together in the sea?"

Filier responded by kneeling as well, his pants and the bottom of his jacket getting soaked in the process.

"Of course, I do," he replied excitedly, "it will be an honor to be by your side for an eternity and so I hope my family will approve."

They both smiled and leaned forward. As their lips met a thunderous cheer accompanied them. They both stood up, Katienne began to walk out of the pond.

"Wait, I have something for you." Filier revealed to her, as nervous as he was happy. He fumbled clumsily with the inside pocket of his jacket, until he finally managed to slip his agitated hand into it extracting something.

A bright, beautiful blue ring rested upon his palm. Katienne exclaimed in surprise. She quickly picked it up, fastened it on her index finger as was customary and inspected it.

"It's incredibly beautiful, my beloved!" She said contemplating the jewel with a beaming smile, "you didn't have to."

"Nothing is too much for you, my dear." He replied breathing a sigh of relief that he had gotten the size right.

Filier knew the exact details of the ring's composition. It had been manufactured under his exhaustive instructions, which is why ordering it had cost him an absolute fortune—a price he paid with pleasure. The crystalline blue semi-transparent stone held within its core two rainwater droplets, two of river, and two of sea, giving the appearance of being wet. The composition of that piece was not casual, it symbolized the journey of the water from its beginning, the rain, to the conclusion of its journey forming part of the sea.

As he gazed at Katienne admiring his gift, he felt a nagging lump in his throat. It was the best ring any noble could probably acquire in all of Aquadom, why then did he feel it might be insufficient? Why that strange feeling that perhaps it was too little for Katienne? Nevertheless, she seemed to have liked it, and that was what mattered.

They had sworn eternal love to each other.

Filier swallowed, aware of how complicated the next step was going to be, it was time for their engagement to be approved. He approached Katienne, she smiled at him so candidly that he looked like a fool again and then they both performed the Aquo reverence in front of their audience. They took each other's elbow again and walked together before the eyes of everyone there, family, friends and servants stood expectantly watching them.

They stopped in front of the only person still seated, an elderly man elegantly dressed and with prominent white sideburns, his father, Bornabas Delorange, legitimate leader of House Delorange. That man was wasting away, physically he was emaciated, his coughing was almost constant, his blindness was getting worse and worse and his lucid moments were becoming increasingly rare. However, from the fierce look on his skeletal face, it seemed that none of these ailments were preventing him from witnessing how his firstborn son and heir to his title and lands was breaking one of the unwritten rules of the house he was to be in charge of sooner or later.

"Father, may I present my fiancée, Katienne..." His throat went dry as he tried to utter her last name, at the same time being absolutely aware of how his armpits, back, neck and forehead were perspiring as he had never ever believed a man could experience, "Dajalam. I hope you will give your blessing to our future union in marriage."

Under normal circumstances, it would have been his mother, whom he should have asked for acceptance. Unfortunately, his dear mother had long since left them after a bad cold. It would have been much easier if that sweet woman had been there.

His father stared at him for a moment. His gaze emanated equal parts disappointment and fury. In a way, it was not without reason, Filier had destroyed a reputation that went back to the beginnings of his lineage, *the Delorange do not fall before the charm of the Dajalam princesses*, with those words his ancestors had boasted, proud that the royal beauty had not been able to bewitch them. Because of him, their house could never boast of such a feat.

"You have my blessing." His father conceded finally, then began to cough.

Filier's emotions were mixed. On the one hand, he felt an overwhelming relief that his father had not made a scene, which was a scenario he had come to contemplate and which, unfortunately, would not have surprised him in the least. On the other, he felt enormous sorrow, it was not easy for him to be aware that neither his father nor his absent brother agreed to his betrothal, he felt alone, abandoned by his loved ones.

Why can't they understand that I love her with all my being? Is a family name so important as to get in the way of love?

"Filier," Katienne called sweetly.

They walked, holding each other's elbows, and waved amidst applause, kisses and hugs. Everyone present wished them a joyful and promising future together—everyone except his father, the sole opinion that mattered to Filier.

5. Tradition

The dreadful day had arrived. Another year had passed, not marking the celebration of his birth, but rather the day he had been beaten so brutally and mercilessly that he had been on the verge of death.

He was situated on the east side of the central square, in the middle of which stood the immensely long grain tower. His flour-stained black boots stood over a gap in the cobblestone, exactly where it had all started nine years ago.

This time it's different, Girilay repeated over and over again, *this year I'm going to stand up to them and make them swear never to celebrate another anniversary.*

The casserole that protected his skull was thrown forward with the slightest inclination of his head, preventing him from seeing properly. The trays protecting his chest and back were digging into him when he moved his arms, limiting his movement considerably. And, in spite of everything, he didn't mind all that discomfort, this time it wasn't going to be his blood watering the weeds that made their way across the cobblestones.

The incident began in the most banal way; he had simply been in the wrong place at the wrong time. It was mere chance that on that fateful day he found himself alone in that square, where a group of bored undesirables had decided to turn all their anger on him.

Since then, every year such an event had been held. The rules were simple, no weapons, two sides, which any citizen could join. However, nine years had passed and nine years he had fought alone. He knew that this time would be no different, no one would lift a finger for him, no citizen would take his side for fear of possible reprisals from that group of thugs led by the most despicable being he had ever met, Muna, an idiot with a stupid smile and insatiable hatred.

This year something had changed; he had decided that his insomnia would be used in improving his armor instead of simply lamenting that the day of the anniversary was approaching. He knew that he would end up lying unconscious on the ground, as usual, but this time he had promised himself that, before lying passed out in his own blood, he would try to make as many of his rivals fall as possible. And, above all, he would make sure that Muna was among his victims.

His grandmother used to tell him that bad thoughts attract bad situations. Maybe that's why, just at that moment, more and more people began to enter the other side of the square. Young men and women, led by Muna. As in previous times, that vile being appeared with his long bangs held absurdly erect by tree resin. He approached Girilay with a crooked smile, waddling as he walked.

"Too bad, looks like another year you get to fight alone." He sneered, sporting a wicked grin with his perfect teeth. Then he looked him up and down, "I thought last year's beating would make it clear to you that your pathetic armor made of scrap metal is useless."

He loathed his petulant voice, his confident face, and even his very existence. He knew that Muna was a coward; that he would not face him alone, he was simply a rat, a vile being who took advantage of the vermin that fought beside him, under his orders.

"I'm... I'm ready." He said, trying to keep his voice from shaking, to no avail. He had practiced in front of the mirror for several nights, trying not to stutter, something that only happened to him that day, when he faced Muna and all the undesirables who had chosen to accompany him in that macabre celebration they had decided to baptize as the *Anniversary of Pain.*

"I'm glad you're ready, because today I have a special desire to get the blood flowing." Muna revealed to him, throwing his shoulders back to warm up his muscles. "Or maybe you want us to wait a little bit longer in case someone joins you this time?" He added, then letting out a chuckle.

Girilay swallowed. Then he examined his arms, making sure that both black ribbons were still securely tied around each wrist. A precaution against the tricks he anticipated Muna might attempt, if he skirted the rules, then this time he would too.

His opponents had already positioned themselves in the middle of the square, Muna in front of everyone, his henchmen behind, ready.

Girilay took a deep breath, ready to put an end to it as soon as possible. He positioned himself at a short distance from his numerous opponents, alone, as always.

"You know, Girilay," Muna began, "as soon as you fall unconscious on the ground, we'll march off in search of Tizai. One of the Onriseay brothers claims to have spotted something shiny in the swamp. And guess what we'll request if we get the Royal Favor..." he let slip, with an even more terrifying smile on his face than usual.

Girilay's blood froze. *He's just playing with me, it's another one of his wicked games,* he tried to convince himself. *Of course they won't find the sword, nor would they waste something like a Royal Favor on simply hurting me... or maybe they would?* He felt his strength failing, manipulated by his rival's malicious words.

"Looks like no one's coming to help you, as usual, huh?" Scoffed Muna with a shrug of his shoulders and raising his hands as if in resignation. "Shall we get started?" He proposed.

Girilay pursed his lips, merely nodding just enough so that the casserole would not block his view. He crouched his body, ready to defend himself.

"Wait!" Said a voice.

Everyone turned around, equally confused.

"Can I still... still join?" Asked a black-haired, brown-eyed young man, gasping for breath and clutching his knees.

A Fireo? Girilay thought, surprised.

"Sure," Muna said with a smirk, "join in kicking this chubby guy."

"I'm not talking to you, scum," he said looking at Muna with a grimace of disgust, "do you mind if I fight beside you?"

Girilay could not believe what he was hearing, was he dreaming or was that Fireo addressing him?

"Is it... is it me?" He replied, pointing to himself as much as the trays protecting his arms would allow.

The Fireo nodded. "I'll join your side, Girilay." he replied placing himself next to him. "If you want me to, of course." He added, resting his palm on his other fist, making it crack.

Surely, it's Muna with another one of his games, Girilay pondered, *pretending I've gained an ally, only to reveal later that it was another one of his ploys.* It had to be that, but then why was Muna staring at the Fireo in puzzlement? Maybe...?

"Su... sure." He ventured to say.

"Great," the Fireo replied. He put his hand to his chest. "You can call me Noakh," he then looked straight ahead as if trying to read the situation, their rivals staring at one other in utter confusion, "you take care of the idiot with the bangs, I'll take care of the others, understood?"

Girilay wanted to ask him again why; however, instead he just nodded, clutching his casserole to get a better look.

"Concentrate, here they come." Noakh instructed him, his fists ready to begin that confrontation.

Girilay looked ahead, feeling how under the casserole the cold sweat began to run down his face. They were running towards them, all those young men who followed Muna's orders. His stupid opponent always followed the same strategy, first send his vermin, then him to finish the job.

A pock-faced boy went to attack him, Girilay raised his heavy arm, his armor of knives and forks clinking stridently as he moved. He clenched his plump fingers, ready to defend himself, however, before he could throw his punch, Noakh appeared out of nowhere, charging his shoulder so hard into the pock-faced boy that the latter began to roll across the floor uncontrollably.

Faced with such a confrontation, their rivals went for their ally. Noakh delivered a hard headbutt to one of them. Then they grabbed him between two, each holding him by one arm, while a third gave him a powerful punch in the stomach.

I must help him, Girilay thought, coming to the aid of his unexpected Fireo ally. Before he went to assist him, Noakh jumped up with both feet, so as to hit a hard double kick to the one who had delivered the blow to his stomach.

"You focus on the one with the bangs!" He indicated him, just before a tremendous punch hit him in the nose and sent him crashing to the ground.

"All right." Girilay agreed. His eyes roamed the battlefield that the town square had become. Muna wasn't moving, simply watching as his allies swooped down on Noakh without the slightest mercy.

It's my time, he decided.

Girilay charged at his distracted enemy, taking advantage of his greater weight to knock him to the ground. He shouted, placing himself on top of him so that he could not move, and then he clumsily slapped him in the face. His heavy body, coupled with the additional weight of his crafted armor, caused him to attack very slowly. By contrast, he was aware that his heavier weight and beefy arms allowed him to land more

56

powerful blows than most of his opponents, including that skinny idiot Muna. He was not a fighter, Girilay only knew how to bake delicious cakes. He had practiced punching a sack of flour, but it wasn't the same.

Muna struggled to pull away from his blows.

Girilay turned to see how Noakh was faring. His unexpected ally continued to face several opponents simultaneously, he seemed to be fighting quite well, however, the numerical advantage was too overwhelming.

He focused on Muna again, he knew that if their leader fell the rest would flee like cowardly rats. He raised his heavy fist to strike a blow, unfortunately, the casserole on his head moved, preventing him from seeing.

Damn, he thought, trying to adjust it in time. He brought both hands to his casserole. As he regained his vision, the first thing he saw was how Muna's tremendous punch was directed towards one of his eyes.

He felt the blunt impact in his right eye. Girilay groaned in pain and fell to the ground, landing face-up with a deafening metallic screech. Muna seized the moment to stand, slipping his hands into his pockets.

"That... that's cheating," Girilay complained, noticing his rival pulling out two steel pieces with holes for his fingers. Now Muna's knuckles were protected by that strange weapon that, unfortunately, he had felt impacting his body on previous occasions. "You know weapons are not allowed." He reprimanded him, standing up as best he could.

"Yes, well," he replied raising both metallic fists, "but can this be considered a weapon? It's a suit of armor, just like the one you wear, only these protect my fists and allow me to hit you relentlessly by not hurting me." He said, smiling mischievously.

Girilay gritted his teeth.

"I knew you would cheat, but this time I come prepared to repay you in kind!" He waved his hands and waited.

Out of nowhere, two saucepans appeared flying in the direction of Girilay. The plump young man managed to catch both on the fly. He raised his new weapons towards Muna. "What now, you idiot?"

His opponent snorted. Then the attack began. Girilay raised his saucepans, ready to defend himself.

* * *

Noakh was lying on the floor with his mouth open, those saucepans had appeared flying from some corner, landing in Girilay's hands. What kind of amazing sorcery was that? Engrossed as he was, he didn't notice the shadow sinking over him, the huge sole of a boot was approaching to crush his head, taking advantage of his distraction. He rolled on the ground, dodging the blow as best he could. His ribs, arms and every part of his body ached, many of which were bleeding profusely.

Especially painful was his nose wound, whose blood dripped onto his lips, causing him to feel a foul metallic taste. Similarly, the wound on his head looked quite serious. His knuckles were swollen from the blows he had delivered, his head was thundering from the headbutts he had both received and dealt. But he couldn't care less.

"Come on, Girilay, rip that guy to shreds!" He encouraged him. As he did, he dodged a blow from his opponent, a young girl with pigtails, and delivered a hard kick to her back.

In truth, the altercation between Muna and Girilay could hardly be called a fight. Girilay limited himself to protecting himself with the saucepans, while his opponent attacked with his steel fists with the fury of someone ready to kill.

Noakh wanted to intervene, but he was too busy being subjected to multiple blows that were starting to wear him down. It was difficult to defend oneself while trying to keep an eye on Girilay from a distance.

Muna was ruthless, he attacked sharply and without any qualms before the victim of his blows. He made an attack towards Girilay's guts, the plump young man lowered his arms to protect his stomach, Noakh opened his mouth to warn him from afar, but did not do it in time, the opponent stopped his attack halfway and, taking advantage of the fact that Girilay's face was now unprotected, directed one of his metal fists towards his cheek.

A rattling of metal announced Girilay's hard fall to the ground. The ground was stained with blood.

Noakh clenched his jaw. As fate would have it, one of Girilay's saucepans slipped not far from where he stood; he bent down slightly, grasping it by the handle.

With Girilay's fall, he was the only one left standing. It should not have been like that, it should have been the plump young man who would have put an end to that story, however, he had failed. Now it was Noakh's turn to impose some sanity and justice on the world.

His kidneys burned from the kicks they had received; the toes of his right foot begged him to stop walking and give them a break. But there was work to be done.

He witnessed his opponents gradually surround him, smiles breaking out on their faces as they became aware that the numbers were in their favor. *Eleven against one*, Noakh counted. Piece of cake with his swords, no more hassle than swatting away a fly if he could count on Distra's powers, however, his beloved weapons were far from his reach, sheltered in the deep hollow of a tree too far away, a saucepan was the only thing that allowed him not to have to face all those undesirables with his bare hands.

For an instant, his opponents transformed into blond-haired, blue-eyed children. Pushing him, spitting on him, pulling his hair or holding him so that others could take advantage of the opportunity to hit him.

At such memories, his fingers gripped the handle of the saucepan tighter.

"Finish him off!" Muna ordered.

All his opponents charged in unison. *Of course, they'd attack all at once,* thought Noakh. Was any different behavior to be expected from such vermin?

He stood in his position, on guard, his legs slightly bent, right leg in front, left leg further back, and his right arm extended holding the saucepan.

The first one charged, his war cry silenced by a blunt blow that struck his temple so hard, he immediately dropped to the ground. Unconscious or dead, it was hard to say.

Noakh threw his body back to avoid the violent attack of a young woman with horse-like teeth. Taking advantage of his opponent's momentum, he struck her a hard blow to the back of the neck with his weapon.

Noakh looked at the saucepan with admiration, *who would have thought that a kitchen utensil could turn out to be such a good weapon!* He thought with a grimace of recognition.

However, it was not all good. Yes, his blows with the saucepan were undoubtedly forceful, but the range was far less than that provided by either of his swords, and his opponents still outnumbered him.

If I had both saucepans in hand, the confrontation would be much easier, he told himself. He moved out of the way of a punch, trying to spot the second saucepan. There it was, near the still unconscious

Girilay. How easy it would be for his ally to stand up for an instant and throw it at him....

Then he remembered something: Girilay had managed to get both saucepans to fly towards him. Maybe he could achieve the same? Instinctively, he whistled towards the saucepan, a shrill and annoying sound. The metal utensil did not move in the slightest.

He continued his fight. A blow in the tibia of another opponent was enough to get rid of him. At this rate, he would soon get rid of all of them and the only thing left to do was to give Muna what he deserved.

"Drop that saucepan on the ground or your friend will pay dearly!" Muna threatened from a distance.

Noakh's face turned white, that rotten man was aiming his knife at the unconscious Girilay's neck. He gritted his teeth in rage, he did not want to give Muna the satisfaction of victory, but he had no choice, the young Fireo dropped the saucepan to the ground and raised both hands in surrender.

Muna grinned wickedly before turning his gaze to his comrades, who, with a mere glance, understood their leader's instructions.

Three of them pounced on Noakh, the first one punched him in the liver. He fell to the ground, in pain, aware that he could do nothing to defend himself if he didn't want to see Girilay get hurt. As his face touched the grayish stone, he felt a strong kick in his kidneys, then another, and a third even harder than the previous ones.

He gritted his teeth, trying not to scream, he knew that, if he did, he would be hit harder and harder. These people fed on the pain and suffering of others and, as long as he could bear it, it would not be his screams that would replenish their energy.

"Leave him alone!" He heard Girilay say in the distance. His voice broken, full of anguish, probably at the thought that he was the one who, indirectly, was causing him all that pain.

For a slight moment he stopped feeling any more blows; was there any room for a little compassion in the hearts of those despicable beings? The strong kick he felt in his ribs answered him.

"And let such a lesson pass? Let the people learn that this will be the fate of anyone who fights by your side." He heard Muna say.

"No!" Girilay lashed out, managing to knock the knife held by Muna to the ground.

Muna punched Girilay hard, then bent down to pick up the knife. However, a bolt urged him to stop his actions.

"Enough is enough," said the tavern keeper, folding his arms, "it's time to end this barbarism."

Muna turned. The entire village stood there, Hilzen at the head with the crossbow still in his hand.

"No!" replied Muna indignantly, "it's a tradition, you can't interfere!"

The village began to walk, in absolute silence, behind Girilay. Muna understood, leaving, just like the fleeing rat he was, followed by his miscreants.

Hilzen offered Noakh his hand to help him up, who gladly accepted it.

"You look a mess and we only just got into Aere Tine," Hilzen said looking at him disapprovingly.

"Trust me, it was worth it." He said, nodding towards Girilay.

The plump young man was on his knees, his mouth hanging open not seeming to believe that finally the people had come to their senses and sided with him. The tavern keeper walked over to Girilay and grabbed his arm, helping him up, then bowed his head.

"Sorry, boy. We've been blind for so many years that we know a mere apology isn't enough. Luckily, these foreigners arrived like a powerful gale, strong enough to blow away our blindfolds."

A man, older and with a grayish beard, approached.

"We have decided to change the name of this day. From now on, today will be known as *The Day We Opened Our Eyes*. We want you to create a cake to commemorate such an event."

Girilay fell to the ground on his knees, nodding as tears of happiness flooded his face.

6. Battle front

War cries echoed through the sky, as the cracked, greenish earth below became soaked with the blood of the Aquo and Fireo soldiers fighting for their lives on that island. They clashed fiercely, some trying to extinguish the flame, others trying to evaporate the water. Each side was resolute, willing to do anything to ensure they were the last ones standing on that remote battleground.

That Aquo settlement had been assaulted, Fireo troops had landed in imposing and menacing ships with coal-black hulls and maroon sails during the early morning. Such an attack would seem insane to any military strategist, the Fireo soldiers were considerably outnumbered. However, at the front of that reckless army, stood an elite troop. Relentless warriors, led by a man with a broad back, a fierce gaze and two swords wreathed in flames.

King Wulkan had arrived, prepared to administer justice and death.

The mysterious voice through the sapphire had spoken again. Information that had been even juicier than usual. In addition to revealing the island's location as a meeting place for enemy troops, which had led to Wulkan now attacking it, an even more significant piece of information emerged: Queen Graglia was already somewhere on the frontiers, still without her sacred weapon. This fact was an advantage that Wulkan had to capitalize on. He had to flush Graglia out of her burrow with fire and steel.

The uniformed Aquo formations of silver and purple armor fought against those Fireo warriors, who seemed to attack with utter undiscipline. Not all those men and women with furious brown eyes and black hair were soldiers; many were civilians with little or no armor and weapons of all kinds, from mere knives to axes that not long ago had been used to cut down trees, some even fought with sticks that they had sharpened with their razors. Humble people, willing to skewer several Aquos before being bestowed with the honor of dying for their kingdom, their king, and their god.

In the middle of the fray, where the fiercest combat was taking place, stood the king; as it could not and should not be otherwise.

Wulkan felt invincible in his gigantic armor. Blackish metal with light golden trim, and shoulder pads so large they made his already muscular shoulders appear even more imposing. Surrounding him were his faithful elite soldiers, led by a standard-bearer who fearlessly waved a black flag. It featured a vivid flame rising into the sky, transitioning the upper part of the cloth into red, where a phoenix was depicted. The other end of the pole where the flag was proudly displayed had been duly sharpened, ready to skewer the head of the bravest enemy warrior once he lay lifeless. Which of those Aquo warriors would enjoy such an honor? For now, the king and his guard were making their way with sword, spear and shield without finding anyone worthy of such recognition.

Wulkan's entourage was perfectly suited to accompany him into battle: his personal guard, known as the Chosen by Fire, comprised of sixteen men and women, the fiercest and most resilient among the already revered Sons of the Flame soldiers. All of them clad in black armor, with orange-edged trim that made their plates appear to be on fire, and a flame in reddish metal engraved on their right shoulder pad.

Some would think that this fierce elite troop acted as Wulkan's escort; that they were experienced soldiers who had been entrusted with the protection of the king during the battle. However, that assessment could not have been more wrong. A Fireo monarch did not require protection as the weak Aquo queen did. The Incandescent had chosen Wulkan to protect his people, not the other way around. Precisely for that reason, the Chosen by Fire instead walked beside the king to make sure that he was not encumbered in his lethal advance. They would be in charge of guaranteeing him space for his combat and of carrying out the orders that he would signal. Such a notorious detachment was making its way along the battle front, leaving a string of blue-eyed corpses in its wake.

Both blades of the king's swords were engulfed in flames. In his left hand he wielded Sinistra, with which he enjoyed launching both powerful and lethal ranged fire attacks at his enemies. In his right hand, he wielded Distra or, as only he knew, an exact replica of it. In the steel of this had been poured a thick oil-like substance from Tirhan lands that, except for the handicap of not being able to call upon its powers, seemed quite convincing.

Wulkan delivered a blunt headbutt into his opponent's face, the unfortunate Aquo's nose exploded in an eruption of blood. He then made a swift movement with his left hand, a puff of fire engulfed a whole row of purple-armored enemy soldiers in flames.

Not a single complaint, the king lamented to himself, as he watched his rivals being consumed by fire without uttering the slightest cry of pain. The dexterity and skill of those opponents was accompanied by an admirable devotion. Those troops covered with purple plates were part of the Temple Guard. Soldiers renowned for their unwavering faith which, much to Wulkan's disappointment, prevented them from showing any signs of distress. Even when their bodies were consumed by the flames, they still did not utter the slightest groan.

He was old and wise enough to know why the respectable troops of the Temple Guard had joined the fray. Somehow, Queen Graglia had managed to get whatever the name of her ecclesiastical organization was, to declare that war a holy one, a battle fought in pursuit of the Aqua Deus. And Wulkan could not be more pleased with that decision, he was going to show them why the Incandescent was a deity to be feared.

Sinistra pierced the neck of a pathetic rival. With the contact of blood on the fiery blade it emitted a *fssh*, as if the sacred steel was enjoying the contest.

"Where is your queen?" Roared Wulkan. His deep voice breaking through the heated clamor of battle, "why does she hide behind her weak subjects! Has she forgotten that it is she who must protect them?"

Distra's blade penetrated the skull of an Aquo soldier with a resounding *crack*, lending further weight to his words.

Reigns such as the Aquo's found it more logical to position their monarch at the rear, guarded by their army and focusing their work on military planning and strategy. This was not the case with the Fireo rulers. They were still advancing, causing death. An example of how an absolute massacre should be conducted. Wulkan took the lives of two soldiers who rushed at him in unison. The standard-bearer tackled one soldier, biting off his ear and then striking him with the flagpole. This allowed one of his comrades to end the soldier's life by stabbing him in the chest with his sword.

The slaughter incited a frenzy among the platoons of Fireo warriors who had the honor of witnessing the bloody spectacle delivered by their king and his escort. Wulkan was a good representative of what was expected of a Fireo king: lethal, bloodthirsty, a whirlwind of fire that delighted the Incandescent.

The monarch raised the sacred sword aloft, the fiery edge of Sinistra challenging the heavens. It was one of the signs, the glare of battle did not always allow the voice orders to be as enlightening as they should be, which is why they had created a code based on indications according to the position in which the king positioned the swords.

The captain of the Chosen by Fire interpreted Wulkan's signal.

"Accompany the king, advance, earn your place in hell!" She cried out fervently, just before her hammer blew the head of a wretched silver-armored enemy soldier into a thousand pieces.

Accompany, the words of that elite warrior were carefully chosen. For a true Chosen by Fire knew that a Fireo king did not require protection, on the contrary, they knew that if the Incandescent had blessed a Fireo with the power of fire, it was so that he would be the one to protect his people.

Protecting the king was one of the many forbidden orders of the Chosen by Fire, to resort to its use would be shameful, though it was far from being the most humiliating proclamation of all. Such a degrading honor was held by no less than two other orders. On the one hand, *retreat*, a word that only the king could invoke and which, it was believed, was so outrageous that, if used, a monarch might even lose the favor of the Incandescent. There was only one word even worse, *Akhail*, surrender. No phoenix had ever used it, and Wulkan was not going to be the first to do so.

The Fireo monarch pinned Distra to the ground for an instant, then drew back his large right fist and punched a vivid blue-eyed soldier with such force that it seemed, for a moment, as if they were amidst a spray of blood and teeth.

"Earn your place in hell!" The captain encouraged them, ripping the spearhead that had pierced the black armor from her chest after plunging the head of her weapon into the face of the wielder. Her words of encouragement were answered by a rousing shout from the rest of the Chosen by Fire.

No worthy opponent, thought Wulkan in frustration. He performed several movements with Sinistra, thus throwing discs of fire against his enemies to alleviate his disappointment. His reflection reminded him of something, a sad message that had come to him tied to the leg of a huge crow, not long ago.

66

The venerable Daikan Burum Babar has passed away, his body now resides with the monarchs before him. His spirit resides proud and peaceful in Tir Na Nog.

He never knelt down, he always did his best for his people, to preserve peace both in his land and with the rest of the kingdoms. His life was honorable until the last moment, facing a worthy opponent.

Arbilla, Daikan of the Queendom of the Moon.

Remembering that text, Wulkan felt a deep sense of nostalgia come over him.

My old friend, you finally found your way to your beloved Tir Na Nog. He was gone, he knew he should feel good for Burum Babar. That his suffering had lasted too long, and that with his death he would finally leave behind that illness that had been able to bend his inspiring mental and physical strength. However, that did not detract from the fact that his fall made Wulkan aware of his own mortality. Something that did not please him too much.

The legendary Daikan had been succeeded by his granddaughter. That young girl with the huge emerald eyes. She would surely reign with wisdom.

It was not his friend's demise that disturbed him most, nor the uncertainty of how worthy the new Daikan would be to receive the baton from the great Burum Babar. It was some of the haunting words included in that message that had managed to catch his mind.

Facing a worthy opponent, so read part of the message.

For some reason, he felt that those words held more importance than they were intended to. It was merely a hunch, maybe he was starting to be paranoid or was such uneasiness justified?

Who could have been powerful enough to have stood up to Burum Babar himself? He wondered. Certainly, the Daikan's death was not the result of a confrontation with the kings of Aere Tine, nor against Queen Graglia, so had Burum Babar succumbed to someone with no power in his sword? True, his poor friend was ill and had lived a long life, one already full of ailments due to age. Even so, it was hard to believe that the eternal monarch Tirhan no longer walked the world of the living.

How many years had the revered man lived? More than three hundred, he calculated. Considering his friend's advanced age made him more aware of his own. *I am young in comparison,* he told himself. Then he gave a snort at his witticism, *young...* he boasted, reminding himself that he was already over a hundred years old.

67

An axe through his neck brought him out of his deep introspection. He pressed his knuckles to his neck, feeling them get wet with his own blood.

The memory of his friend fallen in combat had distracted him for an instant. Long enough for the blade of an axe to have found its way into his flesh. The blood gushed ominously, yet the king's experience and history of countless wounds told him it was a more alarming looking gash than it truly was.

He glanced to the front. His gaze fixed on the audacious soldier who had inflicted such a wound. A man of short stature, heavy worn purple armor full of illegible writings and a huge axe. Wulkan smiled when he saw the black tear tattooed under his right eye; a symbol only worn by warriors of the Divine Protection.

Jerhen the Taisee, he recognized, at last a worthy opponent.

Both swords, wreathed in flame, rose to the sky. Their blades clashed, twice. A loud *clank, clank*, after which both sword tips pointed towards the man who had managed to wound him. The Chosen by Fire fought more briskly, trying to provide space on the battlefield for their king. They knew perfectly well what that signal meant, a face-to-face confrontation in which they should not intervene under any circumstances, on the contrary, they should die before allowing anyone to interfere in that duel to the death. Their monarch had chosen his prey and they had to step aside and gain ground so that he could play with his victim.

It was Jerhen who initiated the combat. A roar anticipated his attack, that man of short stature moved with alarming gracefulness for the weight of his armor and the size of his axe. The warrior of the Divine Protection charged at Wulkan with swift determination. The king pointed the tip of Sinistra at him, launching several flames that the taisee dodged with dexterity to continue advancing in search of melee combat.

Did he feel he was wrong to resort to a fire weapon that provided him with such an advantage? Not at all, the Fireos used to say that every being was born with the blessing of a talent. So, how could it be his fault that his particular gift was to wield a flaming sword? It was a sin to feel bad about the grace with which one had been blessed, so he wielded the red-hot steel with honor.

His opponent's axe met his flaming steel. The face of that elite soldier looked more temperamental than Wulkan supposed a warrior of the Divine Protection should have. *More fun that way*, he thought.

The king of the Fireos lunged, ready to slit his opponent's throat with a single blow, but Jerhen deflected the attack with his axe. Wulkan noticed how his movements were not as agile as in his youth, but who was he kidding? After all, he was over a hundred years old—he was the oldest living monarch by far! His still black hair could fool others, but not himself, just as his aching bones couldn't.

They were engaged in an epic battle. Some soldiers of his personal guard could not help but look in the direction where the duel was taking place, even if such an act meant being skewered by their opponents. The axe and the flame-wrapped swords clashed again and again.

That taisee fought fiercely. He leaped at Wulkan, wielding his gigantic axe with both hands. The king countered the attack with Distra, and then tried to pierce his heart with Sinistra. However, that Aquo warrior knew how to postpone his death, dodging it at the last moment.

"You fight well," Wulkan conceded to him, "but not so well that you could end the life of a Fireo king."

The taisee, on the other hand, continued in his eagerness to take the victory. He made a feint, and then tried to drive the edge of his axe into one of Wulkan's legs. An attempt that was countered by a forceful kick, throwing the soldier of the Divine Protection rolling on the ground.

Wulkan pointed Sinistra at his enemy. Jerhen tried to turn away when he saw a flame emanating from the tip of the sword in his direction. But he had no strength left. His eyes lit up at the color of the fire that was about to consume him completely.

Not a grimace of fear, not a cry of pain, admirable, Wulkan acknowledged, watching as the flame impacted his target.

His opponent lay on the ground motionless, his armor now red-hot, his body completely charred.

Wulkan advanced, enraptured by the fervor of the combat, continued the march, indicating with his swords to follow him. His personal guard went after him without the slightest delay, imbued with a murderous fury at witnessing the triumph of their king's duel against such a worthy rival. They advanced, stepping over the bodies of countless slain Aquo soldiers.

However, the soldier carrying the standard, paused; placing his dirty boots just in front of the charred body of Jerhen the Taisee. He raised the standard-bearer as high as he could, then roared, his teeth still stained in the blood of one of his enemies. The sharp point of the wood descended, ready to impale the charred head of the brave warrior.

* * *

Two black-armored soldiers laid the lifeless body of the Fireo woman on the huge pile of brown-eyed corpses. The deceased woman fell face up, her neck craning backward due to the tilt on which she lay. She was looking at Wulkan, watching him with her unmoving eyes.

His people had fought as they were expected to fight. With courage, bravery, fury and hatred. It had been a crushing victory, and yet that did not mean that there had been no casualties. Men and women who had given their lives for their kingdom, for their king.

Wulkan watched as the ritual took place, solemn, grieving for the fallen.

"That was the last one, my king," Turuma informed him, the captain trying to appear upright and unchanged despite displaying an ugly chest wound.

Wulkan nodded.

Now, it was his turn. His people had fought under his mandate. It was time to honor them and return the favor. He had to make sure that the stay of those warriors in hell was appropriate.

Wulkan had always found it amusing how the paradise of the Fireos was used in the common tongue by other kingdoms to describe a horrible place of suffering. As far as he knew, they described it as a fiery place, where everyone who was sent there suffered eternal torture.

The truth was that they could not have been more wrong. Hell was a cold place, as icy as the peak of the highest mountain. When dying and appearing in hell, every Fireo was accompanied by a flame that arose between the palms of his hands, the size of which was one or the other depending on how dedicated he had been in the material world. That was why it was important for the Fireos to act as good citizens, otherwise, their flame would be weak and insignificant after their death, one that would eventually extinguish, their soul suffering the icy onslaught for an eternity.

He unsheathed Sinistra, ready to perform the ritual. He pointed the tip of the sword at the fallen Fireos. Sinistra's blade began to turn red-hot. He made a motion with his left wrist. The pile of corpses began to burn brightly.

70

It was said that those incinerated by the power of one of the twin swords of fire would appear in hell with a fanned flame. This flame was far more impetuous than what would have been bestowed upon them had they not died in pursuit of their king.

The Incandescent was fair.

The lifeless bodies burned, the gray smoke claiming its place in the sky. The king said his prayers, praying that the flames that accompanied the souls of those brave Fireos would dance forever.

"What do we do with the bodies of the Aquos, my king?" Said the captain of the Chosen by Fire, "throw them into the sea?"

Wulkan gave a snort, turning to his subject with a faint smile on his face. Turuma laughed, pleased that her quip had amused her king.

Those Aquos would not find the sea. It was the price of defeat; they had lost the right to choose the destiny of their souls. Now their fortune was in the hands of Wulkan, and he was not willing to please any god but the Incandescent.

Just at that moment, he heard footsteps behind him. He turned around, two Chosen by Fire were grabbing the arms of an Aquo soldier who was trying to resist. However, as the man's blue eyes fell on Wulkan he ceased his rebellion, now looking down at the ground, trembling like a frightened lamb.

"We found this one, my king," one of the warriors stated, "intact, save for his thumb and forefinger, of course."

It was a common maneuver performed by Fireos warriors on their captives, to remove from both hands those two fingers that a soldier made most use of, the thumb to control the sword, the index finger to handle the bow.

Wulkan looked at the prisoner's armor. *Silver, so much the better,* he thought. He stepped closer to the cowering soldier, who kept his eyes fixed on the bloody ground beneath his feet.

"We will offer you a boat and you will be allowed to escape from here, safe and sound." Wulkan looked to Turuma, who nodded, thus ensuring that no one would touch the man, "I want you to give a message from me to Queen Graglia."

71

7. Empty nest

Vienne looked up, taking in the majestic palace. Its five towers and walls, built from white rock, stood in stark contrast to the blue conical roofs reaching towards the cloudy skies. From her hazy memories of the dreary architecture lessons given by her caretaker, Igüenza, that singular structure was designed to mimic an immense wave. Originating from the sky and breaking apart, its whitish stone depicted the foam.

That architectural work had a certain creative logic in the eyes of the princess, for the Aquos the sky and the sea symbolized respectively the beginning and the end of life. Rain fell from the sky; the Aqua Deus blessed the world with sweet, pure and crystalline water that irrigated the fields, filled the rivers and from which living beings drank. The seas, on the other hand, were the place where their deity would receive them at the end of their journey. That was precisely why sea water was salty and made those who drank it sick, for one should not consume the water destined to venerate the dead.

She approached two guards. The two women stood motionless, positioned between a small palisade and the deep moat behind them that prevented access to the palace from the front and sides. They stood with their heads held high, their austere blue gaze peering out from between their helmets as they lost themselves in the horizon. Each held a spear—one with her right hand and the other with her left. They wore silver armor tinged with blue, upon which a wave was carved, topped by a crown of three peaks. The symbol of the Guard of the Sea, when adorned with a crown, signified that those soldiers were indeed members of the Royal Guard.

Vienne bent down and picked up Zyrah. She approached the guards and opened her mouth to introduce herself.

"No begging at the palace gates," one of the guards said, shaking her head and shooting a glare from beneath her helmet. "You think a trick as old as bringing a dog with you is going to get us any more grief? Get out of here." She pointed at her, tapping the damp earth with the shaft of the spear.

"Is this how you treat people who don't have enough to eat?" Replied Vienne apologetically, stroking Zyrah's little head, "with contempt and bad manners?

"Did you not hear my companion, you filthy beggar?" The other guard reprimanded, stepping forward. "Get out of here or we'll throw you in the pit!" She threatened Vienne, pointing the tip of her spear at her.

Vienne pulled back her hood, fed up with so much insolence, "my name is Vienne Dajalam," she revealed, glaring angrily at those soldiers, "Lacrima, rightful heir to the throne. The last time I was here this palace was my home, I am astonished that I am now mistaken for a beggar." She added sharply.

The guard who had threatened her frowned. Both guards exchanged a nervous glance.

Before they were to question if it was really her, the princess reached out the arm she wasn't holding Zyrah with towards the cloak, grabbing the fabric at her hips and pulling it away far enough for them to see her belt. She placed her index and middle finger on the pommel of her sword, tapping it twice. The unhinged faces of both soldiers were enough for Vienne to assume that they had recognized the hilt of the sacred sword.

"Prin... princess Vienne," faltered the soldier who had threatened her, backing away thus returning to her position. "Forgive us for our insolence, I beg of you." She added, executing the Aquo reverence so abruptly that her spear slipped from her grasp and clattered to the ground.

The other soldier mimicked her. Then the latter turned. "Lower the bridge!"

The two guards then addressed the princess, probably enunciating a new apology, but their words were muffled by the clattering sound of chains that the drawbridge produced as it moved. As the bridge descended, Vienne reflected on how curious the layout of the Aquo palace was. On one side, the walls of the palace were protected by a freshwater moat; on the opposite side, they were guarded by a private beach. One might think that placing the palace next to a sea entrance would make it vulnerable to attacks from the waters. However, should any enemy's pride cause them to overlook that the sea is home to the god of the Aquos, probably the mighty naval force of the Aquadom would serve as a deterrent to even the most avid conquerors of glory and fortune.

After a moment's gradual tilting, the bridge settled completely. The thick bluish wood struck the earth with a resonant thud.

The princess nodded to the two embarrassed soldiers. "I hope this lesson has served you well in dealing less rudely with beggars who approach to ask for something to eat." She admonished them, then crouched down, leaving Zyrah on the ground, both of them walking across the drawbridge.

She passed through the parade ground and proceeded to the barbican. She stopped for a moment, confused; she didn't feel anything, shouldn't she feel at ease for having returned home? For being back among the whitish rock walls that had been her home since she was conscious? She did not perceive any kind of attachment, everything seemed cold, surprisingly far from the warm feeling she had felt in that Tirhan tavern. There, she had lived an endearing moment together with Alvia and Gelegen, laughing and having fun as she assumed a normal family should do... it was true that, not long after, that pleasant experience had been cut short after meeting Siere and who she insisted was still her boyfriend... How easily life could swing from offering you pure happiness to profound sadness! The princess considered. However, there was one thing she did look forward to, she would soon meet Aienne!

It's early in the morning, so she would surely be along with the rest of my sisters in their classes, she considered.

She wandered absently, her feet instinctively navigating corners they knew so well. Zyrah, on the other hand, took her time to sniff every nook and cranny, then lightened her pace to follow the princess.

While her return had already caused a stir, the presence of a little white dog in the palace only heightened the expectation. It was no secret that her mother detested dogs, to the point of prohibiting their entry into the palace.

She climbed one of the towers, the one where her classes were taught, and looked out. There was no one there, neither her sisters, nor Igüenza, not even the cushions on which they sat to attend her lessons. She went into the room and opened the window to look out onto the royal garden, perhaps they were sitting there, enjoying the music or poetry of an artist invited to the palace. An intense and fresh scent of flowers overwhelmed her, beyond that, in that garden there was no one except a long-haired troubadour playing a beautiful melody with a harp.

The princess frowned, *where are my sisters?* She descended from the tower and continued her tour of the many rooms of the castle, closely followed by her faithful canine companion. Every servant and soldier she encountered showed the same expression on their face, morbid interest.

They know, she thought, *somehow, they know that my journey was made to awaken the powers of the sacred sword and they are eager to ask me if I achieved such a purpose....*

Rumors, whispers, gossip... Vienne hated all that insidious chatter, she had always disregarded all those meddlesome and manipulated malicious comments whose aim was none other than to cause harm.

She entered the princesses' bedroom. A spacious room with large windows; thick, shaggy light blue carpets, and thirteen beds, all with soft, uniform vanilla-colored sheets. Vienne had always found Sendarienne's bed peculiar. Her sister slept with two pillows instead of one, positioned vertically on the bed—one parallel to the other, in contrast to the horizontal arrangement of the others.

She walked around the room until she reached the back. There lay her bed and Aienne's, the penultimate and the last respectively. She ran her hand across what had been her bed until she had been named Lacrima, feeling the amazing softness of the fabric in her fingertips, until she stopped at a particular spot. She smiled, wistfully recalling the smear of ink that permeated all the sheets once an inkwell had been knocked over while she and Aienne were drawing flowers on parchment. How many whimsical conversations they had had late at night.

"Woof!"

Vienne looked around for the little dog and shook her head. Zyrah had climbed onto the first bed in the room, looking at her with her tongue hanging out as she rested her bottom on the sheets.

Suddenly, Vienne's face changed completely. Zyrah had not sat down; she had placed herself in such a position to urinate.

"No, Zyrah, no!" The princess urged her, running to stop the dog. That bed belonged to none other than Katienne.

She tried to avoid it, however; as she lifted Zyrah out of bed, she had already finished her needs. The urine began to seep between the sheets, leaving a wet yellowish stain that gave off a strong odor reminiscent of rancid fish.

She had to do something. They might assume it was intentional, that it was a way of taunting her sister Katienne. She looked around, maybe she could change the sheets? No, these were stored in a room in the remote laundry room, it would raise too much suspicion.

She nodded. There was only one thing she could do. She headed for the door, grabbing Zyrah. She stepped out and closed it very gently, taking care not to make even the slightest noise. She began to walk down the corridors, as if she had never entered that room before.

Luckily, no one had seen her, she thanked the Aqua Deus for her fortune. She turned around a corner, slamming her face against the wood of a ladder on which a man was climbing, dusting with a grayish rag the golden frame of a huge painting showing a ship docked in an Aquo port.

The servant paused in his cleaning.

"Oh, Princess Vienne," he said with a broad smile that caused dimples to rise in his ruddy cheeks, "it's you, what a pleasant surprise!"

The princess smiled, recognizing the always-polite servant, Pokondu. He had an affable, round face that seemed too small in comparison with his big body.

"It's good to see you, Pokondu. Do you know where my sisters are?"

"Gee, didn't they tell you?" He replied quizzically. "None of your sisters live in the palace anymore, princess. From what I hear, your mother urged them to carve out a future for themselves now that you are the Lacrima."

Vienne frowned. Had her mother really thrown all her sisters out of the palace? It sounded like a somewhat drastic measure, however, she remembered that such a course of action was perfectly in line with the queen's own.

"You wouldn't happen to know where Aienne resides?" She said, without any hope.

"I haven't the slightest idea," he replied with a shrug, the ladder creaking with his slight movement. Just as the princess went to thank him, he continued. "But I do know where she works! Your younger sister is part of the Research Team."

"Really?" The princess replied with a smile. Things had certainly changed a lot since she had left. "Great, thank you very much!" She said goodbye.

The servant smiled warmly at her and continued his work. The princess lightened her pace followed closely by Zyrah. She was eager to head to the research workshops and hug her sister tightly.

Aienne devoting herself to research... what a great profession for a mind as eager for answers as hers! She was glad, surely Aienne would have much to tell her about her experiments.

Her steps led her to the throne room. That was the shortest way out of the palace. She entered through a side door, she caught the scent of lilies, she knew that they periodically refreshed the rooms with different scents to enhance their cheerfulness.

She closed the door to the royal hall. She walked quickly, followed by Zyrah. Suddenly, the little dog barked, looking toward the throne. Vienne frowned, turning to the royal chair. It was not empty, sitting on the throne was none other than Katienne.

"Isn't she the one no one remembers anymore as the Lacrima?" scoffed Katienne, situated with both hands on the armrests of the throne and her back straight.

"What are you doing here?" replied Vienne, unable to hide her disgust, "and why do you think you have the right to sit on our mother's throne?"

Katienne tilted her head slightly and looked at her with a grimace of disgust, "is it that you think I have to explain myself to you?" She said angrily. "I heard that you had returned from the Kingdom of Earth safe and sound. I wanted to verify if such rumors were a lie, but, apparently, you somehow managed to survive."

Of course, Vienne thought, *for of course my ambitious and conceited sister has eyes and ears all over the queendom.* She noticed something; beside the throne, Katienne had a sheathed sword. Vienne clenched her jaw.

Her older sister was still watching her with utter contempt. Then she bowed her head, diverting her attention to Zyrah, who was approaching her.

"And where did this mangy dog come from?" She said boastfully.

Instinctively, Vienne moved her hand toward Crystaline's grip. For an instant, she considered doing nothing, allowing the little dog to approach her sister closely enough for Katienne to reveal her true nature with a cruel act, like kicking the animal. Such a vile reaction would provide the perfect pretext to reach for her weapon.

She began to feel bad about herself. Allowing Zyrah to be beaten as a consequence of their sibling feud seemed to her a tremendously disloyal act.

"Silbai," she commanded. At the sound of her voice, Zyrah turned around, taking quick strides to stand beside her with her tongue lolling out.

"Ha!" scoffed Katienne, "a skinny, pathetic, weak dog. They say dogs take after their owners, so your pet fits you perfectly."

Vienne's breathing quickened. "Well, if so, your ideal pet would be a pig. A fat, greasy pig that wallows in its own feces and grunts at anyone who tries to get near the garbage it's been fed!"

As that sentence left her mouth, Vienne realized that she had made a tremendous mistake. Katienne swiftly grabbed the sword, rising as if spring-loaded.

"Do you think you're somebody just because you came back alive from Tir Torrent?" She reproached her with a sneer. "You must feel very brave to have survived a few days away from home. I'm sure the only reason you're still alive is because our Aunt Alvia made an immense effort to keep you safe, so you're already wiping that defiant look off your face right now."

An inner voice urged Vienne to let her comment slide, to look away and not fall for her provocations. However, she also felt something different this time, a new sensation that had come over her since she had awakened the powers of the sword and that seemed to have grown stronger since she had met Noakh. The need not to feel crushed by anyone.

"You're good with words," Vienne began, "I'm not. You're especially good at manipulating people. However, I think I know why the Aqua Deus chose me, as well as why he granted me Absolute Power."

"And why is that?"

"Because even the Aqua Deus is aware that, even someone like me, is a better alternative than leaving the reign in the hands of a being as petty as you, capable of bossing around an entire people just to get what she wants."

For a moment, Katienne just looked at her without saying anything. Her mouth open, as if trying to find the right words, her eyes barely blinking, as if trying to affirm to herself that the words Vienne had just said were not true.

"Your ego has swelled since your visit to the neighboring kingdom," she managed to finally say, "you might impress a handful of naive individuals with your changed attitude, but I know you are as pathetic as ever," she added, drawing her sword and letting the sheath fall to the ground.

"It's time someone took you down a peg or two and showed you how weak and pathetic you are and will forever be."

If that's what you want, Vienne thought. The princess reached for Crystaline. She tightened her fingers around the hilt firmly, then glanced back at Zyrah, tilting her head slightly to the side.

The dog obeyed. Crystaline wielded a metallic sound as it was released from its sheath.

Both princesses looked at each other. Crystaline's edge was still dry, *not yet the time,* Vienne decided.

"What are you waiting for, coward?" encouraged Katienne, holding her sword in two hands.

"It is you who wants to usurp my right to the throne," she reminded her, "come and get it!"

That provocation was enough. Katienne gritted her teeth and charged her sister. Vienne also ran swiftly, her sword held high, its edge unsoaked. The footsteps of both princesses echoed in the palace hall, its blue walls full of paintings witnessing how their weapons were about to cross, how the destiny of the queendom was about to be forged.

"Ladies!" cried a voice that boomed resoundingly through the ornate palace roof.

Both princesses stopped dead in their tracks. Vienne felt a chill, that voice had resonated throughout her entire being. It was a voice that reminded her of the past, of the many reprimands she had received since she was conscious. From Katienne's unhinged face, she had felt exactly the same.

At the main entrance to the throne room, still holding the door, stood their elderly caretaker, Igüenza, pursing her wrinkled lips as she shook her head.

"I don't remember teaching you such manners," she chided them.

"It was her, Igüenza," complained Katienne, "her mere presence is a provocation."

"It's not true!" defended Vienne, "it's she who won't leave me alone!"

Both princesses offered explanations for their actions. Aware that they were defending themselves as if they were two little girls before a mother who was scolding them.

"I don't care who started it, I just know that I will be the one to end it. This is not the place or the way for two ladies to settle their differences. So, apologize to each other, and go your separate ways."

"But..." Katienne began to reproach her.

"No buts," Igüenza cut her off, "you are the elder, Katienne. Show your maturity and apologize to your sister." At the slight smirk that faintly tugged at Vienne's lips her caretaker continued. "And you will go next, young lady."

Katienne glanced at Vienne, poised to speak. Soon after, her gaze shifted swiftly to Igüenza. It was a look filled with the intent of reproach. However, it was met with sternness from their caretaker. The eldest of the sisters turned to Vienne.

"I'm sorry."

For a brief moment, Vienne felt a tremendous sense of satisfaction. However, that feeling vanished as soon as Igüenza's stern gaze indicated that it was her turn.

"I'm sorry too." Vienne replied, lowering her head.

"Well, I'm glad that two well-mannered young ladies know how to put their differences aside," Igüenza continued, the caretaker probably knew perfectly well that neither princess was the least bit sorry; however, it had been a way to have quelled their desire to confront each other. "I'm heading out for my morning snack, for me it would be an honor to have you join me." She invited them.

"I can't," Katienne said, "I have important business that requires my attention." She said walking towards the door, sheathing her weapon.

For a moment, they stood silently, watching as Katienne vanished behind the royal hall's door.

"At least tie that animal up." Igüenza ordered her, turning her gaze to Zyrah, who was sniffing the throne.

Vienne went to protest, but ceased her efforts. She knew perfectly well what Igüenza's answer would be, that these were her mother's rules and that as long as she was present, she would see to it that they were followed to the letter. The same statement that Vienne had heard her make on countless occasions for as long as she could remember.

Igüenza reached over, grabbed Vienne by both cheeks squeezing them hard, her baggy eyes examining her closely.

"You've lost weight, but I also see newfound confidence in you." She added proudly, "I'm glad it is so. You have a lot to tell me, young lady." She went to hug her and, as she did so, wrinkled her nose. "We'll have some cookies together, but first, have a nice bath and, while you're at it, have that animal washed and tied up."

8. A complicated step

Coins of bronze, silver, and even some gold began to fall on the folded jacket she had left under the stage. It was a cheerful and simple song, *The Merchant Woman*, she had titled it. It was not her best creation, but its jocular tone made it a perfect choice to lighten the mood of the crowded and noisy tavern she had chosen for her performance.

The applause was still going on, even people who had paid and were about to leave the establishment had stayed until the end of her song. However, Halftal was not satisfied with her performance. The strumming of her lute had been less brilliant than she would have liked. Moreover, her voice faltered in the third verse, even though it was a simple song....

She was still on the stage, a wooden platform so worn that it gave the impression that it could break at any moment. The *Grand Piglet* was the name of the noisy, spacious and dirty tavern she had chosen to test her musical talent. The proprietress had been somewhat unpleasant when she introduced herself as an artist, grimacing at her brown hair as though she expected little from a unickey like her.

Luckily, the applause from Halftal's performances had served as a pretext for that annoying proprietress to allow her to continue playing, postponing her confrontation with destiny.

Dabayl had accompanied her, simply for the kindness of doing so. She had left Noakh and Hilzen behind in order to go with her into Aere Tine and lead her to the mythical city in which she now found herself, Stirrup. Dabayl's company had been most pleasant, she was a somewhat coarse and very independent young woman, though kind. However, what had surprised her most was the only condition Dabayl had given in exchange for accompanying her: *please, do not play or sing any song in my presence*, those had been her words. It had not been an abrupt and impertinent demand as someone like Garland might make, she had simply asked her to be so, *what could have happened to Dabayl to not want to listen to a single musical note?* Emisai could not help but wonder.

She threw her lute behind her back and jumped down from the stage. Then she bent down to pick up her jacket and the coins that had been deposited on it. She quickly counted the coins, *there's enough for a night's stay, and perhaps to try the famous spicy, greasy suckling pig of this establishment*, she estimated. She was shocked at how expensive everything was in that city, with so many coins she could have lived peacefully in Tir Torrent for weeks, maybe it was her impression, but she would even say that every day the prices of food and drink were higher.

"Lute girl," said a voice.

Halftal raised her head. A young woman with braided reddish hair and a giant bow behind her back had approached her.

"My girls and I are going in search of the sword," she said, pointing with her thumb to a table where several women in armor were drinking with astonishing energy. "We could use someone to liven up our evenings and sing of our exploits when we deliver the sacred weapon to the queen. We are sponsored by my family, we can't compete against the big families, but I assure you that you won't lack for food or a warm place to spend the night, you'll live better than what you make playing in a dingy place like this." She said winking at her, trying to tempt her.

"I thank you very much, but I'm afraid I have to decline such a generous offer, I'm already sponsored," lied Halftal, putting on her jacket and stashing the coins in a grizzled leather pouch.

The young woman merely nodded. As she walked away, Halftal breathed a sigh of relief. Ever since her arrival in the chaotic city of Stirrup, she had been approached countless times to join expeditions. Her rejection had been followed by insults, reproaches and even a few blows, as she reflected on that she brought her hand to the stitched wound on her right eyebrow, which had been healed by a kindly cloth seller, an assault carried out by a heavy-set woman who had not taken kindly to Halftal's refusal to join her troop.

After that incident, she had discovered that responding to such overtures by indicating that she was already sponsored was a simple way to avoid any kind of confrontation, though it did not always prevent a few frowns.

A curious thing was that, with a few exceptions, the inhabitants of those lands seemed usually indifferent to her brown hair. They didn't seem to care in the least that she was a unickey, their treatment was the same as with others. Discourteous, sometimes aggressive and sometimes strangely kind, perhaps that was why it was said that the Aertians changed their minds as much as the wind blew.

She left the tavern, taking a stroll through the streets of the busy city.

Groups of heavily armed men and women were making their way through the already crowded streets of the main promenade. One woman was trying to make herself heard to sell her vegetable wares over the fishmonger across the street. In general, the mix of raw materials of all kinds, combined with the constant influx of livestock, endowed those streets with a smell somewhere between nauseating and vomitous. So unpleasant was it, that her creative mind had composed a little tune about it.

Was such turmoil in the city of Stirrup a common event, or did it have to do with the incident of the sacred sword? The fall of The Tower of Concord had been both unexpected and surprising news. The sword of the Kingdom of Air had disappeared, and with it, numerous groups of people had formed a team to find it. Glory, ambition and the desire for adventure; a combination as fiery as it was dangerous.

On more than one occasion she had been tempted to join one of those expeditions. Surely they would live fascinating adventures worthy of being recalled in the verses of a beautiful song. However, she had already found her muse. A young man with brown eyes and a flaming sword. A tale that had inspired her to write the best song she had ever composed. One that she could not play before anyone if she wanted it to be part of history, one that would be archived in that place to which her aimless steps had led her, in a totally unconscious manner.

The imposing reddish building of majestic dimensions, the Cloister of Music, the revered temple where songs were created to be heard by the very kings and queens present, past and future. It was an impressive square construction with four towers at its apexes, on top of which stood the same sculpture, a barefoot woman whose body was covered in a wide robe and whose right arm was stretched high up, brushing her fingers against a jade-colored bell, the result of advanced copper oxide.

From the day her popoi gifted her the lute, she had dreamed of being there. And, since Dabayl had guided her to the city of Stirrup, she had not yet mustered enough courage to enter it.

85

Halftal was very insecure about her own talent; many times, people had complimented her voice, her lute playing and even her compositions. Gond had reiterated to her on several occasions that her nickname, Half Talent, did not do justice to someone as skilled as she was. Even Garland, in his crude and impertinent way, had praised her musical gifts.

However, as much as they had praised her skill, there had been only one person who had managed to fuel her desire to fulfill her dream, Noakh. The young Fireo had listened to her intention to write the most epic song ever written and had not mocked her, on the contrary, he had encouraged her to fulfill her dreams.

She swallowed, observing the Cloister of Music. It was so easy and yet so complicated... she only had to enter through the entrance, request and await an audience with the representatives of this esteemed institution to present her melody.

She would have the chance to perform for them. If her composition was of sufficient purity to delight the ears of the demanding and illustrious members of the Cloister then her song would not only enjoy the honor of being performed in front of the kings Zarta and Lieri, it would also be a song preserved in the archives of the Cloister, where they would see to it that its melody would live forever. It was said that the musicians who managed to have one of their pieces preserved in the cloister's archives would be acclaimed by the Lady of the Bell herself when the day of her death arrived.

What did you come here for? To stand trembling in the doorway? She said to herself, those would probably have been the words Garland would have said to her, but probably accompanied by an expletive or two.

She nodded, determined, it was time to fulfill her dream.

86

9. A not so golden tower

Fortune seemed to be on her side, the leaders of that organization had received her message and had scheduled a visit on that cloudy and foggy morning. The invocation of the Chosen Lineage Preservation clause, along with the invitation to Katienne's proposal ceremony, had prompted Aienne to hasten in her efforts to gain support for Vienne. She had to hurry now that she knew that, at any moment, soldiers of the Royal Guard could capture her and force her to set sail for an island lost even to the Aqua Deus.

Dornias and Aienne stretched their necks to admire the expanse of the Golden Tower, then turned, trying to compare its height with that of the Hymal cathedral that stood directly opposite. The rumors were true, that building managed by the bourgeoisie was now of lesser height than the one destined for the cult of the Aqua Deus after the sculpture that not so long ago had lain on its golden top had been removed.

It was no secret what had happened there; on the contrary, it had been the talk of the whole queendom. The Knight of Water Gant, under the queen's orders, had taken the lives of three of the four guild leaders, and had gone in search of the fourth member. *A lesson in humility*, so had several servants Aienne had heard categorized it. It made sense that it had been so, the princess knew more than well that her mother liked such lessons to reach as many ears as possible.

"Well, here we go," Aienne said taking a deep breath and heading for the door.

"Aienne, do you really think it's a good idea for me to accompany you?" Said Dornias, stopping at the entrance.

"Of course, everything will be fine," she reassured him with a smile. The princess perfectly understood the nobleman's concern. One did not need to have studied in the royal palace itself to know that nobility and bourgeoisie did not get along at all. The nobles, rich from birth, looked down on the bourgeoisie, who in turn held their own disdain for the nobles, considering that the latter had done nothing to achieve their fortune and status other than being born into the right family.

She proceeded to enter the Golden Tower, but thought better of it and stopped. "Whatever they say, let me do the talking," she added, anticipating any clashes there might be between the parties.

They entered the building. The strong smell surprised her, at the entrance there were several bovine skins lying on the floor. The walls were bare, not a single painting, no sculptures adorning the corners. It was a strange feeling, like a place that had been built to house the greatest of luxuries and had been stripped of all wealth and dignity along the way.

They walked up the marble stairs, meeting a man with haggard eyes, yellowish teeth and worn clothes in shades of gray. The man stood with his hands behind his back. It was a room without any kind of decoration, only a simple table full of documents and a chair, equally lacking in any detail or luxury.

"I was hoping that we could be met by the four guild representatives." Aienne indicated matter-of-factly, "we can wait for them if they haven't arrived yet."

The man shook his head. "The era of four guildsmen operating this tower came to an end with the lesson your mother blessed us with, princess. I alone manage the Tower now."

"Just you?" Said Aienne, puzzled, "I thought the Tower always had four representatives." She added, careful not to mention the word *Golden* as the leader had avoided.

"That's the way it usually is," he said, "when there are at least four candidates to fill such positions. After what happened, after the bloody death experienced by these four walls in which we find ourselves, only I had the courage to volunteer for the job."

Aienne was able to read between the lines. A tower led by a cautious man, not much given to conversation, and wearing humble and wide robes that did not disguise his slim figure... it was obvious that those guilds had made a major effort to hide any ostentation that reminded of their past, and that included their representative.

If they are making such efforts, it is because they fear further reprisals from my mother. She realized. *How stupid of me, how could I have thought that scheduling a meeting with the busy representative of the bourgeoisie was a mere matter of luck? They think I am coming on behalf of my mother...* such a discovery made her intellect start to work, how should she approach that matter?

"You are probably thinking that I am here on behalf of my mother, that my visit is just a pretext with which the queen intends to make sure you learned your lesson. Believe me, that is far from being the case."

The representative raised his eyebrow, interested. "What is the reason for your visit then if I may ask?"

"The queen rules through fear," said Aienne, the representative's eyes widened, as if surprised that anyone would dare enact such dangerous words aloud. "I can see that this majestic edifice has succumbed to the terror of being punished. I am not disturbed by your ostentatious past, any more than I am captivated by the present modesty within the walls of this place, but I wish to speak of your future. Are you terrified of my mother's form of rule? You will be surprised to learn that it is nothing compared to the reign of terror that is to come if my sister Katienne rules.

Many say that Katienne has the same character as my mother, but it is not true, my sister is far worse. She is ruthless, selfish and cares for no one but herself. And if my mother didn't have the slightest qualms about ending the lives of guild leaders imagine what she could be capable of.

After all, even her fiancé's own brother was not spared imprisonment," she indicated, pointing to Dornias, who stood idly by. "Why should she treat the bourgeoisie any better? That is why I come to offer you a more attractive alternative..."

The representative raised a hand, urging her to stop.

"An impressive speech," he acknowledged, looking slightly more nervous now, "I'm glad to know that the substantial money I pay in taxes at least goes towards providing the princesses with an education of the highest standard." He took a deep breath, visibly annoyed, "you are looking for us to make public our support for Princess Vienne to the throne. Do you really expect us to take a stand against the Church after what they did to the previous heads of the guilds?" He spat, completely indignant, "this may be difficult to understand for mere nobles and girls born in the delicate fabrics of the palace but, we, bourgeois, work hard to be able to eat; we have amassed wealth based on effort and sacrifice..." he pointed his index finger at the marble of the floor, "I can still see traces of the blood of my murdered comrades. This tower has already endured a heavy blow, another of such magnitude will cause it to fall, and I will not be the one to bring about such a fateful destiny!"

Aienne pursed her lips, making a pretense to turn and walk away, but Dornias grabbed her arm. The nobleman looked at the representative seriously. "Do you realize that it is only a matter of time before Katienne sets her sights on this organization?" He remarked gravely.

The representative gave a snort. "She already has." He revealed to them, then his gaze returned to the princess, "I'm afraid your sister is ahead of you."

Aienne couldn't help but open her mouth in disbelief.

"Princess Katienne offered a large sum of money and promises of prosperity for the Tower once she was the one to reign. More than an offer it sounded like threats, even so, I managed to dissuade her from her attempts without myself ending up bleeding to death in the middle of an alley..."

"You are very brave then." Dornias flattered him.

"I wish my wife saw it the same way," he confessed in annoyance, "there is not a night before bed when she does not reprove me for refusing her offer, and in how much danger I am putting our son in." He turned again to the princess, "so this is the most you can get from me, princess, the bourgeois will not ally themselves with any side, perhaps it is less than you expected in coming here, but it is what I can offer you."

Aienne merely nodded, completely demoralized. It was a small victory, but it wasn't enough.

"I thank you," the princess finished by saying, followed then by an Aquo reverence that Dornias mimicked. "I won't take up any more of your time then, thank you for listening." She said turning to leave.

"Wait." The representative indicated, Aienne turned, hopeful. "The Tower has already paid hard for its sins in the form of blood and offerings, I don't think Princess Katienne will take any notice of us, unless we meddle in family confrontations that do us no good. However, I appreciate that requests made to me as a representative of the Tower are made with respect and words rather than intimidation. That is why I will tell you something else; even if it is at the cost of risking my own safety. Your sister is not only willing to pay to get our support, she is also offering a juicy reward for ratting out those who go against her choice for the throne. And that puts you in grave danger."

Aienne's eyes widened. The rest of the nobles were in the Cathedral of Hymal and it was more than likely that the Sisters of the Church of

Water would take action. She caught Dornias' fleeting glance; he too had noticed the danger of his companions.

"We greatly appreciate it." Dornias indicated.

The representative nodded, walking to his desk. "It's been a pleasure to receive you, you know which way is the exit of the building." He said politely, yet firmly.

They went down the stairs quickly. They did not speak on their way out of the Golden Tower. Aienne could not believe what was happening. She had hoped the bourgeoise would take her side, that they would support Vienne, but she felt she hadn't done enough to help her sister.

I failed again.

Gorigus, Laenise and Arilai appeared from the Cathedral of Hymal. Aienne sighed with relief to see them safe and sound. They crossed the busy square, finding the five of them in the center of it.

"Well?" Asked Aienne hopefully.

Gorigus shook his head.

"The Sisters of Hymal want nothing to do with earthly matters." Arilai indicated.

"However, as soon as we revealed the noble houses we belong to, they did not hesitate to ask for a generous donation." Laenise added sulkily.

Another failure. Aienne was on the verge of tears, she believed she had talent, that she could develop a plan with which to help her favorite sister. However, they had achieved nothing more than to put themselves in danger.

Clonk, clonk, clonk, clonk.

A boy no more than eight years old was standing on the saddle of his scrawny spotted horse, waving a rusty bell with fervor, trying to catch the attention of everyone in the square. He continued ringing the brass bell a couple of times, then took a deep breath.

"News from the Queendom of Water!

King Wolukan has razed several settlements of the Aquo army, the casualties among our soldiers is incalculable. The situation is so drastic that some believe that the Holy War is on the verge of being declared in favor of the Fireo army.

Further news about the Kingdom of Earth, the death of Borenm Bobar is confirmed. According to the rumors, he died after a terrible murder by the heiress to the throne, Jarbila, while he was sleeping.

Princess Vienne has been sighted in Aquo territory, the heir to the throne is back to the Aquadom after having fought against a powerful fire-breathing dragon accompanied by the Knight of Water Alvia and an albino wolf with gigantic fangs."

Aienne was stunned by the news, not knowing what to think. The inaccuracies in the names of representatives from neighboring kingdoms made her doubt the news's reliability, but she had to know more. The princess went to run after the young man before he left, she wanted to know more, to discover any details she might have overlooked. However, she felt her arm being grabbed.

She turned around, indignant, "Laenise, why are you...?" She didn't need to ask her why, as she was witnessing it with her own eyes. One of the nuns from the cathedral was talking to some guards, pointing in their direction, they had to disappear from there if they didn't want to get into more trouble.

10. Palace affairs

The princess's feet felt the chill of the beach water. Her pinky toes cocked outward, a peculiar appearance she'd had as long as she could remember.

Maids had carefully combed her hair, giving it a silky shine. It was a far cry from the frizzy mane she had when she disembarked. Her hairstyle, despite being more elaborate with some waves in her long hair, still showed both eyes visible, denoting that she had not yet forgotten the lesson of her Aunt Alvia on the trip to Tir Torrent.

On the palace's private beach, Igüenza stood with the sheathed Crystaline cradled in her arms. She watched with indignation as Zyrah, her fur now much whiter and softer from her bath, ecstatically dug into the wet sand.

The princess retrieved the bluish stone from her dress pocket, placed it in her palm, and leaned forward, letting the waters wash over the sapphire. She waited with bated breath, would Noakh have heard her message and answered her? She wanted to hear from him; she wanted him tell her the reality of his confrontation with Burum Babar, everything.

She watched the sapphire, hopeful, seeing it sway slightly in the current. Then her heart skipped a beat, hadn't it been illuminated? She moved her head closer to make sure. Then she turned to the sky, squinting her eyes, *no, it hadn't lit up, it was just an untimely ray of sunshine sneaking through the clouds.*

She gave a snort of disappointment, *maybe Noakh wasn't the least bit interested in talking to me? I thought there had been a connection, someone who could understand that being chosen by the sword did not bring the happiness many would expect.*

She felt furious with herself. She had had to ask Gelegen to do her the favor, a request that had caused the kindly veteran not to be with them. Zyrah missed her master, and so did she, and what if something had happened to him on her way? She couldn't forgive herself...

She waited. She continued to wait. The sapphire was still not blinking in the slightest. *Really?* Her mind posed a thousand hypotheses, from Gelegen never having found Noakh, to the Fireo or the veteran ending up lifeless, or perhaps Noakh had simply decided to refuse the sapphire because he didn't want to talk to her?

"Whoever it is you're hoping has spoken to you, he clearly hasn't." Igüenza indicated from the shore.

"It would seem so," she replied grumpily, Vienne pulled the hand with which she held the sapphire from the water and walked to the shore, drying the stone on her dress and then putting it in her pocket. Waiting for her there were Igüenza and Zyrah, who sat her white fur down on the sand with her tongue hanging out.

"Come on, walk with me," Igüenza invited as the princess neared, "the wet sand soothes my old joints." She added as she handed her the sacred sword.

They walked for a while in silence as Zyrah scampered back and forth chasing the seagulls that landed on the sand to feed on the crustaceans that inhabited the shore. The slight rays of sunlight made the crystal-clear water seem even more magical, especially when contrasted with the colorful corals; these served as a natural barrier on the palace's private beach. She smiled as she remembered in her lessons that those natural walls had been designed by Burum Babar; it was incredible to think that she had come to meet that man.

As she recalled her trip, she remembered one detail, "Igüenza, I had a strange experience on our way home."

She then recounted the incident with the mermaids and how she had ended up under the sea to heal the mermaid that had been injured by her Aunt Alvia.

"They said it was time to unleash the storm, they seemed especially interested in me doing so, as much as I try to mentally go over the manuscript my mother gave me, I don't remember it compiling any blessings bestowed on my ancestors that had anything to do with releasing a storm."

Igüenza pursed her wrinkled lips. "There's a reason they're called blessings, Vienne, we consider that these, in one way or another, help the bearer of the sacred sword. What you're talking about, releasing the storm, isn't something that's very helpful..."

94

"So, do you know what the mermaids were referring to?" She asked with extreme interest.

Igüenza just looked at Vienne without saying anything, as if weighing whether she should tell her the truth. Finally, she nodded.

"*Nazar te acto, the storm that unites sky and sea.* It is certain that none of your ancestors has had such power, except the one who began it all."

"Dajalam, the Lady of the Mountain," Vienne understood. There were countless legends about her predecessor, the one whose steps were guided by the Aqua Deus until she was granted the power to control the water, so many stories, and yet she was shrouded in an unparalleled halo of mystery. "And what did she use such a blessing for?" She dared to ask.

Her caregiver looked at her with fear in her eyes, uncertain if she should answer. "Well, it's only fair that you know what it's all about," she decided. "But don't take it lightly. Using this blessing was the reason the Lady of the Mountain passed away."

"Dajalam died from releasing the storm?" Vienne said unable to believe what she was hearing.

* * *

The day was getting particularly busy. Igüenza's shocking revelation was followed by a meeting with Counselor Meredian. The visit didn't promise much entertainment, but according to her caretaker, it was a must.

She was in the throne room again, fortunately, this time she had not met Katienne there. She was alone; Zyrah was under the watchful eye of a freckled young servant with a mischievous smile, who had willingly agreed to walk the canine in the royal garden while the princess had an audience with the counselor.

She walked around the room, bored. Why was Meredian taking so long to arrive? Her aimless wandering brought her directly in front of the throne.

The truth was that she had never stopped to observe it in detail. It was as if that seat gave her respect, so much so that she had not even deigned to admire it carefully until that moment, or maybe it was fear? Looking at it, she had to admit that it was impressive. Seat and high back upholstered in sapphire blue contrasting with a beautiful white wood, its arms ended in a carving that simulated breaking waves, the

95

feet of the throne, however, were decorated in such a way that the wood acquired a very light bluish tone, showing the silhouette of a mermaid's tail that twisted until it was lost in the back of the seat.

She rested her index finger on one of the armrests, appreciating the delicate carving of it, she could feel the grooves in the wood, as if she were sailing on the waves. It was a commendable piece of cabinetwork.

A doubt assailed her, how comfortable would that seat be? Would it be wrong to test how good it felt to settle into the throne?

Her reflections were severely interrupted by the opening of doors to the royal hall.

"Ah, Princess Vienne, glad to see you are already here," said Counselor Meredian performing the Aquo reverence, "forgive my tardiness, but some errors in the palace books required my absolute attention." He looked her up and down and added. "You don't know how glad I am that you have returned safely from your mission in Tirhan territory, I trust everything went as your mother had hoped?"

Vienne gave a slight nod. The truth was that she had no informed opinion of that ungainly-looking man other than to be sure that he had a deep respect, and perhaps fear, for his mother, the queen. In a way, she felt sorry for him, Meredian was in charge of managing the taxes and everything related to the expenses of the reign. A task that, from what little she had witnessed, her mother did not make easy.

However, Meredian was now acting not only as a tax counselor, but her mother had empowered him to act as her representative in her absence, making him the Crown's Favourite.

"I'm sure by now you are aware the situation of our troops on the Fireo borders is complicated, to say the least..." he said cordially, smoothing over the situation as would be expected of him.

"I have heard a bit about it. Surely my mother will want to dispose of Crystaline as soon as possible," the princess assumed. "Tell me where I am to depart, and I will set course for the border with the least possible delay."

"I welcome your enthusiasm, princess," said Meredian, "it is true that the latest news about the status of the conflict with our hated Fireo neighbors urges that you deliver the sword to your mother with as much haste as it is in our power to dispose of. However, the queen was incisively insistent that I make it clear to you that, while it was crucial that you set sail for the front with alacrity, before doing so you must demonstrate your blessings to the other members of the Congregation of the Church."

Vienne merely shrugged her shoulders. She could perceive the interest in the crown counselor's face, the morbid desire to discover if she had succeeded in controlling the sword and thus disposing of her right to rule or if, on the contrary, she had failed and embarrassed the queendom.

Of course, Queen Graglia wanted her to prove her blessings. Beyond the relevance of the war, it was understandable that her mother, both as High Priestess and as Queen, would make sure that the ecclesiastical organization was kept under control. Her mother had mentioned to her the deal she had agreed with Priest Ovilier, if she was able to control Crystaline's powers she would be entitled to the crown, now she had to prove to the Congregation that this had been the case.

"In fact," Meredian added, " She made it clear to me that it's of utmost importance for you to give your best in demonstrating your blessings to the Congregation, to leave no doubt about your worthiness."

The princess could not help but furrow her brow. Those words did not sound like her mother. Something told her that Meredian was softening the words the queen would have actually used. Surely insisting that it was very important that her laziness and disdain could not get in the way of her mission to demonstrate her blessings. Yes, those adjectives sounded more like her mother's speech talking about her.

"I understand," Vienne replied, "How can I show the Congregation what I am capable of?" She asked. She certainly had no idea how that ritual worked—if it could even be called that. Something told her that her predecessors had not been called into question as she had been. Perhaps because they had a more robust character, or because they were lucky enough not to have a manipulative sister weaving treacherous plots behind their backs....

"Don't worry about that, Princess Vienne," Meredian reassured her, "that's what I am here for. I am pleased to say that I have taken it upon myself to manage everything. Let me tell you how the normal course of events will unfold. Initially, you will have to attend the sword celebration, which will take place tomorrow at dawn. Under normal conditions, it would be held well in advance, as such an event requires, and important families of the queendom, relatives of the crown and so on would be invited. However, the urgency of war demands a certain haste that leads us to skip the protocols and leave aside the cordialities.

That is why, instead, we will perform an intimate ceremony, where only you and the members of the Congregation of the Church will attend.

In the meantime, I will organize the preparations for your journey to the border. If everything goes according to my estimates, you will be allowed to travel from here three dawns. You must embark promptly for the front lines and reunite with your mother, however, not only are you incredibly valuable, but you also carry the sacred sword of the queendom. That is why such a journey must be made with due planning and discretion. Do not be in a hurry, princess, plotting the best route for your journey requires our utmost attention."

In three dawns, Vienne thought. She had several things to do, she had to hurry.

"All right, thank you for taking care of everything, Counselor Meredian," Vienne said, performing the Aquo reverence and preparing to leave.

"One more thing, princess," the counselor put one of his hands to his pocket extracting a small parchment from it, "there is a certain matter I would like to discuss with you before you leave, it is about your little sister, Aienne."

11. Remnants of war

The wooden mermaids in shades of violet and dark blue were crowded on the island of Ciana. Suddenly, they were swept away as if nothing, replaced by a derisory number of phoenixes in maroon, led by one whose head was painted in gold. Graglia gazed at the table in stupefaction, simply watching as Counselor Galonais gathered up the pieces representing the soldiers of the Aquo army and put them in their respective leather pouches.

She looked again at the map spread out on the table in the command tent, trying to come up with some explanation for such a disturbing scenario. Firia, located to the east, was surrounded at both ends. Figures in shades of blue on one side, yellow on the other. The number of phoenixes located near the Aquo borders had decreased by a third; these now relocated towards their borders with the northern kingdom of Aere Tine. And all this thanks to the plan of her daughter Aienne.

The expedition across Finistia into Aertian territory had been confirmed a success. They had destroyed the Tower of Concord and, as a consequence, the Kingdom of Air had been forced to send its troops to its borders with Tir Torrent and Firia as a precautionary measure. Faced with such a threat, Wulkan had been forced to send part of his soldiers to the other end of his kingdom.

They had not yet provoked a worldwide conflict, though her informants had reported to her that the situation was incredibly tense. Any false move would lead to a declaration of war by the Aertians. The only reason the Kingdom of Air had not gone to war was because they seemed to want to find out who had carried out the attack first.

Queen Graglia had assumed that, with such a reduction of Fireo troops on her borders, things would become easier for her army. But, against all odds, this was far from being the case. King Wulkan was attacking key Aquo settlements, destroying them with his characteristic ferocity.

Although she would never state it out loud, she had to admit that they were losing the war; one that had only just begun.

Utterly unhinged, reckless, absurdly rash... as much as she liked to live up to the countless insults to the Fireo people and their monarch, she knew for a fact that King Wulkan was, unfortunately, no fool. In fact, she was able to admit that, in his own way, he was a strategist.

But the war's progress, as depicted on that table full of colorful figures, didn't seem like the work of someone with an overwhelming talent for military strategy. Rather, it seemed to be someone capable of anticipating any of their movements.

Has Wulkan succeeded in obtaining the gift of predicting the future?

She did not want to admit it, but, as Queen and High Priestess, she could not deny what seemed most obvious. Someone in her entourage must have been informing Wulkan of the Aquo army's movements, their advances, the location of their settlements, everything. It was hard for her to accept it as much as it pained her that it was so, but one thing was clear to her, whoever it was, she would personally make sure that his remains would never rest in the sea.

She looked up from the board. Her sister, the commander of the Sea Guard, looked at her with eager anticipation. Bravia, the least graceful of her sisters, had a square jaw and an eternally unfriendly face, a combination of features that was ideally suited to lead the most powerful faction in the Queendom of Water.

"Well, your majesty?" Bravia began, raising one of her bushy eyebrows.

"Well, what then?" replied Graglia irritably. While placing the Aquo troops under the command of one of her sisters secured their loyalty, it came at the irksome price of enduring her sister's overfamiliarity.

"King Wulkan is crushing us, and we stand here." She said, extending both hands towards the roof of the command tent, "sheltered, doing nothing but witnessing our troops being slaughtered."

"And what do you expect me to do?" replied Graglia indignantly. "Do you have any ideas?"

"To begin with, it would be helpful to know when we can rely on the powers of the holy sword," interceded her other sister, Sastria, commander of the River Guard. The latter stood next to Bravia; her smaller size in both height and shoulder width making her look almost

100

childlike in comparison to her rough-hewn sister, despite the extra heel her boots always carried.

"That's not up to me," Graglia replied, more reserved than usual. Vienne's whereabouts were not unknown to her. Meredian had informed her, she and Alvia had landed in Royal Harbor. While she did not have much more information, everything seemed to indicate that her daughter had awakened the powers of the sword. However, Graglia would not believe it until she saw it with her own eyes.

"It wouldn't hurt to have all of our Knights of Water, either." Sastria continued, shaking her head.

The Defense Counselor sat in a chair, simply contemplating the scene with her arms folded. Probably in her experience leading the Aquo armies she had learned that this was going to be more of a fraternal dispute than a military one.

"Precisely," Bravia supported, "when does Miss Knight of Water plan to grace us with her presence?"

Here we go again, the queen thought, rolling her eyes. *How many years has it been since I named Alvia Knight of Water? So long ago that I don't even remember*, the queen reflected. *And, no matter how much time passes, it seems that they will never forgive me for having done so.*

She just looked at her sisters, without saying anything. They, likewise, remained silent.

"Oh, excuse me, are you really asking the queen for explanations?" said Graglia with feigned innocence. "As far as I remember, it is I who must demand explanations, not the other way around. I will not allow any more distractions related to our sister, if you manage to defeat Alvia in single combat I will be happy to dismiss her as Knight of Water, until then, lead my troops, which is what you are here for. Well, have either of you come to inform me that you've defeated Alvia?" Her two sisters pursed their lips and lowered their heads, "well then, let's focus our efforts on winning this war. I don't want to be remembered as the queen who lost a Holy War."

Just then a female soldier appeared at the entrance. "Pardon the intrusion, my Queen," she said hurriedly, "but a survivor from the island of Ciana comes to bring you a message."

Graglia frowned, *has Wulkan allowed someone to survive in one of his bloodthirsty attacks? That is most unusual.* Her sisters looked at each other, equally confused at such an event.

101

"Bring him in." Graglia ordered. Counselor Galonais stood up, placing herself next to Bravia and Sastria, who still seemed affected by the reprimand.

The soldier entered the command tent, frightened, eyes fixed on the ground, trembling. *Without performing the Aquo reverence, without dignity,* Graglia observed. He looked at the man's mutilated hands. *And without some of his fingers, Wulkan has dispossessed him of everything.*

The queen approached, placing herself in front of him. "Do not fear, you are safe now." She reassured him, "speak."

"King Wulkan left me alive in exchange for delivering a message to you..." the man began, his eyes fixed on the floor of the command tent.

"Go ahead." Graglia urged him calmly, hiding her haste. She wanted that man out of her sight as soon as possible, the mere presence of someone so devoid of spirit made her uncomfortable.

"He proposes you... a pact." He continued. "He declares that you can continue to hide in your lair while he destroys one by one all our settlements, or you can face him with dignity on the beach of Ghandya, army against army, king against queen."

Graglia gritted her teeth. Counselor Galonais could not help showing surprise at such a bold request.

Damn bastard Wulkan, this is no pact. He simply wanted fear to grip the hearts of the Aquo soldiers, fighting on the beach of Ghandya is not an option...

12. A second chance

Gant Blacksword uttered a cry of fury, making a powerful attack with his sword. The blade descended with a faint flash, catching the sun's rays that managed to break through the clouds.

Pieces of the log he split flew in all directions.

An impressive strength, the princess acknowledged from a distance. She watched him from the shadows, sheltered behind a damp tree. Its canopy was filled with flowering blue pompoms that emanated a scent so sweet it was reminiscent of honey. However, Katienne was too nervous to admire the beauty of that tree, as well as the vast greenish grassy landscape that stretched along the remote mountain range, where the Knight of Water had been exiled.

Clank! Another log suffered the uncontainable rage of Gant.

Katienne's heart was pounding, aware of how important it was going to be to measure her words. Vienne had returned, obviously thanks to the protection of her Aunt Alvia, and such a return required precautionary measures that would allow her to make sure that her sister would not get in her way. And among those measures was Gant....

She emerged from her hiding place, threw her shoulders back and walked towards the outcast Knight of Water. She made her way quickly through the grass. She had chosen her attire well: comfortable pants and boots suitable both for the field and for visiting a man to be brought to terms with reality. Such a revelation could be extremely dangerous if she did not resort to all her cunning.

Gant's black blade rose above his sweaty, shiny bald head, ready to finish off his next wooden victim. Up close, it was Katienne's first time seeing him out of his heavy armor. He now wore a soaked white shirt that hinted at his massive muscles, paired with slightly short, wide pants.

"Is smashing logs the best thing a Knight of Water can do in times of war?" The princess began, positioning herself behind Gant's back.

The Knight of Water paused in his attack, his sword held high. He turned quickly, his face drenched in sweat, the blade of his sword ready to execute whoever dared to mock his misfortune.

His angry eyes met the princess'. Unwillingly, the princess' gaze passed over the ugly burns on his face and on the part of his chest peeking through the unbuttoned collar of his shirt.

"What are you doing here, princess?" He said, his face becoming less aggressive. Gant lowered his weapon, resting its tip on the ground.

A meek response, Katienne thought, grateful for such a good start. The princess could not have known how the Knight of Water would react to seeing her appear. Their relationship had been nothing more than cordial—mere protocol greetings between a soldier sworn to fight for the queendom and a princess he was bound to protect with his life.

"I came as soon as I heard of your fate," she replied, looking gravely at him, "of how my mother removed you from your position as a Knight of Water to condemn you to this sort of ostracism." She added, taking care that neither in her face nor in her tone was there the slightest trace of mockery.

The soldier stuck the tip of his weapon into the grass and released the hilt, leaving the blade of his weapon embedded in the ground. "Not true," he said shaking his head and crossing his arms. "The queen indicated she had a mission for me, it is simply not yet time for me to find out what it is."

Katienne smiled candidly at him, trying to emulate genuine concern and pity.

"Oh, come on, Gant, someone as smart as you must have figured out by now that my mother only told you that so you wouldn't feel bad about yourself..."

"That's not true!" He replied, upset.

Katienne's heart was pumping so hard that it seemed as if it would burst out of her chest. She was acutely aware of the danger and the weight of her words. Her speech had to be sufficiently provocative and at the same time cautious so that the soldier would understand her situation without damaging his pride and without the princess having to fear that his sword would make his head roll. Gant was like a ferocious beast that had been wounded and cornered, he knew that his end was near, but his dignity would make him fight to the end.

"I'm sure someone as perceptive as you has figured it out, you just don't want to accept the facts. I have no doubt you already know why my mother won't allow you to participate in the war against the Fireos..."

Gant gritted his teeth, then grabbed his weapon with two hands, wrenching it out of the ground. The princess recoiled, unable to hide her fear. With unbridled fury, the soldier launched his attack, slamming brutally into his target.

"I'm in perfect condition!" He declared with such rage that he spat with every word, his body swelling with intensity. "I am more than capable of tearing as many Fireos in half as are put in front of me, as anyone who questions my abilities will discover."

The princess observed how the trunk against which the soldier had vented his fury had been completely shattered.

"I can see that, an impressive attack," she complimented him, trying to sound unperturbed. "However, I think we both know that the reason you have not yet embarked eastward has nothing to do with your state of health. I know it, my mother knows it, and even you know it. Those burns that show on your face and chest... would discourage the hearts of our Aquo troops, they would provoke..."

"Silence!" Gant cut her off. "If you have come to mock me, I assure you that not even your title as princess will save you from being run through with my sword." He threatened her, his eyes determined to make good his words. He was like a wild creature ready to lunge at a moment's notice.

The princess summoned the courage not to take a single step back, it was important not to show weakness. Blacksword unleashed his fury on the logs, striking once, again, and then a third time. Several logs fell from the pile, brutally cut in half, causing a shower of splinters in all directions.

He is tormented, and I must take advantage of such frustration, Katienne told herself.

"I can see that you are suffering, that you are distressed at having been cast aside by my mother."

Katienne merely raised her hands to allow him to explain before he acted. She was aware that she had to be cautious, Gant's temper was well known in the palace. The fine line between provocation and insult could make the difference between gaining a powerful ally or a fearsome executioner.

"My mother lied to you to make you content so that you would not be a nuisance." She said with her head held high, with assurance and solemnity in her voice. "I, on the other hand, am willing to offer you a mission to match your abilities. The war against the Fireos is not the only battle the queendom is engaged in, and in this one I would be

105

delighted to have you as part of it. No great deed has ever been achieved without a great warrior, and you are the bravest of all I have ever known."

Gant frowned, a gesture Katienne took as an invitation to tell him more.

"Soon I will be queen, it is inevitable." She stated emphatically, "Fight for me so that my victory over my sister will be indisputable, and I promise you that he whom my mother turned away from his duties and honor as an outcast, will rise as the most laureate Knight of Water of all time."

Gant's knee touched the ground.

"My sword is yours."

A Knight of Water kneeling before me, the princess could not contain her joy.

"Well, I have a mission of vital importance that I want you to take care of."

13. Unexpected course

That kitchen was a spectacle to behold. Pans, casseroles, and wooden utensils covered the walls and shelves of the large room. In the center, a rectangular table filled with flour, which gave the kitchen a pleasant smell, eggs, creams and various pots and pans that Girilay used with amazing skill.

Meanwhile, Hilzen and Noakh sat near a huge wood-fired oven, next to a large hourglass whose fine granules were about to reach the bottom surface. They just watched, engrossed as Girilay went back and forth in his culinary process. The young Fireo was still sore, one rib was hurting excessively, but, in his experience, it would soon heal.

"I need a bigger pan," mused Girilay. An instant later, a large frying pan appeared flying from one of the shelves. The young man raised his arm without looking, and the frying pan glided over to him. He caught it by the handle in mid-air and placed it on the table, then grabbed an egg, tapped it on the edge of the kitchen utensil, and dropped its contents into the pan.

Girilay glanced at the hourglass, noticing the sand had fully settled, and quickly moved to the oven. He grabbed a wide wooden shovel that was leaning against the wall near the oven and introduced it into the oven, using the shovel to extract a tray from inside.

"You have to taste this." Girilay invited them, leaving those sweets on a small wooden table next to where his guests stood. He had insisted that the least he could do for them was to thank them for their help, by treating them to a tasting they would not forget.

Noakh bowed his head at the sight of the food Girilay had prepared for them. They resembled bread but were much thinner than any loaf he'd ever seen. Moreover, Girilay had coated their surface with a generous layer of melted, whitish sugar. In a way, their suggestive smell caused the bruises from the blows he had received to fade into the background.

"I've named these buns fartuns," he revealed to them as he passed the sweets from the tray to a wide plate, positioning them to form a tower.

Hilzen reached for one, but Girilay stopped him.

"Not yet, the best is yet to come." He indicated to him, after which the pastry chef walked out the door and reappeared with a bucket, the base of which had traces of ice. He took two glasses and filled them to the top with a ladle.

"Dip them in this and see."

Noakh inspected his glass curiously, it was a cold, white liquid. He brought his nose close to that drink, guessing what it was, it smelled fresh and sweet.

"Of this we also have in the Aquadom, Girilay, we call it milk." He informed him.

"It doesn't taste like milk." Hilzen, who had a full white mustache after taking a big gulp, pointed out to him.

Noakh nodded, taking a sip. That drink made its way down his throat, leaving a fresh, sweetish aftertaste. It was much more pleasing to his palate than milk, of which he had never been much of a fan, "It tastes so much better than milk!"

"That's right," Girilay nodded proudly, "oroxiat, a typical drink of this shire. Dip the fartuns in it, come on!"

Hilzen was the first to grab one of those buns, Noakh followed, noticing how his hand was soaked in the sticky sugar. Those fartuns were fluffy, he brought it close to his glass of oroxiat and inserted the tip of the sweet into it. Then he put it in his mouth.

The refreshing taste of the drink combined with the sugar and the warm, fluffy bun sent his mouth into a frenzy.

"This is delicious!" Hilzen praised, and then immediately poured the rest of his fartun into the oroxiat and popped it into his mouth, white dribbles running down his beard from his eagerness.

Noakh, equally captivated by the delightful gastronomic combination, took the opportunity to satisfy his curiosity. "Girilay," he managed to say between mouthfuls, "how do you make cooking utensils fly at you?"

"Ah, that," Girilay walked over to one of the saucepans he had used in the fight and handed it to Noakh. The young Fireo finished what little he had left of his oroxiat, set the glass aside, and then grabbed the saucepan. He began to inspect it; at first glance it looked like an ordinary kitchen utensil. In fact, it was similar in manufacture to the ones he had seen in the Aquadom, although the handle of this one was slightly longer and heavier. Upon turning it over, he noticed a small detail: a bright yellow stone embedded in the saucepan's handle

"What is it?" Said Noakh, perplexed, pointing to the stone.

"That's a citrine. I am not entirely sure how it works, but apparently there is a way to make a citrine attract another one." He showed them the palm of his hand, in those gloves several citrines were tied together. Using the tip of his middle finger, Girilay tapped one of those stones. This caused the saucepan to break free from Noakh's hands, flying through the air towards Girilay, who deftly caught it.

"Unbelievable!" Noakh said in amazement.

He remembered how, in Tir Torrent, he had discovered that emeralds emitted light; it made sense that stones from other realms would also have unique characteristics.

"This is for you," Girilay said, thus interrupting the young Fireo's thoughts.

"Really?" He said looking up at Girilay, the pastry chef had rested on his palm two citrines brimming with flour. He watched the bright yellow stones, moving back and forth in his palm, dancing just above the scar he had gotten when he was just a baby.

"Are you sure? It doesn't look like these stones are easy to find."

"Not only are they rare, but I'd end up hanging from a tree if the authorities found out I used them to help me with cake baking," he revealed with a silly laugh, "however, I don't care. They were a gift from my grandfather and I'm very fond of them, but it's the least I can do."

"I really appreciate it," Noakh wiped the stones on his pants, thus adding a whitish stain to his already dirty clothes. Then he put them in his pocket.

"Do you want any, Hilzen?" Girilay said turning to the latter. "If it hadn't been for you bringing the townspeople..."

"No," he said, taking a bite of another fartun soaked in his nearly finished oroxiat, "if you'll treat us to a good portion of these buns to take with us on our journey, I'll be content."

Girilay smiled and nodded. "Oh, I almost forgot, those stones will be useless to you without this, Noakh." The pie maker walked over to the shelf and picked up two saucepans, handing them to him.

The young Fireo inspected one of the handles in which was also embedded a small citrine.

"But they are embedded to the saucepan, is there any way to dislodge them without damaging them?"

Girilay twisted his lips, trying to think. "My grandfather told me that the only ones who can dislodge and anchor them wherever you want are the dwarven craftswomen, only they have the knowledge to do it without damaging the stone."

"And where will we find one of those craftswomen?" Asked Hilzen with interest, picking up one of the saucepans to observe them.

"You will be able to hire their services in the larger cities of the Kingdom, they tend to settle where there is the most work." He said looking at the ground as if distracted.

"Is something wrong, Girilay?" Noakh said, confused, "you don't seem very happy despite having just finished that nightmare they called an anniversary."

The pastry chef put a hand to the back of his neck, releasing a cloud of flour, "don't misunderstand me, I am deeply happy and I thank you enormously for your help. It's just that I can't forget certain words Muna said..."

Hilzen picked up both saucepans and clipped them to the side of his belt, "what did that despicable being say?"

"Maybe it's nothing, but I can't help but think how horrible it would be if it were true... Muna mentioned that, after our fight, they would leave in search of the sacred sword, they say it lies in a nearby swamp... just the thought that he might get the Royal Favor makes my skin crawl." Girilay raised his eyebrows as he saw the confused faces of Hilzen and Noakh. "You have no idea what I'm talking about, do you?"

Noakh shrugged, Hilzen chewed the last piece of his fluffy fartun with bewilderment in his eyes.

"I'm surprised you haven't heard," Girilay said perplexed, "Tizai, the sacred sword of Aere Tine, has disappeared. No one knows where it is, and a reward is being offered to anyone who finds it and delivers it to Kings Zarta and Lieri. The monarchs have sent a message to every city, town and village, inviting citizens to participate in the search for the sword, offering a substantial reward to whoever finds it."

"A large sum of money?" Hilzen asked.

"Something more amazing and unusual, a Royal Favor." He revealed to them. Girilay waited, as if expecting some sort of reaction from them, seeing that Noakh and Hilzen merely looked at each other he continued, "to have a Royal Favor is something that is not seen very

110

often. Whoever is granted it will be allowed to request anything and it will be granted, whatever it is, without consequence."

"Anything?" repeated Noakh, crossing his arms, "that sounds dangerous."

Girilay nodded. "Especially if it falls into the hands of someone as vile as Muna," he concurred. "They will grant any request that is within the power of being granted by the kings of Aere Tine and that does not endanger the security of the kingdom," he clarified.

"Couldn't one who disposed of a Royal Favor ask for an entire village to be exterminated?" Hilzen said with a grimace.

"They could very well," Girilay acknowledged, "I have not the slightest doubt that Queen Zarta and King Lieri would commit such a slaughter if, in return, they would retrieve the sword that makes both the kingdom and their own skins safe."

Noakh nodded. Without meaning to, he wondered what he would use such a concession for. Gold? Land? He was not interested in any of those things, certainly the only thing he would be more than happy to ask for would be a guarantee that his friends would come to no harm, and that would obviously not fall within the monarch's capabilities....

"Oh, if I were to find that sword, I know exactly what I'd ask for," Hilzen said enthusiastically, "that they erect a Church dedicated to the Aqua Deus around here, so that people like me could have a place to pray. Or, better yet," he added turning to Noakh, "that the Aertian army would escort us and help make things easier for our dear friend Fireo on his arrival in Firia." He said winking at him.

"I'm no expert, but... I suppose something like that could not be granted to you," Girilay clarified, "I would say that using Aere Tine's troops to escort you to Firia would conflict with the condition that you cannot request something that would jeopardize the security of the kingdom," Girilay sighed, "people usually ask for more common things, being rich, a song that speaks of them being archived in the Cloister of Music, revenge... something like that."

"And you're afraid that Muna will get hold of the sword and request something that will endanger your life?"

"That's right, I'm terrified he'll use Royal Favor against me or, now that the village has stood by me, against all its people."

Hilzen stood up.

"What?" he said, stretching his arms towards Noakh upon seeing the Fireo's confusion about his sudden movement. "We all know how this is going to end, so why delay it any longer?" He then turned to Girilay.

111

"Tell us how to reach that swamp. Oh, and it wouldn't hurt to be able to take those delicious buns with us to liven up the trip."

14. The best unexpected visit

Aienne diverted her attention from the vast map on the wall, glancing at the thick, old-fashioned book of yellow pages. It rested on a white wooden stand, seemingly too small for such a weighty document. She tilted her head, looking at one of its pages, which detailed the rivers and tributaries of the Aquadom.

She was slightly distracted, knowing that at night she would have to fulfill her deal. She had managed to convince Lampen to allow her to sleep in the same workshop. It had not been easy, nor had it been for nothing. In exchange for the counselor turning a blind eye, Aienne had to sweep the entire workshop night after night for a month. An arduous task, but one she was happy to do in exchange for being able to hide there and not having to deal with either the dreaded Chosen Lineage Preservation clause or the danger of her sister Katienne. After having escaped from the Golden Tower, she was sure Katienne was also looking for her to, at the very least, ask for explanations for having freed the nobles she had imprisoned.

Her curious eyes returned again to her map. She climbed onto the stool and rested a worn wooden ruler on it, tracing with a charcoal pencil a pair of blackish lines that began at a river, went around a mountain and continued until they were near a village. She had been entrusted with the task of studying a canalization that would provide water to some villages located at the southern end of the Aquadom, near where the Void was located.

She studied her markings, shaking her head when she realized they didn't offer an optimal solution. It was not an overly complicated task and it frustrated her that she could not solve it, almost as much as that Lampen had assigned her a simpler-than-usual project.

The counselor had hinted to her on more than one occasion in the last few weeks that he noticed she was more distracted than normal.

And, although she had flatly denied it, she knew perfectly well that he was right. How could she not be distracted after all? Her attempts to help Vienne had not only been unsuccessful, but quite the opposite.

Those stupid bourgeoisie who refused to help me! Aienne cursed, accompanied by two rough taps with the tip of the charcoal on the map. To make matters worse, she had heard that Vienne had landed in Aquo territory and, try as she might, she had been unable to find her.

Has Vienne forgotten me? No, that's impossible.

"That sounds tremendously complicated," said an unexpectedly familiar voice from behind her.

Aienne's face lit up completely. She turned around with her mouth open, finally, after so long. Vienne had come to visit her.

They both ran, melting into a longed-for embrace. Aienne wrapped her arms around her sister as tightly as she could, in doing so, she realized that she could hug her even more easily than before.

"You're even thinner," she pointed out, with some concern. She pulled away slightly, to look into her eyes. She said nothing more, but even Vienne's look had changed slightly. Her eyes looked the same color, yet something about her gaze was different.

"Don't think my trip was exactly a bed of roses." Her sister replied with a smile. Then she reached out, placing her palm on Aienne's head. "You, on the other hand, are taller!"

Aienne smiled, gratefully. "Really?" She said excitedly, for her it had always been an annoyance to be the shortest of all her sisters. She was aware that part of the reason for her shorter stature was due to her inferior age, however, Vienne happened to be the tallest of them all despite being the second to last in birth.

Vienne nodded. For a moment, Aienne silently thanked the Aqua Deus for finally being taller. However, a moment later she realized that she was tilting her head up so that she could look her sister in the eye, she still had a long way to go to match her in height.

She glanced at her belt, confirming that Vienne was carrying the sacred sword. She pressed her lower lip to suppress a smirk. "You did manage to unleash its power, didn't you?" She said, mischievously.

Her sister needed no more; understanding perfectly well what she was getting at with that question. She unsheathed Crystaline before Aienne's expectant gaze. She extended her bare arm and brought the blade of the sword close to her forearm.

"No!" Rushed Aienne.

114

Vienne stopped just in time for the blade to pierce her flesh. Then Aienne rolled up her sleeve, placing her arm close to the sharp blade.

"Do it to me, I want to feel how my sister is able to heal wounds." Aienne added excitedly.

"Fine, but a tiny little cut." She conceded after smiling candidly at her.

Aienne gritted her teeth as she felt the blade on her white skin. She tried to appear brave, however, she couldn't help squinting. She felt the blade cut into her flesh; blood began to gush from her forearm.

"Don't move." Vienne instructed her.

Then she placed the tip of the sword over the wound. Water began to flow from the blade, lightly, like dewdrops on the leaves of a rose bush leaves in early morning. Aienne watched the miracle with her mouth open. If she thought she could not admire her sister any more, that moment had just proven her wrong. The drops made their way into the small wound, which began to close little by little.

A slight stinging was the only thing Aienne noticed when the wound was completely closed. She ran the index finger of her other hand where, until a moment ago, the cut was located. She stared at the place where the wound was supposed to be and where it did not show the slightest mark, absorbedly captivated by the miracle her sister had performed. It was a peculiar sensation, the cut had disappeared, however, the slight itching from the cut remained.

She gazed at Vienne with unconditional admiration. Marveling at both what she had just done and what she had become. She had managed to master the blessings of the holy sword; she couldn't be happier to see that her favorite sister was doing well.

"Oh, Vienne, I have missed you so much!" She cried, hugging her again with all her might, then pulling away as she remembered the news she had heard. "You don't know how many rumors I have heard about you! Is it true that you were accompanied by a ferocious beast with great fangs that gave chase to a dragon that spat fire so fiery it looked like lava?"

Vienne frowned, then smiled in understanding, "in Tir Torrent, there was fire, a dragon, and as for the ferocious beast with big fangs..."

Gentle taps on one of her sandals caused Aienne to look down at the floor.

"There you have it," Vienne revealed to her with a chuckle.

Aienne turned to her sister, totally perplexed. "She's Zyrah, the Dragon Slayer?"

"I suppose so," Vienne replied amused at the absurdity of that title.

Both princesses observed the canine, who scratched her head vigorously with her hind paw. Completely oblivious to the fact that the Aquos breathed with greater relief when they thought of the war against the Fireos, for a new heroine had emerged among their ranks.

"Why, she's adorable!" She exclaimed with utmost excitement, then bent down and picked her up from the ground, so vigorously that the animal gave a start.

"Achoo!" sneezed Aienne over Zyrah's face, an act that caused the little dog to start squirming back and forth to get her off the ground. Aienne bent down, releasing her, only to perform an even more intense sneeze than the first.

She felt an annoying itch in her eyes, as unpleasant as the stinging deep in her throat and the sudden runny nose that assaulted her. She brought both index and middle fingers to her face, their fingertips wet with tears from the irritation.

"Don't tell me you have an allergy to Zyrah," Vienne lamented sadly.

"Ob course nod!" She replied, snot preventing her from speaking clearly. She sniffled repeatedly to stop the insistent and annoying runny nose. "Ib's juds dad I slebd wid de windoh oben yestohday," she said as best she could.

Aienne tried to approach Zyrah again, but the dog, either out of concern for the princess's health or to escape the rain of snot and drool from her sneezing, took shelter behind Vienne's legs.

* * *

The two horses trotted in parallel in the gentle rain, a leisurely ride in which they took the opportunity to catch up. It was Aienne who led the way, she wanted to introduce her sister to some very special friends, so much so that Aienne had asked her not to tell her story until they reached them. That's why during their walk, it was Aienne who was updating her on how busy she had been in her absence.

"You did what?" Vienne dropped the reins with her right hand, pressing her index finger and thumb to her temple; an intense pain surfaced after hearing her little sister's tale.

"I did it to protect you!" Excused Aienne, her eyes still slightly watery from the allergy.

Aienne pressed another silk handkerchief to her irritated nose. Zyrah walked away, snooping and sniffing at any flower, feces, or other scent that caught her interest along the route.

"Oh, Aienne," Vienne lamented, shaking her head, "I know you did it to help me, but I don't want a decision like that to weigh on your shoulders." She added, looking at her gravely.

To provoke a world war... to go so far as to start a war of such magnitude... In a way, Aienne and Katienne are not so different, she considered, *two young women willing to do anything to achieve their goals.* True, Aienne seemed to have at least some remorse for her actions, or perhaps she only saw it that way because the youngest of her sisters was on her side?

They arrived at the house. In a spacious cottage with a boarded floor, four people were playing cards in the living room. Seeing that Aienne was accompanied, they interrupted their game, standing up quickly.

"Vienne, these are the nobles who were imprisoned for supporting you. Arilai Rosewood, Laenise Naudine, Arigus Emsai and Dornias Delorange." Aienne introduced them, the four nobles offered the Aquo reverence.

Vienne first bowed to Arilai. Though they had never spoken, Vienne recognized her. Arilai had captured many gazes at the ball where she, Vienne, had been presented as the Lacrima.

"Aienne told me how much Katienne gave you a hard time and the terrifying fate that would have awaited you had it not been for the courageous intervention of these nobles, who also proclaimed their support for my right to the crown despite the risk of expressing such words in the presence of my vile sister." At such words the brown-eyed young woman bit her lower lip, while the other three puffed out their chests at such recognition, "I hope that having met Aienne has served to make you realize that Katienne does not represent the ideals nor the values in which the rest of us Dajalam princesses have been educated, in any case, I beg you to accept my apologies on behalf of the crown."

The nobles smiled, looking surprised at the speech.

"You look like someone worthy of calling queen," Dornias acknowledged with a broad smile.

"Yeah, you don't look weak at all." Arilai added, receiving a rebuke in the form of a glare from Laenise and Gorigus.

"From what I hear, sooner or later, you will be our brother-in-law." Vienne remarked, turning to Dornias.

Dornias gave a chuckle. "Unfortunately, so. I hope you're not offended, but it's not something I'm eagerly anticipating."

"I am not offended, on the contrary, I am sorry that your brother has fallen for Katienne's manipulations."

"I pray to the Aqua Deus that the day will come when Filier will come to his senses..." replied Dornias in a regretful tone. "But enough with the regrets, I think you owe us a story, princess."

It was Vienne's turn to tell them everything that had happened in the Kingdom of Earth, starting with the awakening of her powers, to her various battles and, of course, to tell them about Noakh. Aienne looked at her absorbed with each of her stories, the nobles seemed equally intrigued, asking her all kinds of questions to know more details, except for Arilai who just listened to her.

"How amazing you are, sister! With you here, everything will be so much easier," cried Aienne enthusiastically once Vienne finished telling her story, "I've been considering various ways to tarnish Katienne's reputation and..."

"I think you've done more than enough." Vienne politely cut her off.

"What?" Replied Aienne in surprise, the rest of the nobles were also dumbfounded.

"Princess Vienne," Gorigus began, "is it that you do not want us to help you?"

"Of course, I do. That's why I would like to ask you a favor that I have no right to ask: to take care of Aienne and ensure her safety. Can you fight?"

"Of course we know how to fight," Laenise confirmed, crossing her arms proudly.

"We are all nobles here, princess," Dornias clarified to her, "that entails many rights and privileges, but also certain obligations. Among them, that of having combat training available should the queendom require our services."

"I couldn't leave Aienne in better hands then, I'm glad your paths have found each other." Vienne thanked, sounding much more relieved. Seeing that Aienne was about to complain, she quickly continued, "Little sister, I am beyond proud of you. To think that you saved some nobles from a fateful destiny at Katienne's hands, that you've even been able to provoke a world conflict for me... it's far more than I deserve," she said, smiling sweetly at her. "But it's risky, Aienne, and I dare not think that anything could happen to you because of me."

"Don't worry about that," Aienne replied, waving her hand dismissively, "it's true that vulcanite has its dangers, but I've been practicing and I've got it under control now, or so I think..." she added

118

with a mixture of confidence and a grimace that suggested she didn't have it all together.

"I wasn't referring to the vulcanite," she said, shooking her head, "it's not all those trinkets I'm afraid of. I'm sure a mind as fascinating as yours will be able to tame any contraption that gets in your way." She flattered her, then rested her hand delicately on Aienne's thigh and looked at her gravely. "It's Katienne I'm worried about. She locked up her betrothed's brother, she tried to burn a noblewoman alive... our older sister has lost her mind, she's willing to do anything to get what she wants. Soon I will have to show my powers before the eyes of the Congregation of the Church. It is possible that this will allow me to snatch the support of the Church from her in an instant. How do you think she will respond as soon as I try to take away the power she has sought to acquire at any cost? I am sure she will not hesitate to harm my loved ones in order to blackmail me. I could not forgive myself if you should suffer the least harm on my account." At that moment she reached a hand into her pocket and extracted a folded piece of paper. Aienne's unhinged face at the sight of such a document anticipated that she knew what it contained, "Meredian handed this to me, I know you are not the least bit amused, but I want to ask you to please travel and get to safety. That Preservation of the Chosen Lineage thing is nonsense, but it serves me well if with it you are protected, away from any danger, and I will be reassured that the person I love most is away from Katienne's ruthless clutches."

Aienne pursed her lips and frowned. Vienne knew for a fact what was flitting through her sister's sulking mind, that she didn't want to do it, that she was willing to suffer any evil if she could help her.

"Your sister is right, Aienne," Dornias interjected. "Right now, we are more a hindrance than a help. If your sister feels she can wrest power from Katienne on her own, then the best thing we can do is make sure she doesn't have to worry about us and especially you."

"Arilai, are you all right?" Arigus said, watching her with concern. "You haven't said a word since Princess Vienne began recounting her adventures in the Kingdom of Earth."

Arilai scratched her head. "I'm sure it's a mere coincidence, but the Noakh you spoke of... is he by chance a brown-eyed young man named Noakhail?"

The two princesses opened their mouths, completely dumbfounded. Certainly, the brown-eyed noblewoman had a story worth listening to.

15. Views to the past

The children surrounded her, many bending down to pick up the wet clay. They molded it with their hands into spheres, creating the perfect projectiles. Children of nobles and servants played as equals, regardless of the wealth or privilege of their families, there was no nobility when it came to children. They saw no value in titles, their twisted childish minds only allowed them to see that they all had blue eyes and blond hair. Except for her.

"Take that, poop eyes!"

A mud ball hit her right cheek.

"Yuck! I almost got touched by the unickey!" A golden-curled girl exclaimed with a disgusted look on her face.

Arilai's brown eyes flooded with tears.

"Leave me alone!" She implored them in tears.

"Or what, poop eyes?" A boy sporting a black eye asked.

"Or... I'll call my mom's family and they'll teach you a lesson!"

The children looked at each other and started pointing at her, bursting into laughter.

"Your mother's family couldn't get into the Aquadom even if they wanted to." Replied the golden-curled girl.

"Yes! Your Fireo relatives would be crushed by the Knights of Water, stupid..."

"That's not true," Arilai continued, terribly angry, "one day they will come and then..."

A figure suddenly appeared, right behind Arilai. The children's faces suddenly changed from mockery to utter terror. Their unhinged faces were the last thing Arilai saw moments before scattered in panic in all directions.

Arilai was also startled, she slowly turned around. This time it was her eyes that couldn't believe what they were seeing. A man, with blond hair and... brown eyes, *exactly like me!* She thought excitedly.

"Hello, little girl," greeted the man affectionately squatting down and giving her a few friendly taps on the head, "what pretty eyes you have, what's your name?"

"Arilai," she indicated, wiping away tears with her fingers, "and you?"

"My name is Lumio, how old are you, about five?" he asked her, Arilai looked down and looked at her own fingers doing the math, then showed him the result of her calculations. "Oh, six? Just like one of my daughters, you're already a young lady."

Arilai smiled at the compliment. Then her face changed to one of terror, "have you come to hurt the children who pick on me?" She said fearfully, "don't harm them, please, they were just playing..."

Lumio let out a laugh. "A very noble spirit of yours to want to protect even those who pick on you. You know, my son has brown eyes like you, he's still a baby, but maybe when he grows up, I could bring him over one day for you to play together? I'm sure you'd be pleased to see another child with different colored eyes for a little change, would you like that?"

Arilai nodded so many times that her neck ached.

"All right," Lumio said, kneeling to wipe the remnants of mud from her cheek, then stood up, "is your mother around?"

Arilai nodded.

"She doesn't know me, but I'd like to talk to her. Could you tell her to come out? Tell her that a man with brown eyes and an ugly scar on the palm of his hand has come asking about her," he said showing her said scar, "I'm sure she'll understand." He added, winking at her.

"My mom has a scar just like that!" Then she looked at her own palm, "but I don't, look." She said, showing it to him.

Lumio smiled. "What a sweet little girl, you remind me so much of my daughters..." he said sighing, "could you call your mom?"

"On it!" She said, disappearing in the direction of the door of her house to fulfill the order. Arilai hurried inside the house, heading straight to the living room where she found her mother resting on the sofa with a cloth on her forehead.

She is ill again, she thought sorrowfully.

"Mommy! Mommy!" She said, coming up and grabbing her by her skirts, "a man with a scar has come; he has a baby, could he come over and play sometime?" she was speaking so fast and vaguely that it was hard to understand her.

"Calm down, Arilai," her mother said, removing the cloth over her forehead and leaning back with much effort to sit on the couch. "Did you say there's a man out there asking for me?" She lay back down on the couch, "I'm not feeling very well right now, why don't you tell him to come another time?"

"But, mom," she said more calmly, "the man said he wanted to see you," then she remembered, "he told me to tell you he had a scar on his palm and..."

Before she could finish the sentence, her mother was on her feet. Her gaze looked fearful, "stay here, Arilai," her mother instructed, then walked over to a cupboard and pulled out a silver pommel sword.

Her mother hurried to the door. Arilai sat down on a chair, trying to obey her mother's instructions, but she was so curious! Was that man really evil? Impossible! He had been kind to her, he had told her to play with the baby. No villain in the stories her parents read her behaved like that.

She fidgeted with her fingers for a moment, then got up and ran to the same door her mother had exited. She peeked out slightly, just enough to see. Her mother was pointing her sword at Lumio, who stood with his hands up, attempting to calm her. They were talking, Arilai wanted to know what they were saying, so she started to tiptoe behind an apple tree, made sure her mother hadn't seen her and peeked her head out to hear better.

"I have already told you, I am not here to capture you or your family."

"You lie! Why would you come all the way from Firia, then? You were sent by King Wulkan, are you not?"

Lumio shook his head, smiling. "You don't know how wrong you are. King Wulkan is less fond of me than he is of you, I guarantee you..."

"And why is that?" She asked, lowering her weapon slightly.

"How about treating me to some hot drinks, and I'll explain it to you in detail? It's a bit chilly here, which is not pleasant for me, nor advisable for you." Lumio proposed, "you can keep pointing the sword at me while we talk inside."

Her mother had agreed to let him in, but not without being alert. Arilai had been allowed to be with them; as long as she didn't make any noise and was quiet, they were dealing with grown-up matters. Lumio told them about that boy, Noakhail, and his destiny linked to a flaming sword.

"This Turay tea is delicious." Lumio said once he concluded his story.

"It better be, it's not at all easy to import. It's getting more and more complicated to acquire raw materials coming from Tir Torrent. The boy, where is he right now?"

"He is safe," Lumio clarified to her, "being cared for by an elderly couple, they are happy to look after the little one." Seeing the noblewoman's stunned look, he added, "don't worry, they are trustworthy people."

"And the sword?"

"Guarded in a safe place." He indicated. "Listen, I understand that you don't know me and I have no right to ask anything of you. I also know you owe Firia nothing, but Noakhail is just a boy who doesn't deserve to die. The Incandescent chose him through one of his steel blades."

"How exactly do you intend for me to help you?"

"As I have mentioned, I am on my own in this queendom. I will take care of him and raise him to become a good man, a great swordsman and a better king. I simply ask that, in the unlikely event that Noakhail should require help and I am unable to assist him, he may turn to your family for shelter..."

Arilai's mother looked upset.

"Like you," Lumio continued, "I have been taught to hate these blue-eyed people. However, I believe we both feel that Aquos and Fireos are not as different as we have been led to believe. It's just another place where idiots and nice people coexist."

"What you are asking me... would be putting my family in danger, I don't know if I can accept something like that..."

"I know I am asking a lot of you, but as soon as I heard that there was a Fireo woman married to a nobleman I could not let such an opportunity slip away. I am asking you for something that is unlikely to happen, I simply want to make sure that, should something happen to me, Noakhail would not be left alone in this world. He is a good boy. Since you are married to an Aquo, I am sure you would love to see a world where the two peoples are not at odds, where your daughter can meet her ancestors."

"I would love to visit Firia and meet the grandparents, mom!" interceded Arilai, excited to be able to travel to such a distant land.

"Be quiet, Arilai!" She scolded her angrily. Then, she turned to Lumio, "I'm sorry, but I can't put my daughter in danger for anything in the world, not even for the Ascending Phoenix himself."

Lumio snorted, stood up in frustration without saying anything.

"But there is one way I can help you."

* * *

Everyone in the room looked at Arilai in amazement.

"I'm sorry, it happened a long time ago." Said Arilai, scratching her head, "that's all I remember."

"Did you see him? Did you ever get to meet Noakh?" Vienne asked with interest.

Arilai shook her head. "After that visit, I never saw Lumio again. I was just a child, I guess as time went by his words remained hidden in my memory. Please don't think badly of my mother," she said feeling bad for tainting her memory, "she only wanted to protect me."

16. Sword in the mud

The citrine emitted a beautiful golden glow as it came into contact with the sun's rays that were breaking through the cloudy sky. Noakh held the stone aloft, gazing at it with the utmost curiosity.

"All sacred stones have power; It's still hard for me to believe." Hilzen said, marveling. "I wonder what the rubies will do, something evil surely, dealing with the stone that represents the Fireos..."

Noakh raised an eyebrow, "do you know what sapphires do?" he asked. As far as he could remember, Hilzen had, like him, only known the power residing in emeralds until their arrival in the Kingdom of Air.

"Ah, of course! We haven't seen what sapphires do yet. I'd almost forgotten about my own queendom! Too long away from home, eh, Noakh?"

It was at that moment that he remembered Hilzen had a sapphire when they were searched at the village entrance. He stashed the citrine in his pocket alongside the other stone, then folded his arms. "Hilzen, are you hiding something?"

The devout Aquo tried to justify himself, but, seeing Noakh's solemn expression, he instead sighed. "All right! Here, this is yours." He confessed, extracting the sapphire from his pocket to then hand it to Noakh.

"And why is it mine?" he said as he contemplated the bluestone in his hand.

"Fine, I will tell you." replied Hilzen, looking tremendously guilty, "When Gelegen visited you in the Misty Forest, he not only inquired about your health and presented us with the Holy Water. But also wanted to give you that sapphire to facilitate communication with Princess Vienne."

"What?" Noakh exclaimed indignantly, "and may I know why you've been hiding it from me until now?"

"You are the Phoenix Ascendant and she is the Lacrima!" he excused himself. "Our peoples are destined to clash, Noakh. Why make friends with someone you are going to have to fight sooner or later? I am not able to comprehend it."

Noakh shook his head. In part, his words made sense, but it bothered him to no end that Hilzen had kept something like that from him.

"How does it work?" He asked still annoyed.

Hilzen explained how the sapphires worked. After hearing that they needed a water source in order to communicate, they wandered back and forth until they found a stream that, fortunately, did not take them too far off course.

Noakh placed the sapphire on the water and arched his head curiously. Suddenly, the bluish stone illuminated, and he heard a voice. He hurried to place it with his ear.

"*Noakh, I hope you are well,*" the message began, he couldn't help but smile, it didn't sound like the voice of the princess, but, somehow, he could perfectly perceive that it was her talking to him. She was telling him about the confrontation she had with princess Arbilla, about how incredible she found the wall of fire that had divided the royal garden of the Tirhan palace in two. "I *just wanted to know what had happened and if you were safe and sound. If you want, you can use this sapphire to talk to me.*"

The message concluded. It was his turn. "Am I only to introduce the sapphire back into the water to answer her?" He said, turning to Hilzen.

Hilzen nodded, "don't forget to ask her if she was able to perform the ritual to Marne and Lynea yet."

Noakh put the sapphire back into the water, ready to tell her in detail why he had confronted Burum Babar and recount everything that had happened since their paths had parted.

* * *

Noakh drew his steel sword to clear the leafy branches blocking their path. As he smoothed the way, Hilzen showed off his best guidance to find the swamp as soon as possible, all while eating one of what seemed to be his new favorite sweets.

The young Fireo made two vigorous swings against a thick branch that seemed unwilling to break in two. He attacked more forcefully, filled with renewed strength after knowing that Vienne was well.

128

They had delayed their arrival at the swamp because of their insistence on finding a water source, so they had to hurry to make sure that the sacred sword Tizai was not in the swamp and, even worse, that it fell into the hands of someone like Muna.

For some reason, Noakh had a strange feeling about what happened to the sacred Aertian sword. Girilay had told them everything he knew about the incident: how it lay on top of a tower that had ended up being destroyed, without knowing by whom or why, resulting in the disappearance of the sword. The war of Aquos and Fireos, the death of Burum Babar... it was as if the world was rushing to leave all its past behind.

More branches fell to the ground, cut by the sharp edge of his weapon. They made their way through the leafy path, until they came to a wide, greenish garden inhabited by large purple flowers that seemed to sprout from the ground. Noakh went to place his foot on the garden; however, Hilzen hurried to block his way with his arm.

"This is not a garden." He said pointing, "look over there."

Noakh frowned, looking in that direction. He saw a bubble of mud that gradually grew larger. It expanded to a considerable size before bursting with a *plop*, soaking the surrounding moss and what he now realized were water lilies—appropriate, given they were in the swamp.

"Great," Noakh said satisfied as he saw that they had reached their destination, he glanced ahead trying to locate any objects among so much green and purple. Not a trace.

"And how do we know if the sacred sword really is here? I'm not about to go looking for it in this endless swamp." Hilzen refused, crossing his arms.

We could have thought about it earlier, Noakh admitted. He put a hand to his chin in a thoughtful tone, then rummaged through the ground, found a rather heavy stone and threw it. It landed on the mud, barely sinking.

"I'd say the mud is too thick for a sword to sink in." He concluded. "Though, perhaps there is only one way to be entirely sure," the young Fireo reached into his sash, unsheathing one of his swords. He looked closely at the hilt, thus making sure it wasn't Distra, just in case, then leaned forward.

"Throw it a little farther than the stone, in case it's deeper there." Hilzen suggested to him.

"All right, but you'll have to go retrieve my sword then." He swiftly hurled the sword upward before Hilzen could voice his opinion on the

129

matter. The weapon flew through the air making a parabola, until it landed with a *thud*, sticking in the surface of the mud, right next to a water lily.

"Well, well, if it isn't the two meddling idiots." Said a voice behind their backs.

Noakh and Hilzen turned around, discovering that behind them stood Muna and four of his thugs, all of them with a knife ready to be used.

"You may have saved Girilay, but I assure you that you will now be the object of my wrath," Muna said malevolently. Then he tilted his head and frowned, peering intently at something behind Noakh and Hilzen, "isn't that..." He rushed past, striking Noakh forcefully as they crossed paths, "yes! It is the sword, and I have found it!" He celebrated, laughing loudly.

"No, that sword is..."

"Damn it, Noakh," Hilzen cut him off, "how could we have been so stupid not to have noticed the sacred sword was right under our noses!" he said with a snort of presumed indignation, "on top of that, we are outnumbered, there is no point fighting over it, there will be better luck next time."

Noakh chuckled to himself, understanding Hilzen's ploy to not be the one who had to dive into the mud to retrieve the steel sword. Muna began to wade deeper into the mud, however, before he turned around.

"You two," he said pointing to two of his henchmen, "make sure these idiots don't do anything weird," he ordered them, then he hurriedly jumped into the mud while two of his thugs approached Noakh and Hilzen with unfriendly faces and knives ready for any move.

Muna's boots gripped the moss as he advanced towards the weapon he believed to be Tizai. With each step the mud covering more and more of his legs, until it was almost up to his waist.

Hilzen folded his arms, nodding proudly at the fact that they were doing the dirty work for him.

Muna is in for a disappointment, though he deserves it for being so vile and despicable, Noakh thought, following with his eyes how Muna was trying to get the sword. Then he frowned, had it been his imagination or had he sensed a strange movement in the mud? It had been very fast, as if something was crawling under the muddy surface.

Muna had made his way through the heavy mud and had almost reached the sword. However, Noakh was no longer contemplating his advance. His instinct urged him to watch the mud, alert. Just then he detected another movement, this time much more obvious and quicker. It was heading towards Muna.

"Get out of there!" Noakh alerted him, "there's something in the mud coming towards you!"

Muna paused for an instant in his advance, turned around with a grimace of displeasure. "Do you think I'm going to fall for such an old trick, stupid?" he sneered.

Noakh turned to Hilzen, who shrugged indicating that he had seen nothing. Muna's minions, although they did cast fearful glances into the mud after hearing his warning, also seemed to have seen nothing. Perhaps he had imagined it?

Muna meanwhile continued anxiously, reaching out to grab the sword. He grabbed it swiftly and raised it, triumphant.

"The Royal Favor is mine, you idiots!" He jubilantly celebrated by turning around and raising the sword to the heavens with both hands.

His henchmen celebrated Muna's triumph with applause, sure that Muna had promised them that they would be part of his prize for delivering the sacred sword. Noakh spotted another movement, he unsheathed Distra.

A slight oscillation was the only thing that anticipated its appearance. Behind Muna, a monstrous head began to appear and slowly rose out of the mud, it was an aberrant being, it seemed to be made of mud, with a mouth brimming with gigantic fangs.

"Muna!" said one of his henchmen, "behind you, run!"

Seeing that now it was one of his own who warned him of the danger, this time Muna turned around. He gave a scream of terror, then began to advance through the mud, trying to get out of the swamp, without letting go of his sword at any moment.

The mud monster thrust forth a gigantic hand, its fingers ending in incredibly long claws. It extended its arm, ready to impale Muna. However, its monstruous arm fell into the mud, severed by a disc of fire.

"Run, you stupid idiot!" Noakh urged him, launching a second fire attack that hit the chest of that being. As the creature began to melt into the mud, he watched in awe as three more monstrous beings replaced it.

Hilzen went to assist Muna, "you guys, give me a hand!" he said turning to Muna's minions, but they just stared in terror at the creature, until finally the four of them ran terrified out of there.

"I have an idea, Noakh, the citrines!"

The young Fireo failed to discern Hilzen's plan, however, he reached into his pockets and threw both citrines at him. He then launched a fiery attack, turned his wrist, the fire consuming two of those creatures. But, again, several monsters took their place.

Muna screamed in panic, one of those claws had grabbed his leg and was dragging him backwards again. Noakh rushed forward, an accurate disc of fire prevented the monster from continuing in its attempts.

Hilzen ran back to shore, unhooked one of the saucepans from his belt and tossed it to Muna. "Trust me and hold on tight to the saucepan." He instructed him, then moved as far away from the shore as he could.

"Drop the sword and grab the saucepan with both hands, you fool!" Noakh reprimanded Muna while throwing several discs of fire at those nasty creatures.

But Muna was too greedy to let go of what he thought was the coveted Tizai, clutching the saucepan with only one hand.

"Hilzen, do it now." He said throwing several flares of fire. "There's no time!"

Noakh deployed the full power of his sword, fortunately he had learned to handle Distra with greater ease thanks to Burum Babar. As the wise monarch had said, by taking the pothai he had managed to make his mind strong, now the killer instinct that enveloped the blade was still there, only Noakh could use it at will. He and the sword had become one.

A powerful flame blew a gigantic creature into a thousand pieces. He felt his strength fading, that power was a great use of his energy.

Hilzen slammed both citrines hard against a tree trunk. The saucepan moved in Muna's hand, however, as he did not have a good grip on it, it slipped from his hands and flew quickly towards Hilzen. The other saucepan, still hanging from Hilzen's belt, pulled sharply, causing the Aquo to fall, while the one thrown by Muna swiftly followed its course, hitting him hard on the head.

"Hilzen!" Noakh yelled, seeing that the latter now lay unconscious on the ground.

Noakh continued to launch fire attacks, without rest. Muna tried to advance, but the mud increasingly engulfed him as the monsters multiplied. Finally, common sense came to his being, Muna ended up throwing the sword to the shore to be able to advance with more speed.

He was approaching the shore, maybe he could reach and save himself? Just at that moment, a jaw appeared from the mud and grabbed one of Muna's arms and pulled. His torn arm flew through the air until it landed on the mud, where it remained for a brief moment before being devoured by another one of those creatures. The piercing scream of pain gave Noakh goose bumps. A second monster appeared behind Muna's back, ready to devour him completely.

"There's nothing to be done now," said a hooded woman who had appeared out of nowhere, then drew her bow and fired.

"Wait!" Noakh urged her.

The arrow had already been shot, hitting Muna's forehead. He fell dead in the mud, being devoured by those creatures. Noakh looked away, not wanting to witness such a bloody fate. He felt bad for not having been able to save him, yes, he was a disgusting human being who enjoyed causing pain to other people, but that death had been too cruel.

If he had grabbed the saucepan with both hands instead of continuing to grip the sword he would surely have been saved, he pondered.

He turned to see who the hooded woman who had fired the arrow was, however, at that moment Hilzen seemed to wake up.

"Hilzen, how are you feeling, friend?" he said. Rushing to help him to his feet. "Muna has fallen into the hands of those creatures..."

The Aquo grimaced, shaking his head, equally unhappy that this had been Muna's fate.

"The sword is not here." The woman revealed to them, "surely some prankster must have thought it amusing to send people into the lair of some slime morlods."

That voice... thought Noakh.

The young woman turned around, removing her hood. Her hair was of such a radiant reddish color that it rivaled the very rays of the sun. She stood looking at them smiling wordlessly, gazing at them with familiar yellow eyes. Hilzen and Noakh grimaced in surprise.

"Da... Dabayl? Is that you?" Hilzen managed to say. "What are you doing here?"

"I was on my way to look for you in town and heard the rumors about the sword being here, so I was curious."

"Aertian!" exclaimed Noakh at the sight of Dabayl's hair color. He then jabbed several elbows into Hilzen's ribs, "I told you so! I told you from the day we met her at the tournament that her attitude fit right in with the citizens of the Kingdom of Air."

"Aren't you a unickey?" Hilzen asked perplexed.

Dabayl merely shook her head, handing Noakh the mud-strewn sword that Muna had thrown a few moments before he died.

"I'm sorry about your friend." Dabayl said.

"He wasn't our friend," Noakh clarified, looking at a mud that now seemed to be calm again, as if nothing had happened. "Though I'm not pleased that he died like this..." Then he turned to her friend again, contemplating her reddish hair. "Why didn't you tell us, Dabayl?" said Noakh, chagrined.

"You guys aren't the only ones who might have secrets." She remarked.

Fair enough, Noakh agreed. Distra's power, his Fireo origin... they had kept so much from her that they were in no position to demand anything of her.

"I'm glad you shared your secret with us," Noakh said, smiling at her.

"I see that you have decided to accept that you are a Fireo," she said, pointing to his black hair. "It suits you better than I would have imagined."

"You look good with long hair; it sure has grown a lot since you left with Halftal." Hilzen pointed out.

"Well, I really just wanted to impress you guys."

As they both frowned, Dabayl reached up, gripping a clump of her reddish hair, and pulled it away. In place of her long hair, she now sported equally reddish hair, but barely a finger's length. Suddenly, Dabayl burst into loud laughter.

"Just seeing the shock on your faces was worth it," she said putting her wig back on and then running a forefinger across both eyes to wipe away the tears.

"Did you put on fake hair just to leave us with our mouths open?" asked Noakh, by now he knew that Dabayl was certainly peculiar, however, that seemed too much effort even for her.

"Yes," she nodded proudly, "but also no." She added, her face becoming much more somber, "the truth is I have to ask you for something and for that we're going to need this." She said, pointing towards her wig, which was swaying in the slight wind.

"We are going to need your wig?" Hilzen asked blankly.

"That's right, because you're coming to a wedding."

She then removed her cloak, revealing that it was so thick because she was wearing more than one.

"This one is slightly longer, perfect for you." She said handing a cloak to Noakh, then handed another to Hilzen.

"Are these cloaks for the wedding too?"

"They're for getting to the wedding on time. It's not like I wanted to carry three cloaks for the fun of it," she let slip, winking at them.

* * *

They stood on the edge of a cliff. The views were as breathtaking as they were intimidating, the trees and rivers below looking incredibly small from there. Their cloaks fluttered fiercely in the strong wind.

Dabayl took a deep breath, then put both hands to her mouth, "Loredan!" she shouted at the top of her lungs.

The cliff repeated that word, echoing over and over again.

"Loredan?" said Hilzen, "that name you mentioned on several occasions while we were captured in Tir Torrent, who is he?"

"Loredan was my older brother." Dabayl revealed to them.

"Was?" Noakh said. "What happened to him?"

"He is now part of the wind." Replied Dabayl, "as long as his name continues to echo in the mountains, he will remain with us. Loredan!" She repeated once more, "why don't you honor your fallen as well?"

Hilzen folded his arms, "I don't think the Aqua Deus will be angry for simply mentioning their names," he weighed, then clasped his hands to his mouth, "Marne! Lynea!" he shouted loudly as he clutched the pendant he wore around his neck.

"Lumio!" Noakh shouted, wanting to be part of that memorial ritual. He felt slightly bad; he would have liked to honor his mother, unfortunately, he didn't even know her name.

They stood for a moment in silence, simply letting the wind commemorate those they had lost.

"See that tiny road down there?" Dabayl finally said, pointing her finger down. Noakh nodded. "That's our path to the village of Pianga, our destination."

Hilzen looked one way, then the other, perplexed. "It will take us days until we reach that path, Dabayl, it does not look as if descending from this lofty place will be an easy task."

"On the contrary, we'll get there in no time at all."

135

"Dabayl, have you lost your mind? Even if we walked day and night, it would take days to get there."

Dabayl crossed her arms and showed a mischievous smile. "Do you know how eagles teach their chicks to fly?"

Before Hilzen even opened his mouth to answer, Dabayl had already placed her hands on his chest, pushing him off the cliff. Noakh's face paled, Dabayl pounced on him, giving him no time to react, her arms and legs trapping Noakh's body then leaning down and letting inertia take care of the rest.

They both plummeted down the cliff, their cloaks billowing wildly as they descended. Noakh screamed. Dabayl laughed, taking the opportunity to remove her wig and quickly tuck it into her robes.

"I'll kill you, Dabayl!" Noakh cursed, drawing on all the air in his lungs.

The young woman shook her head, then spoke into his ear to counteract the strong wind, "You'd better learn to fly as soon as possible, if you don't want the ground to be the one to kill you!" she said, letting out a laugh.

"Hilzen first!" he said, aware that his friend was closer to the ground.

Dabayl rolled her eyes. Then she leaned her weight on Noakh and then threw herself downward as if she had dived headlong into a river.

Noakh's mouth was filling with air, his eyes watering from the same wind that was noisily ringing in his ears. And the worst part was how he was moving arms and legs, a pathetic instinctive movement that made it look like he was trying to swim in the very heavens. He felt his heart pounding so hard that he felt dizzy from the intensity with which it was making his blood beat. His body was aware that if he did nothing he would be crushed to death on the ground.

Dabayl appeared out of nowhere, followed by Hilzen, who seemed to glide through the air, albeit awkwardly. Then the Aertian made a movement with her legs, her cloak billowed out, throwing her upwards, allowing her to position herself very close to Noakh. She grabbed one of his legs and forced the toe of his boot into what looked like a sort of pocket in his own cloak, then helped him to slip his other foot into the opening at the other lower end of the cloak.

"Stretch your legs!" Dabayl instructed him.

Noakh obeyed, extending both of them backward. As he did so, the cloak swelled with air, throwing him slightly upward.

"Ah!" A sharp crack resonated from his back, which groaned in protest from the jarring movement. He had gone from falling sharply to

136

descending much more gently to a ground that was still countless feet away.

Dabayl moved gracefully through the wind. The young Fireo watched her intently, trying to understand the technique behind her movements. In order to turn to the side, she would slightly tuck her leg in that direction, thus causing the cloak to deflate on one side.

He tried to imitate her, picked up his right leg slightly and, in doing so, began to move in that direction abruptly and awkwardly.

"You learn fast!" praised Dabayl coming close to his ear, "how about this?"

After her words, the young woman grabbed her legs, starting to somersault back and forth uncontrollably. Then she extended her legs again, allowing her to glide normally.

"Enough of showing off, Dabayl!" Hilzen reprimanded her, "we're getting dangerously close to land. How do we land on the ground without hurting ourselves?"

The Aertian widened her eyes. "Oh, I'm afraid landing carefully requires a lot of training, just stretch your legs to break your fall. You'll survive."

"What are you..."

Before Noakh could put some sanity into his friend, she threw herself headfirst into the ground, then somersaulted into the air and stretched her legs out. Landing on solid ground as gracefully as if she had just leaped from a boulder.

For a brief instant, he thought he could imitate Dabayl. Then he thought better of it. Preserving his own skin seemed the wiser choice.

The ground was already very close. Dabayl, like the dragon Gurandel, seemed to find some satisfaction in torturing those who, unlike them, were not much given to soaring the skies.

The trees, it seems the least painful landing zone, Noakh decided. He slightly bent his left leg, precisely enough to ensure a smooth glide into the canopy of leafy trees with yellowish leaves. However, apparently his movement had been too abrupt, crashing hard into the branch of a twisted tree.

Instinctively, Noakh placed his hands in front of his face, trying to protect himself and minimize injury. His arms hit a branch hard. He tried to grab it, but the force of his fall made his palms scorch as he slid down. He tumbled from one branch to another until he finally crashed to the ground.

137

He remained on the ground in pain. From there, he could see that Hilzen had landed on some bushes which, from his face, must have been full of spikes.

"Congratulations, my fledglings," Dabayl teased, "you have survived your first flying lesson."

17. Family duty

Aienne sighed as she walked through the deserted Royal Harbor, flanked by the Crown's Favourite Meredian, and Vienne. It was an official ceremony, as much as denoted by the impressive procession of Royal Guard soldiers walking behind them.

The princess had visited that port on countless occasions, hoping to catch a glimpse of a ship from which her favorite sister would finally disembark. Ironically, now it was Vienne who accompanied her to ensure that she was boarding a ship. Usually crowded with sailors, soldiers, crates, nets, barrels, and a long etcetera, now the harbor had been cleared for her farewell.

On that cloudy morning, there wasn't a soul in sight, except for the seagulls pecking at the debris on the white cobblestone ground. They took flight as soon as they heard the commotion of the accompanying caravan.

Certainly, any visitors had been prohibited on the premises, allowing them to celebrate her departure without any form of intrusion.

No one in this world would have succeeded in convincing her: neither Lampen, nor Meredian, who watched her every few moments as if he expected her to try to escape at any moment. She still didn't like the idea of leaving, but, unfortunately, she knew that Vienne was right. She would be a nuisance, a distraction in a duel in which she had no part. It was time to step aside and let her sister fight for herself, no matter how much it hurt.

She had thought long and hard about it and had finally agreed to Vienne's request to accept the invitation, to enlist on that ship and comply with the stupid Clause of Preservation of the Chosen Lineage. Luckily, it wasn't going to be any convoluted event, something that Aienne gladly appreciated since she hated the pomposities that took place in events related to royalty. She simply had to get on board that ship and thus fulfill her task.

"Don't be sad, Princess Aienne," Meredian reassured her, probably the princess's sour thoughts had been reflected on her face. "I assure you that before you know it you will be back to your normal life, take it as a vacation where you can rest."

Aienne nodded and looked ahead, they had reached the end of the dock. The ship that was to transport her was in front of them, imposing, swaying in harmony with the tranquil sea's movements. Her luggage was already on board, except for the gray leather bag hanging from her shoulder in which she carried some delicate belongings.

The Crown's Favourite and both princesses watched the boat. The soldiers of the Royal Guard stood behind them, acting as a barrier. It remained unclear to her whether their mission was to ensure her safe boarding or merely to guarantee she boarded, despite her strong reluctance.

A whole brigantine put at my disposal. What an honor, she thought ironically. Probably, the choice of such a vessel was due to its combination of speed and simplicity of maneuver.

She had to admit the vessel's elegance. Its jade-painted wooden hull complemented the glossy sail adorned with a graceful design of a mermaid cresting a sea wave. Meredian cleared his throat, as he pulled out a scroll.

"Princess Aienne," Meredian began, reading the document, "on behalf of the Queendom of Water, we thank you for the sacrifice you make in pursuit of safeguarding the Dajalam family lineage. We wish you a safe journey and a pleasant stay. On behalf of the crown, its people, and its Church, I thank you." He concluded, performing the Aquo reverence.

Aienne was aware that perhaps she should return the gesture with a reverence. However, she simply nodded her head. Then she embraced her sister, holding her tightly as if she never wanted to let go.

"Thank you for heeding me, Aienne, you will see that, when you return, I will have defeated our vile sister." She whispered to her.

I have no doubt that you will give her the lesson she deserves, Aienne wished to say, but she was too close to tears to say anything. Instead, she just nodded and watched her face, wanting it to be the last thing she saw before setting sail.

Aienne set out to climb up the ship's ladder.

140

"Safe travels." Vienne wished her. Aienne could sense from her sister's words the difficulty of this moment. It was evident that parting after their prolonged separation was challenging for both.

Just as she was nearing the end of the railing, a soldier held out a hand to help her into the boat. She positioned herself on the starboard side, remaining silent. She simply leaned against the gunwale, watching Meredian and Vienne sadly as the soldiers aboard hurried to remove the ladder, cast off the lines, weigh anchor and announce to the helmswoman that it was time to leave.

Slowly the brig separated from the dock, Meredian, her sister and the soldiers becoming smaller and smaller. One of the soldiers accompanying her on her journey stood beside her.

"Are you sure it wouldn't be better to heed your sister's words, Aienne?" asked Dornias, removing his helmet. "I don't think she'll be too amused when she finds out..."

"She won't find out." She assured. "We all win. The queendom ensures the royal family lineage is safe, my sister gets peace of mind that I'm out of Katienne's reach, and I don't get bored on an island lost at the hand of the Aqua Deus."

Dornias just smiled and shook his head. Two other soldiers approached, already stripped of their helmets. Gorigus smiled and winked, celebrating that the plan had gone well.

"We are not being followed; the maneuver was a success." Arilai confirmed, her long, perfect golden hair swaying in the wind. The four of them, along with Laenise at the helm, would embark on a voyage no one expected.

Everything had gone according to plan. They had managed to bribe the soldiers who had been in charge of taking her to the lost island. It had not been easy, but, above all, it had not been cheap. Luckily, the four nobles had gladly paid for the silence of those soldiers.

Aienne smiled, proud of herself for having been able to deceive those adults. Besides, she was aware that a lie was only useful if it was hidden from the world. That was why only those who were on that ship knew about her little mischief. She had not even dared to tell Lampen for fear that he would reveal it to Meredian or, worse, to Vienne. The truth was that she felt bad about deceiving her sister, but did she have a choice? Vienne would have told her that her plan was crazy, that she shouldn't risk her life in such a way, but it was something she believed in and wanted to do.

141

She glanced at the small bag hanging from her sash. A parting gift from Lampen. She opened it to admire it once more. In one pocket were several bright reddish stones, beside it, a sapphire, a twin of the one in Lampen's possession with which she had made him swear to inform her of any danger her sister might encounter, and an intriguing acquisition, an emerald.

"Are you sure you want to come with me?" The princess asked them.

"You saved us, little princess," Gorigus reminded her. He had taken to calling her by such an annoying appellation.

"In a way, I feel an obligation to help," Arilai indicated, "Lumio seemed like a good man, if I can help his son so be it."

Aienne nodded. It was precisely the unexpected connection between Noakh and Arilai that had been the trigger for this journey. They would navigate the waters of Tir Torrent and then Aere Tine to reach the Kingdom of Fire, a necessary detour to avoid the warring waters and, in turn, position themselves at the other end of Firia. Helping Noakh was only part of the stratagem. If they assisted him, they believed King Wulkan would surely be forced to retreat, an ideal scenario to prevent Vienne from being in danger by confronting the king of the Fireos.

The plan made as much sense as it was likely to end badly. It was highly probable that they would not even reach the Fireo lands by sea, but they had to try, especially when the alternative was to die of boredom on an island.

18. Proof

The cool sea breeze sent shivers through her hair. She looked down; the sea swayed gently, ready to receive her to its bosom. Her feet felt the roughness of the white rock, her gaze fixed on the Flumio inscription that read: *Welcome into your bosom the one who gives everything for you and with his humility faces the wrath of the ocean,* the words she had been able to decipher the last time she had been there, on the great Rock of Salt. From that same location she had jumped to discover what her blessing would be in what seemed like an eternity.

Everything was similar to the last time; she was to make the leap while holding Crystaline, a way of symbolizing the passage from life to death. Only this time there would be far fewer people to greet her once she surfaced.

It was early in the morning, so early that the moon was still reluctant to give way to the sun. Vienne, however, could not have been more lucid. She was aware that this was a crucial moment, the Congregation supported her sister, if she could prove to them that she had been able to control the sacred sword of water she would surely get them to withdraw their support for Katienne. The mere thought of finally getting rid of her petty sister made her ecstatic, she threw herself into the void, ready to put an end to this farce as soon as possible.

She remembered what she had felt the previous time she had had to throw herself from that rock. The blood throbbing in her head, the discomfort for not remembering the phrase in Flumio that she should pronounce to start that ritual. This time none of that mattered to her.

Her body sank into the water. To say it was freezing cold was an understatement, her skin crawled with goose bumps. She dived and surfaced, caught her breath and swam to the only ship anchored there.

A ladder was laid out for her to climb, and once on deck she knelt down, placing the sacred sword in front of her.

She continued kneeling as several footsteps advanced across the deck and stood in front of her, there was no doubt in her mind that it was the Congregation of the Church.

"Rise, Princess Vienne," said a voice, sounding somewhat worn.

The princess ignored her request. It was a singular sensation, to find herself in front of the members of the Congregation of the Church, the same ones who had decided to show their support to her sister Katienne in her intention to usurp the throne. Had they fallen for the accumulation of lies and manipulations concocted by her ambitious sister or did they simply consider that she was not worthy to reign? At another time she would have felt bad, she would have assumed it was her fault, for her flighty look, for her lack of character to give orders and show authority. But not this time, they didn't know her, she had barely exchanged words with them during the ball where they had celebrated that the sacred sword had finally chosen the Lacrima and, in spite of that, they had judged her.

She raised her head. The four members of the Congregation were watching her, only one member was missing, her mother, the High Priestess and representative of that religious organization. She knew all of them, slightly at least, she did not remember having had a conversation of more than five words with any of them. In front of her was the elderly priest Ovilier, an also decrepit Marune who had especially caught her attention because she was missing an arm. Followed by the young Estear and a somber Leeren.

Behind the Congregation were ten soldiers of the Church Guard. The impassive and fervent warriors clad in purple armor stood in line, erect with their swords sheathed, without moving an inch of their bodies.

The princess reached out and grabbed Crystaline by the sheath from the wet deck, then stood up.

"Allow me to convey what a tremendous source of pride it is to see you back, princess." Marune began, stepping forward. She watched her with her serious countenance, her blurred black teardrop tattoo placed under one of her eyes trying to break through a sea of wrinkles and age-induced blemishes. "Do you know why you're here, Lacrima?"

Of course I know, because you supported Katienne, because you judged me without knowing me and considered me weak.

However, Vienne knew that this was one of those occasions when it was best to keep her opinions to herself, so she simply nodded. Then, seeing that the members of the Congregation were waiting for an answer, she opened her mouth.

"To prove my worth and ensure that I am a worthy representative of the Aqua Deus." Vienne replied, given to not saying what she really thought what less than to offer a pompous and convenient affirmation.

"Well?" said Father Ovilier clutching the wide sleeves of his grayish robe with his wrinkled fingers, "did you succeed in releasing the powers of the sword?"

"Of course I did," Vienne replied contentedly, looking him straight in the eye.

The members of the Congregation exchanged fleeting glances of concern, which made the princess even more jubilant. They had claimed she was weak, incapable of invoking the sword's blessings, and not only would she prove them wrong, but she also intended to relish in doing so. Counselor Meredian had conveyed to her the words of her mother, *leave them no doubt of your worth*, and so it was to be.

For some reason, Father Ovilier was the one who stirred the most resentment in her. It was a vague sentiment rooted in nothing more than a hunch because, as far as she knew, beyond having been the one who had informed her mother of the decision made by the members of the Congregation as a whole to support Katienne, he was no more to blame than the rest.

"Can you prove it, my Lacrima?" Estear asked respectfully. He was the youngest member of the congregation, his tousled hair hiding one of his eyes.

Marune looked toward Father Ovilier and, and upon noticing that the latter was too engrossed in watching the Lacrima wield the sacred sword, she spoke instead. "You have been blessed with the *Absa Poestas*, please, Princess Vienne, grant us the honor of beholding the gift of that one with absolute power."

Vienne stood watching their tense faces one by one, she was tempted to remind them to have faith, however, she bit her tongue to restrain her impulses. Instead, she bowed her head. "How many blessings would you like to witness?" She asked them.

"Three will be more than enough." Marune replied. The rest of the members nodded, Ovilier seemed especially nervous.

"All right," Vienne agreed. Three was a small enough number. She wanted to show them as few blessings as possible, let them know of her

145

power just enough to convince them and make them feel embarrassed that they had supported her sister instead. The light clank of metal announced the unsheathing of the sword. "Crystaline, release your powers, please." She said in what was almost a whisper. Her face changed, now looking completely solemn, the edge of her sword moistened.

At that instant the ship rocked abruptly. All the soldiers of the Church Guard had knelt in unison. They were witnessing how the Aqua Deus manifested his powers through his chosen one, the Lacrima. Only the four members of the Congregation were standing, their faces showing looks halfway between devotion and awe.

She walked to the gunwale, the soaked blade of the sword now lying over the sea, allowing several drops to fall into the salty waters. Vienne turned, watching the members of the Congregation.

One.

Her undaunted eyes looking at them with the most absolute indifference.

Two.

Boom!

Behind her, a powerful torrent of water emerged and rose into the skies. Droplets began to fall on the ship, as if it were rain. The younger members of the Congregation murmured among themselves, while Marune and Ovilier looked at her with wide eyes. Vienne walked back and stood again in front of the Congregation members, ready to continue her demonstration.

"Good," Marune continued, satisfied. "Two more blessings to go."

"I will need a volunteer to show the second of the blessings." She indicated. "Father Ovilier, perhaps you would like to witness firsthand how I have been able to awaken my abilities?"

The elderly priest stepped forward to speak, his lower jaw trembling slightly as he prepared to likely decline such an invitation. However, after a glance at the other members, he realized he had no choice, nodded resignedly and took a couple of steps forward.

"Come closer." Vienne indicated, her voice void of any trace of emotion.

Father Ovilier nodded with his face fixed on the ground, as diligently as a man who knows he is sentenced to death. He took one more step, still with his gaze lost in the soaked deck of the ship. Then he raised his head, as if ready to accept his fate.

146

The fingers of Vienne's right hand held the hilt firmly, her gaze never leaving the fearful eyes of the priest. The princess prepared to proceed with her demonstration.

"Please don't overp..."

Before Father Ovilier could finish his sentence, Vienne had already given him a deep cut in the chest. The priest's own clothes began to turn dark, soaking in his own blood.

The priest Ovilier uttered a deep cry of pain, then looked to both sides, but no one came to his defense. Surely for that man it must have been a singular moment to say the least. There he was, soaking the deck of the ship with his own blood, and none of the devout soldiers who had sworn to protect him had moved an inch of their body.

Vienne extended the arm with which he was holding Crystaline. Her now imperturbable eyes watched the priest Ovilier with the most absolute indifference. She brought the tip of the sword close to the wound and raised the elbow with which she wielded the sacred weapon so that some of the drops emanating from the blade fell on the bleeding cut on his chest.

Drops of water made their way through the overflowing blood, diluting the reddish liquid. Gradually, the wound closed, leaving only the tear and the wine-colored stain on his clothing as evidence of the deep cut.

A grimace of indignation appeared for a slight moment on Father Ovilier's face, as if he wanted to reproach the princess for having made such a slash at him. However, his ferocity vanished the moment his old pupils met Vienne's empty eyes, a gaze as cold as ice that seemed capable of freezing his aged heart. Instead, he merely retreated by walking backwards slowly, thus rejoining the rest of the congregation, who were now staring with astonishment at the closed wound in his chest.

Two out of three, Vienne thought. Her mind was now focused on absolute analysis. She had to perform one more blessing to prove her worth, she could make it rain, yes, however, her sharp reasoning urged her to believe that she should resort to a more forceful invocation than healing rain, but which one?

Perhaps... a blessing occurred to her, she had never made use of it, at least, not consciously. It was risky, but something told her it was exactly the one she should invoke if she wanted there to be no doubt of her worth in the eyes of the Congregation.

She turned her gaze back to the sea, pointed the tip of her sword toward the calm waters and made her request. Then she walked the deck, calmly, contemplating the members of the Congregation, who watched her without knowing what she was up to. One of them, the youngest, even fiddled with his fingers not knowing what to do or what to expect. Vienne didn't care, they would wait for whatever it took.

The water began to churn. What had been a flat sea gradually became rough, and then quickly became choppy. The purple sails began to rattle, the ship now rocking from side to side abruptly.

Black tentacles appeared out of nowhere, rising like pillars from the bottom of the sea. They ascended into the skies, until they stood like imperturbable towers of a glowing jet hue around a vessel that, in comparison, looked like a mere child's toy.

A piercing scream as high-pitched as any human throat could ever utter silenced the sound of the ocean waves. The creature's glowing dark-colored head poked through the water, countless eyes, countless saw-like teeth and countless tentacles as thick as the most ancient tree began to coil around the ship's hull, ready to tear it to pieces.

The soldiers of the Church Guard stood again; their hands close to the pommels of their swords ready to give their lives for those they had sworn to protect.

However, they were not looking at the members of the Congregation, but at the princess. Vienne remained calm, totally unperturbed by the attack of a beast that, at any moment, could break the boat into a thousand pieces as if it were a toothpick.

The princess took delight in observing the Congregation, who, probably unconsciously, had crowded around each other; only Marune seemed to maintain her composure. The princess's steps were firm, controlled and lacked urgency.

She stood in front of Father Ovilier.

"I hope the third blessing pleased you." She said condescendingly, her sword still held high.

"Make it stop!" Leeren pleaded her, talking for the first time. Her eyes looked from one tentacle to another, as if she was weighing which one would be the one to end their lives.

The gestures of the other members of the Congregation supported this request. Father Ovilier's saggy chin could not stop trembling, while Marune's hard eyes harbored a certain panic in the depths of her pupils.

The tentacles of that terrifying sea creature continued to twist the ship. The wood began to creak, a warning that the hull would soon succumb to the force of that sea beast, bursting into a thousand pieces. There was no doubt, if the ship exploded, everyone would die. All except the one chosen by the Aqua Deus.

"Please, princess, stop." Marune begged, trying to sound firm.

No one would know... Vienne said to herself. The conclusion of her mind clouded by the logic of the power of the sword was absolute, those people had conspired against her and nothing could guarantee that they would not do it again. They had committed the greatest sin a devotee could commit, to use the name of God for their own worldly interests. They had gone against the choice of Aqua Deus himself....

The ship creaked again. A *crack* that announced the imminence of destruction.

I am not an assassin, she managed to make herself heard before the control of her sword. Her eyes roamed one by one across the trembling faces of the Congregation.

"You will imminently announce your retraction of your support for Katienne's right to assume the throne and instead second my legitimate claim to the crown." She indicated to them. Under normal circumstances Vienne would have asked a question, accompanied by a nervous smile and an elusive glance that would end up fixed on the floor. But this time she spoke with the assurance that came with the power of the sword.

Three of the members of the Congregation nodded without the slightest delay. However, one of them alternated his frightened gaze between his companions and the deck.

"Father Ovilier, only you are missing." Vienne pointed out. A resounding *crack* of wood highlighted the urgency of his response.

The old priest nodded once, then again. But it wasn't enough for the princess, not anymore.

"Father Ovilier," she repeated, "I want to hear you say it, I want you to confirm that you will support my right to the throne, looking me in the eye."

The tentacles stopped squeezing for an instant, a small truce granted by the princess. The old priest raised his head slowly, as if a lurid debate was taking place in his mind.

"Fine, we will renounce our support for Princess Katienne and publicly announce that you are the rightful heir." He accepted in defeat.

149

Vienne just looked at him for a moment, without making any movement, without even blinking. Then she nodded. As she did so, the tentacles gently left the vessel in the sea, then twisted and retracted back into the water, as if they had never been there.

Seeing them disappear, Estear fell to the ground on his knees, his chest swelling with intensity.

It was then that Vienne sheathed her sword, her face regaining its humanity, she tried to avoid smiling, not to show even a deserved look of jubilation.

The way they looked at her... had changed. *Is it fear I see in their eyes?* Vienne pondered. Maybe it was just her impression, but she thought she sensed a certain uneasiness in their faces, as if they had accepted that having distrusted their abilities, having supported another instead of trusting the one chosen by the Aqua Deus, deserved a punishment equal to the sin they had committed.

I've done it, she thought, unable to contain her joy. *I have succeeded in wresting the Church's support from Katienne. And I have done it on my own.*

Without the Congregation on her side, her sister had nothing to do, true, she was still supported by House Delorange and thus by part of the nobility. But that was a battle they had not yet fought.

She felt the intense beating of her heart, so energetic and powerful that it felt like it might burst out of her chest. She was aware of the danger, that Katienne was not going to stand idly by and fight back. But this time she wasn't going to be the frightened little mouse her sister thought she was. She was ready confront her.

19. Faith above all else

On the wide bed, five sky blue wedding dresses lay, each incredibly beautiful and captivating in its own way. What kind of neckline would look best on her? Katienne wondered, perhaps asymmetrical or more of a scoop neckline? She had to choose the perfect outfit for her wedding, the one that would enhance her figure the best, an elegant choice, but without sacrificing comfort and trendiness. It was a complicated decision, after all, the wedding of someone destined to be queen required that every detail be impeccable. They had not yet scheduled a date to make their engagement official, too many distractions lately...

"You'll look amazing in any of them, sister," Lorienne flattered her, Bolenne merely nodded. Her two sisters had enthusiastically offered to help her choose a dress. "But as far as I know, the teardrop-shaped one is very fashionable," she said, bending down to retrieve the exquisite dress from the bed, a garment that had been designed with such a graceful neckline.

"The sapphire one isn't bad either, it's the most daring," Bolenne contributed, "I'm sure Filier will love it." She added, mischievously.

"I don't know, they're both pretty." Katienne replied.

"Is something wrong?" Lorienne asked her worriedly, laying the dress she had picked up on the bed again. "You look discouraged."

"Yeah, you sound distant." Bolenne pointed out in a sad voice.

She clenched her jaw. Choosing the wedding dress was supposed to be a beautiful and endearing moment of enjoyment with her sisters. And she was ruining such an event, not only for her, but also for Lorienne and Bolenne.

That idiot is ruining everything.... Katienne thought.

"I'm fine!" replied Katienne with a feigned smile, "I think the sapphire one will fit me better, why don't you two try some on and see

151

how they look?" She conceded to them. Both of her sisters' faces lit up; of course, they were looking forward to trying on a wedding dress.

The two leaned over the bed, trying absently to choose which dress each would try on. A perfect distraction so they wouldn't notice her. She was indeed downhearted; how could she not be? Things hadn't gone as she had planned.

Vienne had returned safe and sound from her journey in Tirhan territory. As soon as she heard of her landing she had rushed to the palace, she had to see it with her own eyes to believe that someone so pathetic had been able to survive her journey. And she hadn't just returned; she came back with a newfound self-confidence that did not bode well. Vienne was supposed to be timid and vulnerable, incapable of meeting anyone's gaze. On the contrary, in that encounter at the palace she had felt something different, Vienne had not been daunted by the sight of her, and would even have said that she was more than eager to confront her.

What could have happened to her in Tirhan territory that she has changed so much? That she has gained so much confidence in herself? She wondered. She didn't know the answer and she didn't like that. Nothing looked good for her since she had discovered that her sister had landed unharmed in Royal Harbor.

Knock, knock.

"Come in." Katienne indicated.

"My lady," said one of the Delorange family maids appearing through the door, "someone in a carriage has come to see you. The driver has insisted that it was urgent."

Lorienne and Bolenne looked at each other, then gawked at Katienne with devotion. They admired how busy her new life was.

Katienne frowned, she was not expecting anyone. The visit was unexpected, she disliked the lack of control, she had to find out what it was about. She thanked the maid with a warm smile, the maid then took her leave after an Aquo reverence. Katienne looked at herself in the mirror, lightly combed the curls of her hair with her fingers and marched off in search of finding out who the sudden visitor was.

"I'm sure it's some surprise gift from Filier, he's such a sweetheart." She heard Bolenne say as she left the room. Katienne descended the stairs, leaning against the elegant reddish-wood banister, whose turned balusters were a delight to behold.

She walked out the door, her arm hair standing on end from the morning chill. She blamed herself for not having grabbed some jacket to shield her from the morning frost, but there was no time to go back. She walked through the Delorange's spacious rooms, meeting no one on her way, Filier had given most of the servants the day off, in her opinion her fiancé was sometimes too good-natured.

Only a few soldiers were in their elevated guard posts, positioned facing outward from the walls surrounding the grounds. Since that fire followed by the escape of the nobles they had locked up, security had been reinforced, her fiancé insisted that the fire had been a circumstance that Dornias and the rest of the captive nobles in the cellars had taken advantage of to escape, for Katienne it was just the opposite, that fire had been a distraction to carry out a rescue. Until recently, who had helped them had been a mystery to her, however, she had recently been informed that they had sighted Aienne with the nobles.

Resolving the matter of the elusive Aienne and the nobles was only a matter of time. Now she had to focus on the present. She stood at the entrance, where two guards were positioned in their distinctive orange and blue robes, the colors of House Delorange, with the tips of their halberds resting on the ground. When they saw her, they let her pass without the slightest delay, greeting her with a mere nod.

Just in front of the door stood the carriage. Elegant, neat and, at the same time, lacking any pomposity, pulled by two gray horses with black spots and white manes. Leaning against the back wheel was a young page boy with a beak-like nose, who was half yawning when he saw her approach. He immediately straightened up and hastened to open the carriage door for her to enter.

Katienne had many questions. However, deciding to seek answers within, she climbed into the carriage, using the small staircase inside and leaning on the young man's willing arm. Once inside, she encountered an elderly face that, despite looking terribly pale and disheveled, she recognized instantly.

"Father Ovilier, what are you doing here?" she said sitting down opposite him in the carriage. For an instant she was furious, that visit was highly risky, far removed from the caution and preparation with which all their encounters had hitherto been held. She frowned, ready to reproach him for the inappropriateness and danger of his action, then she noticed the large reddish stain on his robes at chest height, "is that blood?"

"She..." the old man began. He brought both hands towards Katienne, the princess leaned down and grasped them, they were

153

incredibly shaky. Ovilier was older and at his age certain tremors were to be expected, nevertheless, the princess had never seen him this unsettled. "She is strong, she has beaten us, Katienne."

"She? Who are you talking about, Father?" replied the princess with a frown, "please calm down and tell me in detail."

The priest took a deep breath, once and twice. Visibly calmer, Katienne released his hands. Ovilier leaned against the backrest and began to tell her what had happened, how Vienne had shown her blessings before the Congregation. Katienne listened with rapt attention. Her eyes opened wider and wider, her almond-shaped fingernails dug deeper into the palms of her hands until the blood gushed out.

How could that idiot have been able to unleash the powers of the sword? She felt her heart race as she realized how her dream of being queen was slipping away...

"It's over, Katienne," Ovilier said in a tired and desperate tone, "she made us declare that we would support her as rightful heir to the throne... Vienne now has the support of the Congregation. There is nothing we can do."

"Let's not be hasty, Father." Replied the princess, shaking her head. She was not willing to accept defeat, there was no doubt that Vienne had changed, daring to hurt a priest of the church... endangering all the members of the Congregation... What audacity! It seemed that her lazy little sister was awakening from her lethargy and had more character than she appeared to have. But if her sister was willing to fight, she was not going to be any less so.

For a moment, she lost her composure. Aware that she had to act with alacrity if she did not want all her plans for the future to be thrown overboard. Losing the favor of the Church would be too hard a blow. The support of the nobility alone would not be enough to seize the throne....

"Father, all is not lost," she told him in a calm voice. "The Congregation's support for Vienne has not yet been officially announced, am I wrong?"

The priest shook his head. "Not yet. First, we must write to the High Priestess, your mother, so that she is aware. It is so commanded by protocol."

"And who will be in charge of writing to her?"

"Marune, why?"

"Because we have to make sure that message never reaches my mother." She said flatly, catching a glimpse of hope. She felt a tingling in her stomach, the burning impatience to come up with a plan that would bring the situation back under her control.

"How?" said the priest bowing his head, "I don't think you understand, Katienne, your sister not only unleashed the power of the sacred sword but also demonstrated her diligence in front of the entire Congregation."

She had lost him, she could see it in his fearful, tired eyes. Ovilier had helped her convince the rest of the Congregation that she, Katienne, was the best choice for a strong reign. And now the priest seemed to regret his decision. What he did not know, however, was that it was already too late.

"Katienne... I've been thinking..." continued Ovilier, without looking her in the eyes, "I think it's time to accept it, Princess Vienne has been able to release the powers of the sacred sword. No one is going to see her weak after something like that..."

"Powers awakened or not, Vienne remains fragile and carefree. Believe me, Father, you would not like to watch helplessly as our queendom withers at the hands of that inept ruler." Katienne exerted an extraordinary effort to replicate her mother's tone, pronouncing each word with authority and decision, yet managing to sound kind. She was aware that if she lost Ovilier's support she would have no say in the Congregation of the Church and with that not even the power of the House Delorange would be of the slightest use. "We have come too far, Father, too far to back down, can't you see how close we are to achieving our goals? This is a test! A test from Aqua Deus himself to test our resolve!"

"I don't know anymore, Katienne..." he replied with a weary sigh, "maybe it's best to let it go, it may be time to accept our defeat and bow out gracefully before we..."

"Absolutely not." Katienne cut him off sharply.

"I understand, in that case, Katienne, I'm afraid I no longer want to be part of this alliance. I think it's time for me to step aside and save my skin, I advise you to do the same."

Katienne took a deep breath and smiled. It was time to show off her charms. Some would think she was simply referring to her beauty, but beauty was only the starting point. Her sisters were all beautiful in their own ways. Dambalarienne perhaps had the most harmonious face. Bolenne boasted the finest skin. Aienne, still a child, held potential.

And even Vienne, she begrudgingly had to admit, could look striking if not for her elusive gaze. She, on the other hand, was aware of her beauty, but knew that relying solely on her looks was insufficient, that was like a diamond that has not been polished to extract its maximum splendor. The princess knew how to make good use of the language of her body, the tone of her voice, the movement of her eyelashes, her smile... Her entire body was a tool, a vessel with which to make men and women fall prey to her charm. And that was an ideal moment to show off her arts once again.

"Does that mean you are no longer on my side, Father?" she asked, tilting her head to one side with feigned innocence. "Has Vienne's wound not only marred your garments but also stolen your courage?" she added, trying to humiliate him.

The priest looked at her in surprise at such insolence.

"My courage is as unimpeachable as ever, young lady!" he replied so irritably that his face reddened. "It's just that... perhaps we misjudged Vienne, even you must be able to see that your sister has changed. It's time to accept that we have lost and beg for forgiveness."

"Oh, I am sure that the rest of the members of the Congregation will seek to atone for their sins by not relying on the Lacrima's abilities, and it is possible that they will be redeemed. For them, mere forgiveness might be enough. But how do you think the High Priestess and Queen will react upon learning that your motives for supporting me were none other than to take away my mother's precious ecclesiastical title?"

"Perhaps my old ears are deceiving me," said the priest scandalized, "aren't you trying to blackmail me?"

"I would never dare of such a thing." She said, smiling tenderly at him. She leaned down to place one of her hands on the older man's thigh. "I am simply warning you of the risks of your decision, Father." She indicated, shrugging her shoulders as she tried to make him see that it was simply pure logic. "My faith is such that nothing and no one will prevent me from ensuring that the queendom is in hands as competent as mine. Interpose yourself in my vision and I assure you that losing your priestly title will be the least that will happen to you."

For an instant, the priest's eyes were filled with anger, his mouth opened to probably reprimand her for her threats. But Katienne's determined gaze seemed to be able to break him.

Father Ovilier tried to speak, attempting to escape the snare the princess was setting for him. But before he could utter a word, Katienne gently placed a finger on the priest's aged lips.

156

"Hush, father," she said soothingly, "it's all right, for you and me there is no more forgiveness, we played our cards and now we have to continue the game to the end. Whatever it takes..."

Ovilier intended to reproach her, but instead, he ended up ducking his head. Becoming a frail and manipulable old man. Katienne smiled inwardly, she had once again subjected him to her will.

"And what do you expect us to do?" the priest finally said.

"It's time to stop the nonsense and address the problem at its source. Bring me before the Sons of the Church."

Ovilier looked at her puzzled, "you don't pretend?"

"My faith is above all else, Father, above all else."

20. Making sense

White stone walls, violet-tiled roofs, and large outdoor courtyards with manicured gardens filled with colorful flowers. The village of Pianga was ostentatious, just as the Aertians were said to be; for some reason, they seemed to be attracted to the bright colors and the combination of tones.

An old woman appeared to be teaching twin girls, about eight years old, how to water plants in her garden, each carrying an identical small watering can. Three little birds with orange plumage alternated between fluttering and frolicking around them, and perching on the shoulders of the old woman and the girls.

Dabayl lead the way, they turned a corner, passing two young girls carrying baskets, who, seeing that Noakh was looking at them, began to put their hands to their mouths and giggle. The young Fireo looked back, seeing that those young girls had turned around to look in his direction and continue laughing.

Noakh frowned. "Dabayl, is it just me or are there scarcely any men in this village?"

"My, my, Noakh, what things we notice, eh?" Dabayl raised an eyebrow smiling. Once Noakh reddened, she continued. "But you are right, in Pianga it is very rare for a man to be born, we don't quite know why. My mother told me that when my brother was born, he was carried around the village being greeted with applause and cheers." She recalled with a nostalgic smile. "Which, reminds me of one thing, it's not easy to find a husband in these lands."

"How curious," Hilzen said, just before taking a bite of one of the last of the luscious fartuns Girilay had given him and to which the devoted Aquo seemed to have developed something of an addiction. "See if you can find companionship for our dear prince of fire, so he stops leading us down the path of bitterness."

159

Dabayl waved to an elderly man, then changed course, heading down a cobblestone road.

"Precisely, because of the lack of men, it would be relatively easy for you to settle down in this place," she turned around, walking backwards as she watched Noakh, "what do you say, Ascendant Phoenix?" she said amused, "maybe it wouldn't be a bad idea to find an Aertian wife and get some rest instead of setting out to take on Daikans, Knights of Water and every being that comes your way?" she proposed raising her eyebrows.

"Tempting," Noakh acknowledged, "but I'm going to have to decline such a proposal. Not to mention that Wulkan killed my mother and if it weren't for Lumio he would have finished me off as well, I would not live peacefully knowing that I have such an outstanding debt to repay."

A dilemma, Noakh recalled. That was what Burum Babar had called it. After the revelation the Daikan had made to him, he had no doubt that behind the incident the day the flaming sword chose him was King Wulkan. And all for fear that whoever succeeded him would not be a good king. A cowardice that had been paid for in blood....

"What about you, Hilzen?" said Dabayl turning to him.

The devout Aquo looked at her with utter indignation, "You've got to be kidding! Me marrying? I'm already married! Marne is and always will be my wife, until we meet again at sea."

Noakh nodded. As far as he knew, in Aquadom it was far from atypical for a widowed person to marry after a certain period of time. Hilzen, on the other hand, was not only very devout, but also professed a deep love for his wife, so it made sense that he would not want a new life partner.

Just then, a group of armored women on horseback emerged from one of the properties. Their steeds were making their way down the cobblestone street, looking imposing, protected by colored cloth fences, packed with bundles in which they were probably carrying provisions. It seemed that they were ready to go to war.

The first of them tugged on the reins of her steed at the sight of them. "Dabayl? Is that you?" She was a beautiful young woman, with lively, cheerful eyes brimming with curiosity.

"Laylaya, long time no see," Dabayl greeted, "don't tell me you've joined the search."

"That's right, we are going in search of the sword. My family has made a pact with several nearby houses, so we have a patronage. We have agreed to use the Royal Favor to help our people prosper," she

160

lifted her head slightly, "I see you still carry a bow! If you continue to be as accurate as when you were little you have a more than earned position in our troops," she then turned to Noakh and Hilzen, "your handsome friends may also join us if they wish." She said, giving them a nice smile.

"I'm afraid not, Laylaya, we have a wedding to attend." Dabayl excused herself.

"Yarna's wedding?" Laylaya said without hiding her surprise, "I'm glad you took it well. Many of my female companions don't, how few men there are around these lands and she's been able to captivate two of them!" She said with a mixture of jest and slight indignation.

"She must have something special, I suppose," she said with a shrug, "best of luck on your journey, Laylaya, go carefully."

Laylaya gave them a smile and left, walking away with the rest of the knights.

"Perfect for Noakh," Hilzen remarked, taking a last bite of his beloved fartun as they walked away.

"What's gotten into you about finding me a mate?" Noakh said in annoyance. "Besides, what's the point of finding me a mate, if I have this?" he teased, showing him the sapphire.

Hilzen snorted. "Don't even think of trying anything with the princess!" He said grumpily.

Noakh smiled, pleased that he had been able to annoy Hilzen with his retort. He had immersed the sapphire in water before arriving at that village, but Vienne had left him no message in return. Surely, she was too busy kicking her annoying sister's ass.

"It's here," said Dabayl entering a large white house with several pink flowers on the sides of the entrance. As she walked into the yard two little yellow birds with funny crests came flying out, fluttering around Dabayl until they landed on the Aertian's outstretched index finger.

"Did you miss me, little ones?" She said bringing her finger to her cheek, allowing both little birds to chirp as they innocently pecked at Dabayl's skin.

"Welcome to my home," Dabayl said, once she opened the door. Behind it were two old men, watching them in wide gray robes, each with a little bird also on their shoulders. "These are my parents." She introduced them. "Bum, Noakh," She said in Aertian, pointing a thumb at the Fireo, "Bum, Hilzen," she indicated, pointing this time at her other companion.

161

Her parents looked very old, so much so that they could very well be her grandparents. Dabayl was young, she had never mentioned her exact age, but, according to Noakh's calculations, she must have been three or four years older than he, a couple more at most. That meant that the couple must have had their daughter at a fairly mature age.

He felt a slight movement on his shoulder. He turned, observing the yellow-crested bird pacing his clothes as his head watched him making small, yet constant neck rolls. Four birds, one for each member of the family, he assumed.

Dabayl's mother said something. Noakh could not understand her as she spoke in Aertian but, from the way she was looking at them, it seemed she was talking about them in expletives. Her gaze was fierce.

"Welcome to our home. Make yourselves comfortable," Dabayl's father indicated, much more politely.

* * *

Hilzen took a swig of his hot drink, while Noakh leaned back in his seat to pick up one of the delicious anise-flavored pastries piled on that plate, an act that caused both crested birds to fly from Dabayl's shoulder to Noakh's head in an attempt to join the feast. They sat in Dabayl's bedroom, small, somewhat dusty, but with a skylight that illuminated the room amply.

"Founa, ensuna yu naaa." Dabayl complained from her bed.

Noakh did not need to know Aertian to discern that Dabayl was complaining to her father to stop appearing at the door of the room to offer them more hot drinks, something to eat, and anything else with which to show off his hospitality. Her father seemed to get the message, disappearing out the door, but not before offering a smile to his guests and nodding to them.

"Take strength, fellows, there's a wedding we have to attend." She said, resting her dirty boots on top of a cushion.

Hilzen set his purple tea down on the table, "yes, regarding that wedding, what business do Noakh and I have being there?"

Dabayl sighed. "You guys really have to know everything, don't you?" she grumbled, leaning over and resting her feet on the ground. "All right, I'll tell you. Our attendance at that wedding has little to do with amusement, but rather we are going in search of Tizai."

Noakh frowned, "and what does the sword have to do with the wedding?"

162

"Precisely the wedding is the key to start the search for Tizai with certain guarantees. I have a plan to meet there with someone to sponsor us. Searching for the sword in an entire kingdom is already an arduous task, without having a sponsor, that is, without financial backing for the journey, it becomes nearly impossible. Yes, a peasant could set out to find the sacred sword on his own, but it is a long, costly and danger-filled quest, to undertake such an expedition without someone to pay for our journey would delay us and cause us great hardship, the price of everything has drastically risen due to the euphoria over the crusade in search of the sword."

"Wait a minute, your friend..." Noakh made an effort to rummage through his memory for the young woman's name, "Laylaya, she said she had a patronage and they were going in search of the sword. Why not just accept your friend's invitation and be done with it?" Noakh suggested.

"I knew it..." Hilzen said, beginning to whistle a renowned Aquo love song known as *The Two Lovers.*

Dabayl did not laugh, instead she swallowed, "for she who leads a patronage is the one who has the right to request the Royal Favor," she revealed, "Noakh, Hilzen, I know I have no right to ask such a thing of you, but I would like to be the one who has the privilege of choosing the reward for finding the sword."

Noakh shrugged, "fine."

"Really? Just like that?" Dabayl replied, in bewilderment.

"Hilzen would ask for a church, I wouldn't even know what to ask," Noakh began, "who better than you to ask for the Royal Favor? Besides, we owe it to you."

"What do you mean by that?" replied Dabayl, confused.

"Have you forgotten?" the Fireo said, smiling, "the tournament in the city of Miere, Vileblood was going to kill me, but one of your accurate arrows saved me from being torn to pieces by that merciless man."

"True, you tried to save me too when Gelegen was interrogating me." Hilzen added.

Noakh walked over to her and squeezed her shoulder in a friendly manner. "You may have forgotten, but we haven't, the Royal Favor is all yours, we owe you."

"Searching for the sword..." Hilzen mused aloud, "it seems an impossible task to find it, it could be anywhere. From a ravine, to the top of a mountain... it's like finding a needle in a haystack."

163

"Only that the haystack will be teeming with tiny insects ready to devour you, should you try to take their precious prize," Noakh added.

"Though at least we have the advantage," Hilzen said confidently, "we have Noakh's flaming sword! That will make us unstoppable."

Dabayl quickly grabbed one of the pastries from the table and, without warning, threw one at Noakh, hitting him in the chest.

"Dead." Dabayl indicated, as the two little birds hurriedly pecked at the bits of dough now spread out across the worn wooden floor. "As convenient as Noakh and his flaming sword may be to us, he is still a human. One accurate arrow and say goodbye to our dear Fireo prince." She threw a second pastry. "Dead again," she declared as it impacted Noakh's head.

Noakh saw no flaw in his Aertian friend's logic. No doubt in melee his sword provided them with a considerable advantage, however, the Aertians' known skill with the bow could allow them to pierce his heart with an arrow even before he could make an attempt to unsheathe his weapon.

"Well then, let's go get that patronage and start our quest." Noakh said enthusiastically. "Sounds like the most fun."

Hilzen snorted of derision. "Meddling in another kingdom's sword-finding endeavors? Of course, you'd find it amusing."

The door burst open; revealing her father's face once more.

"Founa, ensuna yu naaa dare!" Dabayl complained, probably urging him again not to interrupt them. However, the man's face was white, "yo sai?"

"Surtu sae na daruga sua kue Sui Lana," her father replied, looking worried.

This time it was Dabayl's face that paled. She turned slowly to Noakh and Hilzen, looking at them in horror.

"They have found the location of the sacred sword." She translated, looking stupefied, "it lies at the edge of the Void... and you won't believe what's guarding it."

21. Eternal glory

The hooves of war horses clattered through the snowy terrain. It was a sight to behold: an amalgamation of half a hundred soldiers on horseback, all ready for combat. The mountain glittered, a result of the vibrant sun reflecting off the radiant armor in a striking combination of colors. Different breastplates and helmets displayed a myriad of colors, including shades of yellow, gold, red, silver, blue, and orange. The barding of their portentous steeds also matched the clothing of their riders, thus achieving together a design that was as spectacular as it was not very discreet.

The display of knights from various families trotting together was an uncommon sight. However, the news of what was hidden on the edge of that mountainside made this unique gathering worthwhile.

It had all started as a rumor, mere hearsay that had spread from town to town as if it were the catchiest song ever written. These words, embellished by some romantic minstrel, dictated the following: *What the entire kingdom seeks, what every citizen craves, is found on the slope of Sui Lana anchored in the rock bordering the dreaded Void.* A few verses had been more than enough to mobilize all those knights.

The rainbow of soldiers did not cease on their march. It was an ominous route, a place no knight would ever want to trot to, Sui Lana, the last slope of Aere Tine, hostile and abandoned from Shiana's divine hand.

A few verses had been enough to ride there together. Some in search of glory, others of eternal memory and many, why not, of the Royal Favor.

The road to Sui Lana had been hard, icy and long. But at last, they were there, riding along the slight slope of that hillside that divided the Kingdom of the Air with the Void, where Tizai was said to be located at its limits, anchored on top of a great rock. The snowy mountains full of

165

caves behind them, witnessing how they were closer and closer to accomplish their feat.

They rode in wedge formation; led by the venerated Jolana. An avid warrior, skilled with the spear, prodigious with the bow, versed in the art of the sword. At thirty-five years of age, she was not the oldest, nor did she belong to the most powerful family, simply her talent in combat and her innate gift for leadership had earned her the respect of all those men and women who had decided to follow her in pursuit of glory.

Jolana couldn't keep her golden eyes from glancing back and forth nervously. They were close to their target and everything was calm, too calm. The icy wind howled, the passing of the soldiers caused their armor to rattle, but nothing else. That tranquility gave her a very bad feeling.

Her eyes, shielded by her reddish helmet, peered intently towards the horizon; at some point, there would be no more snow, and Tizai would appear in front of them, embedded in the rock. She thanked Shiana for her blessing, it was a clear day. The moment when the sword in the rock appeared on the horizon would be key, they had to act fast and make sure Tizai was recovered, whatever it took, no matter how many fell.

She took a deep breath, her lungs freezing from the cold of the place. She had to be alert to be able to give the proper orders if necessary. The lives of the entire formation depended on her instructions and her ability to command.

Jolana strained her eyes, searching for any sign in the distance. The helmet was beginning to bother her, a necessary evil when the purpose was to get out of there alive. She squinted to see better, finally spotting a figure in the distance, wasn't it? Yes! A large black rock on the edge of that slope, into which a sword was embedded.

Her heart skipped a beat. *Tizai, there it is, the rumors were true*, she said to herself still in disbelief.

She spurred her horse with impetus. "Courage brothers and sisters, glory is within our grasp!" she cried, her angelic voice booming before the mountains.

The gigantic, colorful triangle of knights advanced with decision. The leader of the formation took her hands to the horn hanging from her neck; the one with which she would give the order to retreat as soon as they took possession of the sword and left that hidden place without looking back for a moment.

So many frozen nights, so many doubts about the expedition... finally rewarded.

Jolana was already able to hear the chants that would narrate how she and her brave knights had ridden up the slope of that frozen hell to retrieve Tizai.

For the kingdom, reclaim the sword, Jolana and her knights, worthy to be received by kings, worthy to be led by the Maiden of the Bell. Jolana and her knights, glory! Glory! Glory! Glory!

They were already very close; she could even discern the silhouette of the sword on the rock right at the edge of the cliff, welcoming the Void. The thunderous sound of the ride was music to her ears. A celestial melody that anticipated the success of their expedition. Jolana could not believe her fortune. Just like that, had Shiana intervened to pave the way for them?

Almost there, she motivated herself, her eyes fixed on the sword stuck in the rock getting closer and closer.

It had gone better than they expected. No casualties, no complications beyond the distance and the biting cold. Those songs would recount how they succeeded without losing a single rider.

An eerie roar erupted from the skies.

For an instant, Jolana stopped spurring her horse, shocked at what her eyes were witnessing.

A tailless dragon was heading toward them, soaring through the skies.

The most veteran knights drew their bows, while others pointed to the sky in disbelief at what was heading their way.

The first arrows whizzed past. Some were effortlessly dodged by the monstrous beast, and the rest ricocheted off its scales as if they were mere pebbles.

"Disperse!" Jolana commanded, bringing her horn to her lips to execute two high-pitched sounds so that all the riders without exception would hear her orders.

The triangle began to spread out, until the knights were spaced apart from each other. That slope was incredibly extensive, perfect for maneuvering and thus facing a dragon in the most convenient way.

The dragon descended, its jaws wide open, an orange glow foretold the fate of its victims. An entire line of knights was consumed by the flames, terrified neighs and cries of anguish and pain broke through the echoing mountains.

167

You will be remembered, brothers and sisters, she said to herself, clenching her jaw and continuing to ride towards the sword, accompanied by the rest of the knights who were still alive.

"Take back the sword, become worthy of the call of the Maiden of the Bell!"

She felt a shadow pounce on her, she leaned over her horse's mane. The soldier on her right screamed in panic as he was caught in the dragon's claws, only to immediately have his body explode into a thousand pieces as he was thrown violently against two other knights in the formation.

That bastard creature is attacking from the skies, Jolana reflected, looking up to see that the dragon was once again gliding through the air in search of new victims.

It is not descending to the ground at any time, she observed. he knew it was no coincidence; that being was intelligent. If it fought on the ground, it would be overcome by overwhelming numbers. If they damaged its wings, then it would be a much fairer fight.

She analyzed the situation, trying to keep a cool head while his companions fell prey to the flames and claws of the dragon. The powerful creature kept flying, sowing death, hunting one by one, without pause.

We have no choice, she decided, bringing the horn back to her lips. She took a moment to blow it, aware of what she was asking of these men.

Poooooooooooooooooooooooooom.

The low sound echoed through the mountains. The rest of the knights raised their fists to the sky twice. Jolana puffed out her chest with pride, they were ready to die.

The strategy was simple. A bloodthirsty dragon, all her knights prepared to fall lifeless. The horn signal had given a clear order, none were to offer battle, they were simply to ride, fearless, ready to succumb if in return one of them was able to retrieve the sword.

None of us will truly die if one of us survives and reclaims Tizai. There is no death when you live on in noble songs, Jolana encouraged herself. It was only necessary that one of them returned alive, that would be enough for all of them to earn a privileged place in the melodies of the kingdom.

She felt the heat of the flames ravage her right flank, tugged on the reins, managing to pull her tired mare out of the way in time. The fire

168

devoured a young man in bright green armor, someone she had known well for a long time.

She turned her gaze forward, gritting her teeth. Urging her horse to ride even faster. She was so close that she could appreciate the beauty of Tizai's harness, its gold guard with the slightly curved quillons contrasting with the black square pommel.

She pulled hard on the reins, rushing abruptly from her horse to fall on the snow. She did not want to look back, aware that behind her there was only death, fire and blood.

Jolana stood in front of the rock; the embedded sword was before her blissful eyes. Ready to be pulled out and transported to a safe place, returned to its rightful owners.

Worthy to be guided by the Maiden of the Bell. Jolana and her knights, glory! Glory! Glory!

She took a deep breath and reached out her arm, ignoring the screams of terror behind her.

I will see to it that your death will not be in vain, she promised. They had fought well; with their death they had distracted the tailless dragon.

She clenched her jaw, ready to pull and tear the blade from the rock. *Shiana, grant me strength.* Her gloved fingers wrapped around the hilt.

Glory, glory...

Her hand slowly began to lose its grip. Her arm fell onto the rock and then onto the snow. On the other side of that limb there was no longer Jolana's body, only a huge pool of blood in whose reflection one could glimpse how the dragon's jaws were tearing apart the mutilated body of such a valiant warrior.

22. Comrades

Alvia leaned against the bark of a tree just outside the stable, the toe of her boot drumming on the yellowish leaf litter impatiently as she waited for her mount to be saddled. She had received a most atypical message. The parchment indicated that Gant Blacksword wanted to see her as soon as possible in a shelter located in the nearby mountains of Lanjara. Under normal conditions, she would have ignored such a vague request; however, she was curious.

Although, to be honest, she had also decided to pay a visit to her companion for a slightly more devious reason. Not long ago, she had met Noakh, the boy who had defeated Gant, and she saw this as the perfect opportunity to taunt him for being defeated by such a scrawny young man.

The young page boy with the crooked nose and shy look appeared from the stable, holding the reins of a beautiful white mare with a long mane and blue eyes.

"I'm glad you remembered my preferences, kid," she thanked him with a smile.

She climbed onto her mount, feeling the steed's eagerness to begin riding. She tugged on the reins, then tossed a coin to the page and winked—a combination enough to make the youngster blush. He made sure to catch his reward and avoided letting the coin get lost in the straw and mud that covered the stable floor.

She rode away from the stable. She felt the enthusiasm of her mount, the nervousness of the animal's gallop pleased her, it was a feeling that resonated with her perfectly. She positioned her body straight, adjusted her legs properly to be able to follow the mare's movement. A light tap of the heel of her boot on the back of the girth was enough to make the mare ride with frenzy.

171

She knew those forests perfectly well. She had visited those mountains on several occasions during her childhood, her caretaker had taken them there to pick mushrooms, a way for them to breathe fresh air and get away from the palace walls. She remembered how she picked a striking mushroom with a purple cap and yellow granulations, so beautiful she thought it was that she decided to offer it as a gift to her mother, the queen. *A most beautiful gift, if what you want is to kill me*, those words and a look of disappointment had been her mom's answer and, consequently, the first moment in which Alvia had considered her mother a bitter and ungrateful witch. The first of many such moments.

She felt the wind in her face, the trees appearing and falling behind in an instant. She smiled, happy and free, enjoying the solitude. After accompanying Vienne for so long, she needed to feel independent again, to get as far away as possible from an arduous job as a nanny.

She had to admit it. She had been impressed with her niece's evolution. Not because she had mastered the powers of the sword, not even because she had been able to survive the confrontation against the boy who had managed to defeat a Knight of Water. She could not deny that the young girl had matured. The skill to begin to demand and assert herself had surfaced within her, and though she found it annoying, she knew it was a quality Vienne needed to develop if she was to stand up to her sister Katienne in her conflict.

Of course, there was much to be polished in her. Nevertheless, she had no doubt that her character would continue to toughen. She wondered what it would be like to reign under her command, perhaps she would become someone worth taking orders for? The thought of retiring plagued her mind more and more intensely.

However, the fact that Vienne had earned her respect did not detract from the fact that she was still upset with her. Her adolescent whims had caused Gelegen to fall behind. That idiot had agreed to Vienne's request, accompanied with a submissive *of course, Princess Vienne, anything you ask of me*. At the thought, she frowned. During their journey in Tir Torrent, she had noticed a small detail that she knew she had to clear up with her dear sister, the queen, as soon as possible.

In front of her was the trunk of a tree that had fallen and as a result had succumbed to moss and fungus. She tugged on the reins, urging her fervent mare to leap over the obstacle.

Some would feel bad for Gant. He had been excluded from his duties as a Knight of Water almost entirely, he had not traveled east, as

172

the rest of his companions had done, nor had he been given any mission beyond doing nothing. One could almost say that, except for still enjoying the title, he had been relegated from his post. However, for Alvia, it all came down to a matter of attitude, if Gant had wanted to, if he had given everything not to be relegated, she had no doubt that he would have marched east no matter how many burns had covered his body.

She pulled on the reins, bringing the mare to a halt. She had arrived at the designated address. A cottage of white and brown stones with a large fenced outdoor yard. She dismounted, tying her mare to a leafy tree with reddish berries that quickly caught her mount's interest.

Her companion stood there, striking blows against unseen opponents with fervor. Gant was clad in dark blue armor. Had he ever worn such equipment before? Not that she could remember, however, it was true that she did not pay particular attention to the attire of her companions either.

She stood watching him for a moment, the soldier was showing off his strength, wielding his bulky sword with dexterity. His thrusts were forceful and as powerful as she was used to seeing him perform. He seemed to be fully recovered, although it was something she would never admit to Gant; it was much more fun to humiliate him.

She walked toward him. The mere anticipation of teasing him filled her with a wide grin.

"Trying to prove you're still good for something, aren't you, Gant?" she scoffed after taking up a position at his rear without him noticing, "face it, your time has passed, it's time to make a change and start a new chapter in your life. Hey, why don't you trade your sword for a shovel? I bet you could plant this whole yard full of tubers! Knight of the Potato Field! What do you think of such a title?" she proposed with a loud laugh at her witticism.

Gant turned around, his bald head and forehead drenched in sweat. Part of his face slightly deformed and with pink skin due to the burns he had suffered against Noakh... and a grumpy countenance as was usual for him. The latter merely frowned, jabbing the tip of his gigantic weapon into the ground, as if he was restraining himself from skewering it. Such signs would have been warning enough for any person with sense to cease his taunting, but not for Alvia.

"I had forgotten how ugly you had looked after the terrible burns," Alvia taunted contemplating his partially burned face, "well, what am I saying? Almost like that guy did you a favor, so at least you have an

173

excuse," she corrected, "but what does it matter how you look as long as you keep your strength, right? Or did you also lose your energy after that confrontation?"

Not a word from Gant. He simply exhaled deeply through his nostrils, like a raging bull about to charge at his victim.

"What's the matter, did you become mute after being terribly humiliated by that boy?" Alvia feigned surprise, "Don't tell me he burned your tongue too!" she said making an exaggerated grimace of astonishment in mockery. "And I still have the best part left, guess who stood up to your little brown-eyed friend, Vienne! And she doesn't even sport a burn on her face!" She teased, winking at him.

"Insolent worm!" Gant replied, grabbing his weapon by the hilt and snatching the blade from the ground.

Alvia leaned her body back slightly, narrowly avoiding the sharp edge of Gant's sword. Using the momentum, she executed a backward somersault, using her hands to aid the movement. As her feet touched the ground again, two daggers had appeared in her hands and a wide grin on her face.

Finally, a bit of fun.

There was no better way to dispel the hangover of inactivity she had suffered on that long voyage aboard the Merrybelle than by engaging in a fight against an opponent like Gant. Rough, astonishingly strong, and now, thanks to her clever provocations, incredibly choleric.

She extended her left arm, pointing her dagger at Gant, then provocatively waved her weapon at him, urging him to attack. An uncontrolled shout of fury followed by a fierce charge indicated that it had been a sufficient lure to motivate his companion.

The bluish armor did not prevent Gant from advancing toward her with firmness and rage, his sword raised in both hands. She waited patiently, a broad smile revealing the excitement she felt about engaging in combat. One leg forward, the other behind, supporting the weight of her body only on the tips of her boots.

Gant's sword came down right where Alvia was positioned, striking so hard that the blade pierced even the earth just below. However, the Knight of Water was no longer in that spot. She had swiftly moved to the side, avoiding being split in half by such a blow.

Fighting Gant was going to be fun. He was probably the strongest and most resilient man in the entire queendom. She, on the other hand, made up for her deficiencies on those areas with unparalleled speed and reflexes. That made their fighting style very different, he was

174

slower, yet his blows, so devastatingly powerful, could easily end her life with a single strike.

Of course, Alvia knew for a fact that this confrontation was the reason Gant had asked her to visit him in that remote place. A way to prove his worth without his pride being affected. She did not expect pleas, not even words from her companion except perhaps the occasional insult. Nor did she need them, for Alvia it was enough to test what he was capable of, the training she was to take part in was Gant's way of proving he was fit and worthy of being sent to the front with the rest of the Knights of Water.

The fight was intense. One of her daggers made a deep cut in Gant's face, a second cut in the neck, very close to the carotid artery. Gant, for his part, had managed to seriously wound her in the back, a blow that, had she not partially dodged it, would have broken her spine. She enjoyed the fact that Gant was taking this training with the necessary seriousness, she could sense his exaltation and this only provoked a combative outburst in her own guts.

With all her might, Alvia hurled her dagger aiming for the sweat-drenched forehead of her furious adversary. While Gant blocked the attack from a distance, Alvia took the opportunity to move swiftly, placing herself in front of Gant, dodged his sword by pivoting on her boot, and then had to retreat to avoid his headbutt.

Both were bleeding profusely. Alvia was especially sore all over her right side: her shoulder, the deep wound on her back and the irritating puncture in her thigh... Nevertheless, it had been an interesting confrontation.

"Fine," Alvia said with a smile without trying to hide that she was breathing with some difficulty, "as much as I'd like to keep picking on you, I can't deny that you're clearly in excellent shape." She acknowledged.

Did she believe in redemption? Only when it was properly deserved. Gant had been defeated by Noakh and deserved to be mocked for it. However, having seen the Fireo boy in action fighting Vienne, she could understand why his companion had ended up paying for underestimating the scrawny, seemingly helpless young man.

"You win, I will talk to my sister the great queen and tell her that you deserve to be sent to the front along with the others." She conceded.

For a slight moment, she watched her companion, waiting for some simple gesture of happiness or, at least, gratitude. She knew for a fact that Gant was far from emotional, she didn't expect him to be jumping up and down in happiness, clapping or any such nonsense. What she also didn't expect was that he would remain motionless, just holding his sword with both hands as if he were absent.

"What's the matter with you, you idiot?" Alvia asked quizzically, situated opposite him. "Wasn't that what you were looking for? To stand up to me to prove your worth so you could be respected again?"

Gant made his move. Alvia tried to pull away, but he had caught her completely off guard. Gant's sword had pierced her stomach.

"Your dear sister treated me as if I were an outcast," he said digging the tip of his weapon even deeper into her belly, "and, you worm, you have nothing but taunts to hide how lonely you feel. Now I've found someone who respects me and treats me as I deserve."

Alvia could not answer. Instead, her mouth only emitted a blood choked scream as she watched in stupefaction as Gant's sword further cleaved into her guts.

23. A death request

Her footsteps echoed up the deep, twisting spiral staircase. Katienne descended with care, ensuring the tip of her foot found secure purchase on the uneven stone steps. In front of her stood the priest Ovilier, who carried a torch with ease despite his advanced age.

It had been a struggle, but the pious man seemed to have come to his senses. His faith had been restored, fortified by the belief that Vienne would not undermine their power and plans, as long as they remained true and faithful.

She wrinkled her delicate nose again as she felt that intense smell of dampness invading her nostrils. Her head grew cloudy, so much that she had to place her hand on the rough and cold limestone wall so as not to lose her balance.

Ovilier, noticing Katienne's pause, halted.

"Are you all right?"

"I've been better," she replied, still stricken. "It's this suffocating smell... no," she corrected, "it's this whole place itself, it's so stifling."

"Indeed, it is tremendously hostile," he confirmed, just before turning and resuming his march down the stairs, "but I understand that, being a prison, it is a most appropriate characteristic, wouldn't you say?"

The princess remained silent. She merely breathed through her mouth, leaning her hand on the wall to descend as soon as possible. The mere touch of the moist porosity in her fingernails made her cringe deeply.

At the base of the stairs stood a jade-colored door, its edges seemingly gnawed away by time. A lock barred access.

"Here we are. I warn you; it is a somewhat disturbing sight."

Katienne nodded. She had heard rumors of how horrible the ecclesiastical prison was, a place where those who had committed the worst crimes were sent, not those committed against the queendom but

177

against Aqua Deus himself. An unforgivable act that, it was said, was paid for with a sentence that entailed the most horrifying tortures. The princess, on the other hand, was sure that the horrors that took place there had been exaggerated.

Ovilier offered the torch to Katienne, once she held it, the priest extracted from his neck a thick chain from which hung a large rusty black key that seemed very heavy. He inserted it into the lock and turned it, the robust *clonk* announced that they could gain access. He pocketed the key again, then pushed the door with both hands, causing it to slowly give way.

If she found the smell of the staircase unpleasant, the one that emanated when Ovilier opened the door made it look like the most select perfume of roses in comparison. The priest stepped in, and Katienne followed, her eyes darting side to side, her morbid interest undeterred by the foul stench.

They walked down a narrow corridor. The iron bars took on an orange hue as the torch passed. Cells, to her left and to her right. She felt a shiver, it was certainly an eerie sight.

Katienne approached one of the cells, seized by morbid curiosity, she approached the torch to the large black bars to see what was inside. She made a grimace of displeasure, a completely naked man lay chained by the ankles and wrists to the floor, robust and short chains that forced him to be positioned on all fours.

Ovilier approached her, grabbed the torch and pointed with his index finger to a small, badly rusted slit at the top of the cell.

"A drop of water falls on his head every few seconds without a break, day and night. An interval long enough for you to forget about it, lose yourself in your thoughts, and then..." Just at that instant, a drop fell from the slit, rushed into the void until it landed on the prisoner's head. The latter laughed hysterically, so disproportionately that Katienne's hair stood on end, the prisoner's uncontrolled laughter was accompanied by an intense moan, followed by cries and screams as if possessed. "Precisely that. Funny how sometimes the simplest forms of torture can become the most macabre."

"Please! I beg you... kill me!" The prisoner cried in a high-pitched voice. "Kill me, I beg you!" At that instant another drop fell on his head, this caused him to stop talking, instead he laughed frantically until he stopped and began to pull the shackles that held his wrists to exhaustion.

178

"This way, Katienne." Ovilier urged her, illuminating the wet cobblestone path with his torch.

"Why are they here?" asked Katienne as she inadvertently stepped in a puddle, "are the Sons of the Church treated as prisoners?"

Ovilier gave a chuckle that mingled with the wailing coming from the nearest cells. "The truth is that they are the ones who decided to live in here, apparently this place gives them peace."

Peace... How can such a sinister place appease anyone? The princess pondered, her skin crawling as she heard an agonized cry coming from some nearby cell.

The path ended in a hall. Damp, completely empty, except for a bald man in a brown robe who was kneeling before a statue of a cracked white stone mermaid with a large part of her belly and one arm missing. Up close, the princess heard a faint murmur, that man was praying.

They stood there, motionless, doing nothing. Finally, the man stood up, looking at them through one ice-blue eye and one completely white eye. Ovilier gestured to Katienne, urging her to let him carry the conversation.

"Greetings, Commander, man who has given his life for the Church of Water, we bring a petition on behalf of the Aqua Deus."

Katienne noted the respect and caution with which Father Ovilier dealt with the members of the Sons of the Church. As far as she knew, these men obeyed the orders of the Congregation of the Church, of which Ovilier was one of the oldest and most respected members, so why such deference?

The Commander stared at the priest; then his gaze shifted to Katienne, who had to make an effort not to look away. Despite being around fifty years old, the man had a strong and tremendously intimidating bearing.

"Any work in the name of the Aqua Deus can be done." He conceded, "but you know what the price is for our services."

Price? Katienne thought, her gaze drifting slightly to Ovilier, the priest had not mentioned anything to her about any payment.

"I don't have any coins with me," the princess began, "but I'm sure..."

Before she could finish the sentence, Ovilier placed his wrinkled hand on her mouth, preventing her from continuing. Then, with his other arm, he grabbed her wrist and pulled her back, away from the Commander.

179

"It's not that kind of price they expect," Ovilier whispered nervously, "gold to them is nothing more than an earthly commodity, they are above that." Ovilier pulled his hand away from Katienne's mouth. "There is only one way to pay for the services, a water offering that shows how much this mission means to us."

Katienne frowned, Ovilier, understanding that the princess did not know what she was referring to, continued. "We must offer them pure water as well as corrupt water."

One of Igüenza's lessons resonated in Katienne's mind. *Pure water, a water as crystalline and salty as that of the sea, a sign that the ocean is inside all of us. Corrupted water, the living reflection of how human beings are capable of staining everything, even the purest...*

Ovilier approached the Commander and recited a few words that Katienne could not hear; the latter, after nodding, rummaged in a drawer of the table and gave him something. Then Ovilier approached the princess again and held out his trembling hand, showing her what the Commander had handed him, two elongated glass vials and a dagger whose blade was curved.

"A couple of drops of pure water will suffice," he revealed to her while showing her one of the flasks, "the container of corrupt water, on the other hand, has to be delivered completely full, can you do it?"

"Of course," Katienne said, resting her hand on one of the vials. Ovilier stepped back just enough so as not to disturb the princess in the ritual.

Katienne took a deep breath, first focusing on offering the pristine water. She began to rummage through her memory, seeking a sad or emotional moment. She didn't have to dive far into her memories to find one bleak enough to bring tears to her eyes. She remembered the time Vienne was chosen by the sword, subsequently designated as the Lacrima, and how, with that, her dreams of reigning had almost completely collapsed. Her eyes became blurry, she felt her cheeks moisten. She brought the vial to her right eye with her hand, leaving it there for a few moments to make sure that several of her tears made their way through the glass container. She handed the offering to Ovilier, who nodded in satisfaction.

She had delivered the pure water; it was time to offer the corrupt. She took the other flask and the dagger from the trembling hands of the priest. She remembered why she was in that place. She had to stop Vienne from reigning and to do that they had to enlist the services of the Sons of the Church. And nothing was going to stop her wishes from coming true.

She remained upright and brought the tip of the curved dagger blade close to her belly. She felt the cold steel work its way into her gut, she let out a moan of pain as her pretty linen dress began to stain with blood. She ripped the dagger out and placed the vial under her deep wound, gushes of dark blood began to slowly fill the vial.

Ovilier approached her, grabbed her wrist in a sign of support and then picked up from her hands both the dagger and the vial filled with blood. Katienne could see in Ovilier's eyes what appeared to be a look of concern. However, she stood her ground. The wound hurt, but she had to endure the pain, that pain and much more, in order to make sure that the queendom would one day be under her rule.

Both offerings were handed to the Commander. The man left the dagger on the table, still stained with Katienne's blood, and began to walk carrying both vials. He stopped in front of the mermaid where he had been praying before being interrupted by his visitors.

"Oh, Aqua Deus, bear witness to the offering your humble servants present to you." He began. He lifted the vial containing the tears with both hands. "Pure water, representing the sea we harbor within us. May the best that resides within us be sufficient to cleanse our sins." He recited, tilting the vessel, Katienne's tears fell over the mermaid's right eye, causing the stone statue to feel as if it were weeping.

Then he raised the flask overflowing with blood likewise showing it to the mermaid. "Corrupt water, representing the imperfection of the human being." The Commander poured the contents over the statue's left eye, causing immensely more sinister tears to form.

Blood trickled down the stone face. The Commander turned to them after performing the ritual.

"We accept your offering with pleasure." said the man, after which he made an Aquo reverence. Ovilier and Katienne imitated him. "I can only offer you one Son of the Church, the other two have already left on a mission of faith."

"We know," said Ovilier, "one will suffice for our purposes."

The Commander led them into an adjoining room, then returned the way he had come. The dark blue cobblestones that covered the floor of that room moved slightly when they felt the weight of their footsteps, revealing water protruding from the unstuck mortar. Completely smooth walls, without any kind of decoration, the only decorative element was a huge amount of smoke.

No, steam, Katienne realized, sensing the intense heat. She felt her hair frizz, in another scenario being aware that her stylish hairstyle had been totally ruined would have been tremendously annoying, but the prickling in her bloodied belly and her desire for triumph allowed her to disregard such an inconvenience.

The Son of the Church was kneeling with his arms folded, leaning his bare back against the bluish wall. His solemn face was slightly bent forward, while over his shaven head a stream of water fell steadily from an opening in the ceiling, which, from the amount of steam visible in the room, must have been painfully hot.

What kind of training are these men subjected to? The princess couldn't help but wonder.

Katienne noticed how her heart was beating faster, it was a feeling hard to explain, a complete exhaustion as she felt that she was close to having everything under control again. Just thinking that such a feeling of power would be greater when she was in charge of the queendom made the hairs on her arms stand on end.

The bony hand of the priest was on Katienne's waist, trying to help her walk. The wound in her belly was bleeding with some insistence, yet her eyes could not have been more alert. She was so excited with that moment, with her voracious desire, that a stupid hemorrhage was not going to stand in her way.

The princess glanced sideways at the priest. He responded with a slight nod, extending his trembling arm to urge her to approach the Son of the Church.

Katienne's footsteps echoed on the empty walls of that dank room. She moved to the side of the Son of the Church, knelt down and, as she stood so close, the burning drops of water falling on the head of that servant of the Aqua Deus splashed on her, slightly burning her face. She tried not to grimace; it was another price to pay for her desires.

She leaned to whisper her request in his ear. She took her time, sparing no detail, making the Son of the Church understand why someone sworn to protect the faith should act on her behalf. The Son of the Church merely remained motionless at the words he was hearing.

Once Katienne finished her plea, he nodded. He stared into the void for a slight moment and then turned to the priest.

182

"Father Ovilier," he began, his voice sounding more powerful than his slender, yet remarkably athletic, build would anticipate, "does this woman speak on your behalf and for the Church of Water?"

The priest swallowed, as if considering the gravity of what they were about to do. Then he nodded slowly.

The Son of the Church stood up and, without a word, left the room. Willing to carry out the assassination order.

24. Secrets

Noakh climbed down from the bed, taking care not to disturb Hilzen in the process, who was sleeping peacefully on a cot on the floor. He walked, barefoot, out of the guest room where they had been kindly accommodated. From Hilzen's snoring, he confirmed that he had not disturbed his sleep.

He wandered through the corridors, immersed in his thoughts.

It was very early in the morning; the sun was barely filtering through the windows, but that was not the reason why he could not sleep, nor was the fact that today was the wedding they were to attend accompanying Dabayl. The reason he could not rest was none other than Gurandel, the tailless dragon had decided to use the freedom he had granted her by ensuring that the sword Tizai was not recovered by the Aertian monarchs. Certainly, he could not assert that it was Gurandel; Dabayl's father had not indicated that the dragon had no tail. However, who else could it be? Of course it would be Gurandel. The Queen of the Dragons had sworn to exact vengeance. Was this her way of initiating it? He felt bad thinking about the number of people who could have already died under her jaws and flames, wasn't all that pain his fault for having decided to release her?

Without realizing it, he had stood in front of the entrance to a room, Loredan's bedroom. For some reason, the door had been left open. He did not dare to enter, but it did not take him long to discern the notable difference between Loredan's bedroom and Dabayl's. Loredan's was crammed with instruments strapped to the wall, from flutes, lutes and other exotic instruments that Noakh didn't even know how they could produce music. Any gap where an instrument did not rest was covered with notations of sheet music and also long writings in what Noakh assumed must be poetry or song lyrics.

Is this why you don't like music, Dabayl? Noakh wondered, his heart shrinking, *because the brother you lost loved it?* It made sense, probably listening to melodies reminded her of her older brother, a wound that opened again and again at each new song her ears heard... he felt bad for his friend, thinking that every time the music played, she would relive her torment.

"Loredan was a good boy." A voice said from behind him.

Noakh startled, turning around. Behind him stood Dabayl's father, watching him from his short stature with both arms behind his back and three little birds on his shoulders.

"I'm sorry, I didn't mean to be lingering in your son's room, the door was open." He apologized in embarrassment.

The man shook his head. "We Aertians think there is no better way to honor those who have left us than to speak of them. That way their name becomes part of the wind again." He said, walking into the room. Two of the birds began to fly away, fluttering off down the halls of the house, the third, one with a crest, hovered at his shoulder. Noakh stood still in place, however, Dabayl's father urged him with his hand to follow, once Noakh did so he continued. "Loredan's death was a hard blow to all of us. As parents it was very hard to take, no matter if your son's lifeless face is lying in front of you, your insides keep urging you to think that he is not gone, that he is still there... however, for Dabayl it was especially painful."

The man moved his hand to the shoulder where the bird resided, extended a finger on which it landed, and then moved his hand upward, causing the bird to roam freely around the room until it landed on one of the many flutes on the wall.

"Dabayl is also a very good girl." He said sitting on his son's bed, "she used to be much more cheerful; she loved to spy on her older brother while he was composing and playing new songs. She loved Loredan with all her might, she admired him to such an extent that she wanted to be like him."

He pointed to a corner of the room, a corner Noakh had overlooked, a very small lute, the size a child would probably use, rested on a larger lute.

"After his death, Dabayl lost all interest in music, since then her efforts were focused on learning to handle the bow."

Noakh's stomach lurched. To think that Dabayl's impressive handling of the bow was nothing more than the vivid reflection of the deep pain she carried....

186

"I'm impressed by how happy she looks with both of you. Thank you for restoring the music Dabayl had lost from her heart," he said, offering a pleased smile that caused even more wrinkles to appear on his face. "I know my daughter can sometimes be a little complicated to get along with, but I'm glad to know she can count on you."

Noakh nodded, "I assure you that Dabayl can always count on us." After a pause, he dared to ask a question he knew he had no right to ask, "excuse the boldness, but how did Loredan die?"

"That's the worst of it," Dabayl's father replied, looking at him sadly, "that we never really knew how and why our son died, we simply received a letter from the palace stating that he had passed away."

* * *

The two young women were looking at each other in the mirror, finishing the final touches before the party. Dabayl was tightening the corset of one of them, gripping its laces so tightly that her face reddened from the effort.

"Hey, I don't look bad at all," Noakh said amused, looking at himself in the mirror that sat right next to where Dabayl was tightening Hilzen's corset. The young Fireo ran his fingers around his reddish hair, combed in ringlets that fell to his shoulders. That hairstyle matched his pink-dotted, wide-sleeved white dress, to which a cloth-filled bra had been added as padding, and an ostentatious necklace that looped countless times around his neck, thus concealing the neck bulge.

The worst part was the heels; Noakh took two steps and had to hold on to a chair to keep from falling face first to the floor. Then he kept walking, determined to get the hang of walking in them. He felt an obligation to learn how to wear them, after listening to Dabayl's father about Loredan and his strange death he had to do everything in his power to make Dabayl satisfied, including disguising himself as a woman.

"This is ridiculous," Hilzen complained, taking a deep breath as Dabayl continued to tighten the corset. The devout Aquo attempted to cross his arms, however, he ceased in his attempt as he noticed that the fabric began to creak from the pressure. His dress was yellow and long-tailed, a garment that, according to Dabayl, had belonged to her great-aunt Sandayna.

Although their clothing was not similar, both had on their clothes a kind of white cloth in the shape of an inverted triangle running across

187

their shoulders until it ended just above their stomachs. A garment that, according to Dabayl, denoted that they exercised the profession of servants.

In Noakh's case, the reddish wig had been styled in such a way that he had straight bangs that hid his black eyebrows, which in turn, severely limited his vision. As for Hilzen, he wore his hair pulled back in a ponytail, had fully shaved his beard, and now sported reddish eyebrows, thanks to a cream makeup that colored his blond brow hairs.

"Do you intend to explain to us why we have to go disguised as women to accompany you, or are you simply mocking us?" Hilzen said in annoyance.

"Yes, Dabayl, I think you owe us an explanation." Noakh supported him, stepping across the floorboards of the room with his arms outstretched for balance.

"Oh, come on, you look divine."

Frowning looks from Noakh and Hilzen were their only response.

"While it is true that I find the idea of disguising yourselves as women absurdly amusing, the truth is that your attire also obeys a much more important issue than my entertainment. I have only one invitation, however, you can accompany me if you will act as my maids."

"And what does that have to do with being disguised as women?" Hilzen demanded to know trying again to cross his arms, but ceasing as soon as he realized that it would rip the dress.

"It has a lot to do, in Aere Tine, a woman cannot have male servants. Likewise, a man cannot have female servants." She informed them, then leaned her body to the right and reached for a small makeup box that sat on a three-legged chair. "You need more makeup, Hilza." She said as she picked up the sponge, then dabbed it in powder from the box and brought it close to Hilzen's face. "And, in anticipation of your annoying questions, yes, you have to come with me, because she has to meet you."

"She?"

"The patronage I seek is from none other than the woman who is to be married. Yarna, a beautiful woman who happened to be my brother's fiancée or, rather, was until he passed away. Now she is marrying another man, as if my brother never existed."

Dabayl's annoyed tone assaulted him. He was about to ask her about Loredan and his fiancée, however, he felt remorseful for discovering her past from her father and not discussing it with her, so he decided to keep quiet.

188

"And we are to appear at their wedding to do so?" Hilzen insisted, tilting his head obediently to one side so that Dabayl could continue with her makeup application, "we could wait after they're married so..."

"It has to be today, during the wedding." Dabayl declared. Seeing Hilzen and Noakh look at each other with a puzzled grimace, she let out a sigh and continued, "since you want to know everything, we did not end on good terms. When my brother died, she did nothing. She didn't complain, she wasn't even shocked... and I made sure she didn't forget him by putting an arrow in her chest. We haven't spoken since."

Noakh shook his head disapprovingly.

"So, why are you attending her wedding?" Hilzen continued, uncomprehending. "Or, worse, why are you invited?"

"It is part of the Aertian tradition; one must invite all the people and forget the grievances of the past." She clarified to them. "But there is more. That same tradition dictates that the betrothed, on her wedding day, cannot refuse to heed the requests of her guests. She must listen to everything that anyone who attends her wedding has to say to her, it is a tradition that has always been carried out. And we will take advantage of it to get her to sponsor us."

"You expect someone you ended up on such bad terms with to sponsor us?" said Noakh, perplexed.

"Yes, though for it to work we'll need your flaming sword," she revealed to him, then pointed to a long umbrella leaning against the wall.

25. A change of plans

This time it had been a *C Major*. The early morning sun was beginning to warm the stagnant water in the trough of that small abandoned barn where they had played so often as children.

There was Lieri, leaning on the gnawed wood, looking more nervous than usual. It was no wonder, this meeting was more than necessary. They had discovered the sword's whereabouts, and rather than joy, they felt absolute despair.

"A dragon," Lieri merely said. "What have we done to deserve this, Zarta?"

"Nothing, brother," she said hugging him, "at least we know where Tizai is." She comforted him. She shared that helplessness with her brother, they knew where the sacred sword was located and could do nothing to retrieve it.

"Without the sacred sword, all we have is our cunning..." said Lieri, "and trust in the valiant knights who seek Tizai in pursuit of glory and the Royal Favor."

"I think it's time to change strategy, brother," Zarta suggested, trying not to be affected by Lieri's saddened look. "Now that we know where the sword is located, we simply have to face that dragon with the combined power of our armies to retrieve it."

"Leaving our borders defenseless in the process..." punctuated Lieri, "It would be too risky."

Zarta gave a snort, "you worry too much, if there is a dragon in our domain it was surely this one that destroyed the tower and stole the sword..."

"It may be simple for you to say, but remember that Fireo troops have begun to camp on my borders."

He is right, Zarta conceded. It was all so confusing... After the attack on the Tower of Concord, Lieri had deployed a large number of troops on his border with Firia, thus protecting himself from any attack. Ironically, it had not been until her brother Lieri had made that move that Wulkan had responded in kind, encamping Fireo soldiers on his borders with Aere Tine. It appeared that Wulkan was more focused on defending himself than launching an offensive. In any case, there was no point in pondering about it; the result was the same: Lieri could not withdraw his troops from the border with Firia as it would leave them unprotected.

"I may not have to call upon my army to help you," Lieri mused, staring into the void, "I have come up with the perfect people we could make use of. Hundreds of newcomers to the sword quest that could help your army."

Zarta inclined her head, interested.

"Prisoners." Lieri unveiled to her, "each and every one of them. We offer them freedom and the possibility of obtaining the Royal Favor, how could they refuse?"

Allow prisoners who have caused the most cruel and bloodthirsty crimes to roam free in the streets in exchange for a measly chance for one of them to regain our sword? Zarta pondered, many people would die, several of their citizens would suffer the consequences of freeing the most despicable beings from their prisons. It seemed a price only someone desperate would be willing to allow.

"All right, Lieri, we will release the prisoners who agree to go in search of Tizai."

26. In the name of Aqua Deus

The shadow made its way into the room, stealthy, trained not to make the slightest noise. He synchronized his steps with his victim's breathing, ensuring his presence went undetected.

The old woman slept peacefully, lying on her back, letting out a slight hiss with each exhalation. For an instant, the Son of the Church contemplated the woman in her dreams. She was missing an arm. What struck him most, however, was the tear tattoo under one of her cheeks. He clenched his fists angrily, recognizing that symbol, that woman had once been a member of the Divine Protection, how could someone dedicated to the Aqua Deus have been corrupted to such an extent that she deserved death as punishment?

He drew his dagger. *I wonder how sinners can sleep*, he thought, gritting his teeth.

His dagger sliced into the old woman's chest. Piercing her heart. An accurate blow; it could not be otherwise, for his hand had been directed by the same implacable justice of the Aqua Deus.

The Son of the Church wiped the blade of his dagger on the sheets of his victim. The blood soaked the white cloth, staining it near the neck. He ran the blade several times over the sheets, making sure that the impure water did not stain his weapon. He was in no hurry. Having entered her home with stealth, he intended to leave with the same discretion, mocking the Temple Guards who, consciously or not, protected a sinner.

He did not feel bad for having ended her life. He was only following orders, that member of the Congregation had sullied the honor of the Aqua Deus; and those who had decided to speak in the name of their deity with false testimony deserved death for having succumbed to human greed. Fortunately, he had been entrusted to cleanse the world of its sins.

He mentally crossed that member off his list. He only had one visit left to make.

The night still had a lot to say.

The Son of the Church disappeared through the window, launching himself to the top of a nearby tree with the same dexterity of a wildcat. He descended it, steadily, now absorbed in thought. For some reason, his mind carried him back to his meeting with Father Ovilier and the princess.

He could not get out of his mind the beautiful face of the young woman who had accompanied Ovilier. Of the sweetness of her voice. He wondered if she knew who he was, if among the lessons he assumed the princesses of the palace would receive there would be at least a few lines dedicated to revealing to them who the Sons of the Church were.

He slapped his face. Chastising himself for being so sentimental. Since he had learned of the fall of his two brothers, he had not been the same. Baise and Noben... they had sacrificed their lives on a mission for the Aqua Deus. Now, at last, he had been assigned a mission to mete out justice in the name of his revered deity.

He was not ashamed to admit that he had wept for the loss of his brothers. To pour pure water for those you cared about: was there any greater proof than that that goodness resided in human beings? He would forever miss Baise and Noben, but he was proud of their deed.

The night was coming to an end. Fortunately, he was no longer to raid any more houses. He walked through the alleys, taking advantage of the shadows and night noises to pass completely unnoticed. The last person he had to pierce with his dagger was just below the stone bridge he had just reached. The moonlight allowed him to distinguish his silhouette.

"It is done, my lord." He informed, bending down to kiss his ring.

Priest Ovilier seemed incredibly nervous. It was a peculiar sight; in the few times they had met he had given him the impression of being a man as pious as he was self-confident.

The lack of faith of his fellow members of the Congregation undoubtedly disturbs him, the Son of the Church assumed, feeling moved.

"Well done," said Ovilier, "your hands have acted under the will of the Aqua Deus, may the deaths of this night not weigh on your conscience. Go back to your home sheltering in the darkness of the night and rest, you have done well."

I have done well, the Son of the Church was proud of himself, *I have acted in the name of the Aqua Deus. Are you watching me from the sacred waters, brothers? I too am worthy to have my remains rest in the sea.*

However, the job had not yet concluded. He reached for his dagger.

"Father Ovilier, my mission included you." He reminded him feeling sympathy for the old man, he had surely forgotten.

"Oh, yes, that's right."

"You are the only member who will have the honor of receiving this question, where do you want my dagger to pierce you?" He said raising the weapon.

"On the arm," he proposed, then raised his hand. "No, better do it on the belly, it must be convincing."

"It will be painful." The Son of the Church warned him.

"Pain is more bearable when endured for Aqua Deus."

The Son of the Church nodded, inspired by the priest's courageous words. He approached the pious man, ready to conclude his mission.

* * *

He gritted his teeth, dragging himself through the streets in pain. It was a constant pang, making itself present with every beat of his heart. At other times in his life, he would have begged the Aqua Deus to make him strong in the face of pain. But it was becoming increasingly clear to him that his deity was not going to listen to him. They had gone too far and now he had no choice but to continue this farce to the end.

"Help!" he cried out with difficulty, crawling over the bridge.

"The light of the torches drew nearer, their glow accompanied by the increasingly audible clank of armor in the night's silence.

He squinted as the powerful light from the torch hit his face.

"Father Ovilier! Are you all right?" said one of the soldiers in terror.

"By the Aqua Deus, you are bleeding!" said the other soldier, "who has dared to attack you?"

The priest recounted the events in detail. Aware that his lies would probably prevent his remains from resting in the sea.

195

27. Wedding

Dabayl handed her invitation to the stout, elderly butler, who stood in front of the entrance to the property. She had chosen a spectacularly daring outfit, green fabric with an open back, tight at the waist, with bare arms on which she wore several golden bracelets that adorned both forearms and matched with her copper hoops as earrings. That outfit, combined with her short hair, made her especially conspicuous, especially in comparison to her maidservants. Hilza and Naka did not wear any jewelry and their reddish false hair was partially covered by a cloth.

The butler looked up after reading the invitation, then wrinkled her already furrowed brow as she looked with little conviction at the two maids that accompanied her. For a moment, her eyes lingered on the umbrellas that were part of the two maids' attire. She opened her mouth to say something, perhaps to inspect the accessory, but she was interrupted as an elderly couple dressed in fuchsia pink appeared behind them. Clearly people of importance, they were quickly ushered through by the butler, who gave an effusive welcome to the newcomers. An attitude far removed from the terse welcome they had received.

After taking a few steps, Noakh felt like it was an eternity, especially walking in heels. They descended via one of the two identical stone staircases on the sides. It was a beautiful place full of people, tables with drinks and food, servants carrying dishes back and forth. The great protagonist was a kind of round wooden structure located at the back of the whole setup, which was adorned with white and light-yellow fabrics.

Noakh had heard that the Aertians liked to attract attention and, in view of those guests, such a description had fallen short. Guests throughout the gathering flaunted their hair, styled exuberantly. Several female guests were similarly styled, hair slicked back and set with colorful green glitter that contrasted with their reddish manes. Their attire was no less striking, glittering jewels adorning their robes, necks and limbs. To such an exaltation of costume jewelry, there was a plethora of brightly colored dresses with various cuts and drapes, particularly in shades of yellow, reddish, orange, and lime green.

They descended one of the staircases, with Noakh and Hilzen leaning on the railing to maintain their balance and avoid causing a scene. They passed behind a group of people laughing and joking amicably, Dabayl gave a nod and continued walking, her two maids imitated her. However, a member of the group, an elderly woman who had covered her gray chignon with an orange hairnet, gently grabbed Dabayl's arm.

"My dear, we did not think you would come," she said stepping in front of her and grasping both of her bare shoulders. Her eyes inspected Dabayl warily, while Hilzen and Noakh stood behind their mistress, like mere passersby. Noakh felt slightly dizzy from the strong perfume that must have come from that woman. "And that short hair? Well, everything looks good on you," then she pinched one of her cheeks, "you have enviable colors, I'd even say you're a bit plumper since the last time I saw you, but don't make that face, it looks great on you." Then she glanced at Noakh and Hilzen, "oh, but what divine maids! Each one with eyes of a different color, your family always so funny, I'm much duller," she said leaning with her head towards a plump woman with yellow eyes and a triangle on her chest standing to one side of the group, "I'm convinced that this humor of yours was the reason why my dear Yarna took notice of your brother Loredan... this young man she's engaged to is not so given to the arts, but his family is very rich and influential so..."

The woman continued in her endless and formal yet insolent speech. At that moment, Noakh noticed a detail that particularly caught his attention: there was no music. Did a kingdom so well known for its love for such arts really celebrate their marriages without an orchestra?

Hilzen tapped him lightly on the shoulder; a touch so delicate in comparison to the usual that the young Fireo could not discern whether it was due to the limitations of his dress or to maintain the appearances required by their disguise. Once Hilzen got his attention, he pointed to a table laden with plates of food.

"Dabayl will be busy for a while, let's enjoy ourselves a little." Hilzen said quietly to him.

Hilzen extended his arm, and Noakh linked his with it. That act of survival allowed them to walk with enough ease not to cause an embarrassing spectacle. On their walk, the young Fireo inadvertently hit with the tip of his umbrella a short, scrawny woman wearing a headdress with what looked like peacock feathers on her head, she accepted the apology with a grimace of reluctance and contempt, accompanied by a comment pointing out how unfortunate it was that some of the guests couldn't afford better-quality servants.

He eyed a skewer of meat with orange peppers, drizzled in a sauce with a honey-like texture and greenish hue. He took the skewer and put it in his mouth, the meat was more raw than he would like, but delicious. The sauce, although Noakh was not able to discern its composition, had a mildly spicy flavor that he enjoyed so much that he decided to take another one.

Suddenly, the room erupted in applause and cheers. The bride and groom stood directly in front of the wooden platform at the back. They were elegant, though, of course, equally striking; he in a yellow jacket and she in a tight-fitting yellow dress, but of an immensely more garish hue. After greeting their audience and smiling happily, they walked to stand behind the platform. She climbed first, and then he did after his fiancée leaned down to help him up. Now they were both standing on that narrow round platform. Their lips met in a prolonged embrace, neither of them moving an inch.

"They make a good couple," Hilzen acknowledged with a smile. "It reminds me of when I got married, of course this strange ceremony has nothing to do with the elegance and class of an Aquo ritual, needless to say, but the feeling of love and unity they both give off is similar."

Just at that moment, a full-figured woman in a yellow cassock with white borders appeared carrying an astonishingly long pole, anchoring it somewhere at the back of the platform. That pole extended high up, reaching just behind the heads of the bride and groom. At its apex was what appeared to be a bell as white as ivory.

The guests had ceased their chatter, the servants had completely disappeared. They were all engrossed in watching that couple joining their lips on that platform. They remained in that position, without moving. What Noakh initially thought of as a beautiful scene began to look more like martyrdom. He turned when he noticed a presence behind him, Dabayl had made her way through the audience to join her beautiful and obedient maidservants.

"What are they waiting for?" whispered Noakh to her, confused.

Dabayl halted the snack she was about to eat, "Shiana has to bless the wedding," then she popped the entire snack into her mouth and

199

began to chew on it, eliciting a loud crunching sound that brought disapproval from the nearby guests. Seeing that her explanation was not enough, she rolled her eyes and continued. " In order for your wedding to be blessed, you must wait at the platform until you are uplifted by a breeze. This is our goddess's method of granting approval for a marriage to proceed."

"What if there is no breeze?"

"They will have to keep waiting, as long as it takes until there is one." Dabayl smiled, "my mother told me that my aunt and her husband had to wait on the platform for five days."

"You've got to be kidding," Noakh replied, surprised at the peculiarity of that ritual.

"The question is, we, as guests, are not to wait that long, are we?" interjected Hilzen with some anxiety in his voice.

"Only the closest relatives are obligated to stay. My maids can take a break when their delicate legs demand it." She said with as much derisive tone as she could muster.

"Ahem," a man in a gold jacket remarked around them, without even looking at them. An act they understood urged them to be quiet and show proper respect for the ritual.

So peculiar, Noakh pondered.

A light breeze filled the place, the bell tinkled for a brief moment before its sound was eclipsed by applause, whistles and cheers. Out of nowhere, a group of musicians appeared, they made their way through the crowd carrying their instruments until they stood in the middle of the crowd and flooded the room with joyful songs to which everyone danced.

The bride and groom raised their arms in celebration and embraced each other effusively, and then descended from the wooden platform helped by several of the guests. After their descent, the groom began to dance effusively with an older woman, while the bride was grabbed by the arm by a brown-eyed man, leaving the room together.

"We have work to do," Dabayl said, turning around and making her way through the crowd.

Hilzen and Noakh followed their companion, who walked briskly, showing little empathy to her companions' awkward gait due to their ill-suited footwear.

They reached the entrance of a two-story building. The door was closed. Just as they stood in front of it, the door opened and a man with brown eyes and reddish hair like braided fire appeared behind it, saying goodbye with eternal thanks to the bride, Yarna, who was smiling in what looked like absolute happiness.

Yarna and the guest continued to chat amiably as they approached, waiting their turn. The man was thanking her in a thousand and one different ways that she had listened to him on her wedding day and that she had decided to help him with his request.

From closer, Noakh got a better look at the young woman. Her silk dress of intense lemon-yellow left her neck bare and matched both her eyes and the golden bracelets on her wrists. No, he did not find her beautiful, far from it. Individually, her facial features could be deemed attractive. However, for reasons he couldn't explain, their combination on her face wasn't particularly captivating. Nevertheless, she looked splendid, a golden tiara trying to tame the curls of her long, reddish hair. Her face itself radiated the image of pure well-being, of the extreme happiness that Noakh understood that woman could feel after having married the man she loved, one of those occasions when not only the mouth but the whole face smiles in unison. It was one of those moments full of happiness that no one could ruin.

However, when she bid farewell to the guest and her gaze settled on Dabayl and her two maids, the liveliness of her face clouded over as on a stormy day.

"What are you doing here?" said Yarna in a tone halfway between contempt and surprise. "You don't mean to..." She added in fright.

"Oh, woman whose winds blow celebrating love!" Dabayl recited, to Yarna's astonished gaze, "on this most beautiful day, when the Maiden of the Bell has blessed your betrothal having as witnesses so many friends and relatives who wish you the best of fortune, I ask you to listen to me."

Yarna's forehead vein became so pronounced that Noakh could feel the beating of the young woman's agitated heart through it. The bride lowered her head, aware of what she had to do to fulfill the tradition.

"Come, on my wedding day, I hear you." She enunciated, with the most resignation Noakh had ever heard. Then, with a dismissive wave of her hand, she prompted Dabayl to enter the room where she received guests seeking an audience.

"Your maids can wait here." Yarna indicated grumpily.

"No, let them pass. They are part of the petition."

Yarna grimaced. She seemed to mull it over, finally agreed and invited them in as well.

The walls of that room were full of large paintings of landscapes, hunting and fishing scenes as well as portraits of troubadours posing with their instruments around the room; turning that room into a wonderful and surely very valuable art gallery. The floor was covered by a carpet with a diamond pattern in different shades of ochre, and right in the middle of the room were two wide armchairs, one facing the other. Dabayl sat in one of them, Noakh and Hilzen sat to the side, expectantly. The meeting was expected to be lengthy, so Noakh rested the tip of his umbrella on the carpet for support, compensating for the lack of balance provided by his shoes.

"Fine, what do you want?" the bride said sharply, pushing the train of her dress aside, to sit down.

Dabayl cleared her throat.

"I have come to propose something to you, as my ex-sister-in-law that you are, only you will be able to offer me what I am looking for. You're not going to believe me if I tell you, so let's start by answering why I'm sure we'll get it."

"What are you talking about?"

"Naka, show him." She indicated without even turning to him.

Noakh obeyed and opened the umbrella, revealing a sword hidden inside. Yarna jumped to her feet, looking terrified.

"Dabayl," she said in fright, "if this is because I have married another man I..."

"If I held a grudge against you for it, I would only need to climb a tree and wait for a favorable wind to shoot you through the skull. So shut up and watch." Dabayl encouraged her, then turned her gaze to Noakh and bowed her head.

Distra's blade was engulfed in flames. The fire was reflected in the eyes of the bride, who seemed to be mesmerized by its dancing.

"You see, I've assembled a small team with unique skills," she revealed to her as Noakh turned off the sword and returned it to its hiding place, "so we have a serious chance of finding Tizai. I don't want to waste your nice wedding day with detours, so here's the deal: your family sponsors us and I get to keep the Royal Favor."

The bride grimaced, "and why would I do something like that? What do my family and I gain from you taking the Royal Favor?"

"I plan to use the Royal Favor to find out what happened to Loredan." Dabayl revealed to her.

The bride's eyes widened, her mouth fell open. Hilzen and Noakh looked at each other in astonishment as they discovered what Dabayl wanted the Royal Favor for.

"Find out what happened to Loredan..." said Yarna, not even seeming to believe it possible, "do you truly believe you can succeed, Dabayl?" her tone had changed completely, from indignation to sounding like she was pleading. "Don't give me false hope."

Dabayl leaned forward, grasping both of Yarna's hands. "I will find the sword Tizai and we will discover why Loredan really died. But for that I need your patronage."

The bride's eyes watered. "I never thought there would ever be a choice to know what happened to him..." she mused, as if in disbelief, she swallowed, "fine, Dabayl, I'll sponsor you."

"Great! Naka, Hilza, go enjoy the party while I finalize the details with our sponsor."

Noakh and Hilzen were grateful for their mistress's orders. They disappeared behind the door, in search of some amusement. The devout Aquo slipped his arm around Noakh's neck, miraculously managing to keep his dress from splitting as a result, urging him to walk towards where the music was coming from.

"While Dabayl takes care of such important matters, there's nothing to stop us from having a good time, don't you think, Noakh?"

The young Fireo adjusted his dress, feeling somewhat foolish for doing so, and then just nodded. It didn't hurt to have a good time in life too. After all they had endured in the Kingdom of Earth—the famine and countless near-death moments—what better way to make up for it than with a little fun?

They drank and tried to dance to the passionate Aertian music. Several guests stood on the wooden tables, which had only moments ago held the feast, stomping their feet rhythmically while others sang sentimental ditties. What fascinated Noakh most, however, was the clapping accompaniment that some of the guests were performing. For a non-music expert like him, it was difficult to explain; on the one hand, it seemed that some of them were clapping to a rhythm, while others were following along, clapping in counter rhythms. In an attempt to imitate them, he leaned his umbrella against the wall right next to him to avoid mishaps, then put his hands just like some unruly-haired children who were partying next to him, trying to replicate the counter rhythm of their clapping. After several futile attempts, he confirmed that it was not his thing.

Hilzen, meanwhile, was sitting in a chair next to an older woman in makeup that made it look like she had pink skin, the Aquo was holding a glass of some liquor as he closed his eyes, whether he was asleep or just enjoying the music with his eyes closed was a mystery.

The effect produced by the music intoned by the band together with the accompaniment of clapping and stomping caused Noakh to be spellbound, amazed at how the Aertians were able to create compositions of the most beautiful and full of feeling. He had heard about the art and passion that people had for music; but any information he had heard paled in comparison to the overwhelming reality of witnessing that talent firsthand.

"Excuse me," a young man in his twenties said as he approached Noakh.

"I'm not interested, thank you," he tried to say politely, modulating his voice to a higher pitch in an attempt to sound more feminine, anticipating.

"Huh?" the man said quizzically, pulling his face back slightly, "I was just going to ask you about your dress, it's really beautiful and I think my fiancée would look great in it."

"Oh," Noakh replied, his face reddening. He had assumed it was a close-up with intentions of courtship, and he couldn't have been more mistaken.

Suddenly he saw Dabayl appear, dancing her way through the crowd. A young man grabbed her by the hand to dance, and she responded with a forceful slap to his chest.

Boom!

A loud explosion blew out the walls on one side of the building. Debris fell in all directions, accompanied by a cloud of dust. The music had ceased, being replaced by a sinister melody of people screaming and fleeing in terror as they witnessed the guests lying on the floor covered in blood after being hit by the explosion.

Noakh started coughing, then grabbed the umbrella, which had fallen to the ground. Something told him he would have to get hold of Distra soon. He checked to make sure that Dabayl and Hilzen were all right. Hilzen was trying to assist the elderly woman who had been standing next to him until recently and was now lying on the ground, suffering from what appeared to be some sort of heart ailment.

"The groom! They've taken the groom!" was heard amidst such commotion. Panic began to spread among the guests.

He kicked off his uncomfortable heels and headed to the stables, umbrella in hand. He pushed his way as best he could through the crowd of guests looking to rush out of there with their steeds and borrowed the first horse he could find, setting off in search of the kidnappers.

"Which way did those thugs go?" he asked a young woman who was covering a wound on her forehead with a rag. The latter was slow to understand what he was talking about, until she finally pointed to a path.

Noakh began his chase, determined to track them down and rescue the groom.

Dabayl had said that the man Yarna was marrying came from a wealthy family, perhaps that was why they had attacked in the middle of a wedding, when these would be most vulnerable? Or were these enemies who had wanted to add some sort of macabre symbolism to a moment as special and unique as a wedding should be? The young Fireo pondered, as he continued riding.

In addition to his lack of riding skills, he was holding on to his wig with his left hand, to keep it from falling off. Then he realized what a stupid thing he was doing, taking the reins with both hands and thus gaining more control of the steed. It didn't take much trotting to send his wig flying through the air.

He looked in both directions pulling on the horse's reins. He had lost them. He made the horse trot, trying to get his bearings.

A shadow emerged from the undergrowth and quickly pounced on him before he could react. Caught off guard, the young Fireo lost his balance and fell abruptly to the ground. He was roughly grabbed by both arms, forced to walk.

"Let go of me!" He demanded. Unfortunately, the umbrella that sheltered Distra had remained tied to his horse's bridles, he regretted not having the citrines to be able to reclaim his sword from a distance as he fought against his restraints.

His captors ignored his request for freedom. Instead, they simply forced him into the forest. Before he could scream again, his mouth was bound with a tight cloth, which gave off a bitter taste.

There, on a small esplanade, stood the groom, kneeling with his hands clasped together as if he were begging. In front of him stood a short-haired woman with a hard face and a pointed nose, showing identical scars on both cheeks. It was a peculiar drawing formed by three stripes, a straight one in the middle, one whose edges end with the tip curved upwards and the lower line downwards. Her stern face turned towards Noakh.

"Suruyana, we found this strange young man, trying to play hero." Said one of the men grabbing him.

"Bring him to his knees, as well." Suruyana instructed them, her orders completely blunt.

Noakh tried to resist, but a sharp punch to his stomach finally convinced him. As he stood up recovering from the pain, he felt the sharp edge of a rusty razor on his neck.

"No." Suruyana instructed, "let him be a witness; it will be better if one of their guests tells everyone what happened here."

"You should be in prison," claimed the groom, "how could they have taken you out of the cell? You should be rotting in after so many murders behind your back!"

Suruyana just snorted, "that's none of your business, your family offers patronage, don't they?"

"Yes! I've already sponsored one expedition group, but I can use my influence in the Wind Council to cancel it and sponsor you if that's what you're looking for." Said in a desperate tone the man.

Suruyana smiled macabrely, as she shook her finger at him. "That wouldn't be right, we don't need a patronage. What we want is to deter other powerful families from sponsoring anyone. And what better occasion than this wedding to teach a lesson? This will show all those wealthy families who believe they can take our prize away from us."

"Wait, no... I can offer you money, gold, jewelry, anything as long as..."

A harsh slap silenced him.

"Don't try to buy what you can't." She said, pointing her index finger at him, "the lesson families are going to learn from what's going to happen to you is priceless."

"No, no..." he tried to say, trembling so much that it was hard to speak.

"But don't worry, because, in a way, you're going to be remembered. For you are going to serve as an example, words and blood... no," she turned to one of her men, "what is the saying?"

"Words are not carried away by the wind when they are soaked in blood." Said one of the men grabbing Noakh.

"That's right."

Then she nodded in the direction of the groom. One of her men appeared with a large steel ball and began to walk several steps. Noakh struggled as he perceived a slight yellowish glint in the metal of that ball. *They couldn't possibly...* he thought, scandalized.

Suruyana reached into an inside pocket of her jacket; the bright yellowish light of the citrine glowed with the moon.

"No, please!"

"You should have thought of that before you joined the sword quest." She said, slapping the groom twice in the face, "now there is only hope that with your death the rest of the families will learn their lesson and back off."

"No!"

A man grabbed the groom by the mouth, attempting to force it open. The groom, in an attempt to defend himself, bit him. That act was answered first with a shriek of pain and then with a resounding punch in the face that made the groom much more docile. He kept trying to resist, however, they managed to open his mouth.

"Happy wedding day, by the way," Suruyana congratulated him with a grim smile. She struck the citrine hard with a nearby rock and quickly popped it into the groom's mouth.

The man struggled, but one hand grabbed his neck and another continued to cover his mouth. He tried to free himself, but could not.

The large steel ball trembled on the ground. Flying powerfully through the air, heading straight for the groom's face.

Noakh closed his eyes, turning his head away. However, that did not prevent him from hearing the horrifying *crack* that announced that the ball had crushed the man's skull. When he opened his eyes again, he saw Suruyana bending over the corpse. She tore off the lobe of one ear in a gruesome manner, stood up as if admiring a trophy, and carefully placed it in a small bag.

Then she turned to Noakh, slowly, playing with her penknife, lightly jabbing its tip into the tip of the index finger of her other hand. With a contemptuous glance, Suruyana looked him up and down.

"A most peculiar dress, you always were a family with somewhat special tastes." Her comment caused her minions to laugh.

Noakh struggled again, but a strong kick prevented him from continuing.

"Tell them what happened here, tell them what is the fate of those who stand in our way of gaining the Royal Favor." Suruyana stood in front of Noakh, "but first..." she said, raising the knife.

Noakh felt the edge pierce his ear, he gritted his teeth to withstand the searing pain.

* * *

Noakh gasped loudly as he felt the burning. Hilzen looked at him, in surprise, still holding the vial of holy water. The eyes of his friend Aquo shifted to look at the flask.

"It makes sense that Holy Water would not heal a Fireo," Hilzen assumed, closing the vial and handing it back to Noakh to keep it safe.

"Don't ever use that on me again," he said, still with bated breath and a terrible burning in the cut of his right lobe.

It had been a rough ride, the men of that damned Suruyana had taken him back to his horse, thus allowing him to return to the place where the wedding had taken place and tell Yarna and the rest of the guests what had happened in detail.

"Try this ointment then," Dabayl's father suggested, offering Hilzen a jar. "I'm sure it won't leave any marks on his ear."

At that moment there was a knock at the door. It was Dabayl who opened the door, Noakh leaned down to see who it was. Meanwhile, Hilzen continued to apply the greasy ointment. The strong smell of the product instantly cleared his lungs.

On the other side of the door stood Yarna. The bride's eyes were so red they looked bloodshot, she had scabs on her face from how much she seemed to have cried, she was even still dressed in her flashy yellow wedding dress, now filthy with mud and blood.

"Dabayl, I can't sponsor you."

28. Promise to a traitor

The tree was adorned with the most beautiful orange blossoms; save for a single branch still blackened from a past fire. Vienne smiled, that was where Noakh and Hilzen's adventure had begun. And it was in that very place that she was to fulfill her promise.

"Silbai," said the princess, preventing Zyrah from relieving herself near the old fence at the entrance. Even though Hilzen had abandoned that place, it didn't seem appropriate for the dog to urinate there.

Nature had claimed the modest house due to neglect; weeds grew at the entrance, and moss spread across the brown walls. However, beyond nature's eagerness to reclaim the land, it seemed that Hilzen's home had managed to stay practically untouched, something that offered some satisfaction to the princess.

She swallowed her breath and walked around the side of the house and into the inner courtyard, followed by a curious Zyrah sniffing with interest. It was one of those things she felt difficult to do, but she had to do it anyway. After all, she had made a promise to Hilzen.

A shiver ran down her spine as she faced the two waterlogged graves. One the size of an adult person and the other much smaller, the latter guarded by a small rag doll that looked very dirty due to the passage of time.

She bent down to grasp the doll. It was damp, the result of being subjected to constant rain. But the doll remained, standing steadfast against the elements, guarding the tomb just as Hilzen had entrusted it to do. She put it back in its place, stroking her cloth hair, as if acknowledging her for her great work of guarding the tomb.

Hilzen had told her about his daughter and his wife. However, being in the presence of their lifeless bodies far surpassed any tale. Marne and Lynea, his two sirens, so he had called them, it was time they received the ritual they deserved.

The noble and bourgeois families were wealthy, as expected; they spared no expense to ensure that the remains of their loved ones reached the sea. A ceremony that was carried out with the utmost care, as the process had to be carried out in a specific, and therefore expensive, manner, so that the remains would not contaminate the water. According to what Igüenza had told her, the putrefaction of the bodies caused the waters to become toxic due to the sins the person had committed, the resounding way in which the Aqua Deus showed his disciples that no Aquo, whether rich or poor, was free of sin.

The truth was that she had never wondered how the humbler families performed the ritual. Now, seeing it with her own eyes, it was evident that there was a considerable difference in charm.

At that moment Zyrah approached the smaller water grave and began to sniff.

"Zyrah, come here," she said, anticipating any move the little dog might make. Not only would it be tremendously sacrilegious, but drinking from that water could be both unhealthy and disrespectful.

The canine obeyed, standing calmly beside Vienne. The princess took a deep breath and unsheathed Crystaline. She knew what to do and what to say, she had watched her mother perform such a ritual once, offering a dignified farewell to an old member of the Congregation of the Church.

She stood in front of the smaller tomb. She stretched her arm up high, Crystaline's tip peering up at the clouds.

"From the sky to the sea, the Aqua Deus accompanies us on our journey down the river of life. Yours was too short a journey, rejoice in the knowledge that it will make your stay at sea longer."

The sword descended, Crystaline's tip now hovering over the water of the smaller tomb. She performed a prayer, dropping a drop of water from the blade of the sacred sword, "may your remains find the sea, may they be welcomed into the lair of the Aqua Deus where you will live forever."

Then she moved towards the second grave, reciting the same prayer and similarly placing a drop onto the tomb of Hilzen's wife. The ritual was completed; she sheathed her sword. Then she stood there for a moment, contemplating the two graves with sadness.

I have kept my word, Hilzen; your daughter and your wife have had a dignified ritual, as they deserved.

A warm sensation welled up inside her. A mixture of peace and satisfaction with herself. Hilzen had asked for her help, for his daughter and wife to have a dignified ritual, and being able to help him had made her feel incredibly good.

If it weren't for the sword, I wouldn't have been able to help him and end his grief, she pondered, *is this the good part of reigning? To be able to help people and to feel such joy at having been of service to someone?*

Just at the moment when the ceremony was over, she noticed a strange sound. A *grrr* that gradually became more noticeable. Vienne turned around, confused by Zyrah's reaction. The little dog was growling, moving slowly toward the path leading to the front of the farmhouse.

There is someone, the princess assumed. She walked on, passing under the tree with the burnt branch. *Maybe Zyrah has sniffed out some wild animal,* she considered, *most likely, this doesn't seem to be a bustling place.*

As she reached the front yard, Vienne realized how wrong she had been in her assumption. In front of her stood more than thirty soldiers.

"Vienne Dajalam," began the captain of that troop, without reverence, without respect, "you are under arrest for the murder of three members of the Congregation of the Church."

The princess opened her mouth in horror at such an accusation.

"Murder?" she managed to say almost in a whisper still unable to believe it, "you accuse me of having ended the lives of three members of the Congregation of the Church?" She added, almost imperceptibly.

Her mind made the connection quickly, *they have just died shortly after I showed them my powers and they assured me that they would support me in my legitimacy to the throne. It can't be a coincidence,* the princess deduced. *But why now, why bring troops to a village far from the hand of the Aqua Deus instead of waiting for me to return to the palace?* She wondered, then she herself came up with the answer, *because here, finding us in the middle of nowhere, with no witnesses, they will be able to tell whatever they want and no one but me will be able to deny it. They will allege that I fled after committing the crimes and they caught me in the middle of the escape, or some other similar lie...*

"You are surrounded, Princess Vienne, please lay your weapon on the ground, we mean you no harm." The captain alerted her, his hand gripping the hilt of his sword, ready to unsheathe it if necessary.

211

Harm me... It was impossible that her mother had issued that arrest warrant, not only was she sure that the queen would know for a fact that she would not have committed such a crime, she was also too far away.

"Who has accused me of such crimes?" she asked, keeping her cool.

"The sole survivor of your assassination attempt, the priest Ovilier." He revealed to her.

Vienne raised her eyebrows slightly in understanding. It had to be Katienne's doing, that was the most logical conclusion, but killing members of the Congregation... it sounded too excessive even for her ambitious sister, *has she lost her mind and doesn't care who suffers as long as she gets what she wants?* She wondered.

Then she took another look at the armor of those soldiers. It had no purple tones.

"You say that I am accused by a member of the Congregation. Your armor, however, is not the usual armor of the Church Guard." She pointed out.

The captain looked embarrassed for a moment. "Surrender, princess! You are surrounded!" He ended up saying.

Vienne lowered her head, her eyes meeting Zyrah's alert pupils. She made a slight neck movement to the left side, a gesture sufficient for the canine to understand that she must get to safety.

Zyrah began to run, slipping nimbly between the legs of two of those soldiers, while Vienne unsheathed Crystaline. She saw her reflection on the blade.

Should I surrender my weapon and trust the truth to come to light? She questioned herself, *surely sooner or later justice will be served.* Vienne then snorted at the naivety of her own occurrence, with her sister behind the ruse, the least she could hope for was that the law would be enforced.

"Surrender your weapon!" the captain urged her in a more nervous and aggressive tone as he saw her draw her weapon, "this is my last warning." He warned her, an instant later he unsheathed his sword. The rest of the soldiers mimicked him, they shifted slightly in position, uneasy.

Vienne stared at the captain. "If you want me to give you my weapon, I invite you to take it from my hands. Crystaline, grant me your powers, please."

Her face changed. She brandished the hilt of her sword with both hands, ready to deliver her own justice.

"Seize her!"

Several soldiers began to run towards her. The princess tilted her sword; the first drops came off the soaked edge of the blade.

The first soldier charged at her letting out a fierce scream as he launched his lunge; the princess made a quick foot movement, moving out of the way just at the exact moment when her opponent's blade was about to pierce her head.

One.

The eyes of the soldier who had attacked her went from absolute fury to fear in an instant. Crystaline's blade slashed into his chest.

Two.

Boom! She jumped at the precise moment over the torrent, dodging the attack of three spear-wielding soldiers who had attacked in unison. She somersaulted through the air, gaining momentum.

In her fall, she landed on the chest of a tall female soldier; causing her enemy to fall hard to the ground. She never got up, as the soaked edge of the blade piercing her neck prevented her from doing so.

The princess moved in search of her next victim. She pushed off with all the strength of her legs, propelling herself forward on the tips of her boots, just as her Aunt Alvia, the fastest in the queendom, had taught her. Her movements were swift, taking two quick steps forward with which she managed to skewer a mustachioed soldier in the belly before he could impale her with his spear.

She didn't have a moment's respite. She felt a presence behind her. She stepped aside, in time to avoid the sword that was going to pierce her heart from the rear. With a palm strike, she broke her opponent's nose, just before she had to duck to avoid an attack from another soldier, who fell to the ground dead after being pierced in the chest.

She danced.

The art of the sword is like a dance. Her aunt had told her. *But it is a solitary dance; one in which no one must be able to keep up with you, where each step must keep you from death and where you offer in exchange the lives of those who dare to dance with you.*

As soon as the toe of her boot touched the ground, she rotated rapidly, severing the leg of a spear-armed soldier. A cry of anguish flooded the sky, without causing the slightest impact on Vienne's impassive face.

Her conscience told her that these men and women were innocent, that they were simply obeying the orders of those who should not. Her mind controlled by the sacred sword, however, insisted that there was a

213

price for becoming mere executing hands, and in that case the price was none other than death itself.

She felt a sharp sting in her right shoulder blade. *An arrow*, she observed. She pulled it out quickly, dropped two drops on the wound. Then she began to run, before the wound even began to close.

She moved with incredible speed, still far short of her aunt's absurd speed, but more than enough to take on infantry soldiers. She parried one attack with her sword, dodged a thrust from behind by moving out of the way as best she could, but failed to dodge the third strike, her opponent's blade slicing into her side. Blood began to spurt.

An instant later, the three soldiers began to fall lifelessly to the ground. Before their limp bodies hit the ground, the princess was already charging at her next target. A young woman whose long hair was sticking out of her helmet. The soldier took aim with her crossbow, the bolt shot swiftly towards Vienne, but the princess dodged the bolt with a swift stride. The soldier tried to reload her crossbow to make a second attack, but before she could even reload, Crystaline's blade had already pierced her belly.

She pulled out the bloody sword and searched for her next victim. There were hardly any soldiers left.

They were more, but they were no match for the Lacrima and the power of her sacred sword. She sliced the neck of another soldier, while the attacker who was targeting her was sent airborne as she stepped into the path of a forceful water torrent that had just emerged from the ground. She looked up in search of her next victim.

Then she stopped in her tracks. A groan. One she recognized instantly. The princess stopped in her tireless dance of death, turning to where the sound had come from.

A pointed knife was held near Zyrah's neck as she struggled to free herself, the captain gripping her by the skin.

"Surrender, or your beloved pet will pay the consequences!"

Vienne stood still for a moment, her mind trying to decide which option was best.

She extended her arm and dropped Crystaline to the ground.

As the hilt ceased to be in contact with her skin, her face changed completely, now filled with concern.

She had lost. She was going to be accused of murder.

29. In the hands of fortune

He peered into the mouth of the wine bottle. Not a single drop of wine was inside it. *The journey will be much more tedious from now on*, he cursed to himself, dropping the bottle, which then rolled.

He turned the rudder wheel slightly to the right. However, the ramshackle vessel veered sharply and inaccurately to starboard.

"Come on, you wretched piece of wood!" complained Gelegen, "sail properly at once!"

The vessel was hopeless in every aspect. Though no shipbuilding expert, the veteran sensed that the vessel's design was far from auspicious. From what looked like a heavy hull to a sail that, although square, did not catch as much wind as it should. It would be absurd to compare it to the Merrybelle, but something told him that even an Aquo vessel built by a child could rival such maritime nonsense.

Despite all these imperfections in design, the worst of all was the smell. The strong stench of rotten fish caused one to curse being aboard such a vessel at every turn.

The irony was that he had little right to complain; after all, things had turned out better than he had anticipated. After ascertaining that Noakh was well and handing him a sapphire, as Vienne had requested, he had headed for the port of New Ternua in the hope of seizing a vessel.

As fate would have it, the Grey Raven, Mahesen, had offered him a ship in exchange for asking him for something in return, to deliver the pothai to the Queendom of Water. Although somewhat untimely, Tir Torrent had finally fulfilled the agreement that Graglia and Burum Babar had signed some time before, having delivered a generous cargo of pothai, which was now stored in the hold of such a dreadful vessel.

He looked at the sky, noting the waters growing cloudier with increased frequency. That detail reinforced his calculations, he must be in the Aquo Sea by now. He sighed with relief, he could finally put his feet on dry land and get away from that stinking smell of marine rot.

Not only that, he could finally see them. Zyrah would surely be jumping around him like crazy, wagging her tail hysterically accompanied by her characteristic barking. What would have happened to Vienne? Had she already managed to persuade those foolish members of the Congregation and the stupid nobles that she really deserved to reign? And surely Alvia would have forgiven him by now for agreeing to the request of a selfish princess, as she had called it.

He loathed being without answers. Unfortunately, this time, it wasn't a rugged case he could solve with his cunning. At least not while he was still stuck on the high seas.

As he turned his gaze to the front, he saw something on the horizon. Were his eyes deceiving him after so many hours at sea? No, there was no doubt about it, that was a ship heading in his direction. With a bit of fortune, they might be generous enough to assist in docking him, thus making his arrival at the port smoother. Finally, a stroke of luck.

In an instant, the approaching ship transformed from appearing as a mere model in the distance to becoming imposingly close beside him. It was in that moment that he noticed the flag of the vessel, adorned in white and blue, depicting a ship and a knight

His jaw tensed; it seemed the sea had a misfortune in store for him.

"Ahoy there!" Was heard from the other vessel. A woman in a peaked hat and a bluish vest with a mermaid on her breast, an attire that indicated she was the captain. "Why are you sailing with such a ramshackle vessel on our sacred seas? Don't you know that this is an offense to our beloved Aqua Deus?"

Ah, typical, thought Gelegen, *seeking conflict based on religious beliefs, of course.*

"It is not my intention to offend the Aqua Deus," Gelegen began, speaking loudly and deliberately to ensure he was heard on the other vessel. "But neither am I devoted to invoking the wrath of the one he chose as his queen," he reached for his neck, intending to show her the pendant with holy water, an object of recognized prestige that would give more weight to his words.

Stupid idiot, he said to himself, *I gave the pendant to Hilzen....*

"The queen?" said the captain bowing her head. "Who are you?"

"Gelegen Hurehall, soldier in the service of Queen Graglia." He said, trying to sound imposing.

Gelegen had seen various reactions at the mention of his title and position in the army, even the most willing to kill looks had become docile upon hearing that he was acting on behalf of Queen Graglia. However, the woman's reaction was far from usual: she was grinning from ear to ear.

"It can't be," she said leaning forward on the gunwale, several figures appeared around the captain. "The Aqua Deus seems to be on our side, all aboard!"

Her men shouted, then began to jump aboard the ramshackle ship.

The veteran reached for his belt, but neither his sword nor his gun was there; both were in the cabin. Before he could even think of running for them, the tip of the sword of one of those ruffians was dangerously close to his neck.

"You'd better not do anything foolish," the captain warned him, her henchman lightly jabbing the tip of his weapon into Gelegen's skin by way of warning.

The veteran raised his hands, he had been captured and there was nothing he could do about it. He felt bad about himself, was it sensible to have stashed his weapons in the cabin while on the high seas, or was he losing his edge?

It no longer matters, he resigned himself, *I have no choice but to surrender, watch them hand me over as a prisoner, and witness how they steal the pothai...* suddenly, a crazy thought crossed his mind, his heart was beating faster now, *maybe it could work?*

"Why the raid?" Gelegen began, "I am only in charge of transporting an important cargo for the queen's private use..."

The captain raised an eyebrow, a gesture sufficient to let Gelegen know that his ruse had worked.

"You," she said pointing to two of her men, "inspect this filthy ship."

Her henchmen hurried towards the cabin. Gelegen took the opportunity to calculate all his next moves, he had to anticipate every possible scenario that could unfold if he wanted to have a chance of getting out of there on his own two feet.

"Well?" said the woman in charge as she saw them appear.

The men wore confused looks on their faces.

"The cellar is full of vials like this one," said one of them, approaching his boss and handing her a vial with a reddish liquid inside.

The captain grabbed the container, wiggling it slightly as she stared at it in puzzlement, "what on earth is this?"

217

"If you don't want to get in trouble I wouldn't drink it, those miracle potions are for the queen's private use..." Gelegen let slip.

"'Miraculous, eh?" she said contentedly. She uncorked the container and tilted it to pour it into her mouth. Then she paused, "Tumbel, drink it." She said extending her arm to one of her men.

Gelegen blasphemed inwardly, he had weighed the possibility that she would give him a taste of the pothai.

"Me?" Said the man in fright, "why not Zuamba?" He complained, pointing to his companion.

"Because I said so, period." The captain replied firmly. "May I ask why you're afraid of a stupid potion, you idiot?"

Tumbel reached for the pothai, then stared at it in bewilderment and opened his mouth, revealing a most imperfect set of yellowish teeth. The reddish liquid soaked his tongue. Gelegen allowed himself a smile beneath his mustache.

It all happened in the blink of an eye. Tumbel clenched his jaw, then screamed heartbreakingly, clutching his hair as the glass containing the pothai smashed against the deck, shattering into a thousand pieces.

All the assailants looked at their companion, terrified. Tumbel's eyes turned white, the veins in his neck swelled. One of the assailants, the one who had been pointing his sword at Gelegen until recently, approached Tumbel to assist him. Tumbel thanked him for his help by delivering a punch that instantly knocked his head off.

Now.

Taking advantage of the confusion, Gelegen lunged at the captain and snatched her weapon. He tried to skewer her, but Tumbel pounced on him. He felt the hard blow, as forceful as if he had been rammed by a bear. His body fell hard against the deck, his already sore back groaned at such abuse.

He went to get up, however, a shadow appeared right above him. A huge fist was heading for his skull.

Crack! The deck timber burst into a thousand pieces, Gelegen had escaped certain death at the last moment.

Things hadn't gone as he had planned; however, all was not lost as long as he could improvise. He positioned himself on the gunwale, climbed up onto it, and then used one of the ropes holding up the sail.

"Hey, you stupid beast, come and get me!"

Tumbel roared, charging at him ready to crush him. The veteran gauged the precise moment, the one that would make the difference between his ruse working or being crushed to death.

He waited, ignoring a survival instinct that urged him to get out of the way. Tumbel was already upon him.

He grabbed hold of the rope with both hands, leaping with all his might. The rampaging Tumbel continued on its course, bursting the wood of the gunwale as it went, finally falling into the sea.

"Oh, my," Gelegen said, walking over to the captain, who was cornered at the bow, "it looks like the tables have turned..."

Before he could continue in his speech, He realized several men had emerged on his ship, leaping aboard to aid their comrades.

His plan had gone awry.

One of them approached him from behind, Gelegen turned to defend himself—an ideal moment for a second to punch him hard in the kidney, forcing him to fall to his knees on the ground.

The sword was back in the captain's hands. "Get those stupid potions aboard and chain this bastard up."

Gelegen tried to get up. To no avail. His ruse had worked, yet it still wasn't enough to prevent his capture.

30. Crucial disclosure

The robust soldier rowed at a steady pace, while the other two escorts were positioned, each one guarding a flank with their bows and arrows ready for any possible assault. The small boat was making its way through the immense trees, in those waters so full of small floating leaves that it seemed as if the boat was advancing over a shining garden.

The queen stood at the back of the ship; a white lace veil covering her face. The Aertian lands had become considerably more dangerous since their last decision to free the prisoners, in their eagerness to retrieve the sword as soon as possible. Precisely because of such risks, her brother had added a sharp to that *F minor*, a musical alteration that meant they had better be accompanied from now on in their meetings. And she could not agree more with taking such a precaution. She had heard real barbarities carried out by the prisoners they had freed, deaths, tortures, revenge, massacres... but she did not feel bad about it, it was simply the price they had to pay if they wanted to recover the sword as soon as possible.

Zarta gestured toward a tree marked with two deep, parallel stripes on its bark. Once the boat stopped under it a rope ladder fell down, only Zarta climbed up it, with the same alacrity as she did when they played hide and seek there as children.

She peered into the hut's entrance before stepping inside; then she went through the opening, observing how Lieri was waiting for her. He was lying down, pretending to be calm, as if he was resting, leaning on a pile of papers. She knew her brother well enough, such seemingly nonchalant attitude was his way of posing, which meant he had come across some important information that she surely didn't know. She quickly retrieved the ladder, carelessly setting it aside near the cabin's entrance before approaching her brother, who leaned back to receive the two affectionate kisses of greeting and later to press their foreheads together for a brief moment.

"What news do you bring, brother?" She said, situating herself in front of him, then sitting on her heels, "at this rate, you're going to deplete your kingdom of troubadours." She added with amusement.

"As soon as I reveal to you what my spies have discovered, you will see that this information is well worth the lives of a hundred thousand and one troubadours." He indicated, visibly nervous, offering her a parchment, the first document in that pile of papers.

Zarta quickly skimmed the parchment, trying not to be influenced by Lieri's characteristic anxiety. She went through the writing, with interest. The report narrated certain events occurred in Tir Torrent, detailing Burum Babar's confrontation against an alarming opponent. She stopped at one point in the reading, scoffing.

"Do you really believe this?" she said, looking up and slapping the paper, "a young man with a flaming sword capable of taking on Burum Babar? Are your sources trustworthy?"

"Unfortunately, they are," Lieri replied, cradling his face in his hands. "And that's not all. It turns out that after Burum Babar's death, this dangerous young man has entered your kingdom." Lieri offered her several documents that Zarta recognized instantly, a report from the city of Tuens Laya detailing the entry of a young man with black hair, brown eyes and a list of all his belongings.

Two swords, Zarta read, *at least he affirmed that he did not intend to attack me*, she noted in the report. Those guard posts had been a suggestion of her brother, a way to keep an eye on the villages of the Southern Kingdom of Aere Tine without having to resort to a whole army, those soldiers collected information of all those visitors who entered those villages and cities, so that, in case they had to trace the route of someone in search and capture, they would be easy to locate.

Zarta frowned. If Lieri had already reviewed such information, it could mean only one thing. "Do you even know where this dangerous young man is?"

"Far from it... he could be in any corner of Aere Tine, but I've requested more reports to try to track him down as soon as possible."

"Brown eyes, black hair..." read Zarta, "although the hair could have been dyed... with such generic information it's impossible to find him, if only we had some more detailed description than that, so we could get a hold of him and keep him from becoming a nuisance."

222

"I have already taken care of that," Lieri replied, showing her a bounty notice with a portrait under which was indicated the name of that boy, Noakh, exactly the same name that appeared in the report from the village of Tuens Laya. "Bounty notices like this were spread throughout the towns of Tir Torrent. Ironically, Hilzen, the one who offered the reward for him, seems to be accompanying him on his journey. His motives? I'm completely unaware."

Zarta nodded, somewhat hurt. The fact that her brother possessed such detailed information, while she remained unaware of it, slightly bothered her. She was in charge of the southern kingdom, which bordered Tir Torrent, how could it be that her brother had information about the Kingdom of Earth that she didn't even suspect? She would have to have a serious talk with her informants and make some adjustments.

"So," Zarta began, collecting her thoughts, "we not only have to contend with a dragon which, as if its mere existence weren't threat enough, happens to be holding our sword hostage; now we also have to deal with a king-killer on our streets?"

Lieri shook his head. "I'm sure we're missing something; I don't believe that young man was capable of ending Daikan Burum Babar's life, no matter how old and sick he was."

Zarta smiled, from a young age Lieri had shown the deepest respect and admiration for the Tirhan monarch.

"This boy, Noakh, is a fraud, sister. I assure you that this young man with a flaming sword is nothing but a vulgar lie." He said, sulkily.

"In any case, allowing someone so dangerous to roam our streets is an intolerable risk," Zarta admitted.

"Yes, that's why I've already set to work." Her brother stated.

31. Family reunion

It was a quiet afternoon, Filier relayed news of the war against the Fireos, and Katienne listened with rapt attention. She was nodding, jotting down every detail mentally, her betrothed expressed his concern about how King Wulkan had seemingly razed several Aquo settlements. She grimaced in surprise at such news. They knocked on the door, after due authorization from the heir of House Delorange, the soldier entered the room, standing in front of them.

"Lord Filier, we have brought in the murderess of the members of the Congregation." The soldier informed them, his body as straight as humanly possible. He then showed them Crystaline.

Katienne jumped as soon as she saw the sacred sword, standing up to take it.

"May I?" she requested, the soldier handed her the sword without the slightest qualm, and continued with his report, now giving details of how Princess Vienne had been captured.

Such information was received very differently by both. Filier grimaced with concern, looking terribly upset after hearing of the number of casualties among his soldiers during the capture of Vienne. Katienne, on the other hand, simply kept a serious countenance, her gaze fixed on the sacred sword while her index finger ran along the dirty leather scabbard that protected its blade. Wielding that weapon provoked an exhausting frenzy inside her, somehow, it was the confirmation that she had triumphed, that the queendom was going to be hers.

"My beloved?" Filier repeated.

Katienne snapped out of her trance. "Excuse me, dear, what were you saying?"

"I was saying that it would be good to send the sword to your mother as soon as possible, certainly, with the sacred weapon at her command, the queen will stand strong against the Fireos and make advances in the contest." He announced, hopeful.

"Quite right, my dear, I will see to it myself to speak to Meredian so that Crystaline is thus delivered to my mother with the utmost haste." She said, sketching a smile. "First though, I have something to do, if you'll excuse me."

She left the room, as soon as she started walking down the corridors her face changed to one of absolute happiness. Her plan had worked perfectly. She descended the stairs anxiously, leaning on the handrail to descend several steps at a time, she didn't have a moment to lose.

She ran through the grounds until she reached a large fenced yard. Not so long ago, this remote place was used to keep livestock. Gant was on guard, and when he saw someone approaching, he reached for his sword, but when he saw that it was her, he continued his patrol.

Katienne made her way across the courtyard. Her heart skipped a beat at the sight of the two of them together. Her Aunt Alvia and her pathetic sister were kneeling on the dusty yellow dirt. Both with their heads and hands blocked by wooden stocks. Next to them, in a corner, lay locked in a small cage that annoying white dog.

"What a delightful sight," she said, gazing at them with the most satisfied smile she had ever worn.

Katienne leaned in, placing her face close to her pitiful sister, who was looking at her with a mixture of hatred and defiance.

"Seventeen soldiers died to capture you, eh, Vienne? Impressive," she acknowledged, then glanced back at the dog and shook her head, "you could have finished them all off, but your kindness got in your way." Katienne looked back, "that's the difference between you and me, you don't have the guts to make sacrifices for the greater good."

"What distinguishes us is that you are vile, envious and a dirty traitor." Vienne replied, glaring at her with contempt.

Slap!

A forceful slap was Katienne's response to such impertinence. If she thought she could not like Vienne's attitude any less, that new personality that had surfaced in her after her return from Tir Torrent was even more insolent and annoying.

The dog began to bark.

"Silence, you dirty rat!" She commanded turning to the canine as she pointed her sword at it. Somehow, the animal must have understood her message, for it ceased its barking, curling in on itself.

Katienne was breathing deeply, her chest swelling and deflating with emphasis. She turned to Vienne again, "I won't tolerate such talk from you or anyone else." She took a deep breath, trying to regain her composure. "I hope you are liking the prestigious corner we have dedicated to keep you comfortable; security has had to be improved since certain nobles escaped, aided by a meddlesome vermin. Unfortunately for you, Vienne, she won't be able to help you escape because she has been left to rot on a desert island to preserve our lineage."

She gazed at Vienne with a confident look that let her sister know that she was perfectly aware that it had been Aienne who had freed the nobles. Alvia coughed, her stomach wound, though healed, was apparently giving her a raging fever. Katienne took two steps, placing herself in front of her.

"Oh, auntie, I'm sorry you got involved in all this." She apologized, her tone now devoid of aggression, "the truth is, I didn't relish the idea of capturing you, but you would have sided with my pathetic sister, wouldn't you?"

"Why are we still alive?" asked Alvia, ignoring her words. "Are you afraid of being scolded by your mom?" she provoked her, bursting into a loud laugh.

"Irreverent, stupid, even in a situation like this." Katienne scoffed, trying to contain her anger. "We'll see if that smile doesn't backfire on you." She threatened her, walking away.

* * *

Katienne walked to the spacious room where she kept all her attire, where she knew she would be alone. She leaned against the closet and rested Crystaline on her belly, taking a moment to regain her composure. She felt nervous, furious with herself. She had captured her sister, and incidentally, her aunt. They had fallen one by one, the result of her sharp wit. Not only had she captured them, but she had also been bold enough to frame Vienne for murder. This was why she knew Meredian would not intervene; it was too important a decision for a mere Crown's Favourite. And, despite all her accomplishments, her aunt had mocked her.

Ending both their lives seemed the most logical decision. However, executing two women with the surname Dajalam... there would not be a single priest who would not consider it a mortal sin, more than enough reason to be rejected in the lair of the Aqua Deus. However, pious threats were far from the reason why she had not ordered Gant to have her aunt and sister appear lifeless at dawn.

There was another reason. It simply wasn't the right time. The death of either would raise many questions and, more than likely, an investigation. Any slip up could put her in the spotlight, but that would only be the case as long as she wasn't queen. It was time to take care of her mother, or rather, to make sure she would be taken care of.

She turned, looking at her reflection in the mirror. As she contemplated herself wielding the sword, she could not prevent a small spark of hope from shaking her heart. It was an outstanding debt, a long-standing resentment that maybe, just maybe, she could make amends for.

She unsheathed Crystaline, observing its bluish edge. Her feelings met, sensing a mixture of devotion and anger. It was the first time she had unsheathed the sacred sword since the fateful day when the cursed Aqua Deus had made the incomprehensible decision to choose Vienne as the Lacrima and not her.

She knew what she had to do; she had performed that ritual countless times. Every morning since she became aware of its significance, she held the illusion that this would be the longed-for day when the sword would finally choose her as the Lacrima. An illusion that had never been fulfilled. She knew it had been a mistake, one that she could make amends for in such a simple way

"Crystaline, grant me your powers." She commanded authoritatively, a tingle in her belly reflecting her nervousness.

She contemplated the blade with eagerness. Her face lit up, weren't those little drops of water emanating from the blade? No, just the mist of her agitated breathing, of how close she had placed the blade to her face in the hope that it would respond to her commands.

She gritted her teeth. Throwing the sword sharply against the floor. The steel clattered loudly as it bounced across the wood before coming to rest in the room's corner.

"All well, my lady?" said Porleas from the doorway. The butler glanced toward the corner where the sacred weapon lay, then back at the princess, arching an eyebrow.

"All good," Katienne confirmed to him.

"If you please, I can arrange everything to deliver the sacred sword to your mother via one of the next ships the Delorange family sends to the front." Proposed the steward.

"Oh no, that would be too risky." Katienne answered him politely with a smile, "this sword has been in my family for generations, I will personally see to it that I choose people I trust to get it safely to my mother."

"As you wish, my lady." He said, performing the Aquo reverence and closing the door.

That's right, stupid old man, I don't trust you. You won't like me, but I don't like you either, and you will regret every moment you have to serve me for the rest of your days.

The princess grabbed Crystaline. Then she bent down, opening a wide drawer, the last one in the cabinet near the window. There lay her diamond-peaked wedding dress, perfectly laid out, without a single wrinkle, pristine and ready to be worn soon. She pushed it aside abruptly, placing the sacred sword under it.

There you will lie until my mother falls, she thought as she closed the drawer, *it is time to make a sacrifice for the greater good.*

32. Harsh reality

The sun beat down on his back with extreme harshness. The grumble of his stomach competed with the incessant noises of bugs and birds that took refuge in the tops of those leafy trees with leaves as bright yellow as Noakh had ever seen.

The young Fireo walked heavily behind Dabayl, who did not seem to want to give them any respite. He didn't usually complain, but he was hungry, thirsty, sleepy, and his feet ached. He put his hand to his right earlobe, or rather, the hollow where it used to be, trying to relieve the annoying itch.

That murderous bastard Suruyana, he muttered to himself, remembering the brutal moment when the bloodthirsty leader of that group of despicable men had killed Yarna's husband and then mutilated him to deliver a message of terror. He clenched his fists, aware that those prisoners were free because of the irresponsible decision of the kings of Aere Tine.

As he reflected on irresponsible decisions, his mind could not help but think of Gurandel and his resolve to end the lives of those who would try to take the sacred sword Tizai from her. No matter how much Noakh thought about it, he could not understand it. Gurandel had vowed revenge. It was precisely because of those vengeful desires that Noakh promised Burum Babar he would assist his granddaughter Arbilla if the dragoness followed through with her threat. But what did Gurandel have against the Kingdom of Air? What did she care about a sacred sword? These were questions he was not going to find answers to, and yet he could not stop them from echoing in his mind over and over again.

He stopped, overwhelmed as much by his thoughts as by his aching feet and the sweltering sun, lying down on the side of the path. Hilzen took two more steps, then stopped as well and rested in the shade of one of those trees filled with such unbearable sounding creatures. The Aquo lifted one of his boots and removed it, revealing a purple sock with a hole through which the yellowish nail of his big toe peeked out.

"She does not seem to be getting over her anger." Hilzen observed, glancing towards Dabayl as he removed his other boot.

The young Aertian kept walking, ignoring her weary companions' need for rest.

She had every reason to be upset; they had secured patronage only to lose it moments later. It was not their fault, far from it, the decision of the kings of Aere Tine to free the prisoners had caused that situation, however, that did not seem to ease the conscience of Dabayl, who, finally, had stopped and leaned her back against a tree while crossing her arms.

The approaching noise made Noakh look up. He turned to see a massive creature approach, a blend of a boar and a bear—a wounk, like the ones he had encountered in the Kingdom of Earth. The colossal animal was pulling a cart driven by a woman who wore a kind of wide headband on her forehead with which she pulled back extremely curly reddish-orange hair. Closer up, there was a constant sound, a *clonk, clonk, clonk,* accompanied by water falling to the ground. In her wagon she carried bulky earthenware jars from which water overflowed. As the cart stood next to Noakh and Hilzen she pulled on the reins, the wounk stopped with astonishing docility.

"Greetings, good travelers, perhaps you would care for a tasty snack to liven up the inclemency of the rough road?" she said in what sounded like a most studied phrase. She pointed with her thumb to her cargo, all filled with earthenware jars soaked by the water that was leaking out during the journey. "I have salmon that's alive and kicking if you want to treat yourselves to a tribute fit for kings."

A tasty salmon... Noakh's mouth watered just thinking about it. He had tasted that delicious reddish fish once, on his fifteenth birthday. His father Lumio had escorted a fisherman and they had been assaulted, that delicious fish had been the gift for having saved him from a certain loss of all his possessions and a more than likely death.

"How much?" Hilzen asked. He seemed also attracted to the idea of a proper dinner.

The young woman looked Hilzen up and down without the slightest impudence, then turned to glance at Noakh, whose equally dusty and threadbare garments did not seem to offer her any greater confidence. She smiled, "I accept credit."

232

"We have none of that," Hilzen replied. Dabayl, who had approached to find out what was going on, walked away with resounding steps, continuing on her own. "Perhaps coins?" Hilzen suggested, putting his hands to his pockets.

"Certainly. Thirty gold coins, and the salmon will be yours."

"Thirty?" Hilzen repeated indignantly. "Are you in your senses? Did Aqua Deus himself hand deliver it to you?"

Noakh grimaced in surprise at such a high price. No matter how fresh the salmon was, the price was too steep, regardless of the quality of the fish. Hexagonal gold coins, triangular silver coins and circular bronze coins. The monetary system was the same in all four kingdoms, for some reason at some point in history the four kingdoms had come together and established a common monetary system. Probably the only thing the four territories had managed to agree on in their entire history. Why they had decided to put their differences aside for this remained as unknown to Noakh as it was uninteresting. Certainly, money had never been of special interest to him beyond seeing it as something necessary to make a living. His life had always been humble, without luxuries or large sums of money. Just enough to survive.

"Perhaps we can escort you in exchange for some of your fish?" Noakh suggested. "The streets of Aere Tine have certainly become dangerous with the royal decision to release all their prisoners..."

The merchant laughed. "I don't think that will be necessary. Shiana will take care of me." She concluded, "and if our goddess isn't enough..." she leaned to the side to then show a crossbow she apparently carried hidden. "Besides, if I were a thief, I'd put all my efforts into snatching credit from the sponsored, I guess that makes you guys safe." She said with a mischievous grin, then tugged on the reins. "May Shiana's breezes guide you on a sure and safe path." She indicated to them, waving the reins, then the wounk resumed the march.

That young woman was willing to give us the fish in exchange for patronage credit; alternatively, she has demanded an absurdly high sum of money from us, Noakh reflected, watching the cart drive away, *day by day is proving Dabayl right.*

At first, Noakh had failed to understand why his Aertian friend considered it crucial to have a patronage; but he was beginning to understand its importance. People were eager to accept credit from a patronage, that meant that if you did not have one and intended to pay with money the monetary sum to be delivered was much higher than before there was this feverish eagerness to find the sacred sword. That situation led to the conclusion that without patronage it was practically unfeasible to move around the kingdom in a minimally dignified manner. A bed in the filthiest lodging, a loaf of bread no matter how hard it was... all these basic necessities had become unattainable except for those who went in search of the sword and had a patronage...

"Bah, to hell with that overpriced fish!" cursed Hilzen, getting to his feet, resuming his march.

* * *

They had reached the city of Mesua. Beneath a white stone archway with yellow flowers poking through the cracks in it and reddish stones stood two soldiers from the southern kingdom who, as had become customary, asked their names and took good note of the reason for their journey and belongings before letting them pass.

The streets were teeming with life. A man carried a curved stick on his back, the end of which was covered with wool, followed by a dozen dark brown pigs that walked in an orderly fashion, grunting constantly under the watchful eye of two large dogs as black as night.

Noakh couldn't contain his amazement. In that place, people with hair and irises of every possible combination were interacting in a hectic but gentle manner. A blonde-haired, blue-eyed woman with several warts on her cheeks was stroking the head of a Fireo girl who was accompanied by a man with the same features.

It was a sight as peaceful as it was strange, as if in that place they had seemed to forget to mention that they had to hate each other. Amidst such a pleasant panorama, he noticed something peculiar, the kingdoms were inhabited by people whose skin colors ranged from the darkest to the palest tone and, shockingly, that had never been a problem. Only eye and hair color seemed to generate tensions. He would have liked to ask Dabayl why features didn't matter in that city. Perhaps, by discovering such a secret, he could replicate it once he was... Noakh smiled at his own occurrence, *once he was king,* he had thought. *Such thoughts,* he reflected, too soon to consider such a thing.

He remembered Vienne's words, Aquos and Fireos were at war again. Wulkan would no doubt be on the battlefield; *how would he have explained to his army having only one of the fire swords at his disposal?* He wondered. Still, something told him that, by one ruse or another, Wulkan had gotten out of the way. Burum Babar had

234

mentioned that they liked to challenge each other with dilemmas, difficult problems to solve with which to test each other's minds. It was precisely one of those dilemmas that had caused him to find himself in that situation, bereft of his family, having lived in ostracism surviving on the kindness of a soldier who cared for him like a son. *When I become king... for that I'll first have to deal with King Wulkan.*

They walked through the busy streets. Noakh waved away the offers of an insistent merchant to purchase his fresh fish, glanced at the freshly baked loaves of bread and also the cloths of an attractive Fireo woman who looked at him with mischievous eyes.

He walked down a wide street that ended at a tall building with an orange façade. Soldiers there ensured the orderly progression of two seemingly endless queues. Men and women were waiting their turn for who knows what, curiosity got the better of him, and he approached. He stood near the building, noting that at the entrance to the door there was an engraving that indicated *Headquarters of the Wind Council*, where at its entrance stood two guards armed with halberds guarding an old woman with hair as white as sparse wearing a wide white robe with silver trim. The young man who was being attended handed the worn woman a sword with a golden pommel.

"I come to deliver Tizai to you." Announced the young man.

"Yes, like everyone else." Scoffed one of the guards, eliciting laughter from his companion.

The old woman, on the other hand, showed no amusement on her wrinkled lips. She simply picked up the weapon, bringing the steel close to one of her ears. After a moment, she shook her head.

Can she listen to the sword? Noakh wondered, *is this how they intend to find out which is the real Tizai and not a mere imitation or a common steel?* He wondered,

Next!" called out one of the soldiers, as the man with the sword walked away crestfallen.

"I come to deliver these credits and collect them..." said the next person in line.

Noakh stopped paying attention, as he began to feel the accusing glances of those who were standing in line, they seemed to begin to suspect that he was trying to sneak in at any moment of distraction.

He walked away, as amazed at the fact that there were people capable of perceiving the essence of a sacred sword as he was at the endless queue of people carrying weapons, they claimed was the coveted Tizai.

His attention, however, was diverted to a noisy and small stall located at the back. Among metals and a forge was... wasn't it? Yes! A dwarf woman. He approached her without delay, he had business to discuss.

He needed to hire the services of that dwarf to extract the citrines and affix them to his swords. The muscular dwarf was hammering away at a breastplate, in what Noakh assumed was an attempt to make all those dents disappear.

"Tell me." The dwarf said without pausing in her work, the water hissed and bubbled as the red-hot piece of metal was plunged into it.

"I'm looking for someone with talent to extract some citrines so I can attach them to my swords, can you do it?"

"I can, as long as the person interested can afford my talent. It will cost you two patronage credits or three thousand gold coins and you will have it ready this afternoon." Affirmed the dwarf without ceasing in her hammering.

"Three thousand gold coins?" Noakh said, widening his eyes. "I can't pay that much."

"Then I can't waste my time."

Noakh snorted, fed up with the growing importance of money in that kingdom. He turned away, ready to leave in indignation, then remembered the word that Dleheim had pointed out to him, of which Burum Babar had told him that the dwarves would know about it. He turned, ready to find out the truth.

"You wouldn't happen to know what the word *Akhulum* means?"

This time the dwarf did cease her hammering. She raised one of her bushy reddish eyebrows, weighing him for a moment.

"Very funny, the price has gone up to eight thousand." She ended up saying. Suddenly, the dwarf's furious gaze landed on Noakh's sash, her face now shifting to surprise. "May I see that sword?" She said with strange interest as she pointed at Distra.

Noakh folded his arms, "Of course," the dwarf's face lit up, "for thirty thousand gold coins I'll let you have a look at it."

"Get out of here," the dwarf ordered him with a hand gesture. Thus returning to her loud hammering.

He passed past a shelf displaying precious stones. Another where they sold breads of all kinds and a third where they offered him what looked like something similar to an Aquo pie, only it smelled like garlic and fish and had a square design instead of a round one. On every shelf, he was bombarded with offers of *free with credits* and other similar promotions.

"Even the most stunted purple carrots are now priceless," Hilzen lamented, appearing behind him, "I think I'm beginning to understand Dabayl's anger at losing the patronage."

"Me too," agreed Noakh, sighing, "where is she, by the way?"

"I saw her conversing with some guards while I was seeking accommodation at a rundown inn. You won't believe it, Noakh, the price of a stable lodging is fifteen times that of any Aquo room, fifteen!"

Noakh laughed at his companion's effusive indignation. Then he frowned, he had a strange feeling, as if he was being watched. He glanced around, a man leaning against the wall wearing a cyan blue robe motioned for them to approach. They waited for a woman to pass with her three woolly sheep, which left a trail of feces on the roadway as a gift, before approaching him.

"Friends, if you want products at a cheaper price, I have a reliable contact." That man told them in a low voice, looking from side to side.

Hilzen and Noakh exchanged glances. The Aquo shrugged his shoulders.

"Show us," agreed Noakh, seeing that they had no choice.

They followed him. The man in the robe was joined by another leaning against the wall, followed by a third, and then two more.

Noakh looked at Hilzen. Something was wrong. All those men walked with their right hand attached to their leg; this meant that these had been, or perhaps still were, soldiers.

They came to an alley and stopped.

"Well?" Hilzen asked, crossing his arms, "where are those cheap..."

More men appeared out of nowhere.

The flour sack caught Noakh's head an instant after Hilzen's. He struggled, reaching for his swords. But too late. He coughed as he felt the punch in his gut. Then they hastened to dispossess him of his weapons.

However, the young Fireo was not willing to give up just like that. He leaned forward slightly, then with a swift motion, he pulled back and landed a forceful punch on the face of the one holding him.

Crack.

By the sound of it he had broken a nose or several teeth.

The impact was enough to free him. He removed the annoying sack, trying to retrieve his weapons and fight a battle. He took a quick look at his situation, Hilzen lay unconscious on the ground with the sack covering his head. He was the only one left. Two of them grabbed him. Unfortunately, those men were strong and seemed well-trained.

But he had no choice. It was either fight or allow those ruffians to capture them.

Then he smiled, grateful for his luck, just at that moment Dabayl had appeared at the entrance to the alley. Noakh allowed himself a breath of relief. Soon, his Aertian friend would draw her bow and rid them of the rogues. His friend did not disappoint him; Dabayl grabbed her bow and then an arrow from her quiver. She quickly notched the arrow, drawing and releasing the bowstring in one fluid motion. The arrow shot out, piercing the abdomen of her target.

Noakh's eyes widened. He glanced down at his belly, watching as his clothes were soaked in his own blood.

He fell to the ground on his knees.

Dabayl approached him, bow still in hand, her other arm resting on his shoulder, ready to resort to a second arrow.

"Why... why?" managed to say Noakh.

"Sorry, my revenge is even more important than your friendship." She replied.

After those words, a stomp from one of the soldiers made everything go black.

33. An unexpected gift

It could not rain any more. Lightning lit up the sky with white light, followed by thunder that roared as if thousands of pieces of furniture were being shuffled around in a massive bedroom. Katienne found herself looking out the window, already dressed to embrace the day.

"Don't you think it's a great day, dear?"

"Of course, my beloved."

Katienne turned away, that parsimonious response a far cry from the devotion with which Filier usually responded to her.

"Is something wrong with you?"

"It's nothing," he said leaning back in his armchair, laying on a small table some parchments he was reviewing. After a pause, he continued. "It's just that the idea of having your sister and your Aunt Alvia locked up in our domain makes me uncomfortable to say the least. Besides, that Knight of Water, Gant... I don't trust him."

"Oh, does that nonsense keep you awake at night, my dear?" she replied leaning her hand candidly on Filier's thigh and then squeezing it lightly. "Believe me, even my aunt is harmless being imprisoned in those stocks, especially with Gant on our side. As for my sister, she's a good-for-nothing who poses no threat."

Filier raised an eyebrow. "My beloved, Princess Vienne was able to defeat seventeen of my best soldiers all by herself. Not to mention your aunt is known for her lethality. I can't stop thinking about those soldiers who died because of us..."

"They died to do justice, my dear, don't forget that. Our mission is to make sure my sister pays for her vile deeds, so we will make sure they did not die in vain."

"Perhaps you are right." Filier agreed, picking up the parchments again and resuming his reading.

239

Katienne smiled at him, pleased that her beloved recognized the costs of seeking justice.

"By the way, do you know if the sacred sword is already on its way to your mother?" he added.

"That is something private to the palace, my dear, but, knowing Meredian's alacrity, I'm sure he will have already taken care of sending it." She lied to him, "I have no doubt that we will soon hear good news from the battlefront."

Such information seemed to please Filier, who turned his attention back to her parchments, these were addressed to each of the families of those who had fallen for confronting Vienne. Her fiancé had informed her that he intended to send them such a message along with a sum of money that, while it might not compensate for the loss of a loved one, would at least ease their spirits. Katienne did not approve of the care with which he cared of his soldiers, but she had to admit that it suited her well that such actions kept him entertained.

The princess left the room, then descended the stairs.

And to think my sister and my aunt are lying helpless under this incessant rain, a wicked smile appeared on her lips. She wanted to see them suffer, to enjoy watching them freeze under such a deluge. She opened the door to find a young, curly-haired soldier, completely drenched, waiting on the other side.

"Excuse me, I'm looking for Filier Delorange, I bring a message for him."

The soldier looked nervous. He certainly did not know what to do, or how to act, perhaps he was a new recruit hired after the casualties caused by her sister's steel? It seemed that this was too good an opportunity to miss.

"I am his fiancée," Katienne informed him, a sweet smile showing on her lips. "Filier is occupied with pressing matters at the moment. You can share the message with me; I'm certain I can assist."

"I'm sorry, but it was insisted to me that only lord Filier could receive the message..." the young man said uncomfortably.

Those words sharpened all of Katienne's senses.

"You seem new here," she observed warmly, "perhaps that is why you have not been informed of my recent arrival in Filier Delorange's life, my betrothed trusts me with his deepest secrets, surely you can tell me what your message is about." Seeing that the soldier still hesitated she hurried to continue, "besides, you must be tired from your journey, not to mention soaking wet," she added innocently, running one of her

240

fingers through the soldier's wet locks, "rest and have a nice hot soup that you so deserve, I will personally see to your well-being and speak highly of you to my dear Filier," she said winking at him.

The young soldier seemed satisfied. He was probably hungry and tired from the trip after such adverse weather conditions.

"All right. A ship has arrived in port Asua, they claim to have brought a cargo that is sure to please the master of the house."

* * *

Despite the raging storm, the men and women continued to unload possessions from the dock. Katienne dismounted from her horse, which looked exhausted after the long and strenuous journey she had forced upon it. No wonder, she had to know what special cargo had arrived. Thankfully, the Delorange residence was close to the port of Asua.

She approached a woman in a hat. The woman's serious countenance, as she inspected how the rest were unloading, indicated to Katienne that she was the one to speak with.

"I have received word from the soldier. My fiancé, Filier Delorange, is very busy," as she mentioned his name, she showed her bluish ring, "so, he sends me in his stead."

The captain looked at that ring with absolute interest. "We seized a ship entering the waters to the west, a stinking vessel. What we found in its hold was a foreign substance..."

The captain told her in detail. Katienne's eyes widened in shock, she opened her mouth without meaning to. Those potions she was referring to, the ones they had seized, must be the famous Tirhan pothai. Just the thought that she had been lucky enough to come across such a shipment caused her to feel an extreme frenzy within herself.

"Great job. I want you to stow those concoctions back in the hold," Katienne ordered keeping her composure, "my fiancé will want to send them to the borders as soon as possible," she lied. "However, it's too soon for you to embark on another voyage. Let your crew visit their loved ones, take rest and await my orders. It is of vital importance that no one knows of your cargo, you will be duly rewarded for it."

The captain's expression shifted upon hearing about the promised reward.

"There is another thing, we captured the passenger of that vessel." The captain whistled, a gesture with which two men brought before them a man with a bruised cheek, a hat with a feather and a large mustache.

It can't be true, Katienne thought, not being able to believe her luck, so much so that she allowed herself to unveil a wicked smile for an instant. She recognized the man instantly. Gelegen, nicknamed the fifth Knight of Water, a sharp-minded veteran soldier who had made a reputation for himself solving mysteries throughout the queendom. She had heard the rumors, that man had accompanied her sister on her crusade through the Kingdom of Earth.

Some might think it was luck that Gelegen would find himself before her like this, manhandled and defeated; but Katienne knew it was not so. Chance had had nothing to do with it, that was living proof that the Aqua Deus was on her side. She had not the slightest doubt that the man would support Vienne. She was aware that her sister's pathetic, sad and insecure face provoked sympathy in those who felt a certain benevolence for the weak.

And now he was also under her control.

* * *

With her head held high and a satisfied smile, Katienne walked through the pouring rain. Behind her walked Gelegen, obliged by Gant, who was especially rough with the new prisoner to the point of carrying his sword drawn in case the latter should think of trying anything foolish.

Her new dress was so extremely soaked that it had probably been ruined forever. Her shoes so waterlogged and muddy that even the poorest peasant would refuse to wear them. And yet, in spite of this, she could not have been happier.

They waded into the swamp that had become the place where their sister and aunt were imprisoned. At first, Vienne and her Aunt Alvia didn't react, probably thinking it was just another of their visits, however, the dog began to bark fervently, a gesture that caused both prisoners to look up.

The stupefied look on both of their faces as they saw Gelegen appear in chains was a memory she hoped would remain etched in her mind forever. Just at that moment, a bolt of lightning lit up the sky,

242

followed instantly by a thunderous noise, an additive that Katienne felt served as the perfect accompaniment to such a grandiose scene. Surely in their hearts there remained the hope that this man would come to save them, she could see such an illusion fading from their eyes.

They stood in front of them. Gant kneed Gelegen hard in the back, forcing him to kneel down in front of Vienne and her aunt. The dog ceased barking, transitioning to a soft whine, a sound that was far more bearable.

"Doesn't it seem symbolic to you, sister? Each and every one of those who aided you on your journey gathered here, together, enduring cold and misery for the mistake of helping you." She scoffed, with extreme enjoyment. Vienne merely glared at her furiously from her position, an attitude that only added to her amusement.

"Release us, Princess Katienne," the veteran soldier cut her off, "you overstep your bounds by imprisoning your sister and aunt. As soon as your mother hears about this..."

Katienne laughed scornfully, pushing a wet strand of hair from her face.

"I know I've crossed a line, Lord Gelegen," she replied with her hands behind her back and her head held high. "But to get what one desires; any lengths must be taken. For the queendom, I'm ready to defy even my own mother." She announced flatly. "We've never had the pleasure of conversing before, I have only heard disturbing gossip about your prowess at solving crimes," Katienne said observing him, "precisely for that reason, I am aware of how very dangerous it would be to let you go free." She looked around, making sure there was no one who could hear her beyond Gant, "I have no doubt you would eventually find out that it was under my cunning to blame Vienne for the murders of the members of the Congregation of the Church who were to support her ascension to the throne." She turned to Vienne. "You didn't see that move coming, did you, pathetic sister?" She said with a superior tone. Turning to Gelegen, she continued. "You would undoubtedly expose the truth, and that's a risk I won't take.

Katienne turned away. "Gant, this man's intelligence is too dangerous, see to it that he can't use his head."

The steel of Gant's sword flashed with lightning, rising to the heavens.

"Don't look, Vienne!" Alvia urged her.

The sword descended, straight for Gelegen's neck.

Vienne uttered a piercing cry of pain, while the dog barked as if possessed. Her Aunt Alvia merely gritted her teeth. None of their wails stopped the sharp blade from continuing its descent.

Gelegen's head came off his shoulders and began to roll on the muddy ground.

Katienne just watched her captives, folding her arms, arms folded, savoring the sheer pleasure her sister's pain brought her.

"You will pay for this, Katienne," Vienne said, her eyes blazing with fury. "I swear that sooner or later you will understand the pain it feels to witness something like this."

Katienne just smiled at her. Then she turned and walked away. "Let's go, Gant, let them say goodbye to their dear friend."

In the pouring rain, Katienne departed, content to leave Gelegen's mutilated body as a haunting presence for Vienne.

34. No alternative

Queen Graglia stood on the banks of that mighty river. She clutched the dark-varnished chest, its wood graced with intricately sculpted mermaids—Lampen's ingenious gift, which lent comfort to her travels beyond the palace. She placed it on the water; the wood swayed with the gentle flow of the river. Yet, it was not influenced by the current, for the handy device had counterweights at the bottom that acted as an anchor.

She opened the lid of the chest, within, several sapphires were set into the wood, meticulously arranged by rank, counselors on one side, Knights of Water at the other end, the three heads of the Guards at the bottom and, in the lower right margin, several empty holes where only a solitary sapphire was located, the one of Gelegen.

She had delayed this moment, as if she expected nothing but bad news. However, she could not delay it any longer, she leaned towards the box and moved a protruding piece of wood moving it downwards, as she did so, a hollow sound was heard, activating an internal mechanism that allowed the water to make its way evenly and carefully through the studied labyrinths designed by Lampen, soaking each and every one of the sapphires. She held her breath, waiting to see which ones would be illuminated. Unwillingly, her eyes remained anchored on the solitary sapphire located in the upper right corner, she had not heard about Alvia and, therefore, not about Vienne. Would they be all right? She examined each sapphire in her collection; Meredian, the Tribute Counselor and now Crown's Favourite, hadn't communicated with her lately either. *Strange*, she thought.

One sapphire did light up, Menest's. Graglia was not surprised, the leader of the Knights of Water took his rank very seriously, offering reports with due depth and frequency, a habit she would have liked others in their charge to take example from. Quickly, she lifted it to her ear, yearning for good news.

"*My queen*," the message began, "*Fireo soldiers ambushed us at night, uncovering our position. It was a massacre. Tarkos and I have been captured.*"

The sapphire stopped. Graglia stood still, her gaze fixed on the horizon, the bluestone in her ear returning to its darker hue. She had lost two of her Knights of Water. Once again, Wulkan displayed an amazing predictive ability. Who? Which damned wretch was revealing the Aquo settlements' positions?

"Excuse me, my queen," said the powerful voice of Galonais behind her back. "We have an unexpected visitor whom you must meet; he awaits you in the command tent."

The queen frowned at the words of her Defense Counselor, whose look was enough to indicate to her that this was an important matter. She merely nodded, gesturing for her to collect and guard the sapphire chest.

She walked back to the camp, guarded by several soldiers of the Royal Guard standing on both flanks to avoid any danger. *Two Knights of Water captured, another one so badly burned that I cannot use him, and my sister's whereabouts unknown*, she could not but sigh at such a bleak picture.

She entered the command tent followed by her guards, meeting a man of strong bearing, bushy beard, brown eyes and black hair. Her heart skipped a beat, thinking that she was in the presence of King Wulkan himself, given his identical appearance.

"Greetings, Queen Graglia," the visitor said nervously, "allow me to introduce myself, I am Minkert, grandson of the mighty Phoenix Descendant and King of the Fireos, Wulkan. My king sends me to deliver a message to you."

At such a presentation Graglia could not help but raise her eyebrows. That explained the striking physical resemblance. It was not easy for her to suppress the instinct that urged her to order that man to be skewered by thousands of spears and then be delivered in pieces to King Wulkan, however, she knew how to repress her craving.

"Talk." She said curtly.

"As you probably already know, two of your Knights of Water have been defeated and taken prisoner by our army." Minkert indicated to her, the latter's voice seemed to try to be as non-threatening as possible, "King Wulkan has sent me to inform you that, to his good pleasure,

246

both knights are safe and sound, having even been treated for the wounds they suffered during such a hard fight.

His previous proposal was disregarded. so, King Wulkan offers you a more palatable deal. Meet him on the beautiful sands of the beach of Ghandya, gather your entire army there in such a symbolic place, and your two Knights of Water will be delivered to you in one piece. And, as a testament to his good will, he offers you me, his humble servant and grandson, as a token of assurance, as proof of the sincerity of his proposal."

Graglia gritted her teeth. *Damned bastard Wulkan*, she muttered to herself. The king of the Fireos seemed insistent in his attempts to confront her in the sands of Ghandya and Graglia was well aware of the reason for such a burning desire. That place was currently Aquo territory; however, in the past, it had belonged to Firia. Wulkan wanted not only to confront her, he also desired both armies to witness him reclaiming those lands from her in an evenly matched battle.

He is forcing direct confrontation and I am still dispossessed of the sacred sword. But I have no choice.

35. Conflict of interest

"Walk faster, you damn idiot!" A voice ordered, pushing Noakh so hard that he nearly fell face first to the ground.

Noakh would have liked to explain to whoever the genius was who was giving him such impertinent orders, that it was difficult to walk briskly when you have your eyes impaired by carrying a dusty bag of flour on your head. Unfortunately, in addition to his impaired vision, a gag had been added that made it impossible for him to communicate as well.

The good thing about those constant orders and expletives was that some of them did not seem to be directed at him. That meant that Hilzen was at his side.

It was difficult to make out the details of their journey without being able to see anything, but at least he had a clear sense of part of the route they had taken. He had been treated for the arrow wound in his stomach then they had traveled in the back of a wagon, with their hands already bound behind their back. Now, from the constant sounds of doors, greetings, and, dare he think, music in the distance, it seemed reasonable to conclude that they were in a sizable residence.

He sniffed, trying to take advantage of his intact senses. Among the smell of flour another aroma crept in, he identified what looked to him like a roast, a strong smell that made him salivate, how good it would be to eat something!

He coughed, the result of the flour entering his nostrils. Then he heard music from what must have been a violin or some similar stringed instrument coming from what sounded like a closed room, it didn't take a genius to conclude that whoever they were being delivered to must be someone of high fortune.

He still could not believe it. Dabayl had betrayed them. After all the experiences they had gone through together, after knowing even her family... why? She had mentioned that her revenge was more important than their friendship, but how could betraying them help her in her revenge? He knew her revenge had to do with Loredan, but what did that have to do with turning them in?

They entered a room.

"Is it him?"

Noakh heard. It was a fine voice, with a pompous touch and, in a way, it even sounded pedantic.

"Well, sit him down there."

Those indications were accompanied by a push into what must have been a corner of the room, followed by a violent squeeze on his right shoulder forcing him to sit down. He felt his buttocks settle on a stool. The annoying flour made him cough again.

"Leave us alone."

"Excuse me, my lord..." said a timid voice, "the girl who delivered this young man and his other friend wishes to be paid for her services."

"Oh, yes, make sure she gets as much gold as she wants."

"She insisted that she didn't want gold, she just wanted to ask you for an answer to a very simple question."

"What? What a stupid request, my time is too valuable to put up with curious commoners, pay her in gold and get her out of here with alacrity."

For an instant all Noakh heard was the sound of several footsteps, followed by a faint *click* as the door closed. He noticed how the one who had asked to be left alone stood in front of him. Suddenly, the sack ceased to cover his face, the light hurt his pupils, causing him to narrow his eyes.

As soon as he got used to the brightly lit room, he laid eyes on his captor. A middle-aged man watched him with interest through intense, sunflower-yellow eyes and a horizontal scar that ran across his forehead from one side to the other. Despite this, it was neither of those features that caught his attention, above his middle-parted hair sat a thin crown where one side was properly ornamented with a citrine set in what appeared to be gold while the other side showed only the base surrounding his head, with no decoration whatsoever.

King Lieri, Noakh assumed. *Half-crown. Half-crown to the king of Aere Tine North.*

His surprise was probably reflected in his face, for the king laughed as he watched him. "I knew you were a fraud," he announced in amusement, turning around and resting both hands behind his back, "when I heard that someone had confronted Burum Babar early on, I doubted that such information had not been maliciously manipulated or, perhaps, exaggerated. It is the price one pays for legends, poems, and songs," he said, shrugging and raising his hands toward the ceiling. "But, what a nice conclusion for a song, right? Young Noakh betrayed by one of his friends, now that's a piece I'd like to hear!"

There he was again. In front of a king. This one was smaller in size than Burum Babar, both in height and width of shoulders, as well as considerably younger. However, while Burum Babar conveyed calmness to him, somehow King Lieri inspired danger. Noakh's teeth clenched the gag so tightly that it creaked.

King Lieri continued on his way through the spacious wood-floored room, whose white walls were lined with rows of what looked to Noakh like surprisingly well-placed musical works side by side. The monarch stopped at a circular table whose legs were graciously carved in what looked like musical notes, upon it were two weapons.

My two swords, Noakh observed.

The king reached for the swords, turned to lock eyes with Noakh, and, without breaking the gaze, grasped Distra's hilt and unsheathed it. He strode back across the room, calmly tapping the flat of the sacred sword in the palm of his other hand.

He returned to stand in front of the young Fireo. Observing him without doing more than continuing his tapping.

"I find myself in a dilemma, Noakh. Perhaps you can offer some insight." He began, now resting the blade of the sword on his bright red velvet robe replete with lace, "you see, I have in my possession one of the sacred swords of fire," he said moving slightly the hand with which he held the weapon, "yes, I am not a fool, I know this sword is Distra and I know you can invoke its power.

You may have a gripping tale to share about it, however, I'm sure a Fireo is not a good storyteller.

So let me be the one to tell you something. The dilemma I'm facing now is quite intriguing, you see," he made a theatrical move after which he quickly placed the tip of Distra on Noakh's chest, right at the level of his heart, "for one thing, I could pierce your chest with the same sword that, for some reason, chose you, poetic indeed, don't you think? It would be so simple," he said squeezing so hard that Distra's sharp point broke through Noakh's shirt, who responded by biting the gag even harder, "then I would dispose of this aberrant weapon, I could have its steel melted down and have the blacksmiths use it for the shoes of our

251

horses," the king laughed at his proposal, "Yes! It would certainly be something worth doing.

With a single motion, I would rid the four kingdoms of the heir to the fiery throne and one of his pesky flaming holy swords!" He announced, raising his hands to the roof and leaning back. Then he pointed Distra's tip at Noakh, so close to his nose that he could almost feel the coldness of the steel.

"I could destroy your flaming sword and, believe me, it would be incredibly satisfying to do so. Wait, I've come up with an even better idea than the horseshoes!" Added King Lieri, amused at his own witticism. "We would melt down the sword and then send Wulkan a gift, my own bust made from the metal of Distra, revealing to him in a jocular note that at last a noble use has been put to the steel of his revered sword. It would be so much fun! Just imagining his reaction makes me happy. So much so that I am seriously tempted to do it.

But here's where the problem lies, destroying the sword would mean leaving the fate of my kingdom, no, of all of Aere Tine, in the hands of luck, and that's something that's not really my style.

My sister Zarta thinks I'm am obsessed with control and she's not wrong, I'm sure you remember all those soldiers asking for information in each of the cities you visited, that was my idea! And thanks to such an ingenious mechanism it has been so easy to find your whereabouts!" he announced, pointing at himself proudly with his thumb, "information is important and I'm sure that with it we can anticipate any situation, but my sister insists that no matter how much I want I can't change the direction of the wind. I, on the other hand, believe that it all depends; depending on how you design the wall, you can even change something as seemingly impossible as the direction of the wind.

Will any of the citizens of Aere Tine finally get their hands on the sword? Perhaps one of the many gangs of troublesome prisoners we freed? Surely yes, but when? How long will not only my sister and I but the kingdom itself continue to be dispossessed of its most powerful weapon?

I have heard formidable stories. Fearsome, cruel and incredibly talented warriors have embarked on a quest for glory trying to get their hands on the sword and all of them have failed, they could not face the dragon! My sister suggests calm and hope, I, on the other hand, believe it is better to fight fire with fire, what better way to face a dragon?

And who has the power of fire?" Distra's tip stabbed into Noakh's chest, "that's why you'll be in charge of retrieving Tizai from that dragon's filthy clutches."

Noakh tried to speak, but the gag muffled his words, making them unintelligible. King Lieri, caught in his interest, approached a shelf on which in addition to a knife rested several books and a skull, picked up the weapon and then used it to cut the gag, thus freeing Noakh.

"Dragoness," Noakh corrected him, "Gurandel, she happens to be the queen of dragons, by the way." He punctuated.

"Huh?" said Lieri with surprise, "how do you know that?"

"Because I cut off her tail." He revealed, taking care not to tell too much. Probably revealing to him that the reason for cutting off her tail had been for the purpose of freeing her and that because of such an act it now prevented them from retrieving their sword would not have been to his benefit.

The king looked at him dumbfounded. Looking him up and down, in what seemed the most absolute astonishment. *I like that way of looking at me better already,* Noakh said to himself, grateful to see King Lieri's superior smile disappear.

To him, the monarch seemed an insufferably arrogant man, overly fond of his wit and, even worse, his nefarious jokes.

"Well," resumed King Lieri, "knowing that you can stand up to the dragoness, you will surely be pleased with this deal: I will give you back your swords to face her," he said, his words sounding confident again, "I will keep your friend Hilzen as hostage so as to make sure you keep your end of the bargain.

I think it's a good deal. I give you back your sacred sword, and I don't order your heads to be cut off for trespassing on my land; in return, you only have to return Tizai to me, is that a deal?"

"No." Noakh replied flatly, his head held high, as a sign of defiance.

"No? What do you mean, no?" said King Lieri with a quizzical grimace, pulling back his face, thus revealing a previously unnoticed double chin, "perhaps I have not been clear enough, are you aware that I could end your life and that of your friend with a snap of my fingers?"

"I am aware. I simply do not believe you are in a position to negotiate. Your kingdom is paralyzed, searching for a sword you cannot retrieve, your citizens are dying at the hands of prisoners you freed or facing a dragon they cannot defeat, meanwhile, you are vulnerable to attack from any of your borders.

The only reason I haven't been killed with my own sword is that you want my help. You have mentioned that you do not leave your fate in the hands of chance, precisely for that reason, you cannot risk that someone who has proven himself capable of cutting the hard scales of the dragon that guards your weapon will not assist you in your endeavor to recover the sacred sword.

You need me. And I will help you to recover the sword, provided you accept my conditions."

Not long ago, he had struck a deal with another despicable being: Garland. He had accepted the terms set by that impudent Tirhan, only to find it was a trap. This time he was not going to be willing to let himself be pushed around, especially by a being as irritating as that king.

"Just who in the hell do you believe yourself to be? Don't you realize that you are at my mercy?" replied Lieri, his face red with anger, "And why should I accept your demands? What's more, who do you think you are to impose conditions on your situation, you impertinent child?"

Noakh remained calm, not letting his pathetic insults affect him, in the least. After having met Garland, any insult seemed insignificant compared to his tongue.

"I am the one who risks his life while you are sitting comfortably in your armchair. So, if you want to count on my services, I will be the one to decide the conditions, as well as my companions." He demanded sharply. "You will grant us the Royal Favor if it is we who deliver the sword to you. Beyond that, you will provide us with weaponry, mounts and any aspect we deem pertinent to our journey."

King Lieri gritted his teeth, terribly frustrated at losing control of the situation. "All right, all right damn it."

"One more thing," said Noakh, amused at the situation, "what will you give me in return for not sending you your sword turned into a bust with an amusing note as an accompaniment?" He scoffed.

"Doesn't a Royal Favor seem enough to you?" He asked, scandalized.

Noakh shook his head. "The Royal Favor is retribution for finding and returning the sword to you. What I ask is what you offer me to ensure that the most powerful weapon your kingdom possesses returns to your hands safe and sound."

"All right," replied Lieri, realizing that he had trapped himself with his own words. "You have an insolent tongue, but your request is just, I am aware that nothing is achieved without offering anything in return, what can I offer you that is of interest to you?

Noakh thought for a moment, *what should I ask for?* That was a good question, then he realized that once he achieved the goal of finding the sword there would only be one thing he would like to make sure of.

"If I manage to bring the sword back to you, my friends and I will be allowed to cross the border of the Kingdom of Aere Tine North to Firia. No tricks, no ambiguity, all my friends and I leave your lands safe and sound, without fear of looking back, deal?"

King Lieri looked at him for a moment, as if pondering his options. Noakh tried to hold his gaze without even blinking or moving in the slightest. He had to be firm and sure of himself, there was too much at stake.

The monarch nodded. "All right, but I intend to alert every guard post from here to the most remote places in both Aere Tine South and North, should you be detected in any city that does not direct you to Sui Lana I will make sure you suffer the worst of the condemnation, is that clear?

"Deal."

36. A slight suspicion

Filier gently drew the curtains closed, shielding his ailing father from the pale, intruding light that seeped through the clouds. Next, he approached the bed, sat on the edge of it and placed his hand on his father's rough forehead to measure his temperature. He shook his head; his fever was raging. His father's health was completely unpredictable; one day he was well enough to gaze furiously at him in his betrothal and, on many other days like today, he lay in bed, his frail form painting a picture of a man on the brink of death.

He held his father's bony hand, trying to make his father see that he was with him, that he was conveying him strength and encouragement to keep fighting.

Please, father, don't abandon me too, he begged inwardly. He was a staunch, tough man, both for his rigorous treatment of his children from a very young age and also for demonstrating a physical strength capable of allowing him to withstand the onslaught of an illness that insisted on taking him away with a frequency that Filier was beginning to find terribly discouraging.

The mere thought of his father no longer being by his side caused Filier terrible discomfort. He knew that his father was significantly physically and mentally deteriorated, that his death would allow him to rest, but, as selfish as his thoughts were, he did not want him to leave. He had lost Dornias, he could not lose him too.

He felt a slight squeeze on his hand.

"Fi... Filier, are you there?" his father said weakly with his eyes closed.

"Here I am, tell me, what do you need?"

"Is... is Bonaite with you?"

Filier's heart shattered at such a question.

"No, father." He said tenderly. "Mother is waiting for you at sea, she left early so she could make sure it was a comfortable place for us." He managed to say. He missed his mother, she was loving, kind and tremendously affable, everything his father had never been.

"And... Dorniaseus? Is he here?" he managed to say between labored breaths.

Filier swallowed nervously. "No, my brother is away on a trip, taking care of our ships." He made it up. He didn't have the guts to tell him the truth. How? How could he tell his half-dying father that his youngest son had lost his mind and was on the run? Words too disturbing for his father's fragile mind. "Rest, regain your strength so you can embrace your youngest son when he returns."

His father nodded and let go of his hand.

Rest, Father. Do not leave me alone, I beg of you.

He stood up. Trying to regain his composure in the darkness that the room offered him. For some reason, he couldn't stop thinking about how much he had lost by supporting her. His father's respect, his own brother's... he loved that woman, so much that he was willing to lose everything for her.

He didn't mind being dispossessed of his right to the inheritance of the Delorange domain, as he couldn't care less about the throne, he just wanted Katienne. Making her happy was his absolute priority, he grinned like a fool every time he saw her smile. However, it was difficult to please her, her strong character was coupled with an inordinate ambition which he admired and, in a way, feared.

He wanted to do whatever it took to make her happy, but how much would he be willing to do for such a task?

The war, his brother's disappearance... what if something had happened to Dornias? Was locking him up in a cell like a common dog really going to be the last memory he would have of his beloved younger brother? The mere idea terrified him to such an extent that he jumped to his feet, leaning both hands on the wall, trying to ward off the nightmares that were beginning to recreate themselves in his mind.

Annoying sounds ended his troubled musings. He frowned in annoyance, knowing that such noises would be disturbing his father's rest. He pulled back the curtains, ready to identify the scoundrel causing such a racket.

Then he found the culprit; that window overlooked the courtyard where Vienne and Alvia Dajalam were being held. From a distance, he observed how the Knight of Water Gant was amusing himself by kicking the cage where the white dog was locked up, causing an uproar of metal noises interspersed with intense barking.

He clenched his fists and reddened with anger. It was one thing to have those two prisoners detained on his land, but it was quite another to make his home a place where torture was allowed. And certainly not at the expense of his dying father's rest.

He left the room like a flash, and made his way through the house to the astonished gaze of his servants, who were not used to seeing him so irritated. He descended the stairs and walked through his grounds, as swiftly as he could. As he drew closer, the intensified barking and clanging metal fueled his growing fury.

He made his way into the place that had become an improvised prison. Seeing him approaching, Gant ceased his amusement, walking until he landed in front of Filier and prevented him from moving forward.

Filier raised his head, so as to rest his eyes on Gant's unconcerned, burnt face.

"What do you think you're doing?"

"To liven up my surveillance work," Gant replied haughtily.

Filier wrinkled his nose at the strong smell of wine coming from the Knight of Water's breath. "For your information, the Delorange domain is not a place where you are allowed to torment anyone. I am aware of the terrible act that Princess Vienne has committed, but that does not give you the right to torture them on my land." He informed him in an indignant tone. Without meaning to, something in his gut told him that everything seemed to be getting out of hand. He had already had to intervene once, ordering the body of the dismembered man to be removed immediately, despite the reluctance of his fiancée, who insisted that it was part of a lesson.

"I don't care what you think," Gant replied, scoffing. For a moment they simply held each other's gaze, a challenge to see if either would bow to the other's fierceness.

His haughtiness, the tone of mockery in his voice, even his look full of defiance... since Katienne had informed him that Gant had allied with her, something had not given him a good feeling and that hunch was becoming a reality by leaps and bounds.

"Step aside, I want to talk to our prisoners." Filier demanded.

The Knight of Water inspected him for a moment, as if weighing whatever intentions Filier might have. Then he stepped aside, allowing him to pass.

He quickly examined the princess and the Knight of Water, feeling terribly relieved to see that they were unharmed, likewise the dog appeared unscathed and now seemed calmer, watching him with her huge black eyes. As much as those women were traitors to their god and their reign, he could not bear the thought of royal blood staining the floor of the Delorange domain, he was sure that the Aqua Deus would reserve a particularly sinister sentence for anyone who dared to commit such an act. He gazed at them, amazed at how, even when they were bound at the neck and wrists, they still sent a shiver down his spine. Those two women were deadly killing monsters.

"Excuse this embarrassing display," Filier said, meeting the eyes of Princess Vienne and Knight of Water Alvia. "Even as traitors, you are still part of the royal family, and it will not be in my domain that you are judged."

"Why are we still here imprisoned?" questioned Princess Vienne, "why am I not locked up in the Church Prison if you assume that I have ended the lives of several members of the Congregation?"

The truth was that Filier had also asked himself the same question, however, Katienne had offered an explanation. She suspected that Vienne and her Aunt Alvia might be released. So, she preferred to keep them guarded in Delorange territory, making sure they were watched until her mother returned victorious from her confrontation with the Fireo soldiers. An explanation Filier had assumed coherent and understandable.

"I have no reason to explain myself to a murderer," he replied angrily, recalling each and every message he had signed informing the families of his fallen soldiers, "do you know how many good men and women died as a result of your weapon? They were only doing their duty."

"Would it help to say that I did not kill the members of the Congregation?" Vienne defended.

Filier sensed a certain sadness in her voice, something that infuriated him.

"With what audacity do you lie to my face? You are nothing but a vulgar liar well given to theatrics," he replied indignantly, "I am surprised to discover such qualities in you, at least it is good to know that you are good for something other than killing innocent people. Have you anything to say in your defense?"

"Don't try to convince him, Vienne," interceded Knight of Water Alvia, then her face fixed on him. Filier had to make an effort not to look away. "You're an idiot being played like a puppet," Alvia sneered, speaking too abruptly to him, "and at some point, you'll figure it out, too bad it'll be too late to save your skin." She said amused.

"I see you are a hopeless case." Filier concluded, "regardless, rest in the knowledge that you will come to no harm while in my domain." He assured them.

He got no response from them. He turned around, standing again in front of Gant, who was now leaning on a fence, his arms crossed.

"Is that clear, Knight of Water? I do not want a drop of Dajalam blood to be spilled on my lands, any more than I wish the animal that accompanies them to be tortured."

Gant shrugged his shoulders.

"I'm just following Princess Katienne's orders," he said. "If you have a problem with it, take it up with your fiancée."

"That's what I intend to do as soon as I see her, where is she, by the way? I haven't seen her all morning."

"She's with Father Ovilier, she wanted to make sure that he is recovering from the assault he suffered during the night."

That's not true, Filier thought. Fate had wanted him to know perfectly well the exact location of Father Ovilier on that day, it had been mere chance. One of the messengers who had returned from delivering the message of death to the family of one of the soldiers killed by Princess Vienne had crossed on his journey with Father Ovilier, who was going to officiate the marriage of the heiress of a noble family residing in the area.

"Fine," he merely said, completely abstracted by the insincerity. The anger on his face disappeared completely, instead, he left the way he had come, trying to convince himself that surely Katienne would have some explanation.

37. Treacherous rat

Dirty liar, treacherous rat, disgusting traitor, unprincipled, backstabbing bastard....

Those insults and many others kept swirling in her mind, in what seemed like a somber chant that sought to make her feel as bad as humanly possible. And she was not going to be the one to stop that atrocious mental beating, for she knew she deserved this torment and worse for the unspeakable betrayal she had committed.

Dabayl walked alone, still unable to believe what she had done. She sniffled, her nose runny. She wiped away her tears, overwhelmed by fury at herself for the betrayal.

It was strange to walk around without hearing Hilzen's songs and having to urge him to shut up, or having to put up with Noakh's constant naive comments. Those idiots...

Dirty liar, treacherous rat, disgusting traitor...

It was difficult for her to digest the swing of emotions she had experienced in such a short period of time. The joy of obtaining the patronage had been followed by absolute desolation after Yarna's decision not to support them in the search for the sword after the death of her husband. And when she had given up everything for lost and her hope of uncovering the truth behind Loredan's death had vanished, some soldiers of the crown had asked her about Noakh. She could not believe her luck; Shiana had granted her a second chance! Excited by the moment, she had not hesitated, she had approached those guards and sold her friends.

She had been overcome by the desire for answers. There was only one reason why she would perform such a dirty deed as turning in her friends. And, it had been in vain. She looked down at the heavy bag of gold coins she had been offered as a reward, gritted her teeth in fury.

"And all for this!" she shouted, hurling the bag of coins to the ground with disdain.

Worthless, dirty money that is good for nothing, she thought angrily, looking at the useless shiny hexagonal coins scattered on the ground. She began to kick them, again and again, as if she wanted to blame those coins, as if she didn't want to accept that it had been her mistake.

She resumed her march, breathing with difficulty after her effort to make those coins disappear from her sight, those serving as cruel reminders of her betrayal. She continued on her way, aimlessly, alone again and, she did not know whether it was worse or not, without an answer.

She advanced; one hesitant step followed by another. With absolute reluctance, wanting nothing more than to get away from there. A dark wish blossomed within her, a longing for the newly freed prisoners to find and assault her, whether she sought to unleash her rage upon them or longed for them to end her misery, she couldn't tell.

She decided what her fate would be, totally dejected. She would walk without rest until she was finally assaulted; it was the best thing to do... she would die as one more, prey of the rusty knife of some ex-convict. A death perhaps too dignified for someone like her.

Suddenly, a flare burst before her feet, halting her pursuit of a death befitting a treacherous traitor like herself.

Dabayl turned around, a smile on her face. *They survived. Somehow, they escaped King Lieri's clutches*, she realized, a wave of joy washing over her. She knew she should be terrified of the consequences, sure that Noakh and Hilzen had come after her to make her pay for her treachery, but despite being fully aware that the release of her companions was going to mean the end of her, she was simply glad that they were safe.

She watched as they approached her. Noakh and Hilzen walked side by side, moving toward her diligently, but without haste. Noakh's flaming sword scraped the ground as he walked, while Hilzen's crossbow sat ready upon his shoulder. They were both ready to settle scores, to finish off the rat who had sold them for nothing.

She felt the wind on her skin, the current was favorable. Noakh and Hilzen continued their advance, coming close enough for Dabayl to showcase her sharp aim. She reached behind her back and unhooked her bow, then took an arrow from her quiver. She placed the arrow on the string and drew it taut, feeling the wind, aiming for Noakh's heart.

She kept the tension, watching how they approached, how they seemed not to feel the slightest sense of danger from her drawn bow.

The bow and arrow fell to the ground; a moment later, her quiver suffered the same fate. She fell to the ground on her knees and arms. It was not a prayer for mercy. She was simply accepting her fate.

I have failed you, Loredan. I hope someday you will forgive me.

The fire behind her vanished, as if the flames had understood that she was not going to escape, that she had accepted that this was the place where she was going to die.

She remained motionless, not shifting an inch from her position until at last she saw their boots appear in front of her. She heard the crackling of the fire from Noakh's sword.

She smiled at her fate. *Looks like I'm not going to offer you the justice you deserve in the end, brother.*

"Last words?" she heard Noakh say. His voice sounded devoid of feeling, which made Dabayl's hair stand on end. She expected fury, uncontained rage, but the mere indifference chilled her blood.

"I know it won't justify my actions, but the only reason I betrayed you was because I was desperate to know what happened to my brother."

Silence fell. A light gust of wind appeared at her back, rushing along the back of her neck.

"Hilzen, you better do it." Noakh said, after his words the noise of the fire faded away.

Dabayl gritted her teeth and closed her eyes. Waiting for the moment when her body would be pierced by one of the bolts from Hilzen's crossbow. She narrowed her eyes even more as she clenched each and every muscle in her body, as if foolishly trying to prevent her skin from being pierced.

She took a deep breath, waiting for the imminent shot. Her heart beat once, then again, *why haven't I died yet?* She wondered. *The click of Hilzen's trigger should have sounded by now, the bolt should have already propelled out of his crossbow and hit me hard in any part of my body, yet here I am, still alive. Are they just playing with me? Making me wait to suffer a little before they kill me? Cruel, but more than deserved as a punishment for a traitorous rat like me.*

She slowly opened one eye, bracing to witness Hilzen and Noakh taking pleasure in her torment.

Tears ran down her forehead, her mouth grimaced tightening her lips. In front of her now terribly snotty nose was Hilzen's outstretched hand. She shook her head, aware that she did not deserve his mercy. Finally, she reached out his arm, both hands came together and, with a strong push, Hilzen pulled her to her feet.

Then Noakh slammed something against her chest. Dabayl, out of mere instinct, grabbed it.

"Come on, we have a Royal Favor to get." Noakh said sheathing his sword and starting to walk. Hilzen likewise placed the crossbow on his shoulder again and followed him.

"What? But... I betrayed you, why don't you kill me?" She said perplexed

"Because I promised someone that when you needed help, we would be there for you." He said without pausing in his course.

She could not understand anything. Her gaze fell, focusing on whatever it was that Noakh had handed her. Her mouth dropped open, her hands trembled with emotion, that was a credit book. They had been sponsored.

38. A dream put to the test

She couldn't believe it, she had finally dared to enter that sacred building, the Cloister of Music. After so many detours, so many self-inflicted excuses, so many so-called last test concerts... she had finally mustered enough courage to take the plunge.

Halftal had imagined such an emblematic place countless times. Always imagining that it must be a building vibrant with life, with rooms full of musicians talking about their works and sharing their love for that art. Instead, the reality could not have been more different, that place was as deserted as it was silent.

It was a round room with an exaggeratedly high ceiling, flat and smooth walls. Thick cylindrical pillars extended upward, converging at the center of the room, around a mosaic of crystals in different shades of yellow through which the sun's rays penetrated.

As she walked through the room, Halftal quickly realized something, despite the lack of furniture and the exaggerated elevation of the ceiling, there was no echo in that place. It made sense, it was a building where music was honored, so somehow the architecture had to allow the acoustics to be pristine.

It was a peculiar room, consisting only of the doors through which she had entered the building; a solitary tall reddish wooden cabinet with a purple cloth in one corner and, in front of the entrance, stood ornate white doors, marked with a pentagram and devoid of any inscription, adorned with a golden knob.

"Come closer," said a voice from the reddish furniture.

Halftal nodded, approaching the place.

"Your name?" was heard through the fabric, it was a worn voice, one of those that clears its throat before and after speaking. Halftal imagined it must have been an elderly man who was sheltered inside that piece of furniture, but that tone could have belonged to a woman perfectly well.

"Emisai Lilac," she indicated, bringing her face close to the canvas, "although my artistic name is Halftal." She added quickly to avoid any confusion.

Her answer was followed by a silence disturbed only by a slight sound that, thanks to her acute hearing, allowed her to understand that whoever was inside that piece of furniture was taking notes. Then she perceived the presence of a face on the other side of the cloth. She could not see it clearly, but she sensed that she was being carefully observed.

"Your brown hair, your stage name, Halftal, I understand there is some connection, am I wrong?"

She merely nodded her head.

"Know then, that our court offers neither favor nor disfavor in any other color than that of music. Your brown hair will not soften the hearts of the members of the court, neither will it harden them..."

"I appreciate that." She nodded proudly. "A trial where only my talent matters is exactly what I come looking for."

"Prior to authorizing you to perform your piece before the Cloister it is necessary that you give answers to the following questions. Answer truthfully, at the price of never being guided by the Maiden of the Bell." The voice cleared its throat several times before continuing. "Do you swear before the Cloister that your melody has hitherto been heard by no mortal at the price of your ears?"

"I swear." Halftal confirmed, showing both hands as if she were begging, it was the gesture her momoi had taught her years ago was the way to swear in the Kingdom of Air.

"Do you swear, before the Cloister, that this song is born of your own ingenuity, and has not been stolen from its true artificer, lest the price be your tongue?"

"I swe..."

A terrifying scream of pain interrupted her oath.

Just then the white doors opened. Two soldiers in pearl armor and gold trim were dragging a man who was holding both hands to his mouth while uttering bloodcurdling screams. *At the price of your tongue*, Emisai recalled as she saw that the man's hands were covered in blood, *that man must have stolen his song from another musician*, she supposed.

268

The exit doors opened, the soldiers roughly threw the man into the street and then closed. Then they went back the way they had come, their boots walking over the trail of blood, until they disappeared through the white door again.

"Do you swear, before the Cloister, that your work is worthy of their ears and time, lest the price be your life?" The voice asked, disregarding the bloody event that had just transpired.

Halftal hesitated for a second, the price for submitting a song that was not up to the standards of the Cloister would be her own life... doubts began to plague her mind harshly, what if her work was not good enough? How could she gauge if her work equaled the compositions of previous artists who had stood before this esteemed courtroom if she had not been able to hear any of their songs?

"I swear." She said unable to keep her throat from going dry.

"Well, you know the price of your testimony, proceed. Knock once only."

She felt like her legs had been anchored to the floor with endless nails, making every step up to the white doors a torture. She stood right in front of the golden doorknob, swallowed hard and rapped her knuckles once as instructed.

The doors opened. The eyes of those soldiers were empty, they had no ears, no noses. She walked into the room, the doors closing behind her, the soldiers kneeling with their faces facing the floor.

She walked along the trail of blood, standing on a stage in front of which the three members of the Cloister were seated behind a table. She felt the attentive gaze of those judges, an act enough to make her begin to question each and every one of her life's decisions.

She tried to calm herself by tuning her lute for the fifteenth time. To any expert ear, that instrument was already perfectly in tune. Yet, Halftal's nerves made her question the tuning of her instrument, despite its perfect pitch.

She managed to muster the courage to stand up straight and look straight ahead. For the first time, she gazed upon the three judges who would determine whether her song merited the ears of kings and queens, if it should endure throughout history.

In the center, a plump woman in her sixties with slanted eyes and such exotic makeup that her skin appeared to be purple. To her right stood a bald man with an open robe, revealing a chest covered in thick reddish hair. The third person, on the other hand, was covered from top to bottom, only showing vivid eyes the color of gold. Halftal did not

269

know who any of them were, however, being the ones chosen to evaluate the works presented to the Cloister, she assumed that they were great artists.

They continued to stare at her without moving, without making any gestures. Despite this, Halftal was able to pick up on their impatience, or perhaps it was her own nervousness urging her to act once and for all. She took a deep breath. She closed her eyes to concentrate better and reminded herself

that her momoi and popoi would be proud to see her playing before the Cloister.

First it was her lute; a beautiful chord initiated her song. As her fingers began to caress the strings, she felt all the tension in her body fade away. Then, after three measures, her voice joined in harmony, it sounded sweet, calm... it was only the introduction, she needed to reserve the full strength of her voice for the composition's climax.

As she progressed in her interpretation, her mind was transported to another place, totally immersed in her art. Her body was still there, in that room in front of the judges of the Cloister, yet Halftal had left the world. She was now in a magical place, alone and isolated from everything, where she could immerse herself in the profound joy that music brought to her heart.

That catchy tune was accompanied by intriguing lyrics telling the story of a young man with a flaming sword—an Ascendant Phoenix making his way in a hostile world full of dangers.

She didn't need to open her eyes to feel how much attention the members of the Cloister were paying. The rhythm of the song was now more frenetic, its verses spoke of epic feats. Lyrics and melody merged into a unison speech as powerful as it was overwhelming.

She kept singing, now with increased intensity, hitting the strings with greater power, to provide her work with more dynamism. The lyrics of the song did not lag behind, mentioning the passage of that young man through Tir Torrent, his confrontation against Burum Babar, the fight as an equal against the Daikan himself. Then came a new verse, the one that mentioned the entrance of that mysterious young man in Aere Tine...

The song ended, abruptly. Halftal opened her eyes for the first time, as if she had come out of a deep trance. Her fingers moved away from the strings with the delicacy that only someone who has seen her performance ruined at the last moment can possess. Halftal looked up not without some trepidation.

"Does it end like this?" asked the purple-faced woman in a powerful voice. "Is not your song concluded?"

Halftal nodded. The three judges looked at each other in utter bewilderment.

"But why?" said a honeyed voice emanating from the person who was covered from top to bottom.

"It is an unfinished ode," she revealed to them, "the person this story is about has not yet concluded his journey, that is why my work is not finished. It will continue as he advances in his adventure."

The purple-skinned woman snapped her fingers and nodded, "Risky, morbid, and challenging." She acknowledged.

"An ode about someone whose deed is unfinished?" The fully covered individual interjected again. "What if he fails in his denouement? Won't you have wasted your time and ours for nothing? A story that did not come to fruition?"

"He will not fail!" replied Halftal, resorting to a more defensive tone than she would have liked, "I believe in him, and I know he will not give up until he has succeeded." She added with determination.

The bald man, who had been silent, arched his eyebrow, his honey eyes seeming to weigh Halftal's words.

"And if you are so sure he will succeed, why haven't you finished the play then? Perhaps some doubt is still harbored within you?" he suggested with a provocative smile.

"It's not that, he must be the one to write the very end of his song. I can't just guess how his story will end. What if the song is not true to reality? No, I will conclude the song when he finally finishes his journey."

"Give us a moment, my dear, we must deliberate." She was instructed by the spokeswoman.

Halftal nodded. Meanwhile, the three members of the Cloister turned around, beginning to talk to each other in low voices.

Once again, nerves had found their way into her whole being. She felt disappointed with herself, that had been the most important performance of her life and she had been slightly off key on the chorus, her fingers had plucked the strings harder than they should have at the beginning of the song causing the music to take more prominence in some parts of the performance than she would have liked.

She lifted her head, observing the judges exchanging bewildered glances. After a time, which for Halftal seemed like an eternity, the three members of the Cloister stood up.

The one in the center stared at her, her nostrils flaring, her chest swelling with each breath. "Your composition, this most novel Unfinished Ode, has managed to captivate the members of the Cloister. We agree that you have achieved a harmony between poetry and music that could captivate the heart of even Shiana herself.

The story narrated in its verses goes from less to more, a mixture of sadness, happiness and drama can be appreciated, thus following a path of adventure that leads us to a climax that never arrives. A formula that, although we found singular at the beginning, has enjoyed our approval once assimilated. In a way, it leaves us eager to know more, to discover what is the conclusion of the protagonist of this journey and how such a feat will be translated into your composition, and isn't the goal of every musician to create in his listeners the desire to hear more of his work?

That is why the Cloister considers that your song is worthy of being listened to by kings and queens for centuries; a piece that not only deserves, but should be kept in our archives to ensure that it will be preserved for all eternity."

Halftal was trembling. She had fulfilled her dream. She had taken a risk; she had traveled to unknown lands with the purpose of fulfilling her dream and she had succeeded. After so many doubts, so much hard work and constant insecurity in herself and her talent, it had finally been worth it.

She felt her eyes mist over with happiness. Her music was going to live forever, every musician's dream. She was eager to see Noakh, to tell him that it was not only his encouragement that had pushed her to go ahead and undertake such a journey, but it was his story that she had turned into the song that had garnered so much praise from the discerning minds of the Cloister.

She bowed, trying to hide her tears of happiness. *Momoi, popoi, I've made it.*

"However," the leader of the members of the Cloister continued, Halftal straightened up like a thunderbolt, "regrettably, despite the previous praises, we must inform you that your song cannot be added to our archives."

A shock of cold water, followed by the trampling of a herd of enraged wounks, that was exactly what Halftal felt in her body upon hearing such a grisly verdict.

"But... why?" she said, almost without being able to say a word. Suddenly she was tremendously exhausted, it was as if her body had suddenly fallen into the most abysmal exhaustion.

"As intriguing as we find your work and as original as we consider your proposal to be, it is, after all, an unfinished work. And this leads us to a dead end.

Its lack of completion means that we will not be able to include it in the archives as it is not finished. Not only would this be a risky precedent, it may also mean that, once completed, it will not live up to what we have heard so far.

That is why we must refuse to include your composition in the Cloister Archives."

The doors suddenly opened. Halftal had to be guided by the soldiers, tears prevented her from even seeing where she was walking.

39. Fidelity

"Are you finished, my lord?" Porleas asked as he took his place beside the table. On a silver tray sat a plate displaying a piece of bread and some melted whitish goat's cheese, with only a few morsels visible.

Filier nodded.

The butler made a quick but polished bow, picked up the tray and made a pretense of leaving, however, at the last moment he turned away. "Forgive the boldness, my lord, but I have noticed that you are eating less than usual lately, I hope you are well."

"I am well, thank you for your concern, Porleas." Filier said with a faint smile, "it's just that I have lost my appetite lately; too many matters assail my head. Father is still in bed, I am not pleased to have a princess and a Knight of Water confined to my domain, and even less pleased that a man dear to the queen has been beheaded in my land." He sighed, trying not to let such unfortunate decisions on the part of his betrothed sap his morale any further. "Any news of my brother Dornias?" he asked, wanting to change the subject.

"Not the slightest, my lord Delorange, the last time I saw him was the day of the fire." Porleas replied, touching the right side of his wrinkled jaw with his index finger for a slight moment.

Filier recognized that gesture, having observed it multiple times when he was a child. Porleas had saved Dornias and him from more than one scolding in front of their parents, telling a white lie to avoid a severe punishment to both him and his then inseparable brother.

His butler had lied to him; he knew more about Dornias than he wanted to admit to him. That revelation did not cause him any anger, something that surprised even himself, but instead caused him to be overcome with a soothing relief steeped in bitter sadness.

"Wherever my brother is, I hope he is safe and sound." Filier said.

"I hope so too, my lord." He replied before retreating.

He tried to show that he was not in the least affected by losing Dornias' affection, he knew that this was the price he had to pay for his decision to become engaged to Katienne. But, not so deep down, he regretted most of the decisions he had made in the last few months.

Even the way his servants looked at him had changed. Their gazes had gone from the utmost respect to somewhere between accusatory and terrified. Worst of all, he could understand them.

He went in search of his fiancée. He was still perturbed by Gant's callous actions, which had disrupted his father's rest through the punishment of the prisoners. But at least he had been able to talk to Katienne and clear up that misunderstanding, the Knight of Water had indicated that his fiancée was meeting that morning with Father Ovilier, something he knew was not true, but, when he asked his beloved about it, she had quickly clarified that she had finally gone to lunch with her sisters Lorienne, Dambalarienne, and Bolenne. An explanation that for Filier had put an end to that unpleasant mistake. And to think that for a mere instant he had come to suspect his beloved, how naive!

He climbed the stairs to the upper courtyard of the house. It was early in the morning and, despite that, several matters had required his attention. Unwittingly, he questioned his brother's whereabouts again, something that led him to admire in Katienne's surprising fortitude. He admired her even more after seeing how she had handled her sister Vienne's betrayal to the throne. The righteousness with which she had been able to detach family ties from what was right was worthy of admiration. He, on the other hand, still felt sick. His brother Dornias had publicly shown his support to Princess Vienne, in his audacity he had cried to the heavens that she was the rightful heir. Perhaps, wherever he was, he would discover that the one he profusely supported had lost her mind. Would that help his beloved little brother to come to his senses and return to his side? He missed him so much...

He walked along the cobblestones of the courtyard. There, in the distance, he glimpsed the silhouette of his beloved bathing in the water. So slender, so sensual, he had no doubt that the Aqua Deus had sculpted in her the living image of one of his mermaids.

Ah, my beloved, all a reflection of virtue and an example to follow, Filier longed. He still couldn't believe that someone as wonderful as she slept next to him. Incredibly beautiful, amazingly intelligent, deliciously educated... how could he be so fortunate to be betrothed to such an absurdly perfect person? The Aqua Deus had wanted to bless him with the ideal life partner. They had yet to discuss the date of the wedding, and while he was eager to marry her, he had unconsciously tried to delay that moment in the hope that his father would recover and his brother Dornias would come to his senses in time and be able to be part of the event.

There she was, immersed in the depths of the very same pond in which they had sworn eternal love to each other. She was leaning with both elbows on the shore, as if she were caressing something with absolute devotion.

Filier smiled, staring at his mermaid in complete rapture. *I'm sure she's admiring the ring I gave her, she liked it so much....*

He approached with caution to avoid startling her, but, at the same time, so as not to tarnish the image of his beloved admiring her precious ring. He wanted to feel the satisfaction of having chosen the perfect engagement gift.

"What have you got there, my beloved?" he asked her tremendously happy. He envisioned her turning around in the next moment, she would turn around, proudly showing him the bluish ring he had presented her with, and he would be immensely pleased that his gift had made her so blissful.

However, Katienne reacted in a totally unexpected way. The princess made a quick movement of her hands, introducing both of them into the water.

"Nothing, dear," she said stroking her hair, "I was just looking at my nails," she replied, pulling one hand out of the water and showing them to him, "do you think this manicure is pretty enough?" she said, showing him her well-manicured sky-blue nails.

"Uh, yes, very nice." Filier answered. "Excuse me, I have something to do." He added, turning away.

She lied to me, he realized in dismay as he returned to the apartment. That bluish, shiny object... it definitely wasn't the ring he had given her, so it could only be....

No, I'm getting ahead of myself, I'm just annoyed because I expected my fiancée to be praising my stupid ring and I am upset that she wasn't, that's all. He told himself. *But why lie to me by telling me about her nails?*

Lately, Katienne's behavior had grown increasingly unpredictable. Whenever he broached certain topics, she would promptly disappear without hinting at where she was headed. And when pressed for an explanation, she would offer flimsy excuses or artfully change the subject to deflect his inquiries.

He revisited the misunderstanding that had taken place a few days ago. Gant had told him that his fiancée was with Ovilier, but it wasn't true. What was going on? Did he have the right to be making conjectures or was he just being irrational?

There was one thing he could do. He knew it was pointless, but something urged him to do it, it was the only way to reassure himself that everything was all right, that he was being an idiot for having the slightest suspicion of someone as laudable as his fiancée.

He glanced around before making his way to Katienne's room; a room dedicated exclusively to the attire of his beloved mermaid. The look of surprise on her face when he had given her that room full of dresses had been a dream. He made sure that none of his servants could see him and entered the room without being seen. The door creaked slightly, fortunately for him, there was no one nearby to hear.

You're being immature and insecure, he insulted himself, picking his way through the pile of dresses. He couldn't help but lucubrate a thousand conjectures, all leading him to the same conclusion, Katienne must have a lover. It made sense, that was why she had hidden her hands in the waters, hiding any gifts from whoever the daring one was who had wooed his betrothed. Then he remembered Gant's lie, he had told him that she was meeting with Father Ovilier, *another crude lie! Surely she was lying with whoever may be the man who has managed to seduce her, who has stolen her away from me!*

He rifled through a closet, sifting through the clothing, feeling for anything out of place. Nothing. Nor did he find any object to incriminate her in the side drawers. A handkerchief, maybe a glove or a pretty pearl necklace. It was a strange feeling, he did not want to find any clue that would confirm his inquiries about Katienne's infidelity, but, at the same time, he felt an irrepressible desire to find anything that would urge him to justify that he was not crazy, that his rummaging through his fiancée's belongings was somehow excusable.

He continued his search relentlessly, overwhelmed by his anxiety and his contradictory thoughts. With each drawer he opened and closed without finding anything, he felt even worse. Despite this, something compelled him to sift through the next one, as if he had been seized by a sick compulsion to find something, to prove to himself that he had been so petty as to rummage through Katienne's clothes for a compelling reason and not because of his simple insecurities.

He kicked a box aside, frustrated. There was only one drawer left to see, he opened it, devoid of hope. He continued his search, with less

278

enthusiasm than before, convinced that he had been a fool to mistrust her.

"Ahem." A voice said from the entrance.

Filier gave such a start that he almost tore the drawer off. His faithful butler Porleas was standing with his arms behind his back. "My lord, I believe you may find the contents of the bottom drawer intriguing."

"What do you mean, I was just..." he began to excuse himself, however, he realized he couldn't deceive good old Porleas. He stood in front of the drawer that his butler had indicated, pointing to it with his index finger, the latter nodded.

Filier opened it and saw a beautiful wedding dress. He felt a tingle in his stomach, she would look so beautiful in it... He caressed it, then his hands came across a bulge. He pushed aside the soft indigo fabric, revealing to the light what was underneath.

There it was, the famous sacred sword. The cause of such a lurid family feud. Filier could not believe it, why had Katienne insisted she sent the sword to her mother, the queen, ensuring its safe arrival? He swallowed hard, something was wrong and something told him that at this point he could not trust his fiancée's word to find out.

He took a deep breath, what should he do, let the matter slide or should he relentlessly pursue the truth? Unintentionally, the words *I told you so* from his father and brother echoed in his mind.

No, I have to prove them wrong, that Katienne wouldn't betray me.

"And that is not all, my lord," Porleas began with notable haste, "I fear that, there is something else and, while I am willing to accept any punishment for it, I want you to know that I did it with the best of my intentions. Your brother Dornias, sent me a letter with a terse request, a request concerning your betrothed, and which he asked me not to tell you about until the blindfold fell from your eyes."

Filier listened, unable to believe his butler's words.

40. Tirhan territory

The ship was making its way through the Tirhan waters. In addition to the calmness of the sea, there was a pleasant clear sky. Such a sunny day caught Aienne's attention, especially coming from a place where it was usually cloudy. However, the reason she found herself looking up at the skies was not because of any weather condition, but because of the worrying number of crows flying behind their ship.

First it had been just one crow, its appearance had simply seemed an amusing pastime, something to distract them as they sailed the waves. In fact, they had even offered it some dried bread, an offering that the blackish bird had gladly devoured. After that approach, however, more of these birds had gradually joined in, to the point where they now seemed to be sailing pursued by a disturbing black shadow.

"They're just crows wanting food, we shouldn't have fed the first one that came along." Dornias said, leaning beside her on the deck.

Surely that's it, the princess said to herself. Despite Dornias' comforting words, Aienne was beginning to feel some trepidation at the sheer number of black birds at the stern of the ship.

"Is Gorigus feeling better?" asked Aienne, wanting to occupy her mind with other, less perplexing matters.

During the course of their voyage, Gorigus had begun to suffer from seasickness. This led to intense discomfort and several trips to the gunwale to make an offering to the Aqua Deus that many members of the Church would surely disapprove of.

"He'll grow out of it," Dornias replied, turning around, toward where his friend was lying. "I'm sure he couldn't be happier, in fact." He added, smiling.

The princess glanced towards Gorigus, who was lying on the deck on a blanket, being attended to by Arilai, who was offering him some water, under the watchful eye of Laenise from the helm post.

Aienne grimaced, then bit her tongue.

"What's so funny to you?" Dornias said.

The young princess smiled, glad he asked. She pointed her index finger at Laenise, who continued to pay more attention to Gorigus and Arilai than to her duties as helmswoman, "she likes him," she indicated pointing now to Gorigus, "he likes her," she continued, pointing then to Arilai, "and she likes you." She concluded as she left her finger fixed on Dornias, "but, as much as I watch, I can't guess who you like." She said, as she tilted her head and watched Dornias as if he were an intricate riddle.

The younger of the Delorange brothers raised his eyebrows, "a very observant girl," he admitted to her, "I am very private about my personal tastes, always have been, though I think as our savior you deserve to know that. My heart always belonged to the young heir of House Olavayan, however..."

"He got married, to a woman," Aienne recalled, "I heard my mother say we were invited to the wedding."

"That's right, sometimes you don't always get what you want." He said with a shrug.

"Unless you're an infuriating manipulator like my sister Katienne..." she let slip.

"Yes, about that. Tell me, Aienne, have you ever seen her with my brother, do you think she really loves him?"

Aienne turned, watching him. In the nobleman's vivid, beautiful blue eyes there was genuine concern. She shrugged her shoulders.

"I've never seen them together, but..."

"But?" repeated Dornias with interest.

Aienne looked away, unable to bear not telling him what he wanted to hear, "I don't know, it seems strange to me that my sister Katienne is capable of really loving someone..." a moment later, seeing that her answer had saddened Dornias, she added, "maybe your brother was able to bring out the best in her."

Dornias nodded, acknowledging the good gesture.

"I told you that getting into the seas of the Kingdom of Earth would be simple." Gorigus said approaching, supported by Arilai's arm. The nobleman's face looked better, though he still looked somewhat discomposed. "After all, what did those tree-huggers miss in the middle of the sea?"

"I am disturbed by the number of crows gliding over our sails." Arilai added without hiding her concern, casting her brown eyes to the sky.

The birds remained deathly silent. Just gliding lightly behind their vessel as if they were chasing them. A sight as peculiar as it was sinister.

"I don't think they will be a problem," Aienne said, trying to convince herself more than the others. "I'm sure they follow us in case we give them some fish, all the harbors are full of seagulls, maybe in Tir Torrent they are crows."

"Ship ahoy!" announced Laenise from the helm station.

They all rushed to see, *what if it is a hostile ship?* Aienne pondered, they carried swords, two crossbows and little else. If they were outnumbered it would be difficult to get out alive... she reached into her pouch, making sure she was ready for any incident.

"Damn, I didn't expect us to have trouble in these waters!" Laenise complained, trying to tack the boat. "Don't worry! Our vessel is much faster than any rickety Tirhan boat!" She said proudly.

Just then, a new crow joined the flock. However, with its arrival, everything changed. The once absolute silence became a tangle of crazed cawing. The birds moved up into the sky, then, as if in a mournful tidal wave, began to fall as one towards the ship.

"Take cover!" Dornias indicated.

First came the sails, swept away in a furious onslaught of wild pecks. Then the birds flew at them with voracious fury.

"To the cabins, quickly!" decided Aienne.

The nobles and the princess placed their hands on their heads, trying to shelter themselves as they ran.

"Aahh!" groaned Aienne in pain as she felt the pecks of several crows on her hands and arms. Luckily, Gorigus approached her and punched several blows in the air to scare those birds away.

They kept running, escaping the thunderous squawking and the incessant attack of pecks and flaps of the countless birds. They were already close to the cabins, where they could take shelter and wait for the birds to leave.

Nevertheless, Aienne stopped, reached into her little bag. She threw an object skyward with all her might.

"Drop to the deck and close your eyes!" she instructed them.

Despite having her eyes closed, Aienne perceived the powerful flash of light, followed by the shrill cawing of crows that must have been fleeing in all directions. It had worked. That was one of her inventions, a device that combined a small amount of vulcanite with an emerald. She had taken it with her in case it was needed on the trip, unfortunately, she would never have imagined that she would use it without even disembarking.

"How clever you are, little princess!" Gorigus flattered her, nervously accompanying his praise with grabbing her by the head and giving her an intense kiss on the forehead.

The rest likewise congratulated her. Approaching Aienne on a deck now filled with black feathers.

Laenise rushed back to the helm, steering the ship in a new direction. The others took their places. Suddenly, the ship began to rise from the sea. It had run aground on a massive coral formation that seemed to appear out of nowhere.

Their captors set down two planks for boarding. However, all the soldiers used only the first plank to board the captured ship, leaving the second plank untouched. Then, a short woman with large green eyes and two swords hanging from her belt appeared and finally used the second plank.

"You had better not make any move that could endanger your lives," a young man bearing a crescent shield urged them. "Before you, the Daikan Arbilla, protector of Tir Torrent under her Queendom of the Moon." He announced.

It's her, she's the princess who fought Vienne, Aienne recalled.

The four nobles, along with Aienne, were now kneeling on the deck, flanked by two men with drawn sabers on either side. This was a way of urging them to continue in that position and not do anything foolish that could lead to losing their heads.

"Look at me." The Daikan ordered them. The five obeyed.

The young monarch passed in front of them, with both arms behind her back, stopping to observe each of their faces. When she found herself in front of Aienne, she stopped and bent down to get a better look at her.

"Your face, it's slightly familiar." Arbilla said.

She had to be cautious, not long ago that young woman who now wore a thin white stone crown with three emeralds on her head had tried to end the life of her sister. She ducked her head, trying to prevent her resemblance to her sister Vienne from becoming apparent, aware that it could cause problems.

"Hey, you stupid girl, can't you see that the Daikan is talking to you?" She was reprimanded by one of the soldiers who had incredibly black teeth.

284

"How dare you speak to a princess like that?" said Gorigus indignantly.

Aienne turned to him, unable to believe he had made such a grave mistake.

"Princess?" inquired the Daikan, "what is your name?"

She did not want to answer; it was so difficult for her that turning to look into those big emerald eyes felt nearly impossible. However, the playfulness of those soldiers with their sabers gave her a hint that she had no other choice.

"Aienne Dajalam." She confessed, utterly dejected.

"Another Dajalam princess trespassing in my domain?" Arbilla spat with expected indignation. "Why does your family believe they can simply invade Tirhan territory at their whim?" she turned away, returning to her vessel. "Laon, you know what to do."

The young soldier placed the crescent shield on the deck.

"In the name of Daikan Arbilla, you are all under arrest for entering Tirhan territory without proper consent."

41. Witnesses to a gift

The servants appeared and disappeared from the room with their usual care, placing on the elegant linen tablecloth all kinds of appetizers that would delight their guests. Filier had organized the evening; he wanted to share something with Katienne and desired her sisters to witness it, except for the princesses Aienne and Vienne, of course.

The eyes of the heir to the House Delorange roamed the paintings in the dining room, witnessing how his ancestors judged him from the comfort of their canvases, especially harsh seemed to him the look on the cadaverous face of his great-great-grandfather Donsur, who appeared to be a most surly man in life.

He slid his index finger to the inside of his shirt collar, attempting to soothe the itch caused by the new fabric and his rising body heat. After this, he rested his hands on the back of his seat. Filier had decided to sit that time presiding over the table, with the door at the other end of his location. That choice of seat had a specious reason, from there he would have a perfect view of his great surprise to Katienne.

Porleas appeared through the door, nodding to him. Everything was ready for that special occasion. *Just in time*, Filier thought as he heard the murmur in the lower room, his guests had arrived.

One by one they appeared through the door. Headdresses, jewelry accessories in gold and silver tones and, of course, beautiful dresses, befitting a visit to a dinner organized by the Delorange family.

The princesses greeted him. They made the Aquo reverence, cordialities for his good attire and how nice everything looked, as expected.

"Oh, Filier, capturing our traitor sister Vienne is an act of immeasurable value for the queendom." Lorienne fawned on him, showing a look of adoration.

"And our aunt being part of her plot, who knew!" Dambalarienne added, looking tremendously scandalized.

"I always said Vienne was going to damage the reputation of our legacy." Added a third princess in a pithy voice, Filier couldn't place whether it was Mimienne or Zurienne, or perhaps she was Dambalarienne and the previous one was Lorienne?

What does it matter who each one is, he said to himself, thus ceasing his attempts to locate their names properly.

In the past, he might have made an effort to recall each of their names. Not anymore.

"But let's stop with the sad news and focus on the good," said another princess whose white makeup was somewhat excessive to heir Delorange's taste, "we are here to be part of the unexpected surprise that the romantic Filier has in store for our sister," she added, receiving several nods from all the others.

"Yes, Filier, very kind of you to want us to be partakers of one of your endearing surprises." Another of the princesses hastened to add.

"I wouldn't want you to miss it for the world." He smiled at them.

It was only then that Katienne made her entrance. Her hair, held back by a silver mermaid ornament, flowed freely. She wore a smile from ear to ear and donned a light blue dress—one Filier now regretted gifting her. She looked spectacularly beautiful, as always.

Her sisters ran to Katienne as if they were standing before the most famous bard in the entire reign. It was evident that they felt a fervent love for their older sister.

It's amazing to see how Katienne manages to attract people and make them dance to her tune....

Little by little they calmed down. Each one sitting down at the table, Katienne was the last to approach, kissed him on the lips and went to sit next to Lorienne.

"No, here better, my dear," Filier urged her, thus placing her in the seat opposite, positioning her facing the door, right next to him.

Filier took a deep breath. Aware of the stares from the royal family, eager to know more about what surprise he had in store for Katienne that they could be a part of.

"Enjoy the dinner that my talented cooks have prepared for you, they took good note of the dishes that dazzled you the most at our proposal ceremony and present them to you again with an improved recipe. The surprise I have prepared will be unveiled at the time of

288

desserts." He announced, receiving excited applause from those present.

He sat down, leaning forward to tear off a piece of black bread which he washed in his mouth with the fruity wine he had selected. It was far from the best of the vintage, yet something told him that any wine he had chosen would have tasted bitter to him on that evening.

Unsurprisingly, the dinner conversation revolved around Vienne's misdeeds and the horrendous nature of her crimes. The princesses seemed to season their succulent dishes with words of hatred, contempt, and rejection. All directed at Vienne, the one chosen by the Aqua Deus, who celebrated her gifts by murdering a large part of the members of the Congregation. It seemed that those unpleasant appellations towards Princess Vienne gave an exquisite taste to the meat, for the venison with cherry and the knuckle with walnut and blue cheese sauce were especially praised during the dinner.

Katienne placed her hand on Filier's thigh, rubbing it candidly. Then she smiled at him. The heir to the House Delorange tried to smile back, to which Katienne responded by leaning toward him.

"Is everything all right, dear?" she whispered to him. "You're quieter than usual."

Filier managed to smile and nod. "It's just that my chest hurts slightly," he replied kindly, "it's a strange stabbing pain, but don't worry, I've already taken a remedy to cure it." He answered her.

"All right," Katienne replied satisfied, "I can't wait to find out what you have planned for me, you're such an amazing man..." she flattered him, giving him a kiss on the cheek, then turned around and burst out laughing at the imitation that one of her sisters was doing of the way the heir of the House Murentu spoke. Filier was annoyed, that man was kind hearted and, although far from being powerful or wealthy, he was a magnificent conversationalist. However, he said nothing.

Eventually, the main courses were finished. Filier had hardly eaten a bite. The princesses' eyes were increasingly drawn to him. It was time for dessert and, with it, the awaited surprise.

Filier took a deep breath, trying not to focus his thoughts on the annoying beads of sweat soaking his lower back. There was little left for his gift, the one with which he hoped to leave both Katienne and all the Dajalam sisters present with their mouths open.

Desserts began to appear on the table. Blue jelly—a very fashionable dessert among the highborn. All the servants had disappeared from the room, except Porleas, the butler was standing by the door in case they required anything that could make the family reunion more endearing.

None of the princesses even pretended to lift their spoons. They hardly spoke to each other, instead gazing at him with a sparkle in their eyes, eager to witness Filier's new act of love, incredibly happy with the luck of their praised sister.

What kind of exciting surprise will Filier have prepared for Katienne and how will we take part? They were probably wondering.

It's time to unveil it.

He carefully folded the napkin, laid it politely next to his untouched dessert and stood up. Some princesses clapped quietly, others whispered. Katienne watched him with radiant light.

He breathed in with all his being.

"Dear Dajalam princesses, I have brought you here because I could not exclude you from such an important moment for your sister and me. I admit it, I am a classic, I like to take care of details, a tradition that unfortunately is increasingly being lost in our revered Aquadom. However, House Delorange enjoys as many privileges as it assumes responsibilities to the crown.

Porleas, please bring in my surprise." He ordered, then sat down.

The butler nodded, made a slight bow and opened the dining room door. The princesses' faces lit up so brightly that they seemed to offer more light than all the chandeliers in the room put together. They seemed so interested in what was going to happen in an instant that they completely forgot any knowledge of manners, placing their elbows on the table and some even leaning so far over the table that they ended up thrusting their hands into their jellied dessert.

The soldier from House Delorange, with his heavy black boots, made his way into the room, until he stood at the far end of the table. His broad shoulders covered several of the portraits of Filier's family ancestors.

The princesses were now confused, exchanging looks of surprise and various whispers. Filier noticed Katienne's puzzled gaze, trying to discern what kind of atypical gift it was, but he did not deign to look at her.

"Proceed to report in detail." Filier ordered the soldier.

The soldier nodded, placed both hands behind his back. He looked straight ahead, his dark blue eyes losing themselves in the walls, "as requested by butler Porleas, I have been following Princess Katienne

290

Dajalam for some time now in her daily activities off the property of this noble house..."

"My dear, what kind of nonsense is this..." Katienne interceded.

Filier didn't even look at her, he merely raised his index finger towards his fiancée urging her to shut her mouth.

"In my investigation, I've noticed some unusual activities by the individual in question, present here. Princess Katienne has met on more than one occasion with the priest Ovilier, as I discerned from secretly listening to several of their conversations, it was they who orchestrated the assassination of the members of the Congregation of the Church, thus seeking to blame Princess Vienne with the aim of ensuring Katienne's ascension to the throne.

Beyond that, I have observed Princess Katienne broadcasting communications via sapphire. From what I heard on one occasion, she was sending information of the location of the Aquo troops."

The gazes of the princesses had gone from looking at the soldier to very slowly turning to look at Katienne with open mouths. There was no devotion in their eyes, but utter stupefaction.

"Excellent. Good work, soldier," Filier thanked, "you're free to go. Take as many days off as you consider, you've earned them." He rewarded him. The soldier performed the Aquo reverence and began walking out of the room.

Once the latter was gone, Filier turned to Katienne, who merely shivered with her mouth open. "I beg your pardon for being spied on in your chores, Katienne, it is a despicable act not to trust the person you have sworn to travel united to rest at sea, though I believe in this case it was for a good reason."

"Katienne," Sendarienne said in a halting voice, "is it... is it true? Is Vienne innocent? Were the murders of the Congregation of the Church really your doing?" She asked, teary-eyed. The rest of the princesses likewise displayed expressions of sadness, biting their lips to keep from crying.

"No, I..." Katienne tried to excuse herself, standing up so hastily that she knocked her chair to the floor, "it's... it's a lie, Filier, what kind of nonsense is this!" Then she turned to her sisters, "I wouldn't do something like that, you believe me, don't you?" she said with teary eyes.

The princesses responded by lowering their eyes, pursing their lips or rubbing their faces in bewilderment.

The strings of these puppets have also been cut.

"A reaction as pathetic and childish as I expected." Filier replied, "Not only are you the mind behind the murders of the members of the Congregation of the Church, you also tried to keep the sacred sword from reaching your mother so as to anticipate her death and thereby seize power as soon as possible." He accused her.

Filier clenched his jaw, anticipating what she might answer. *Go ahead, deny it, have the courage to lie to our faces one more time*, he thought.

"No... that's not true, the sword has been sent to reach my mother..."

Filier did not need to hear another word. Nor was it necessary for him to give any orders. Porleas ushered in a soldier carrying sheathed Crystaline, accompanied by several soldiers armed with crossbows as a precaution. Filier pointed to the sacred weapon.

"Here is the sacred sword that you claimed to have sent by sea to your mother as soon as possible. Apparently, you decided it would be better hidden under your bridal gown..." he added with a sneer.

"Filier, we can still reign," she said, trying to grasp his hands. "What does it matter what I've done if in return we can make the queendom a better place?"

The heir to the House Delorange pushed her aside, gazing at his betrothed with contempt. She looked pathetic, devoid of reason and sanity. She seemed even less beautiful to him, or had he always been blinded by his devotion to her?

"House Delorange has already been too complicit in this monstrous plot. My servants insist that I put you in chains and hand you over to Crown's Favourite Meredian, as a token of my repentance. I, on the other hand, have already abandoned my cause."

His gaze shifted to a soldier carrying two swords in his belt, "proceed," he indicated. The latter approached Katienne and offered her one of his weapons.

"I have given the order to every servant and soldier in my charge not to stand in your way." Filier spoke to Katienne, who clutched the weapon given to her by the soldier with both hands, seemingly in disbelief at what was unfolding. "I invite you to flee from here, for as soon as you leave this room, I will hand over to your sister Vienne the sacred sword and release all our prisoners. They will surely want to settle accounts with you, so I suggest you hurry up and get out of here as soon as possible."

Katienne crossed the room to the door and turned to her sisters, her eyes pleading desperately for them to join her. However, each and every one of them shook their heads in sobs and tears, staring at the floor.

"Katienne," Filier said, the latter paused, gripping the door frame, "I hope... I hope your remains don't..." He gritted his teeth and swallowed hard, aware that, despite everything, he wasn't capable of wishing her such a thing, "go away, please."

The forlorn Katienne disappeared. Her quick footsteps descending the wooden stairs echoed through the hall, reaching the room where no one dared to speak.

I have done it! He thought, still struggling to believe it, *after so many doubts, after so much questioning whether I would be able to stand up to her, I have succeeded, I have freed myself from her spell.*

Ever since the soldier told him about Katienne's wanderings, those had been the hardest days of his life. He had lost weight, both from lack of appetite and from the countless times he had vomited. He felt brutally betrayed by the person he loved most, by the one for which he had defied his family, thereby losing the respect of his father and the love of his brother.

Such was Katienne's manipulative spell that he had even considered the idea of saying nothing; of keeping quiet and pretending that he had not discovered the whole repugnant plan by the one who, even now, was his beloved. Some might assume he was tempted by the prospect of being the queen's consort. But for someone like him, such titles were insignificant. No, it was not the titles, simply her.

Luckily for him, he had come to his senses. He now realized that Katienne had treated him as a mere puppet, manipulating him to gain power, comfortably positioned amid affluence.

Fortunately, or unfortunately, he was not the only puppet, not even in that room. With teary eyes, Filier watched the dejected princesses try, in vain, to console each other.

"What have we done?" said one of them.

"How could we have been manipulated in such a way!" said another, looking even more dejected than the previous one.

Filier could not feel more sorry for them. They had been ensnared just as he was, leading to the ruination of their lives. It was a pain that, unfortunately, he understood perfectly.

He took a deep breath.

"Dajalam sisters," he said, his steady voice breaking through the many wails of the dejected princesses. "I believe you have been subjected to the same farce as I have, perhaps there's still a chance for redemption for those of you who've come to your senses after these revelations." He reached into his pockets, showing them a key, "release your sister, and your aunt. Show your sincere repentance and pray to the Aqua Deus that the rightful heir to the throne will not be as resentful as the one who manipulated us all."

42. Redemption

The open field lay in eerie silence. Vienne didn't feel like talking, her aunt didn't seem to have anything to contribute either. The moonlight reflected off the metal bowl containing an untouched meal. Several chicken drumsticks, slathered in a bluish herb sauce, were placed just within reach of her bound arms. For some incomprehensible reason, the food rations they had received lately had become not only more frequent, but also more abundant and appetizing.

Her Aunt Alvia looked asleep, she was feeling much better from her fever, despite still looking a bit paler than usual. Zyrah lay curled up in her cage, silent. Vienne, on the other hand, was struggling to get her hands up to her neck to relieve that annoying, incessant itching. She should sleep, but every moment she closed her eyes the huge steel blade piercing Gelegen's neck appeared in her mind. She still could not conceive that Gelegen had died. The image of his head, hanging lifelessly from his shoulders, would be a memory that would haunt her for life... she had promised herself that Katienne and Gant would pay for having committed such a vile act.

Not everything was bad. At least that detestable Knight of Water that had taken Gelegen's life did not seem to be in the vicinity, standing guard as he usually did.

Gant... that wicked Knight of Water had fallen for her sister's manipulations; surely, she had tempted him with promises, that dirty game of machination that the filthy Katienne was so good at.

Her body could no longer complain. The pain in her lower back was only made bearable by the terrible numbness in her wrists being even more noticeable. Even her knees were sore from constantly resting on the damp earth.

An earth moistened with his blood...

Gelegen was gone, just like that. The mere whims of a sickly greedy princess who was incapable of assuming her place had been his executioner. That man was a brilliant soldier, a mind to be admired and, more importantly in her eyes, a person of exceptional gentleness. Ever since they had met, Gelegen had treated her with the utmost respect; with an endearing affection that she would now miss forever. She was certain that his kindness wasn't due to her royal status or her claim to the Queendom of Water; it was simply his nature.

She would never again hear him call her *Princess Vienne* with such tenderness. Her aunt was equally affected, she had tried so hard to free herself that Vienne thought she was going to tear her arms off. Perhaps that was why she was now immobile, exhausted by the pain and the effort.

No doubt Zyrah was also having a hard time after witnessing the death of her master, she had not moved one inch from her cell. No barking, not even a slight whimper. She was simply lying on the floor, her head resting on one of her paws. The only thing that showed that the deep sadness had not taken away her will to live was how her body swelled slightly as she breathed.

The emptiness Vienne felt throughout her being was fueled by an uncontrollable rage, an unbridled fury that demanded revenge. She gritted her teeth, her hands struggled, trying to force their way through the small gap through which her hands were blocked.

It was difficult, but she had to keep a cool head, probably there would be no better way to pay homage to Gelegen than to escape from there and avenge his death. However, getting out of that situation appeared to be impossible. It was obvious that they could not free themselves from those traps on their own. But then, who could help her in such a situation? No one would dare to interfere in such a scenario. She had been accused of murder of all the members of the Congregation of the Church except her own mother. Father Ovilier had made a false testimony, incriminating her, so even Meredian himself would not dare to take part. It was too delicate a situation for the cautious counselor to choose sides, he would surely wait for the queen to decide and something told Vienne that her sister would have made sure that the information did not reach her mother's ears and, if it did, it would have been previously manipulated so that even she could come to believe that Vienne could perform an act of madness of such caliber.

Aienne might be my salvation; she's clever enough to devise an escape plan and she knows me well enough to believe that I wasn't

296

capable of murdering the members of the Congregation of the Church. She snorted at her own foolishness. *Only Aienne is out there to free me, and my poor sister will still be in the middle of the sea, heading for an island, oblivious to the trouble I'm in. Even when I try to be in control, I don't do things right....*

A mixture of relief and remorse overwhelmed her. She had been the one to ask Aienne to board the ship and, as a result, her little sister couldn't help her escape. However, this may have inadvertently prevented Katienne from getting her grubby hands on her favorite sister?

In any case, the conclusion was obvious, there was no one who could help her. She had to pray to the Aqua Deus and wait for a miracle to happen. Maybe everything that had transpired would reach her mother's ears, and she would intervene. It was improbable, but...

Her thoughts were silenced by noises. Someone was approaching. Many footsteps, several murmurs. If it was Gant, he must have been accompanied.

It wasn't long before she was blinded by the light of a lamp. She frowned. Weren't those her sisters?

One of them leaned toward her. Glaring light obscured her vision, however, the strong smell of pumpkin perfume gave her away. Lorienne. The sound of metal anticipated a *click*, was she being released?

"Why are you helping me?" she asked in surprise, moments before she was released. She stood up, stretching her back as far as she could to relieve her lower back.

"Oh, Vienne, we are so sorry," Dambalarienne said, moving towards her to give her a hug, however, she stopped midway, as if considering whether or not she had the right to hug her. "We have been blinded for a long time, but Filier opened our eyes by unveiling to us the atrocities committed by Katienne, we can no longer support our big sister's follies! She has lost her sanity; she is a monster who has been controlling us!"

Vienne frowned, unable to believe what she was hearing. She took a quick glance around, all of her sisters were watching her in what looked like regretful glances. Meanwhile, both her aunt and Zyrah were released. The little dog began to bark frantically and wag her tail, relishing her newfound freedom. She then walked over to the exact spot in which Gelegen had been decapitated, lay down, and whimpered.

297

Filier Delorange emerged from the group of princesses, accompanied by two soldiers. He looked at her with a serious expression. Weren't his eyes teary? Filier and the soldiers made their way through the princesses and stood in front of Vienne.

"I believe this belongs to you." Filier said, nodding to one of his soldiers.

The soldier approached Vienne, handing her the sacred sword. Meanwhile, the second soldier had handed Alvia her two daggers and two swords.

"Katienne and the Knight of Water Gant are aware that you are being released." The Delorange heir informed them. "I have given the order that none of my servants are to intervene on their behalf."

"Nor on ours, I hope." Alvia replied, stowing the daggers in her wrists and then placing the two swords in her sash. "Those bastards must fall before our weapons and by no one else."

"Why?" asked Vienne, her gaze sweeping over the somber faces of each and every one of her sisters there present until she fixed her gaze on Filier Delorange.

The heir of the House Delorange knelt down, bowing his head to the ground. "We discovered that it was all a plot articulated by your sister Katienne. I know we do not deserve forgiveness, princess, but I could not leave this world without imploring you to at least understand that we simply fell under the spell of an ambitious and unscrupulous woman. This is not to say that I do not admit my great guilt and involvement in this whole affair. You have the right to wipe out the Delorange family legacy and do with it as you please.

However, I would like to ask for mercy for the future of my family. House Delorange has supported the Queendom of Water since its inception, please, I beg that the foolish acts of a man in love do not tarnish the impeccable name of my ancestors.

That is why I beg you to forgive my family, so that they do not pay for my sins. Hang me, burn me alive, or feed my body to the dogs. I do not care that my remains never find the sea if, in return, my noble house does not pay for my mistakes. You will find in my brother Dorniaseus a far more suitable and loyal heir. I am sure it has come to your ears that he and his friends swore allegiance to you, despite knowing what the price of their actions would be. If you will consider the request of one who betrayed his queendom by falling under a love spell, I hope you will at least respect that wish." He begged.

It was Alvia who approached Filier, he looked up from the ground, his face now drenched in tears.

"You were willing to do anything for her, even betray the queendom itself and shame your family's good name. That shows how deeply you loved her." Alvia acknowledged.

"More than I would like to admit," Filier said, his voice faltering, then he turned his eyes toward Vienne, as if wishing to know what the verdict would be on the fate of the House Delorange.

"You were simply ensnared by my sister's manipulations," Vienne reassured him. "Don't worry about your future or your family's." Then she glanced at her sisters, "the same goes for you, I will do everything in my power to see that our vile sister's sin does not fall on your heads." She assured them.

Tears streamed down Filier's face once more, this time uncontrolled. "Tha... thank you, Princess Vienne, you are indeed the real thing... ouch!"

Filier's words were cut short when Alvia delivered a powerful kick to his stomach.

"I hope this will help you remember your mistake better." Alvia indicated.

Filier raised his hand urging his soldiers not to intervene, however, none of them had made the slightest pretense of defending him from his aggressor.

Vienne was in disbelief. Was it fate's doing, or was it the age-old truth about reaping what one sows? She squared her shoulders, ready for her revenge, while her aunt appeared equally poised for action

"I'll take care of that disgusting traitor who has besmirched the title of Knight of Water," Alvia said. "You already know what you have to do."

"All right." Vienne agreed, walking in search of her vile sister. Hearing Zyrah's footsteps behind her she turned, causing the canine to sit up and watch her with her giant black eyes. "Aunt Alvia, please take Zyrah with you. She too deserves a share of revenge."

The Knight of Water began to voice her objection, but ended up smiling instead, urging the dog to come to her. "All right, but just this once." She then addressed the canine, who tilted her head upon realizing Alvia's gaze, "Zyrah, find the bastard responsible for Gelegen's death."

43. For Gelegen

The Knight of Water trailed closely behind Zyrah, the canine only stopping to sniff again so as not to lose the scent. The little dog appeared to harbor a similar, if not stronger, thirst for revenge.

"Find him, Zyrah! Tell me where that murderous bastard is." Her blood surged so fiercely that she gnashed her teeth in a wild frenzy. The excitement of anticipation of combat was joined by the most burning desire for slaughter she had ever felt.

Worst of all, it had been one of her own who had finished off Gelegen. No, Alvia would never have called Gant a friend, but at least she considered that there was a certain camaraderie. A consideration that had led her to let her guard down, that infamous man had attacked her treacherously, in what she had considered mere training.

It was time for a second round; one from which only one of the two would come out alive this time.

Zyrah's frantic barking broke her concentration. They were at one of the exits of the Delorange domains, Zyrah snarling toward a corner. There, sitting on several stacked wooden crates, was Gant, covered in his bluish armor, the helmet in his lap while with his right hand he held his huge sword with the tip resting on the ground.

Upon seeing Alvia, he used his weapon to help himself stand, leaning forward slightly.

"I got this, Zyrah, good job." She signaled to her. Her words were enough to send the canine scurrying for cover. Then Alvia's gaze focused on Gant, who had donned his helmet and was walking towards her brandishing the huge sword in one hand.

"You haven't run away," Alvia pointed out, "I see that in addition to being a traitor you are also incredibly stupid." She added with disgust.

"Princesses run, while soldiers fight."

301

Alvia let out a snort. "Is that supposed to be an honorable comment? Too late to mention honor, you've long since lost it."

Under any other circumstances Alvia would have waited for her opponent to charge at her, usually resorting to some provocation that would start the fight. This time, however, it was too personal to wait a moment longer. She charged with all her might, unsheathing her blades halfway. This time, she would not resort to her daggers as her main weapon, this was not a combat where she was not going to allow herself the luxury of having a good time.

Gant roared, thrusting his sword forward in an attempt to skewer her. Alvia managed to dodge his attack with swift footwork, directing her blades at the gaps in his armor where the flesh was showing.

She fought with unbridled fury. Her thrusts polished; her technique incredibly refined after years of striving to be a better soldier. Her swords danced gracefully, deflecting Gant's sword while trying to find flesh to pierce with her blades.

Fate had decided that she was born a princess, but she had chosen to live as a warrior. And on the battlefield the courtesies and banal rules of royalty had no place. Only the fight mattered. Kill or be killed, that was the sole rule that governed her life.

She dodged an attack that would have split her in two. It was a battle of strength versus skill. Gant moved fast despite his bulky build and heavy armor; his reflexes were worthy of admiration, were it not for the fact that a traitorous assassin deserved no admiration at all.

She parried the massive sword using both of her blades, gritting her teeth with the effort. Gant was much stronger, that was a fact. She, on the other hand, made up for her lack of strength with her extreme agility, now fueled with hatred and resentment.

Each and every muscle in her legs ached. Wailing twinges that seemed to remind her that she was demanding too much of them after they had been so long unused. She attacked once, then a second time, looking to pierce Gant with eagerness. She felt short of breath, the fever was making it harder to keep fighting, however, she didn't care. She was going to end that sweaty bastard's life no matter the cost. Resting was not an option as long as the man who had decapitated Gelegen was not lying dead at her feet.

Now, Alvia anticipated. One of her blades sliced through the gap in her opponent's armor. Gant was knocked to his knees, the blood on his leg causing a small puddle around him. His huge sword fell to the ground. And, after it, fell the bloodied Knight of Water.

Alvia, breathing heavily, approached her downed opponent and removed his helmet with a swing of her sword. She pointed the tip of one of her weapons at him, placing it near his nose.

"You see the difference between real combat and training now, without attacking your opponent treacherously, don't you? You murderous bastard!" Alvia said contemptuously spitting on the ground.

Gant looked deeply affected. As if he felt wounded in his pride for having gambled everything in a game and having lost what he had achieved in so many years of faithful service to the queendom. Alvia could not have been more indifferent to his lamentations. Under normal conditions, she might not have felt sorry for him; now, she felt even less so.

"Get it over with." Gant demanded of her, his voice cracking, his gaze fixed on the ground. The strength the man exuded was completely gone.

Alvia sheathed her swords. "Oh, not at all," she replied, denying him with her index finger, "someone as petty as you deserves a far more pathetic end than dying at the hands of a Knight of Water."

Alvia pounced on Gant. She wrapped one arm around his thick, sweaty neck and with the other hand, she grabbed his soaked forehead, preventing him from moving. Then she whistled twice.

Zyrah appeared from her hiding place, approaching Gant with a slow pace. She growled, baring her fangs, as if she were a small white wolf. Then she barked and began to charge, pouncing furiously on Gant's face, taking revenge for killing her precious master.

* * *

The moon's light gave her tears a silvery trail. It appeared as if the moon had a radiant yet malevolent smile. *Is it mocking me? Taunting me for failing in my attempts to have a fair and competent ruler for the queendom?*

She ran with all her might. Rigidly clutching the scabbard that held the sword Filier had given her for protection. Everything had fallen apart; how could her plans have been ruined in such a ridiculous way? She had taken charge of her Aunt Alvia, ensuring she was captured and under her control; she had made sure that Meredian did not intervene and that the news that her sister Vienne had murdered the members of the Congregation of the Church reached even the most remote village...

303

so much care in having everything under control and everything had been thrown away because of the suspicions of a man she thought she had dominated by her irresistible charm.

Oh, Filier... We could have had an entire reign at our feet, she lamented, *how could you be so foolish....*

She paused to catch her breath, leaning her back against the rough bark of a tree. Her lungs burned from the effort. Not only was she not accustomed to running; her now tattered and soiled dress, along with her lightly heeled shoes, weren't suitable for it either.

She had no choice; she fled with only the clothes on her back, while the indifferent gazes of the servants and soldiers simply looked away. She took a deep breath, separating her body from the hard, rough bark of the tree. She had to leave, but where to go? She could not ask for asylum in the palace, nor could she turn to any of her sisters after the damning itself... *was there no place where I could be welcomed?* She asked herself, wiping away her tears.

If at least that fool Gant had run away with me, things would have been easier, but no. The soldier had decided to show his honor at a moment like that. *I will stay behind to face my destiny,* those had been exactly his words.

She took a deep breath and started running again. She had to get as far away as possible from the Delorange domains, she would think of a place where she could take refuge. She considered herself resourceful and knew how to make good of her charms, she would surely be able to charm some bourgeois who would offer her protection.

The hopes that all was not lost finally allowed her to stop crying. She hated crying; to her, it was a sign of weakness. Traits that she knew did not define her at all. She was a strong, ambitious and absolutely capable woman. That was why everyone in the palace claimed that she was just like her mother the queen, why then had the sword chosen someone so pitiful in her place?

She stopped suddenly, the moonlight allowing her to make out a figure in front of her. One she recognized instantly. The one who was guilty of finding herself like this, dispossessed of everything. The lucky wretch who didn't deserve her good fortune.

Vienne stood a few paces away, her sword's edge glinting under the light of the mischievous moon. Katienne gritted her teeth and unsheathed the sword Filier had given her. *At least I will take my revenge into my own hand.*

Their eyes met.

"You have lost the support of your fiancé. Even from your sisters who idolized you so much, it seems to me that you are now the pathetic one."

"No!" cried Katienne in despair, her unhinged face brimming with fury. "No matter that you wield Crystaline, you're still weak! And I'll see to it that you're put in your place!"

Both princesses charged at each other ferociously.

Before Katienne could even make a pretense of starting her thrust, she felt something sharp pierce her throat. Suddenly, the world spun around her. She fell to the ground, from where she could watch in anguish as Crystaline's blade was soaked with nothing but her own blood.

She has defeated me, without having to resort to the powers of the sacred sword... How? How can there be such a difference in power? Katienne thought as she pressed the palm of her hand to her neck so as not to bleed to death.

She had lost. No, worse, she had been brutally humiliated.

Her head tried to convince her that the only reason Vienne had been able to defeat her was because of Crystaline's powers. But Katienne knew it wasn't so, it was simply the excuse with which her mind was trying to deceive her so as not to have to face the facts. So as not to suffer having to face reality.

She had gazed upon her face, had felt her blade pierce her throat. Vienne had not called upon Crystaline's powers; she had not needed to. She had defeated her merely thanks to her skill, to an extreme speed she had only seen in her Aunt Alvia.

While I was playing games for the throne, she grew this strong, she acknowledged with embarrassment.

She felt Vienne's feet at her side, meeting her sister's cold, angry gaze.

"You are vile, despicable and an absolute coward," Vienne began, placing the tip of the sword near Katienne's throat, she tilted the blade letting a few drops of water fall.

Instinctively Katienne pulled her hand away, allowing the drops coming from the holy sword to contact her wound. She felt a tingling sensation, she was healing.

She opened her mouth to thank her.

"You're a dirty rat who thinks you're in position to step on others. You killed someone very important to me, do you know how that feels, are you even capable of understanding the pain of losing someone? Of

305

course not, you only care about yourself, maybe I better show you how it feels."

Katienne let out a muffled moan as she felt Crystaline's blade pierce her chest.

"Right there, a sharp and tremendously painful sensation born so close to the heart and yet, it does not stop the heart from beating." She said, roughly yanking the sword from her chest.

Katienne gasped, staring in sheer terror at her sister. Vienne had lost her mind. She had become a monster. This time Crystaline's blade slashed into her side; all she could do to defend herself was utter a bloodcurdling scream of pain.

"I could run you through with the sword a million times and heal you each and every one of them, endless pain, that's what you deserve," Vienne seethed with rage. "No remorse, no looking back, like you did to Gelegen, or have you forgotten?"

Katienne let out an even more terrifying scream as she felt the sword pierce her right leg.

"Mercy, please!" she pleaded between sobs.

Vienne's empty eyes watched her. Katienne's hair stood on end, her body began to tremble as she felt a deep shiver. The sister she had called weak now gave her an indescribable fear.

Her bloodied chest swelled; her eyes reflected the purest terror. Vienne's eyes, on the other hand, expressed no more emotion than an empty condescending look.

Suddenly, Vienne's gaze changed. Hard, furious, but with humanity.

"Mercy, sister, please!"

Vienne stood impassively in front of her as if pondering what to do.

"I don't ever want to see you again, is that clear?" She said sheathing the sword. Then she started to walk away from there without looking back.

Katienne lay on her back, surrounded by a pool of her own blood, not even daring to move for fear that her sister was still there. Her face was streaked with unceasing tears, being watched by a moon that never ceased to mock at how her dream of making the queendom a better place had been shattered into a thousand pieces.

44. Living in the moment

The scissors continued to fly over his head, strands of coal-black hair falling onto the sheet covering his body. The barber seemed little given to conversation, so Noakh amused himself by moving his hands under the sheet in such a way as to direct the hair in one place, where he tried to make a ball of his hair.

The young Fireo's instructions for his haircut were incredibly vague. *I want it short and to fit me well,* had been his sparse indications, guidelines that had allowed the barber to let his imagination run wild.

He turned, next to him was Hilzen, who had his neck full of lather as a second barber ran a sharp razor across his face. Noakh envied him, in a way, he resented not having facial hair, he would have liked to grow a mustache sometime.

"Ready." The barber indicated him, setting the scissors down on a shelf and instead picking up a mirror which he placed behind Noakh so Noakh could see the cut.

"I like it," he said, shaking his head from side to side. Short on the sides, equally short in the back and slightly longer on the bangs and top. It was an aggressive aesthetic, very much in keeping with the Aertian's attention-focused personality. "A modern and practical haircut."

He reached for the credit book. The truth was that it was a beautiful and surprisingly elaborate document, each sheet had a drawing and a different phrase on them, with a dark blue seal in the middle with the drawing of a harp. *Enjoying a drink called solitude,* it said on the bottom of the stamp, it must have been a song or famous quote in the Kingdom of Air he assumed, the drawing was in black and white with a mountain with a tree rushing over a ravine. He folded it in half and put it in his mouth. Wetting the fold with his tongue, he began to break it. At first, he thought the seal wouldn't break, but it cracked in half.

When he saw the loose piece of paper in his hand, he thought he understood how the system worked. The drawing, the phrase and the seal made each credit sheet that made up the book unique. In this way, the bearer kept part of each credit he gave inside the book and the person to whom he had paid the other half. Therefore, once the spectacle that had become the quest for the sword was over, credit books and sheets would be collected at the headquarters of the Wind Council, like the one he saw in the city of Mesua. Surely that organization would be responsible for checking the credit books and the sheets handed in by the applicants for payment would match. May the gods keep the poor wretches who were assigned such an arduous administrative task!

"Here you go," he said handing the barber a credit, "will this cover my haircut and my friend's arrangements?" he asked.

"Oh, of course," he indicated grabbing said document to then approach the window.

The barber held the document up to the light, trying to verify the authenticity of the credit. Noakh was not offended in the least, it made sense that many people would craft false copies of them after all.

King Lieri had provided few details; he'd merely indicated that he couldn't sponsor them directly, as it would compromise the event's fairness. But that he could arrange it by getting a family that owed him a favor to sponsor them. Lies, cheating and favors.

"Hilzen, I'll wait for you by the market, I have something to do." He said, grabbing the two saucepans that the Aquo had carried so far.

"Great, have some fun." He said from his chair.

Noakh did not understand that comment, however, both barbers laughed at his witticism.

He had an errand to run, and fortunately, he already knew the destination; it had been the first thing he had asked when they arrived in that city. He walked through the streets, in an alley a woman and a girl were lying on the ground with a trail of blood around them, instinctively he reached for his swords. He dashed forward to assist but halted when he saw two soldiers from the Northern Kingdom already inspecting the bodies. He felt furious, sure that those deaths had been the consequence of one of the many prisoners freed for looking for the damned sword... he put his hand to his right ear, the one where the wicked Suruyana had torn off part of his lobe.

The dwarf's establishment sat on a corner, marked by a sign that read: *Ronbar, expert in weapon smithing.* She looked stocky, catching what looked like a large nail between her teeth. Noakh detailed the task, showing her the two saucepans with the citrines embedded in them and how he wanted them released from both culinary utensils.

"So, can you do it?"

The dwarf raised one of her bushy blue eyebrows, setting the nail down on the wooden table near countless tools. "Well of course I can do it, what kind of question is that?" she replied angrily.

Noakh shrugged, then handed her the two saucepans and the two citrines that he kept in one of the pockets of his new pants, also financed by the credits. Ronbar took them, but not before grimacing at the discovery that two of those valuable stones were embedded in the cooking utensils.

"Well, extract from here," she indicated pointing with her round head to the saucepan, "and embed them where?"

Noakh unhooked his two swords, handing them over. The dwarf examined the blades intently. Meanwhile, Noakh searched for any sign of realization on her face, wondering if his sacred sword was now in dangerous hands. However, he did not notice the slightest gesture of interest in Ronbar. He breathed a sigh of relief.

"Fine, leave. I need to work undisturbed." She indicated him gruffly, waving him away.

Noakh aimlessly roamed the streets, waiting to retrieve his treasured swords.

"Get out of the way, you idiot!" A female voice yelled at him.

Noakh darted aside, narrowly avoiding a massive gray-coated horse. He glanced at the rider, Dabayl was smiling at him.

"May I present our mounts," she announced, tapping her horse's back. Noakh glanced back, to see two other saddled horses tied next to the first. "The black one is yours."

"Of course," Noakh smiled, he was grateful that Dabayl was calmer. She seemed happy, as if she sensed she had been forgiven.

"These mounts are of a fast and hardy species." Dabayl pointed out to him, "perfect for arriving at Sui Lana fresh, with ample bundles of food, clothing, and weaponry."

Noakh nodded. "We are certainly making good use of the money King Lieri has provided us with, I hope you are pleased." He said, turning serious.

Dabayl's face changed, looking tremendously embarrassed. "Noakh... I, you don't know how stupid I feel for selling you out."

Noakh burst out laughing. "I'm just messing with you." He said winking at her. "I know why you did it. You were desperate for answers about Loredan's death and you were in over your head."

"Still, I want you to know that I am sorry in my soul that I betrayed you." She said in a sincere voice.

Noakh could tell she meant every word. It had not been entirely easy for Hilzen and him to forgive her, after his negotiation with King Lieri and once meeting again with Hilzen they had both shared a terrible desire to teach their friend a lesson for betraying them. However, it had been Hilzen who had tried to understand her motives, which was why they had decided to forgive her.

He shrugged his shoulders, "In any case, fate has wanted to bring us a patronage in the most unexpected way, so don't give it any more thought and let's spend every last credit from that bastard King Lieri."

* * *

"Is it done yet?" said Noakh anxiously, back to the dwarf.

Ronbar just looked at him, her forehead looking incredibly sweaty. Then she handed him the swords. Noakh took them eagerly, observing Distra from top to bottom: the small *D*, the black hilt... its appearance was the same as before, however, as he continued inspecting it, he detected a small detail, at the bottom of the pommel he perceived a small yellow glow.

There it is, the citrine. It looked smaller than when he had given it to the dwarf, perhaps it had been polished so that it could be embedded in the sword, or could it be that the dwarf had played some trick to get her hands on part of the precious stone? In any case, Noakh did not complain. He inspected the steel sword, looking exactly the same.

Then the dwarf handed him what Noakh thought were ordinary dark brown gloves, however, they were not exactly that. He put them on, those leather gloves made their way into his hands, they were certainly glove-like, only leaving his fingers bare except for the first phalanx, he noticed that on the palm part of these garments, near the base of his thumb, were the citrines that connected with those on the pommels of his weapons.

"I've decided to embed the stones in the pommel in a less aggressive way than usual," she explained, picking up one of the weapons to show him better, "it's a second fake pommel, this way, another smith can

310

unscrew them and add them to a different sword in case you want to change weapons."

"How does it work?" he said excitedly.

The dwarf showed him the middle finger, "with the pad of this finger, strike the citrine while simultaneously thrusting your thumb forward," she instructed him while performing said movement to better teach him how it was done. "The movement will always be somewhat controlled since it's not a blow that can be delivered with much force."

Noakh nodded. Then he set Distra down, took five steps and turned around. "I'm ready."

He took a deep breath and tapped the citrine as Ronbar had instructed.

The handle lifted off the ground, propelling the weapon towards Noakh like an arrow. He found the design ingenious. With the citrine located in the pommel, it was this part of the sword that came towards him, far less dangerous than if it was the tip of the sword coming towards him at such speed.

"Keep your hand steady, without gripping too tightly. The citrine anchored in the sword will seek its mate."

The sword was approaching him, he tried to concentrate to grab the sword at the exact moment.

Now, he calculated, attempting to catch the sword mid-air. However, the sword slipped through his fingers, causing a repeated *clank, clank, clank* as it fell against the blackish stone floor.

Then she turned around and walked into the back of her crowded little smithy. Her voice began to carry from inside: "At least you didn't panic and start running when you saw the sword coming your way; you wouldn't be the first or the last."

Noakh tried to keep practicing. He put both swords on the ground and stood some distance away again.

The fingertips of both middle fingers struck the citrines, he thought he hit them at the same time, however, he had struck slightly earlier with his right hand. Distra shot towards him, followed by his steel sword.

He tried to concentrate, not letting the nerves of seeing the hilt of both his swords coming towards him at high speed disturb him. He raised his arms. Ready to take them. He extended his arm and brandished the sacred sword.

"I got it..."

Before he could celebrate, the second pommel hit him hard in the side of the stomach. Noakh fell to the ground, out of breath.

"Are you all right?" said the dwarf.

"I think so." He replied, rising to his feet. Perhaps it was the shock, or simply the dwarf's kindness in taking an interest in his condition that reminded him of a certain question, "Ronbar, can I ask you something?"

The dwarf shrugged, "you can ask, it's another thing if I'll answer."

"An old friend told me of a word, as far as I know, you dwarves know of its meaning, *Akhulum*, would you be so kind as to tell me what it means?"

Ronbar stared at him for a moment, as if weighing whether or not to answer. She had made a slight gesture upon hearing the word, an act that served Noakh well enough to know that she knew exactly what he was talking about.

"One extra credit and I'll tell you everything I know."

Noakh's heart pounded with intensity. Hurrying to tear off a piece of paper and hand it to her. The dwarf kept the credit and nodded.

"*Akhulum* is a peculiar word, for in the common tongue it cannot be translated by a single word, but means several at once."

"And what are those words if I may ask?" he asked anxiously. It seemed that at last, after so long since Dleheim had regaled him with just such a word and after Burum Babar's warnings to disregard it and move on, he was faced with the answer.

"In this case, *Akhulum* means, *sword*, but in turn, it also means *choice*." She revealed to him.

Noakh frowned, "it means both? And what does that mean?" After so much mystery he expected something juicier than that.

Ronbar grimaced, "I haven't the slightest idea; but, anyway, it's a very old language that is no longer useful for anything."

"I understand," Noakh replied, slightly crestfallen at the lax information, "would you at least know of anyone who could tell me more about it?"

"Certainly not in Aere Tine. I doubt there is anyone in the four realms capable of revealing more information to you than that. Only the dwarves who dwell in the Void perhaps know any more."

45. As soon as possible

The palace hall was flooded, nobles and bourgeoise had come to witness that morbid trial in which a renowned member of the Congregation of the Church and the heir of the most powerful noble house of the queendom were being judged. Precisely, because of their desire to hear the disturbing testimony of those two men; the five soldiers of the Royal Guard, who stood in a circle in front of the crowd, did not need to maintain order, no one wanted to miss a word.

Two identical chairs were placed in front of the throne. Crown's Favourite Meredian on the right seat and Vienne on the left; she had placed the sacred sword perpendicular to her feet, as was the Aquo tradition when the sacred sword's bearer had the duty of presiding over a trial. Both men were kneeling in front of them, shackled at their wrists and ankles.

At this moment, it was the turn of the priest, a man who had gone too far in his ambition to the point of having lost the favor of the Aqua Deus.

"Father Ovilier, do you deny the accusations that have been voiced at this hearing?" Meredian asked.

"I was only the object of Princess Katienne's talented manipulations." He testified dejectedly, touching his forehead to the ground, "the support for the regency of Katienne in exchange for granting me the title of High Priest, the order to assassinate the members of the Congregation... it's all true, I was a participant, but it was she who devised it all, I simply did not refuse; I lacked the courage to stand..." His last words ended in a faint trickle of voice that was interspersed with sobs.

To Vienne, the man looked as old as he was frail. Ovilier was already an old man, yet his appearance had deteriorated considerably in a short period of time. He looked exhausted, so thin that his cassock was too big for him.

"Anything else to add before passing sentence?" Meredian offered.

"I just wish this would end." The priest added, in a tone resembling a prayer. "But I want to make it quite clear to you that it was Princess Katienne who masterminded all this charade, I only agreed as a result of my own ambitions, I am guilty of my vanity as I am guilty of having fallen prey to Princess Katienne's schemes. But let not upon me weigh the punishment of being the one who designed the stratagem with which it was intended to take control of the reign."

Pathetic, Vienne thought. That testimony confirmed the reason for the feeling of contempt she had felt for the priest from the very beginning.

"Well." Meredian spoke, "by virtue of the facts of which you are accused, which you have asserted to be true, I sentence you to spend the rest of your days in the ecclesiastical prison."

Such a condemnation would have chilled the heart of any Aquo, and such was the case with Father Ovilier, who began to weep, thus accepting his fateful destiny. Nevertheless, Vienne perceived that, at least in part, he appeared relieved, as if receiving a penalty for his actions had put an end to an eternal pain that clutched his insides.

Two soldiers of the Royal Guard approached the priest, helped him to his feet, and escorted him away.

How many minds have you tormented with your attempts to seize power, sister? Vienne asked herself. She was surprised at her own reflection; did she feel bad about Father Ovilier's fate even though he had publicly confessed that he had done everything in his power to convict her of a crime she had not committed?

"Filier Delorange," continued Meredian. At hearing his name, the nobleman stood up straight, his face solemn, his eyes looked cold, very different from the downcast look of Father Ovilier, as if the latter was willing to accept any punishment, but proud to do so, to make amends for his mistake. "Do you deny that you kept the heiress to the throne Vienne and the Knight of Water Alvia, prisoners?"

"I don't deny it, we did," Filier admitted, nodding, "we also held their dog, Zyrah, captive." He punctuated.

"Do you also confirm that it was in your domain that the life of soldier Gelegen Hurehall was terminated?"

"I confirm this, although it was not a decision I took part in."

314

"Anything else you would like to add before passing sentence?" indicated Meredian.

"While I repent for all my actions and once again seek your forgiveness, I know that my remorse can't undo my deeds."

"Having acknowledged such acts of treason," Meredian continued, "I have no choice but to condemn you to the prison of the queendom and to take you away..."

Meredian ceased his speech when he saw that the princess raised her hand to take the floor. It was not a request; it was more of a command.

"It is true that Filier Delorange was a participant in our imprisonment," Vienne acknowledged, she felt her voice waver slightly under the attentive gaze of the entire room, but this did not prevent her from continuing, "nevertheless, I consider that this man was not acting under his free will, but that his reprehensible acts were the consequence of my sister Katienne's manipulation, an art in which, unfortunately, she is skillfully versed.

That is precisely why, as soon as Filier Delorange discovered my sister's true nature, he put an end to the whole farce. After that, the heir of the house showed repentance, expressing harsh regret and releasing both me and Knight of Water Alvia."

"All right," resumed Meredian, "on the basis of the testimony of Princess Vienne, Lacrima and rightful heir to the throne, you are hereby released from..."

"I'm not finished," Vienne cut him off again. Meredian looked at her, confused, it was hard to tell if his bewilderment was due to the princess's increased self-confidence or from not knowing exactly what verdict she expected him to give. The princess merely gazed at Filier, who looked equally, if not more, bewildered than the Crown's Favourite." Filier Delorange, your support for Katienne resulted in the death of Gelegen, a great soldier and an even better man. Additionally, it jeopardized my mother, the queen's life, given my sister's refusal to surrender the sacred sword and send it to the front.

Your pleas for forgiveness seem honest as does your repentance. However, words are dangerous and sometimes they are not enough. That is why I urge you to let your actions reinforce your words."

Filier opened his mouth and stood even straighter, his eyes reflecting pure hope. "How, how can I beg your forgiveness for my house?"

"You were once willing to risk everything to please my sister, even at the expense of the Aquadom and its queen. It is time to make amends

315

for your mistake; to prove that you are willing to give your all for the Queendom of Water.

Accompany me on this journey to the front, yield to me each soldier who responds to your orders, and give me every ship of your house still anchored in the Aquo seas. Only then will I consider your repentance sincere."

"No." Filier replied, squaring his shoulders. The silent room erupted in sounds of surprise and whispers due to the nobleman's unexpected answer. "It is not punishment enough for me, allow me to command all my ships and soldiers, accompanying you myself to the front." He stood up, a soldier went to stop him, but Vienne indicated with a gesture that it was all right. "And don't think that with that my debt to you is settled. You have saved my life, that is why I take your pardon as a debt of blood. I swear before all the witnesses present that whatever is in my power to be able to help you, now and always, consider it fulfilled, I am your most humble servant."

Vienne nodded, satisfied, "I thank you."

"We hereby conclude the trial." Meredian indicated, at such words two soldiers of the Royal Guard rushed to open the doors while a third knelt to free Filier Delorange from his shackles.

The princess rose from her seat, approaching the nobleman, who was massaging his wrists. "The pain is nagging, but it will fade," Vienne pointed out to him.

"Princess Vienne, I... can't express how grateful I am..."

"Don't mention it," the princess cut him off with a smile, Filier returned the gesture with a grateful nod and turned to walk out the door, "I almost forgot, your brother Dornias asked me, if the occasion arose, to tell you that he was glad his nephew would not bear the name *Treason*, he said you would understand."

Filier's face lit up. "Lessons one gets from one's little brother, princess." He said looking much happier. Then he walked out of there.

In the throne room, only she and Meredian remained. Meredian now appeared visibly more uncomfortable.

"Again, you don't know how sorry I am, princess. I never thought something like this could ever happen... it was simply a situation beyond my control, how could I expect your sister Katienne..." he justified himself.

Since she had arrived at the palace, the apologies from the Crown's Favourite had been incessant. In a way, she couldn't blame him. The man was in a compromising situation. When Queen Graglia entrusted him with managing the reign, he could never have imagined confronting the near-total annihilation of the Congregation, allegedly by the heir to the throne. Not only Meredian's pleas for forgiveness seemed sincere, he also looked in a pitiful state; his dark circles under his eyes were accompanied by a more pronounced baldness than the last time they had met. It was more than evident that the man was not enjoying the burden of replacing the queen.

"If you still have confidence in me," the Crown's Favourite continued, "I can arrange for your embarkation as soon as possible. I am sorry to rush you after all you have been through, princess, but the situation of the Aquo troops at the front could not be more untenable." He sighed, "and to think I was stupid enough to believe that the sacred sword would already be bound for the battle line..."

"Calm down, Meredian, we're sure to be in time."

"Forgive my skepticism, princess, but the situation could not be more dramatic. The confrontation of our troops against the Fireo army on the beach of Ghandya is imminent, and if your mother were not to dispose of her sword come that day, Aqua Deus forbid, I don't want to think what could happen. Unfortunately, we would need a miracle for you to arrive in time before such a contest takes place."

A miracle, Vienne repeated in her head. A crazy idea crossed her mind.

"Meredian, I need the services of an experienced crew that can handle the Merrybelle, this is an incredibly risky maneuver, but, if it went well, we could make it in time."

The counselor rubbed his chin trying to offer her an answer.

"Our best sailors are already on the borders, I can't think of anyone, I'm sorry, princess," he replied, then raised his eyebrows, "the only available thing we have are the two Sea Guard soldiers who carried out the mission orchestrated by your sister Aienne and who retired after carrying out the mission."

Vienne nodded, "I understand that after the retribution and merits they achieved after accomplishing a mission of such caliber they won't even want to see the sea again."

"On the contrary, both refused to receive any merit or retribution for such achievements," the counselor revealed to her with a shrug,

"They refused to receive their reward? Why would they do such a thing? "

"I haven't the slightest idea," Meredian replied, with a quizzical grimace, "although, as the tax counselor, I must admit it was quite a relief, the sum they were to be given was, in my opinion, overly generous."

"Meredian, I need you to find out where said soldiers are located, I must speak with them immediately."

"It won't be necessary to search for them, princess; they are both locked up in the veterans' retreat."

The princess's hope was completely dashed. The veterans' retreat was the place where those who had been deeply shaken by the atrocities of the war resided.

46. Another route

A beggar boy with unruly reddish hair, green eyes and shredded shoes wandered among the agitated patrons of the inn. The walls of the establishment were adorned with the skins of various wild animals. He approached table by table, head down, holding out a bowl in case they offered money, food or, even better, credit. However, that large group of drunken warriors seemed too engrossed in their feast to even be aware of his presence.

"We're going to face a dragon! What better reason to drink than before prostrating ourselves in front of death! Grimm Jala!"

"Grimm Jo Ne!" responded the rest of the table moments before they all embarked on the epic mission of trying to consume their drinks in one gulp.

Hilzen, after turning in his chair to witness the raucous toast, shrugged.

"They seem glad to meet their demise." Dabayl said shaking her head. "At least they're not singing."

They had decided to have a drink in the tavern before deigning to go up to Sui Lana. That inn was crowded, as were each and every one of the streets through which they had traversed.

Noakh felt the stares of those around them. Not all of them were friendly looks. They were in Numuisa, the closest village to the place where Gurandel guarded the sacred sword, there would not only be people who would want to take their credits, but also many who would be happy to get rid of those who would stand in their way to either glory or the vanity of taking the Royal Favor.

We're not up against a dragon, we're challenging all human greed, Noakh reflected, taking a swig of his sour ale.

They had managed to get rooms in that inn. They had to gather strength, eat well and rest properly, their mounts, likewise, rested

319

comfortably in the stable, where they would eat plenty of fodder and would be sheltered from the icy wind that blew in that mountain village. Such a rest was necessary to be ready before challenging Gurandel and, of course, they were going to make sure to spend every last credit of that presumptuous king Lieri before they did so.

"By Shiana's grace, if I could get something to eat..." Noakh overheard. He had been so deep in thought that he hadn't noticed that the young boy begging for alms had approached their table.

Noakh plucked two credits from the book and extended them to him. The boy's gaze lit up, the light in his green eyes rivaling that of the fire in the bonfire that warmed the room. However, Dabayl leaned toward Noakh and blocked his hand.

"Don't even think about it." She warned him.

Those words stopped him in his tracks. The young beggar lowered his head in sorrow, his hope crumbling. Noakh raised an eyebrow, waiting for an explanation.

"If you give him credits, others will assume he has stolen them, or some of the depraved patrons here might slit his throat just to take them."

Noakh nodded. It made sense, he kept the credit book and the two credits he had torn out in his pocket. He got up from the table and started walking toward the bar.

"Boy, come with me," Noakh indicated, the young boy obeyed, walking after him, "are you hungry?" he asked, the beggar merely nodded his head. "Offer this boy whatever he wants to eat and drink," he said to the innkeeper, who was pacing back and forth behind the bar unabated. Noakh raised his eyebrows. "Aren't you looking for a young apprentice to help you in the tavern?" He said, looking at the beggar to see what he thought of the idea, the boy nodded several times.

"I wish I could," the woman replied by placing so many tankards of ale on a tray that Noakh was surprised she was able to lift so much weight, "but everything has become more expensive lately, and this sword fervor won't last forever."

"I understand," Noakh took out the credit book from his pocket, of which only a tenth remained unused, "with this you should have several years' salary once the euphoria of the sword has passed, what do you think?"

"Deal!" she agreed, snatching the book from him, then turned to her new apprentice, "young man, get to doing the dishes, quick."

The boy nodded again and leaned over to go under the bar. Suddenly he stopped, pouncing on Noakh, giving him a grateful hug. The young Fireo smiled, it felt good to use the credits for something noble for a change. Then a noise broke through the tavern's din. His curiosity got the better of him, heading out the door.

"What the...?" he exclaimed in surprise at the sight of such a spectacle. A whole army was walking through the streets of the village, in what looked like a most sinister parade.

The heavy wounks snorted, causing clouds of mist around their furry snouts. They were dragging heavy war machines, from catapults to several bolt throwers, a spectacle followed by an even more striking army formed by units of soldiers walking in perfect formation. Swordsmen walked with their right arms steady, spearmen resting the shaft of their weapon on their chest and archers with one of their hands resting on their shoulder... and, worst of all, the parade was concluded by a disorganized yet vast group of menacing warriors who adorned their clothing and light armor with human remains; arms, fingers, even a half-rotten head hung from the belt of one of them, looking towards Noakh with empty eyes full of flies.

He searched among those miscreants, knowing he was going to find her.

There you are, he said to himself, clenching his jaw and frowning. The despicable Suruyana, the one who had snatched part of his right earlobe and who had brutally killed Yarna's husband, was walking along talking casually with a man with a black tattoo covering his forehead.

I'm sure she still has my piece of ear with her as a trophy. Instinctively, Noakh brought his hand to Distra's hilt. *One thrust and all that scum would cease to be a danger to the world*, he pondered.

He pulled his hand away from the hilt, annoyed with himself.

Why, in spite of knowing full well that these people were going to do nothing but cause death, pain and suffering, did an inner strength restrain him from wiping them all out in one fell swoop?

At that moment he heard a muffled scream. A man was clutching his throat, his legs jerking from side to side.

"Damn bastards!" Noakh exclaimed angrily, rushing up to the badly wounded man. The latter looked at him with fear in his eyes, with the hope of someone who seemed to deny a death he unconsciously knew to be irremediable.

However, Noakh put his hands to his neck, took down the flask of holy water that Gelegen had given them, opened it, and tilted it to let a

321

few drops fall on the man's wound. It closed little by little, the man continued to writhe for a while, until he noticed with astonishment that his wound had vanished.

"Tha... thank you," he said, looking at Noakh as if he were witnessing a ghost, "are you a healer? A wizard, perhaps?"

"Something like that," Noakh replied, hanging the flask back around his neck and tucking it behind his robes. He then turned his gaze back, eyes tracking those miscreants as they retreated. "What did you do to earn a slit throat?" he mused.

"I... I don't know. I just ran into them, and they decided to kill me," he grimaced. "They laughed as they walked away with their knife still soaked with my blood."

Noakh had heard enough. He gritted his teeth, who did they think they were to carry out such a massacre? And why would the Aere Tine authorities allow such a thing? He reached for his swords, ready to reproach them for their despicable acts.

"Calm down," said Dabayl, grabbing him by the hand, "there are too many of them, Noakh, even your flaming sword will not be enough. One arrow to the head and there will be no sacred sword to save you."

The young Fireo tried to reproach her, but, unfortunately, she was right.

"Are we going to let that gang of bastards get away with this?" asked Hilzen in annoyance.

"The only thing we can do is to find Tizai as soon as possible and put an end to this macabre game." Dabayl said. "If this city is suffering these hardships, it is more than likely that other cities are similarly plunged into chaos."

* * *

They had taken another route to avoid crossing paths with that gigantic army. The hooves of their horses made their way through the snow, the route was silent, allowing the *crunch, crunch, crunch* of the hoofbeats and the snorting of the horses to take center stage. Noakh urged his horse to go a little faster in order to get closer to Dabayl, who was leading the march.

"Stop being so quiet, Dabayl." Noakh said. He then turned to Hilzen, putting his hand in front of his mouth. "You think she's plotting against us again?" He sneered, speaking loudly and clearly so she could hear him.

"I'm sure she is," Hilzen replied, "I'm surprised she didn't sell us to the innkeeper in exchange for a drink."

Dabayl shook her head, turning a deaf ear to their provocations. "If my calculations do not fail me, we must be in Sui Lana's outskirts."

"Great, now there's only the simplest thing left," Hilzen sneered, "snatching the sword from a fire-breathing dragon."

The terrifying sight suddenly ended all the fun. Noakh could not believe his eyes, countless men and women were hanging from the icy trees on the slopes of Sui Lana. He felt an immense revulsion. Small vultures were feasting on them, conscientiously pecking at the bloody cavities of a man whose face was as white as snow. This massacre reminded him of the unlit city square, the place where Rivet died in front of his eyes.

They approached, under that carnage hung a wooden sign that had acquired a reddish tone after being soaked in blood. The following message could be read on it: *Your adventure ends here, if you continue you know the price of not paying.*

Behind that display of corpses was a wall made of stone and snow, blocking access except at one end, where several men covered in furs were waiting for them, some pointing their bows at them, others leaning the long handles of their huge axes on the snow.

They rode forward to confront them. They welcomed them with a nod and a smile of superiority that signaled that they were fully aware that they had them at their mercy.

"Price for allowing us to pass?" inquired Dabayl.

"One thousand gold coins or credits." They were informed by a rosy-cheeked woman whose neck was covered in white fur.

Dabayl held out her hand to Noakh, urging him to give her the credits he had in his pocket. The latter shook his head, motioning to turn around, certain there would be another way.

"We can't afford to take a detour, Noakh." Dabayl informed him, "we have no choice."

"You've got to be kidding me." Hilzen replied indignantly.

"I'm not going to give anything to these bastards." Noakh declared, not caring if that band of ruffians heard him. He was sick of seeing what an abhorrent game the quest for the sword had become.

Dabayl offered no more words. She merely fixed her yellow eyes on Noakh, ensuring he understood there was no alternative.

"All right, damn it," he said. Tugging on the reins, his horse made its way through the access. He dropped the two credits from his pocket at the feet of one of the miscreants.

47. Challenge

Vienne dismounted her horse, and took Zyrah out of the leather saddlebag where she had kept her during the journey. This time, she was not traveling alone; After her last solitary journey resulting in her being captured, Meredian had pleaded with her to accept an escort. Though initially reluctant, she had eventually agreed. Five soldiers of the Royal Guard and her Aunt Alvia accompanied her. All had similarly dismounted: three poised to draw their swords and two with bows at the ready, scanning for distant threats. Her Aunt Alvia, on the other hand, merely walked at ease, not showing the slightest concern.

Walking alongside Zyrah, the princess approached the veterans' retreat—a secluded, tranquil retreat for those deeply marked by the ravages of war. The house was three stories high and was of a more than considerable width, although its structure looked old and the wood in certain parts looked decayed, this did not hide the fact that such a house was a mansion that could well belong to a wealthy noble family.

It belonged to House Naudine, Vienne recalled. She then recognized that Laenise, one of the nobles accompanying Aienne, was the heiress of that family. That house had long ago ceased to belong to that lineage, apparently one of the members of that family had become a soldier and, as a result of his passage through some war that Vienne did not remember, he ended up in need of care. That was the reason why the Naudine family had donated that place, so that he and any soldier who required attention would be cared for with the attention deserved by those who fought to defend their home.

It was a beautiful place: flat land with several fruit trees around it and numerous growing areas such as tomatoes, rice, and artichokes. Plantations that would surely not only provide food for those who stayed there, but would also keep their tortured minds occupied.

She found it curious that such a well-intentioned, beautiful domain evoked in her a profound sense of aversion. It was difficult to explain, perhaps it was because that place showed the worst face of the war, those who had been brutally mutilated both inside and out.

Zyrah approached a woman, her tousled gray hair standing out, as she knelt against the trunk of a robust oak tree. The little dog began to sniff her boots, then slowly walked around her. Concerned about the woman, the princess also approached, from closer she perceived that she had her forehead resting on the gray bark of that tree and that she seemed to be saying something, it did not take many steps for her murmur to become intelligible.

"Death, death, death, death, death..." she repeated over and over again.

A chill coursed through Vienne. This woman epitomized the retreat's residents: soldiers who'd given all for the queendom and bore the scars of their sacrifices.

"Silbai," Vienne indicated, thus prompting the canine to cease her interest in the woman and come to her side. "Take a walk with Aunt Alvia, Zyrah." She indicated. Zyrah then began to walk away on her own, searching for the Knight of Water.

On the porch, a middle-aged man, missing both an arm and a leg, sat in an armchair. Beside him, a young woman energetically cut his hair. Glancing her over swiftly, she did not display any symbol in honor of the Aqua Deus on her clothes, nor did she wear the usual mermaid tail symbol wrapped around a cane; this meant she was neither a nun, a doctor, nor a nurse. Perhaps she was a volunteer, it wouldn't be unusual; many people chose to dedicate their lives to helping others. Sometimes it was out of pure altruism; other times, it was in exchange for free room and board.

The only sound that filled the porch was the soft *snip, snip* of the scissors, methodically snipping away at the long golden locks of the injured soldier.

"Excuse me," Vienne began, "I am looking for two soldiers who are staying here, they are Otine and Erin Saboyl."

"Oh, yes," said the volunteer, continuing her task with meticulous care, "two of the last soldiers to arrive in this grim place. They were badly touched after their last mission."

"So I've heard, would there be any chance of talking to them? It's vitally important."

"It depends," the young woman replied, catching the soldier's bangs between her index and middle finger, she began to cut them, "who is asking for them and for what purpose?"

"My name is Vienne Dajalam, and I need their talent to reach the border with Firia as soon as possible."

"Ouch!" The young woman yelped as she accidentally cut her index finger with the scissors, she put her finger to her mouth to lick the blood off, "the heir to the throne?" She said, still with her finger in her mouth.

The princess merely nodded, sensing a release within herself as she did so. She no longer had to feel bad about admitting that she was the heir.

"I'm sorry, Nescar," the young woman said, laying the scissors on the small table beside her, then tapping the soldier on the shoulder twice. "But this young lady seems to have important business to attend to, I'll continue with your haircut later." She began to walk, opening the door to the mansion, "follow me."

They entered the room. It looked exactly the same on the inside as it did on the outside, beautiful and gloomy in equal measure. Elegant pillars curled in the shape of waves, a worn reddish carpet full of both dried and fresh stains that Vienne preferred not to know what kind of fluids they would harbor and an ocher wooden handrail whose knob ended in the shape of a horse riding on the waves whose front legs were broken... an elegance left behind that had been consumed by the most absolute decadence. The smell in that place was tremendously strong and, as much as Vienne wanted to avoid thinking about it, very unpleasant, so pungent that she couldn't help but wrinkle her nose.

Numerous individuals occupied the room, sprawled on chairs, armchairs, and even tables; they being cared for by what was obviously a sparse group of caregivers and nurses. She followed the young woman up the stairs, however, as she climbed the steps, she couldn't help but stop staring at that room, focusing on a woman being attended to by a priest. She felt an emptiness in her stomach, wasn't that woman missing a significant portion of her face? She had to make an immeasurable effort not to vomit before such a shocking sight.

The young woman who was guiding her through the place made her way with brisk confidence. The gloomy atmosphere did not seem to affect her in the least, greeting cheerfully the people she met on her way, whether they were caregivers or the sick.

"My cousin Erin was very disturbed after the incident with the Tower of Concord," she revealed, after giving a friendly pat to a yellow-faced man who was looking down the stairwell with vacant eyes.

Her cousin, Vienne thought, her eyes widened as she realized the identity of her companion.

"Oh, don't mind me," she continued as she turned and saw the surprised look on the princess' face, "I'm simply here in case Erin needs anything, she's the one who will demand explanations from you."

Of course she will want explanations, Vienne mused. The plan to send those soldiers and two Sons of the Church to destroy the Tower of Concord and thus force the kingdom of Aere Tine into action had been hatched by Aienne. If such information had reached the soldiers, they would surely want to know why they had been given a mission that practically sent them to their deaths. In a way, she would have liked Aienne to be with her at that moment, so that she would be aware of the repercussions of her decisions.

They passed through a corridor, where a young woman with several bald patches in her curly hair pointed to a spot on the wall, stood petrified for a moment and then pointed to another. Next to her a man was curled up in a ball, rocking agitatedly on the floor.

Such visions sent a shiver down the princess's spine. *Young men dream of the honor of war, but no one tells them of its horrors,* she considered, overwhelmed by the desolation of the scene. She was aware that many of the soldiers there had not given enough thought to the consequences before enlisting. *I don't even want to think about how many people will be dragged to this gloomy place when the war against Firia is over.*

"It's here," she indicated, situating herself at a door that appeared to have been scratched. Without meaning to, Otine performed the Aquo reverence, showing her soldierly instincts.

"All right, thank you," Vienne said, approaching the door. "Won't you come in with me? It also concerns what I must ask of you."

Otine waved her hand. "My fate is tied to Erin's; her answer will be mine as well."

"I understand." Then she clenched her jaw and opened the door. The room was sparsely furnished, with only an unmade bed, its sheets strewn on the floor, and a rocking chair facing the window. Erin was rocking in it, watching the view out the window, oblivious to anyone who had entered the room.

Vienne closed the door and took several steps.

"Soldier Erin," Vienne said after clearing her throat, "I've come to talk to you."

After speaking, she stood still, waiting for her to respond. However, the soldier seemed not to have heard her, continuing to rock looking out the window oblivious to her presence.

The princess decided to move a little closer, her footsteps now causing the old floorboard to emit an annoying *creak* with each step. She stopped near the soldier, looking out the window as well. She smiled, it was a beautiful view overlooking a huge field of rose bushes in one of which just happened to be Zyrah offering it an extra dose of watering.

"What a beautiful view, I'm sure it relaxes you a lot..."

Slam! Erin's huge swat on the armrest of her rocking chair silenced the princess.

"Don't you dare speak to me with the same condescension that others at this retreat deserve." Erin replied sharply, offering her a furious glare. "I just want a place to rest and forget all the pain we have caused. Leave me alone, the soldier I once was died in that explosion."

"I understand," Vienne replied. "If that soldier were here, I'd tell her that she wasn't to blame, that she was just following orders."

"Well, if she would listen to you, she would tell you that she was the one in charge of the mission and that she has no doubt that the Aqua Deus will judge her for her actions." She replied annoyed.

Vienne raised her eyebrows, realizing a most refreshing detail. Most soldiers did not feel guilty for the deaths they had caused. In part, she could understand the mindset of those who felt that way. Yes, they had been the executing hand, however, they had done nothing more than act in obedience to the orders of a superior officer. A pretext that, for the vast majority, was enough to not feel bad about the brutal and bloody deaths they had committed. This soldier, on the other hand, felt responsible for what happened after the destruction of the Tower of Concord, even though she was only doing her duty as a soldier of the queendom.

"Leave, please," Erin asked her, in what sounded more like a command than a request, looking back out the window. "I've already given up everything. I'm not even a Sea Guard soldier anymore, I just want to rest and reflect on what I did."

"I'd love to leave and let you rest, but I need to ask you something..."

"Ask me something?" she replied indignantly looking her up and down, "who are you?"

"I am Vienne Dajalam," she revealed.

For an instant, Erin's face showed curiosity, a brief sigh before turning red with rage.

"Wasn't it your sister who orchestrated that crazy mission we embarked on? The one who didn't hesitate to have us provoke a conflict of such caliber while she sipped tea and sat her royal ass in a comfortable palace chair? Do you know all that we had to go through to get to the Tower of Concord? All those who will die because of her irresponsible decision?"

The soldier spoke with such indignation that Vienne felt droplets from her forceful words hit her face.

"My sister planned that mission with the aim of saving me, that by doing so I would not have to face King Wulkan." Vienne revealed to her, "you paid for the sisterly love she feels for me, so I apologize on her behalf and also on mine."

"Will your apologies make those who will die because of us come back to life?" She said sharply.

"No..."

Slam!

"Then shove your worthless apologies up your ass!" She replied, rising so violently that the rocking chair toppled over. Erin stared wide-eyed at the princess, her chest heaving with rage, then she put her hands to her head and leaned against the wall.

"Leave me alone and go away... I've already completed my assigned mission, now I just want to rest and try to forgive myself for all the lives that will be lost as a result of my actions."

"Listen to me, I have already apologized to you. Among the many powers conferred upon me by the sacred sword is not that of returning to the past, so I can do no more. But there's one thing I can offer. If the weight of lives lost due to your actions burdens you so, then take the helm of the Merrybelle and take me to the front lines before it's too late. We may save countless lives, including that of the queen herself."

"The Merrybelle?" She said with a frown, "the queen?"

"That's right, it's a suicide mission even for someone as seasoned in perilous assignments as you and soldier Otine."

"No... you're lying to me, I'm sure it's about more deaths," she said shaking her head, "my conscience is already too heavy, princess."

"If you come with me, I will tell you everything in detail, I promise. I simply wish to count on your services to reach the beach of Ghandya in time. I must deliver this to my mother," she said, tapping Crystaline's hilt with her index finger. "We could save countless Aquo lives, soldier Erin, but we need to get there before it is too late, I have a plan that is insane, but perhaps with your talent and that of soldier Otine it can work."

"An insane plan..." she replied with a snort. "Trust me, princess, after descending a gigantic waterfall and crossing a wall of tornadoes I don't think there's anything that would surprise me at this point."

Vienne smiled at Erin's disbelief. "Do you want to bet?"

48. Straight to her jaws

They rode in single file, riding slowly. Dabayl took the lead, followed by Hilzen, who constantly glanced nervously from side to side, with Noakh bringing up the rear.

The wind blew against them, as if urging them to cease their efforts, to come to their senses to not confront the dragoness and turn back.

They had not yet come across anyone descending from that place. *So many go up, none come down,* Noakh felt a shudder as he imagined the fate of all those who had decided to stand up to Gurandel, certainly many of them would have been torn to pieces as brutally as the dragoness had done to the sinister beings with stitched voices and scythe-like hands that once stalked her in the cave, which had been her prison for so long.

It was curious what human greed was capable of, he considered, being even enough to cloud sanity and make all those people believe that they had the slightest chance of facing a dragon and snatching the sword from her. His reflection made his gaze fix on Dabayl, whose reddish hair had already grown slightly, *it is not always greed,* he realized, *many people who are traveling all the way to Sui Lana do it to fulfill their dreams and illusions, for the mere hope.* Thinking about it, there were even those who would have gone to that place without even wanting the Royal Favor... that's how powerful human courage was.

The tall, bare trees lining their path had thick trunks as black as coal. The ground was blanketed in green moss and snow, it was as if nature and sky were fighting their own dispute to decide who reigned in that territory. The slope was getting steeper and steeper, the wind was blowing harder and harder. The whole environment seemed to insist on appearing unpleasant, to point out to them with its grotesque and hostile aspect that they should not be there.

He glanced back. It didn't look like anyone else was coming up the mountain.

Even so, they had to hurry; the army they had witnessed at Numuisa seemed dangerous. Those war machines were really imposing, if they wanted to have a chance they had to hurry before that terrifying army reached Sui Lana. Soldiers and prisoners, a lethal combination.

Fortunately, those giant bolt throwers seemed hardly transportable over that mountain, it would surely take them a long time to be a threat. If all went well—a very optimistic view given the situation—they would have dealt with Gurandel and recovered the sword before such an army reached Sui Lana.

Noakh kicked his heels into the horse's sides, noting that his mount's pace was slowing.

"Easy, Acorns," he murmured, patting his horse's muscular neck. He had named his mount after the horse's peculiar fondness for the tree seeds, often stopping to munch on them with evident relish.

"Come on, walk!" cursed Hilzen to his own mount.

It's as if they knew... thought Noakh, *as if their animal instinct sensed the danger. They are able to detect that they are approaching a dragon's lair. It's funny,* he reflected, *animals act wisely, they know when it's time to flee, to get away from the place where a creature they are unable to defeat is hiding. Humans, on the other hand, seem to find a certain satisfaction in turning their lives against common sense.*

Dabayl descended from the horse. Noakh pulled on the reins to get closer to his companion. They were not there yet, had she spotted anything?

As he reached the height of Dabayl, he could not help but open his mouth to such horror. In that plain there were several bonfires full of people. People without arms, without legs, several being attended to, some crying at the fallen body of a comrade while others seemed to be trying to revive their loved ones, no matter how obvious it was that those people were no longer breathing.

The scenery was most desolate.

A man with a bushy gray beard approached them. He walked steadily, gripping his horse's reins, his eyes so red they looked bloodshot. On the saddle, tied, was a figure covered from top to bottom in a gray blanket.

Upon seeing them, he paused, "listen to the advice of this man who has already witnessed the horror you are about to face. Neither the Royal Favor, nor a thousand songs, nor glory are worth it in exchange for such martyrdom, heed me, turn around and live another day, surrounded by your loved ones. I wish someone had given us this advice when we arrived here." The man said desolately, then departed. "If I had taken my own advice, maybe then my daughter would still be alive."

Noakh swallowed hard at such words.

They took the opportunity to rest on the open plain. They approached one of the campfires, sitting around the fire. Initially, they believed two men were seated there, but upon closer inspection, they realized the men were dead. Their bluish faces staring at the horizon.

They extracted the provisions from the saddlebags of their horses. It was one of the advantages of having obtained a patronage, they had abundant food reserves and varied clothing to face the freezing cold that reigned in such an inhospitable place. In retrospect, Noakh would have considered it impossible to have reached Sui Lana had it not been for having obtained the patronage of King Lieri.

Night had fallen. The flames of the fire crackled, Hilzen brought his hands close to warm them. They heard someone approaching through the darkness as a greenish light grew closer and closer, Noakh reached for his steels in case it was people seeking to lessen their competition by taking advantage of the blanket of stars.

"Would you like a song to liven up the... well, if it isn't you!"

The three turned around, confused. A familiar face carrying a lute stood smiling at them.

"Halftal?" said Noakh, halfway between surprise and joy at seeing her again, "what are you doing here, are you going to confront the dragon?"

"Of course not," she said bending down slightly to embrace each of them, "I am here to encourage with my music those who have decided to face the dragon... or try to ease their sorrows if they return alive grieving defeat."

"But, Emisai," Dabayl began, "if you are here, it means that your dream of having your song approved by the Cloister of Music was not fulfilled..." she said sorrowfully.

"That's right, my song was risky," she replied sadly, "but that's fine! You know? Something told me I'd see you guys around sooner or later."

They invited Halftal to sit with them and tell them about her journey. They also shared their reasons for traveling to Sui Lana.

Noakh took a deep breath, "I've been thinking..." Noticing Hilzen's raised eyebrow and impending interjection, he quickly added, "no, I'm not going to propose to take on Gurandel by myself."

"You are not?" replied Hilzen looking at him in confusion.

"No, we must face Gurandel together. I just think it's obvious that facing her on her turf is not the best option," he said, extending his arms towards all the fallen and depleted there.

"And this is just a paltry sample of the deaths and maimed that the dragon has left in its wake," Halftal revealed to them, grimacing, "so much death..."

"Of course!" said Hilzen, "Noakh, you already cut off Gurandel's tail with Distra. Surel the dragoness will run away if you confront her."

Noakh shook his head, "I didn't think Gurandel was afraid of anyone or anything. That's why I'd better talk to her and, depending on what she tells me, we'll act," he proposed, not coming up with anything better.

"No!" said Hilzen indignantly. "Are you telling me you're just going to talk to her, Noakh?" then he turned to Dabayl. "And what are you laughing at if I may ask?"

"I'm just fascinated you made it all the way to Aere Tine alive with those witticisms you two have." She said amused.

Halftal frowned, turning into the darkness of the night. "Someone's coming." Thereupon, their horses neighed nervously.

It was Hilzen who picked up one of the logs that were on the bonfire and threw it toward where the noise came from. Half a dozen men stealthily approached, their swords ready to slay them in the darkness, as soon as they saw that they had been discovered they charged angrily.

Suddenly, a flash of light illuminated the esplanade. The attackers stopped abruptly at the sight of his flaming sword.

"Any problem?" Noakh challenged them.

In the face of that power, their enemies put away their weapons without saying anything, walking backwards with their hands up to show them that they no longer had bad intentions.

"Noakh, if you don't kill them, they will attack us while we sleep." Dabayl indicated with an arrow nocked in her bow.

"Dabayl is right, Noakh, it's happened many times since I've been here..."

Despite their words of warning, Noakh sheathed his sword.

"In that case, let's continue on our course. It's time to greet Gurandel."

336

49. Awakening the storm

Vienne stood at the bow of the Merrybelle, her gaze lost in a sea that seemed particularly calm that day, as if those waters had no clue what they were about to be part of. Such was its calmness that it faithfully reflected the image of the crescent moon in its waters. A gigantic moon that was in front of them, giving the sensation that, if they continued sailing, they would eventually reach it.

The gentle, yet freezing rain lashed the deck of the Merrybelle, chilling Vienne to the bone. Her aunt approached her, looking at her with concern.

"Are you sure you want to do this, Vienne?" she asked.

This concern on the part of her aunt astonished her. After all, it came from someone who not long ago had not shown the slightest qualms about letting her confront Noakh, who, at that moment, appeared to be a brutal and bloodthirsty killer wielding a flaming sword.

"Yes, there's no other way to get there on time." She replied. Meredian had been clear, her mother was in danger, and, with her, whatever remained of the queendom's army.

She felt a weight on one of her legs; she lowered her head. A soaked Zyrah began to whimper, catching her attention. Vienne smiled and stroked her head twice.

You feel the danger too, don't you? But there's no choice, it's either this or risk not making it in time. In fact, it will be better to hurry and get it done as soon as possible.

She took a deep breath and raised her sword. She heard a whimper again.

"This is going to be very dangerous, Zyrah. Wouldn't you rather be comfortable and safe in the cabin?" she suggested her, however, the little dog didn't move, staying seated next to her even though she was shivering. "Fine then, you can stay and protect me."

She placed the sword even higher. Then she turned for a mere instant, her aunt clinging to one of the ship's ropes, Soldier Erin at the wheel, accompanied by Otine, who was to guide her on what promised to be a wild voyage.

It appears everyone is ready. She then glanced at the stern where twenty ships of the Delorange family sailed. Filier had kept his word, leading the fleet.

It is time, she decided.

She turned to the front and looked up at the gray sky as raindrops ran down her face. She felt a shiver of nervousness at what she was about to accomplish. Crystaline's tip pointed toward the expectant moon.

"Crystaline, please grant me your power."

Vienne's gaze lost her humanity as soon as the blade began to soak in. She stretched out her arm, sword held high, as if she were showing the blade to the immense sea, challenging the moon itself.

"Release the storm."

The sky responded to her demand with a gigantic bolt of lightning that struck not far away in the middle of the sea, the sky was completely illuminated, an instant later came the thunderous noise. The rain began to fall with the intensity of an ocean descending from the heavens. The Merrybelle, meanwhile, began to heave bravely at the increasing ferocity of the swell.

The storm had been invoked and, with it, sea and sky merged as one.

The words of her caretaker Igüenza echoed in her head as if, even from a distance, she was urging her not to do such a thing.

There is a reason they are called blessings, one way or another they help the sword bearer. Your ancestor, however, was blinded by such power. This is something we are not allowed to teach princesses, as it is a black mark on the history of the royal family, but I think it is important for you to know. Dajalam, the first of the royal family, died using the power of the sacred sword.

She wanted to test the limits of her power. That is why she entered the waters and invoked all her power, releasing the storm. Sea and sky become one, beginning and end converge to heed the request of the bearer, resulting in a wave so gigantic that rises to the heavens, Magnazar.

338

Dajalam died for her own thirst for power, ravaging several coastal cities in the process.

That is why, Vienne, Nazar te acto—the storm that unites sky and sea—is not considered a blessing but a curse. A curse that exemplifies how power corrupts, how asking for too much can lead to the perdition of oneself and of what one has sworn to protect.

The water was falling with more intensity, the waves were rocking more and more fiercely. At the bottom, a gigantic wave seemed to be rising from the very bowels of the sea. A flash of lightning illuminated the skies and the water, allowing her to discern how countless mermaids swirled around the Merrybelle, swimming at such a frenetic pace that they seemed to be on a purple and sky-blue whirlpool. Those mystical creatures seemed to be in ecstasy, the Lacrima had finally heard them, the storm had been released.

The water seemed intent on proving it could get even rougher, as if its fury had only just begun.

Vienne craned her head up as far as her neck would allow. The titanic Magnazar had broken through into the sky. Its size, compared to the Merrybelle, made the vessel seem like a mere human toy in the presence of a giant.

She sheathed her sword and, in doing so, fell to her knees on the deck, resting both hands on the dripping wood of the swaying ship. Such an invocation had completely drained her energy. She felt something warm and moist run across her right hand, Zyrah, appearing half her size from being thoroughly drenched, tried in her own way to offer her unconditional support.

She had done her part, now it was up to the helmswoman and the navigator to get them out of there alive.

* * *

Erin's mouth remained open, staring in awe at the majestic and imposing Magnazar. Not long ago she would have sworn that nothing could surprise her after she had crossed a wall of tornadoes and jumped through Finistia itself. Now she saw that this world still had much to amaze her.

She could not suppress a stupid, sickly laugh as she witnessed the gigantic wave that announced itself before her. Even having witnessed with her own eyes how such a monstrosity had originated, it was hard for her to believe that she was in the face of such an atmospheric phenomenon. The sea had become so tumultuous that no maritime term she knew seemed adequate to describe its fury.

"Turn gently to port," Otine managed to instruct her after she came out of her trance watching the wave with awe.

Soldier Erin gripped the helm as tightly as her hands would allow, following the instructions Otine had given her. The Merrybelle set course, heading towards the immense wave, oblivious to any danger.

So much power wielded by a mere teenager, Erin mused, allowing herself to look away from the raging sea for a quick glance at the deck. Knight of Water Alvia was helping the princess walk and leading her to a cabin. Zyrah followed, struggling to move forward on the wildly rocking vessel.

Her attention returned to the raging waters and the huge wave they had to face. *Once again in charge of a suicide mission plotted by one of the Dajalam princesses,* she thought, realizing that no doubt the members of the royal family were of a peculiar nature.

She gladly accepted the challenge. The princess had done her part by summoning the Magnazar wave, and thankfully, not destroying any coastal villages of the queendom in the process. Now it was her and Otine's turn to make sure they reached their destination without that titanic wave destroying them into a thousand pieces.

It was time to get on board such a watery monstrosity. She glanced at Otine, who waved her hand, indicating that she should turn slightly to starboard. The noise of that gigantic wave was terrifying, it was difficult to distinguish between what water was coming from the rain and what was coming from that colossal watery mass. Just as Princess Vienne had described, the sky and sea had become one.

Otine began to move her lips, mentally performing her calculations as her eyes were lost in the titanic wave, then instructed her to stay on course. Erin nodded, trusting her navigator completely. It was wrong for her to admit it herself, but she had no doubt that she and her cousin made an incomparable team. She turned momentarily to check on the Delorange family vessels following them. Suddenly, one of those ships made an abrupt movement, being swallowed up by the fierce waves as if it had never been there before.

She gripped the wheel of the rudder firmly; despite the drama of the situation, she couldn't help but feel excited about steering the Merrybelle. She had heard talk about the ridiculous speed that caravel could reach, and even the most exaggerated rumor had fallen short. The speed with which that light craft ploughed the fierce waters was to be admired. So much so, that there were numerous legends about that ship, her favorite being the one that said that the vessel had belonged to a sailor so devoted that when he died his spirit had not reached the sea, but had refused to stop sailing, dwelling on the Merrybelle forever.

The ship was approaching the titanic wave, they had to be extremely careful in their course if they did not want the Magnazar to destroy them as if they were hitting a wall. As she gripped the helm firmly, she periodically turned her head towards Otine, who simply continued to move her lips, tracing a route that would allow them to climb the wave and, incidentally, not die in the attempt.

"Turn all to port." She finally instructed her.

Erin nodded. Then she clenched her jaw, even for a vessel as formidable as the Merrybelle, this was going to be a challenging endeavor.

The ship plunged into the wave. Erin gritted her teeth, straining to maintain a firm grip on the helm. The Merrybelle quivered, as though the sea were debating whether to yield to the vessel or shatter it into fragments.

"Come on!" cheered Erin to the vessel.

The Merrybelle delved deeper into the wave, shaking and churning so fiercely it felt as if it could be torn to pieces at any moment. Nevertheless, it kept moving forward.

Erin breathed deeply, her mouth agape from the effort. They stood on the crest of the Magnazar, untouched. She felt a tingling in her stomach. Otine moved closer to her cousin, Erin allowed herself the risky luxury of releasing one hand from the helm wheel to melt into an ecstatic embrace with her. Both of them were ecstatic; they had managed to master the world's biggest wave.

"The Delorange ships!" Otine alerted her cousin.

Erin turned, never letting go of the rudder wheel. The ships following them were trying to ride the gigantic wave, several being consumed by it in the process. The soldier paled, *at this rate, none of their ships will survive....*

At that moment her eyes returned to the deck, Princess Vienne was there again, pointing her sword out into the waters while her Aunt Alvia held her so that she would not vanish over the deck.

Her eyes turned back to the Delorange ships. She opened her mouth at such a sight, the fleet was being led to the crest of the wave by sirens and gigantic creatures with countless tentacles.

341

50. Unforgivable rudeness

Countless crows flitted around the garden, several perched on the railing, where Yunea and Winay entertained themselves by feeding them some seed bread.

"Can't we play now, momoi?" said Yunea as a crow pecked at the small pieces of bread in her palm.

"I'm afraid not," Laon, who was watching them intently, replied, "your mother has a very important meeting to attend."

Daikan Arbilla smiled as she watched the two siblings entertain themselves feeding the birds. She and Laon had decided to adopt them, the two siblings who had carried the flag on Noakh's unickey army, as they so proudly liked to boast.

I wish they had met my ayoi, she thought wistfully.

As she remembered her grandfather, her gaze fell on a small wooden table next to the throne, on the white tablecloth that covered it were the three letters of condolences that had arrived. Queen Zarta and King Lieri had each sent a message, both praising the great deeds of Burum Babar. Lieri in particular, had insisted throughout his writing on the profound impact and the great reference that Burum Babar had been for him in understanding how to govern a people with wisdom.

Arbilla had been informed about the fall of the Tower of Concord. As far as she knew, the Aertians had no idea who had been responsible for its destruction and, consequently, this meant that they were surely weighing the possibility that it had been the work of the Tirhan people. She was moved, *even if they suspected that it was us, it did not prevent them from writing a letter of condolences...*

Despite this, the letter from King Wulkan was the most moving and sincere for Arbilla. His words had touched her heart, in his writing he had remembered anecdotes lived between him and her ayoi, how they had shared stories during great dinners full of unforgettable moments.

343

Arbilla could perceive the real regret in his letter, the sadness and affection of a man who was saying goodbye and paying tribute to a friend he would no longer be able to visit, ending his farewell with words of support and strength to the new Daikan.

Three letters, three kings paying their respects. And a queendom that had been indifferent to the death of Burum Babar.

"Mahesen, is it possible that Queen Graglia's letter has gone astray?" proposed Arbilla, striving not to be ill-considered.

"I cannot assure you that this is not so, my Daikan," the counselor replied, clasping his hands together, "however, considering that the Aquos are at war, perhaps Queen Graglia has not had time to write a message of condolence."

"That woman is at war with King Wulkan, and he did have time to write a detailed and moving letter." Arbilla indicated, then sighed, wearily. "Always them, always the Aquos. One way or another, they seem to enjoy belittling us..."

The doors of the royal hall opened. Juray, with his saber resting on his shoulder, appeared leading the march, followed by those who had decided to enter Tirhan waters uninvited.

Of course, yet another discourteous act from the incorrigible Dajalam family—another Aquo princess daring to enter my domain without permission. She had decided to have them locked up for a while, hoping the punishment would dampen their spirits.

"Come with me, I will teach you how crows fly," said the Gray Raven, taking with him an interested Yunea, who hurried to take Mahesen's hand, and a not so enthusiastic Winay, who walked behind them with folded arms as he watched with increased interest those prisoners.

The captives entered the room following Juray. It was Princess Aienne who stumbled on the step, being assisted by that handsome Aquo, Dornias.

Behind their prisoners, Garland followed, "kneel down, you idiots." He instructed with his usual gruffness once the captives were at the proper distance from the Daikan.

The Aquo prisoners obeyed immediately, squinting against the intense morning light filtering through the colored mosaics behind Arbilla, "tell me, what is your motive for sailing through Tirhan waters without my consent? I take it for granted that you are aware that Princess Vienne took the audacity to also enter our waters and walk these lands without the slightest blush, so I will not tolerate any lies about it," before they answered she turned her gaze to her wolf soldiers,

344

"Juray, Garland, at the slightest hint of deception in their speech I order you to cut out their tongues."

Juray needed no further instruction to draw his sharp saber. Garland grinned, his blackish teeth gleaming as he pulled a rusty knife from the side of his pants.

Arbilla's hand rested on the pommel of one of her sheathed swords, "depending on your words, a cell may be the least of your worries compared to the fate that awaits you: death." She made it clear to them.

"No!" said Princess Aienne, her eyes showing terror that such was their fate. "We travel to help a... friend." Her hesitation and lack of precision in her answer caused Juray to take two steps in her direction with saber held high, ready to carry out his judgment. "Noakh! We travel to help Noakh, you know who we're talking about." She revealed, ducking her head.

The Daikan couldn't believe what she was hearing, "Noakh?" she said with a frown, "explain yourself."

Aienne's eyes darted fearfully toward Juray, whose gleaming saber blade was still perilously close to her and her companions. Arbilla waved her hand, an act sufficient for the soldier to retreat back to his position, placing himself back beside Garland. The nobles seemed to look at the princess sideways, as if trying to convey to her that it was not a good idea to tell her the whole truth. However, the young girl did not seem to answer to anyone. She began to speak, narrating in detail why they had decided to set out on their journey.

After hearing the reason for their wanderings, Arbilla could not help but laugh at the idea of such a journey. They did not even know Noakh and yet they were willing to cross the seas for him.

Now she understood why Burum Babar had chosen that young man to end his life. Gond and Garland had told her everything: how her ayoi had asked to engage him in a final combat so that he, Burum Babar, would reach the paradise Tir Na Nog prior to an epic confrontation, as someone like him deserved. And Noakh had agreed to her ayoi's request, not because he enjoyed the slaughter, not to boast of having ended the life of a Daikan, he had simply agreed out of an act of charity, because he wanted to help him. And that was something she could not be angry with.

"I see that your words seem sincere. The reason for your journey, though peculiar, seems to make some sense. However, I fear that, as Daikan, it is my duty to make certain that your extravagant expedition has no ulterior motives that would endanger Tir Torrent or its people."

Arbilla turned again to her soldiers, "Garland, your friend left with Noakh and his companions, didn't she?"

"Halftal," the soldier stated. "That's right, that stupid girl wanted to travel to the Kingdom of Air and decided that..."

"Enough," Arbilla cut him off, not wanting to listen any longer to the tongue-twisting Tirhan, "you will accompany these travelers to ensure that they do not commit any stupidity in our territory."

Garland's face exhibited, in a brief moment, a varied repertoire of emotions. Surprise, disbelief, anger and, finally, acceptance.

"As you wish, my Daikan."

Arbilla's attention returned to the princess and the nobles, who seemed not to believe what they had just heard. "I'm sure you will have no qualms about Garland accompanying you," she told them. "At the end of the day, we both win, I make sure you don't do anything foolish in my domain and you in return get an experienced soldier who, moreover, knows who you are looking for."

Princess Aienne opened her mouth to respond; however, Dornias spoke before her, "nothing to object to that, Daikan Arbilla, it will be an honor to have one of your soldiers on our journey."

"It is decided then, you will leave this very afternoon." Concluded the Daikan. "March on and good luck in your departure."

The captives nodded and stood up. Juray resumed the march, leading them toward the gate.

"Ah, one more thing," Arbilla said, causing everyone to stop and turn around, "I want you to be quite clear about one thing, if another Dajalam princess decides to penetrate my lands without my approval, I will see to it that she ends up on the gallows."

The doors closed, leaving her and Laon alone. Her beloved's mouth was turned into a slight grimace, as if with his teeth he was trapping the flesh of one of his cheeks, a gesture that he had acquired since Arbilla had become Daikan and that she knew perfectly well what it meant.

"Speak, Laon, what is troubling you?"

"I have a bad feeling," he acknowledged after making a sigh, as if allowing him to express his concerns had relieved him of a huge weight, "it's something strange, I get the feeling that a lot of things are happening around us. The loss of the Aertian sword, the war between Fireos and Aquos. I feel like the world is moving forward in a chaotic way..."

"You're right, and here we are doing nothing, stagnating." Arbilla replied with her gaze fixed on the blackish forests that stretched all the way to Mount Ubera.

Laon looked at her quizzically, "that's not what I meant."

But the Daikan was no longer listening to him. The Aertians were in search of their sacred sword and the Aquos had focused all their efforts on defending their borders with the Fireos in their quest to destroy each other. Was this the time? It certainly seemed too idyllic a scenario. Or maybe her annoyance with the Dajalam family's continuous disrespect made her seek a reason to act?

She glanced at the ceiling, reading the phrase that was repeated so many times on the walls. *A Daikan kneels to no one but God*, then she remembered the excerpt added in the room below the Lakai Ma, *unless he does so in pursuit of helping his people.*

Ever since she became Daikan, she had constantly been reminded of her citizen's expectations. The Queendom of the Moon had begun, and when Tir Torrent was protected under the mantle of Modai Tir great things were expected—great achievements with which she had not yet gifted her people. It was time to change that, for the Tirhan people to strike a resounding blow on the game board that the world had become.

"Get your things ready, Laon," Arbilla instructed him with a determined tone, "we set sail in search of the glory of our people."

"What? Where to?"

"To the Queendom of Water."

347

348

51. Fire and scales

His ears rang from the strong wind, he stretched out his legs just enough to keep himself gliding in that draft. He bent his legs, landing his boots more roughly on the snow than he would have liked, but at least he had been able to land gently enough that his knees didn't hurt.

He looked ahead. In the background, just in front of where the cliff began, Tizai was pinned on a large rock.

Simple, I just have to approach and free it from its stony prison, he thought wryly.

His boots crunched as they sank through the thick layer of snow. Noakh could not help but shake his head, refusing to accept what he was witnessing at his feet. The snow wasn't pure white but had a reddish tint, the result of all the blood spilled in that place.

The biting cold whipped mercilessly at his face. His teeth chattered, if he thought it was cold in the Snowy Mountains of the Queendom of Water these looked like hot springs in comparison with Sui Lana.

He staggered slightly, and to his horror, realized he had stepped on a half-buried purple hand. After an involuntary jolt, the index and middle fingers were torn off, now lying on the snow like two shadowy stalactites.

If not for the countless horrifying deaths witnessed there, it could even be said to be a most spectacular sight. The already gleaming reddish snow made it an eerily peculiar place, beautiful in its own way, yet ghastly in every sense. It was even more striking combined with the countless black mountains that stood behind him and counterbalanced with the solitary rock that announced the place where the earth cracked completely, giving rise to the Void.

His eyes focused on the sword stuck in the rock, with each step more and more within his reach. The cause of so much death seemed to have a privileged seat from which to witness how all those who had tried to retrieve it had failed, without exception.

A whole reign in search of the sword except for its rightful owners, he weighed. King Lieri and Queen Zarta had not made the slightest pretense of trying to rescue Tizai on their own. They had simply sat back in their seats, plotting schemes to get others to do the dirty work....

He looked around. No sign of the dragoness. He smiled at the idea that it was really that simple. Just reach over, pull hard on the hilt and rip the blade from its stone scabbard and return it to its rightful owners.

He didn't dare take another step closer; resigned to the fact that there was much to do before he could deign to think of getting out of there alive wielding that sword. He stood there, waiting.

A current of wind announced her arrival. She fluttered, twice, and then fell powerfully on the snow full of the blood of the lives she had already slain. The sword had disappeared from his vision, hidden behind a tailless dragoness with gigantic fangs and intelligent eyes that appeared to scrutinize him.

Every fiber of his being urged him to grip the hilts of his swords. Despite knowing her, despite having saved her from her eternal condemnation to dwell locked in a cave, his own instinct urged him to defend himself, to wield his weapons to resist if he was attacked. He restrained his impulses, fighting against his own survival instinct, aware that if his fingers even brushed their grips Gurandel would see him as a threat, and there would be no choice but to confront her.

The dragoness landed, her wings folded back and the stump of her tail cocked slightly, leaving a furrow in the snow.

It might sound absurd, but, in a way, he was glad to see Gurandel safe and sound. Examining her, he grimaced in surprise. Gurandel was considerably bigger than when he had first met her, she had gone from looking scrawny to looking much more imposing, about three times her size. Even the color of her scales, still shades of purple, seemed much more vivid and vibrant. As a whole, it had become an even more majestic and menacing sight.

Noakh's feelings mixed. He was glad that the dragon queen no longer showed the pitiful, decrepit appearance she had when she was found imprisoned in the cave. However, he could not help but think that such an improvement in her physique was probably due in large part to a diet based on human flesh and the mounts of all those unwary people who, whether motivated by adventure, greed or the honor of appearing in eternal ballads, had decided to confront her.

"We meet again, Gurandel." Noakh greeted her, smiling.

Her lively reptilian eyes watched him.

"*I knew it was you.*"

The voice echoed only inside the Fireo's head, just as it had in the cave where he had met her. Although this time he perceived a slightly different detail from their previous encounter, it was possible that these were mere impressions of his, but it seemed to him that the voice he heard in his head was now more robust, much clearer and powerful.

"*I felt your presence and that of that sword of yours,*" the dragoness continued, "*I have to say I am impressed; your presence is much more noticeable compared to when we first met.*"

Such flattery did not redden Noakh. Instead, his face paled, realizing that his plans had gone awry.

The presence... I'm a stupid idiot! He cursed himself. *The dragoness spoke of the presence when we conversed in the cave. She mentioned that all beings emitted it...* he felt a shudder, being fully aware of the fatal implications of it. *If Gurandel senses the presence in the distance of Hilzen, Dabayl, and Halfial hiding in the cave, she may conclude that we are setting a trap for her, and if that is her deduction, she will take flight and devour my friends, if only to teach me a lesson.*

He had to make sure that his companions did not meet such a bloody fate. He clenched his jaw, conscious of how crucial and delicate each of his next words had to be.

"That minuscule presence you surely feel in the distance are friends of mine believing they are offering me cover from a cave close enough to resort to their bow and crossbow," he revealed to her, "however, it was only a ruse to make sure they did not accompany me to meet you."

The dragoness roared.

"*I see your wit has sharpened just as your presence has,*" she said, despite being a mere voice he heard in his mind, Noakh seemed to sense a certain amusement in her tone. "*I appreciate your sincerity, so I will confess to you that your own presence is preventing me from sensing anyone else's in the vicinity.*"

"Oh," Noakh replied, now feeling like a complete fool for revealing his friends' position.

"*Why are you here?*" the dragoness finally asked, "*it is not in your nature to have traveled all the way to this frozen wasteland to finish me off, otherwise you would not have freed me from the cave.*" She pointed out.

"I'm here because my friend seeks the sacred sword," he revealed to her. "They offer a succulent reward for returning it..." he paused, he had been about to add *to their rightful owners*, however, he bit his tongue in time, aware that such a statement could be dangerous.

"*A Royal Favor, I know. An unfortunate soldier explained to me in detail in exchange for sparing her life.*"

"Why are you doing this?" continued Noakh with genuine interest, "why waste your days of freedom guarding a sword? Did you not find your kin?"

Is this the beginning of your revenge? He had been about to add.

He swallowed hard before continuing.

"Burum Babar died, you will no longer have to take revenge on the Tirhan." He revealed to her.

"*That's not how it works, no matter who rules the Tirhan lands. My bloodline cries out for vengeance and I will be the one to offer it when the time comes.*"

"What about the rest of the dragons, did you manage to find them?"

Noakh felt really bad about that question. He remembered the promise the Tirhan had made to Gurandel, she would give herself up and be imprisoned for eternity, in exchange for the rest of the dragons to go free. While he couldn't say for sure, something told him that all the dragons had been killed and Gurandel was the only one left. A breach of word he saw so capable in the human that he dared not even ask Burum Babar for fear that he would confirm that this had been the case. In a way, he suspected that the dragoness also believed that such had been the fate of her siblings, which was why she sought revenge.

"*I haven't found them yet.*"

"And what do you need the sword for?" he asked, "why stop at searching for your own to guard a weapon that is of no use to you at all?"

"*These weapons emanate a peculiar presence,*" the dragoness revealed to him, "*it is dark and strange, so those of us who can sense it are especially drawn to it. I am sure that just as I was attracted to it, so would my dragon brethren.*

Nor will I deny that the constant source of food that comes to me so assiduously is to be appreciated. After so long in that cave, it is a pleasure to enjoy every meal. And also, it is a strange world, one to which I don't feel I belong." She revealed to him.

Noakh opened his mouth, realizing what was happening.

Gurandel had been trapped in that cave for centuries, if not longer... so long imprisoned that being free felt strange to her, not only that, being imprisoned for so long had probably caused her to find a world very different from the one she knew, a place where it was difficult for her to feel part of. Noakh could come to understand that feeling, he had even experienced it first hand, that time after his father died, he had thrown Distra into the river and lost himself in the woods. Returning to civilization had been shocking at first, cold and strange; something told him that was just what was happening to Gurandel.

"So that's why you protect the sword," Noakh said, smiling at the absurdity. "I freed you from one cage, only for you to cage yourself with this sword. This obsession, this need to guard it—it's become your new prison. Only now, you've chosen this confinement."

He unsheathed Distra. Then he extended his arm backward, the blade of his sacred sword ablaze.

"It seems that, once again, I must release you from your prison, Gurandel."

The dragon roared, taking flight.

She opened her jaws, releasing a puff of fire. Noakh made a lunge with Distra, likewise launching a flare. The fires met halfway. For an instant it seemed that both flames struggled to devour each other, until finally Gurandel's fire prevailed, Noakh rolled on the ground, thus moving out of the path of the dragon's flames.

"*Your fire is nothing compared to a dragon's!*"

Gurandel's claws lunged at Noakh, who made an attack with his swords to try to avoid being rammed. He could not deflect it in time, he felt the power of the blow despite having partially dodged it. He tumbled uncontrollably across the reddish snow, his weapons slipping from his grasp.

He struck both citrines on his palms, snatching the swords in mid-air. As he caught Distra he glanced up at the sky, noting with astonishment that Gurandel had taken flight and was heading towards him at full speed, her claws ready to catch him. He hurriedly launched a disc of fire, the attack speeding towards its target, without making the slightest scratch on the dragon's skin.

He tried to pull away, but it was too late, one of Gurandel's claws grabbed him by the chest, crushing him violently against the snow. He gritted his teeth, feeling the weight of such a brutal creature. He was completely at her mercy; simply by dropping her full weight on him, he would be crushed like a nut.

The dragoness's gigantic jaw gaped open; her giant sharp teeth filled with strands of slime, her purple tongue snaking through that infinite cavity. She roared with such ferocity that Noakh cocked his head to one side and narrowed his eyes at the power of the sound.

"Do you truly believe you're a match for me, boy?"

"I only want to free you from the new prison you live in, Gurandel," he said, haltingly, as he felt the dragoness's grip tighten harder on his chest. "May you stop living trapped and be free."

The dragoness roared again, this time into the skies, releasing him from her grasp and then taking flight.

"For that you will have to prove yourself worthy of snatching the sword from the clutches of a dragon."

Noakh rose to his feet, holding his hand to his aching chest. He called back to his blades as he watched the dragon circling in the sky. Gurandel hovered, waiting for him to recover to continue in that uneven battle. Just at that moment, he felt an object fall near his position. He turned around in surprise.

An arrow? He observed. Then he noticed, the wood of the arrow's body was covered with a white cloth... soaked in blood. However, he had no time for reflection. A piercing roar flooded the sky.

A gigantic bolt impaled Gurandel's tough skin, slicing through her back as she streaked across the sky. The dragoness reacted instantly, roared with such ferocity that Noakh's hair stood on end, she tore out the bolt using her powerful jaw and flew off in search of the culprits.

Noakh's gaze returned to the arrow. A chill ran down his spine as he made the connection. That army, those gigantic bolt throwers... they had assumed too many things. The arrow had been shot by Dabayl, he guessed, such an inaccurate shot on her part could only mean one thing: his friends were in grave danger, he had to go to their aid as soon as possible. He looked towards the distant and high cave where they were sheltering. He would not make it in time. He turned to the dragoness.

"Gurandel!" he shouted at the top of his lungs, "take me with you!"

The dragoness ignored him, continuing in the direction of those who had attacked her.

They had taken too many things for granted. They thought those war machines were heading for that esplanade; they believed the entire army would be used to confront the dragoness. All a mistake. Everything indicated that they had positioned themselves at some high point, from where they could shoot at the dragon and confront her from a distance. But, if that army knew that he and his companions were there, it meant that...

"Please! My friends are in grave danger!" begged Noakh.

The young Fireo dropped to his knees. All was lost.

Suddenly, the dragoness swerved in her course, glided in his direction and headed towards him extending her claws.

"Urrgh!" Noakh exclaimed as he was grabbed by the waist more roughly than he would have liked. "Thank you." He managed to say, trying to disregard the pain of the onslaught.

The dragoness flew at full speed. Dodging the gigantic bolts and huge boulders flying in her direction.

Noakh gritted his teeth. *We are mere puppets in the foolish game of two siblings.* Everything had changed, now he and Gurandel had a common enemy, one who was going to regret meddling in their feud.

They were flying high. From there, Noakh finally spotted the cave where his friends had taken shelter.

"Let go of me!"

The dragon obeyed. Freeing him from her clutches, he began to descend at full speed. He had to enter through the hole in the cave, otherwise he would end up crushed against the mountain. Remembering his previous flights, he swung his body. He was descending too fast, if he continued like this, he was likely to crash violently into the ground or perhaps an air current would blow him slightly off course causing him to crash into the black rock. These were risks he had to take, any second he lost could mean the difference between finding his friends alive or dead.

He shifted his feet, battling against the fierce wind gusts, crossing the cave so abruptly that his head brushed the top of the entrance. Too fast. He stepped roughly into the cave entrance, rolling across the floor violently, finally hitting back and head so hard against the floor that Noakh thought he had cracked his skull in two.

He overcame the pain as best he could, getting to his feet and walking despite his agony.

"No!" he shouted, seeing his fears realized. The limp bodies of his friends lay on the ground covered in blood.

He approached the nearest one, Dabayl. Her back was bathed in blood, she had been stabbed several times. Then he noticed her ear. Noakh gritted his teeth, seeing a piece of her earlobe had been torn off.

It can't be. Her again, my inaction has caused the death of my friends. Please don't be dead, please don't....

He put his hand to his neck and grabbed the flask with holy water. He poured the holy water over the multiple wounds on Dabayl's back, then hastily moved to do the same for Halftal and Hilzen. He felt his breathing quicken, watching as the deep wounds on Hilzen's back and ear slowly closed.

Dabayl was the first to cough, Hilzen merely looked from side to side, disoriented.

"Friend, thank the gods you are well." Noakh celebrated, Hilzen went to speak, but Noakh shook his head at him, "Rest. You too, Dabayl," he said as he saw her move as well, "I know who did this to you, I'll take care of it."

He needed no more. He jumped as best he could through the hole in the cave, ready to hunt down those who had tried to end the lives of his friends.

52. Decisive battle

An anguished scream of terror was the Fireo soldiers' last outcry before the colossal foot of the monstrous giant flattened them, turning them into a gruesome mixture of viscera and blood. The giant hoisted his leg again, preparing to obliterate another unit. The darkening shadow, cast by his towering limb, signaled the impending end for the Fireo militiamen below. Suddenly, the giant emitted a muffled noise, seconds before his head was cut in two by that disc of fire. It lurched, falling backwards, crushing in its path several Aquo soldiers who had, until now, taken advantage of the cover provided by the monstrous being to advance with ease.

Wulkan turned his attention to the front. He walked in the front line of his proud escort of Chosen by Fire. On one side stood the standard-bearer, waving the flag vigorously, and on the other, his faithful Turuma, poised and ready to crush skulls with her mace. They advanced, mercilessly, more bloodthirsty than usual. At last, the beach of Ghandya was to be taken again, watered with the blood of their bitter Aquo enemies.

"Where are you, Graglia?" cried Wulkan fervently.

I know you are here; I just have to flush you out of hiding, the Fireo King thought, his steels cleaving through the chest of a young soldier.

He had kept his word, his platoon was positioned near the coast, as they had agreed. Three members of his escort stood behind the rest of that elite platoon, guarding the two unharmed Knights of Waters who walked embarrassed with chains on their necks and arms. Not a scratch had been made on them, as they had agreed. With that pact, Queen Graglia had agreed to meet on the beach of Ghandya with him, and it was she who was not keeping her word.

He made several accurate thrusts, ending the life of that platoon of blue-eyed opponents. After that, he tried to spot the queen among the tide of soldiers advancing towards them, without success.

Either she shows up soon, or I will see to it that there is not a single Aquo soldier who does not witness how my fiery blades slit the throats of both Knights of Water.

He moved forward, driving the flaming Sinistra through the armor of an Aquo soldier who had looked defiant until a few moments ago. Wulkan felt especially fervent that day, at last, a battle between Aquos and Fireos on the beach of Ghandya. That night the orange flags would flood the coast of that place so important for both kingdoms, as they had done in the past.

But for that, he first had to pierce Graglia's heart with his swords.

He had carried everything. War machines, monsters dragged from their cells and hidden mountains, and a whole army ready to end the life of every last Aquo soldier.

To his knowledge, Graglia had not yet retrieved her sacred sword. However, that would not detract from his triumph. In fairness, he too had been deprived of one of his weapons, was it his fault that the selfish god Aquo had only blessed her chosen one with a single sword? Of course it was not.

The battle on the beach was fierce. Wulkan continued to gain ground as the clash between the Aquo and Fireo troops became increasingly violent and bloody. The mutual hatred that had been repressed for almost two decades was finally being reciprocated with a celebration in the form of blood and glory.

This time the sapphire had not spoken, his esteemed informant seemed to be unaccounted for. However, he had not forgotten her last request. The only thing she had asked of him in exchange for continuing to inform him was something he was already more than willing to do—end the life of Queen Graglia.

He made a lunge, fire and arrows filled the sky for an instant. While his flames struck a large group of victims, he struck a portentous blow with the pommel of Distra to a soldier with vivid blue eyes, who witnessed how he lost his teeth moments before seeing how he also lost his life.

It is time to shake our enemies' morale, he decided.

Wulkan gave the signal, Sinistra's tip being placed perpendicular to the steel of Distra's replica, taking care to be precise enough for the chief artillerist to catch it with his spyglass from the distance from his rearward position.

A motivated opponent charged at him with fervor. Wulkan greeted his enthusiasm by severing both his arms with accurate thrusts and took advantage of the time when the lifeless body of his opponent fell to the ground to allow himself the luxury of looking up at the sky. He wanted to witness the very moment when his opponents' blue eyes filled with despair.

He smiled. Spotting it in the skies, the chief artillerist had picked up his signal perfectly.

A gigantic blackish boulder filled with vulcanite was now passing far above the numerous heads of the Fireo soldiers. The conclusion in its trajectory would cause chaos and death among the Aquo ranks. He felt a shiver of exhilaration, aware of the imminence of the spectacle.

Suddenly, out of nowhere, a second stone appeared from the opposite direction, coming from the rear of the Aquo army. Both stones met in the sky.

Boom!

A spectacular reddish explosion broke through the clamor of the battlefield. Both stones had been shattered into countless pieces upon impact with each other. Fire and rock were now falling from the sky, causing death and pain on both fronts indiscriminately in their descent.

"Damn you, Graglia," muttered the Fireo King, acknowledging the sharpness of that reply. "It seems that, despite my informant, you still have several aces up your sleeve."

As he looked ahead, he spotted a figure he recognized instantly. He smiled, satisfied. Defiant look, eternally young and about to die.

The queen was holding a sword, but Wulkan noticed that it wasn't the hilt of her famous sacred weapon. He could not help smiling.

The battle continued around them, rocks and fire continued to cause death on both sides. Yet, the elite Aquo troops and the Chosen by Fire concentrated their efforts on carving out a space for the two monarchs to meet amidst the chaos.

"At last, you show yourself, Graglia," Wulkan said, speaking to her with deliberate disdain. "It must be rare for you not to hide behind a wall built from the corpses of your own soldiers." He sneered.

The queen didn't reply; she simply regarded him with her customary superior gaze. At Graglia's gesture, two soldiers dragged Minkert next to her. Wulkan quickly inspected his grandson, he seemed safe and sound. There was no scratch on his body or any sign on his face to alert

359

him that he had been mistreated. Wulkan swung his swords. In an instant, the three Chosen by Fire presented him with the two imprisoned Knights of Water.

It was Wulkan who did the honors, waved his hand, signaling his escort to release the two Knights of Water. Graglia then did the same for Minkert. His grandson passed by his side. Wulkan bowed his head, thanking him for his good work. Then he raised two flaming swords, they clashed twice, and then pointed their tips first at Queen Graglia and then at the two Knights of Water. Those who had recently been his prisoners seemed to have soon regained their honor, the Knights of Water were provided with weapons, placing themselves at the side of Graglia.

Three against one. An unfair battle, just the way he liked it.

Without wasting a second, he made a thrust with Sinistra in the direction of Graglia. A powerful flame emanated from the blade, ready to devour its victim.

However, before being consumed by the fire, Graglia and her two henchmen moved out of the path of the flames.

Graglia's only response was a lip-twisting grimace of displeasure.

"Kill him," the queen ordered.

Upon her command, Graglia and the two Knights of Water rushed at him. Wulkan's heart pounded fervently, eager to face such formidable opponents simultaneously.

The Chosen by Fire were expectant, eager to take part in the contest. However, the king had been clear, they were not to interfere or stand in the way of the Phoenix Descendant if they did not want to freeze to death in hell for disobeying his orders.

With a swift move of Sinistra Wulkan deflected Queen Graglia's powerful attack. Then he pulled back before that strange hooded Knight of Water attacked him from the rear.

He parried a second attack from Queen Graglia, and then he lunged at the leader of the Knights of Water. He had to admit it, even without her sacred sword, Graglia was a formidable opponent. Fast, efficient in each of her movements and with a combat style that, even being more focused on defense, allowed her to push Wulkan back on more than one occasion.

Graglia's face, on the other hand, did not show the same condescending look she had shown in many of their previous confrontations. She looked fierce, focused on her movements. This time she could not heal her wounds, nor could she show off those annoying torrents of water.

What a ridiculous situation, Wulkan thought, *me without one of my sacred swords, facing Graglia dispossessed of hers.*

His rivals fought viciously. They dodged his lethal fire attacks, while putting up a stiff fight to the point of having cut his flesh on more than one occasion. His black armor creaked with every powerful blow he had to endure. But he was not lagging behind, his swordsmanship was renowned, and with his flaming blades, he steadily bested his formidable opponents.

He was getting closer to the moment in which he would subdue them to the will of the incandescent fire of his swords.

King and queen fought fiercely. The two Knights of Water also showed a noteworthy talent for combat. But Wulkan had more years of battle experience and, as if that were not enough, a flaming sword with which to consume his opponents at the slightest carelessness.

He felt Graglia's steel pierce his armor at chest level.

"Fireo steel," he acknowledged, only a sword wrought from the metal of the Fireo mines could pierce his armor, "I'm glad to see that even the queen of the Aquos is able to put aside her pride." He added before throwing a disc of fire at her that the queen was able to dodge at the last instant.

Both Graglia and his two elite soldiers were tremendously wounded. One of them, the one with the stupid rag on his face, looked gravely moribund from the burns, the other was bleeding so profusely from the belly that it was impressive that he was still standing.

And Graglia, oh, what a beautiful sight it was to see her beautiful face turning red. One of her eyes was closed due to the abundant blood emanating from the ugly cut above her left eyebrow, her side also looked fatally sore.

Wulkan had not emerged unscathed from such an encounter either. His left arm was bleeding incessantly, as was his neck and chest.

Somehow, his opponents kept getting up, they still had the strength to face him. However, he knew that little by little their lives were running out, soon his flames would consume them completely and they would eventually evaporate.

He gripped the hilt of his flaming swords more fiercely, ready to continue the dance of death. He rushed at his opponents again, unwilling to give them any respite.

Graglia fought with her usual skill and spectacular talent with the sword; even without her sacred sword, she was considerably one of the most worthy opponents he had ever faced. Despite this, he felt bad, disenchanted that his last confrontation with the queen of the Aquos would be without her having the powers conceived to her by her sacred sword. But what was he to do after all? He resigned himself.

He had already played too much with his prey. It was time to put an end to that battle and demonstrate once and for all to these Aquos their futility against the flame. He extended his left hand, the tip of Sinistra reaching toward the heavens, the flames of its blade waving back and forth vividly, as if eager to consume the queen.

Wulkan smiled, enjoying his obvious superiority. Graglia and her two Knights of Water moved much more slowly; bathing the ground with their blood with every step they took. That reddish liquid would be the only sea in which they would be welcomed.

It is time to carry out your death sentence. The flames of his steel resounded loudly, ready to end the duel.

Wulkan raised his flaming blades, ready to finish Graglia off.

A thunderous noise came from the sea. Wulkan frowned, looking out over the water. Was this some Aquo trick?

The next thing was a deafening high-pitched scream, so unbearable that Wulkan instinctively almost dropped his swords to cover his ears. His eyes widened, unable to believe what he was witnessing. A gigantic wave, of such proportions that he would have denied its existence if it were not for the fact that he was contemplating it, was approaching voraciously towards the coast. It was as if the Aquos had summoned the ocean itself to fight by their side.

Enough of these games, Wulkan resolved, weary of the Aquo army's trickery. He made a powerful thrust with Sinistra, and a mighty disc of fire shot out of the blade, heading towards the titanic wave.

Water and fire impacted fiercely. The wave exploded, shattering outrageously. Steam flooded the battlefield, so much so that it was difficult to see. He stood on guard, alert in case any of his opponents took advantage of the confusion and haze to make a move. However, his eyes remained fixed on the shore.

Wulkan frowned; on the shore was stranded a ship whose mask showed a mermaid singing with her arms outstretched. Then he saw a silhouette, brandishing a sword that was swiftly lifted skyward.

Isn't she a young woman? Wulkan wondered, taken aback at the spectacle.

362

That figure was still advancing, with the tip of her weapon pointing toward the clear sky.

The Fireo King felt a light wet tap on his head; he looked up at the sky. A cold drop of water hit his face, followed by another, then two more.

It was beginning to rain. *Is it Princess Vienne that my eyes see?* His spies had mentioned her name, yet they had insisted that she was no threat, quite the contrary.

Suddenly, the sea level rose, and before anyone could react, the battlefield was inundated. The war seemed to stop for an instant. Everyone present was stunned by the strange apparition.

The Aquo soldiers, dejected by their wounds, began to stand up, watching in awe as their cuts closed until not a single scar was visible on their skin. Then they saw her, walking with a grace that seemed nothing short of miraculous.

Princess Vienne walked with her sword held high, calmly making her way while perplexed soldiers from both sides watched her with open mouths. It was as if the battle stopped for a moment. First, it was the soldiers of the Church Guard who knelt down, then the rest of the Aquo troops followed. The Fireos, on the other hand, limited themselves to watch alertly as the young woman walked in front of them, confident, without even deigning to look at them.

The insistent rain did not stop falling.

Wulkan roared with fury, a thunderous battle cry that ripped through the hushed place. Thus, resuming the confrontation. He pointed the fiery tip of Sinistra at the princess and launched a mighty flare with all his eagerness.

The flame traveled across the terrain with great speed. However, when the attack violently struck the spot where the princess had been, she was already gone. He scanned the area in search of her and noticed a faint glow in the distance.

Suddenly, the princess was in front of him. He blocked the powerful attack directed against her neck. He tried to skewer her with Distra, however, a woman showing a wide smile appeared out of nowhere, parrying his thrust.

Such absurd speed, he thought, blocking as best he could that unexpected second attack.

Vienne and the Knight of Water Alvia stepped back. They now positioned themselves in front of the queen.

Why are they here? Wulkan wondered, *the two of them were supposed to have been taken care of.*

"Can you walk, mother?" Princess Vienne asked, not even sparing her a glance.

Wulkan felt Graglia's stunned gaze, watching her daughter. *Even she is not understanding what is happening.*

Rain continued to pour intensely from the sky. The battle had resumed. However, Wulkan heard a faint *fsss*, turned to his weapons. A lump rose in his throat, the flames on Distra's blade had died out.

"Only one of your swords is still burning," Princess Vienne pointed out, looking at him in an insultingly condescending manner, "could it be that the real Distra is not in your possession, but in the hands of the Phoenix Ascendant?"

Wulkan tried to control himself, yet for an instant, fear flashed across his face.

"He's alive." The princess revealed to him, accompanying her words with that repellent condescending look he hated so much, "and he is more than eager to make you pay for your cowardly decision."

Wulkan's heart skipped a beat. *They know, somehow, they know. And he is alive.*

He gritted his teeth.

"Insolent!" He exclaimed furiously, attacking the princess with both of his swords. Princess Vienne moved to parry the attack, but instead of meeting her blade, Wulkan's flaming sword clashed with the swords of the Knight of Water Alvia.

The monarch began to take a deep breath, drawing back for the first time since that war against the Aquos had begun. He felt the cold sweat run down his forehead. His throat, on the other hand, seemed to burn, as if he had been slit by the edge of a flaming sword.

They know, he thought again and again. *He is alive, he survived!*

He had no choice...

Wulkan thrust Sinistra's tip into the ground, its sharp edge cutting its way into the sand. He summoned his power. Fire broke through the earth, and a gigantic wall of fire emerged, splitting the battlefield in two, consuming any unfortunate person in its path, regardless of their faction.

The king of the Fireos raised his two swords to the sky, their tips touching.

The confident expression of the Chosen by Fire vanished; instead, their faces showed the most absolute stupefaction. The musician

364

looked at his fellow comrades, as if to make sure that he had interpreted the signal correctly. Such a signal, *Tanare*, was not one that the Fireos were accustomed to witnessing. The musician breathed in with all his might and exhaled, the low rumbling sound made its way across the battlefield, sending a shiver down the spine of the Fireo troops.

It was a sound that most of the members of the Fireo army had trouble recognizing. For they had only heard of it, never having ever heard it in a battle in which they had taken part. It was the sound that announced their retreat.

53. An eye for an eye

Noakh soared through the sky, both swords drawn. He didn't care that it made it more difficult for him to fly; he wanted to be ready, to pass sentence on those who had made the mistake of trying to murder his friends. He could not believe his misfortune. He had been merciful. and, as a reward, his companions had almost paid for it with their lives. That was a lesson he was not going to forget, sometimes you had to get your hands dirty if you didn't want a greater evil to happen.

Riding the wind currents and adjusting his posture, he propelled himself upwards with remarkable dexterity. He was deeply concentrated, as he had never been before. His mind thought of nothing but revenge. His senses had been sharpened just to make sure that he would be able to hunt those bastards down.

From the heights, he spotted the place from where the attack had been launched. He passed in front of Gurandel. The bolt throwers that had attacked her were consuming in a sea of flames and smoke. The dragon seemed to be doing well, her claws had caught a soldier while her maw devoured the head of another of her unwary human rivals. He identified a group of archers, ensconced in a shelter, unleashing a hail of arrows at the dragon.

Noakh gritted his teeth, making a lunge with Distra, from the blade emanated a flame in the direction of those soldiers. The archer platoon only had time to utter a scream before the flames engulfed them. He had changed. Burum Babar had opened his eyes in their encounter, he had revealed to him that he hid under the power of the sword so as not to blame himself for the deaths caused by his flaming steel. Not anymore.

He continued to glide, trying to spot his prey. He saw uniformed soldiers, but they were not his target. He was specifically looking for the prisoners, but they weren't among them. He frowned, had they left?

Then it dawned on him, it was obvious where to find them. He turned completely around, descending as fast as he could. He angled himself sharply, diving with speed to confront them without delay.

There they are.

They were sprinting across the reddish snow. Trying to get hold of the sword, taking advantage of Gurandel's confrontation with the soldiers. Surely each one of them was pondering about what they were going to use the Royal Favor for.

A flare prevented them from continuing their advance. The whole group stopped, looking up at the sky.

Noakh landed, positioning himself between Tizai and the prisoners. That band of ruffians, armed with swords, axes, and spears, looked on in surprise at his appearance. Surely, they were expecting the dragon, however, they had encountered the Ascendant Phoenix.

He charged at them, furious. Distra pierced the throat of the first of those bastards, then his steel sword cut into the chest of a man with rotten teeth and a necklace full of putrid fingers. As his victim fell lifeless to the ground, he threw a disc of fire that struck the neck of a woman with a shaved half head and a black tattoo on her face, killing her on the spot.

He gritted his teeth, his thrusts full of fury, lethal. This time Distra was not trying to take control, for the young Fireo needed no excuse to finish off that group of bastards. It was his own burning rage and desire for revenge that dictated sentence and death in equal parts.

Out of the corner of his eye, he saw one of his opponents running for his life; but it was too late to repent. He launched a firebolt in his direction, flicking his wrist to make the fire curve, consuming the fugitive.

Several opponents rushed at him. He parried a rival's two-handed sword attack. Seizing the moment, a second opponent attacked him fiercely from behind with a spear. Noakh pivoted on his feet to avoid the thrust but was still thrown off balance by the attack's force, causing him to fall face-first to the ground and release his steel sword.

But he was ready. A tap with his middle finger on one of his citrines was enough to send the sword off the ground and flying toward him. There was nothing that could save them.

He made several thrusts into the air, thus consuming several of his opponents in the fire, they only had time to utter a bloodcurdling scream before they were consumed by the flames. Among the few faces alive, he spotted the one he most wanted to see burn.

368

At last, I found you. The woman in charge, the one who liked to mark her victims by tearing off a piece of their earlobe, Suruyana. He hurried to finish off the few remaining opponents, he deflected his opponent's axe, then moved quickly forward and pierced his leg with his steel sword, splitting his torso in two with his flaming weapon. His fiery discs claimed two more adversaries.

Suruyana was the only one left. Her evil smile had disappeared from her face, the confidence in her gaze had vanished completely. Now, her yellow eyes begged for forgiveness. But the young Fireo had learned from his mistakes. He made several thrusts with Distra.

His victim's pupils lit up as she saw several fiery discs rushing at her, ready to consume her completely.

Noakh breathed with difficulty, the result of the effort. His blades full of blood, Distra satisfied that he had finished with so many enemies. It was over. He had wondered on many occasions how it would feel to be his own hand that ended a human life, now, after having killed those rogues, he could only say that he did not feel guilty knowing that such despicable men and women were not going to cause more evil in the world.

He went to sheathe his swords. Suddenly, he felt something in his chest. A throwing axe had made its way into his heart. He glanced at his attacker, a prisoner with an ugly scar on her face had made the attack from the ground. With a sweep of her arm, the young woman swung the throwing axe back at her.

Distra's blade was no longer aflame. Noakh fell to the ground, slumped. His own blood spilled, staining the snow beneath his motionless body a deeper shade of red.

The woman tried to throw the throwing axe, a second time. Determined to take down the one who had obstructed their path before her own injuries claimed her life. She raised her arm, ready for her throw, however, an arrow through the back of her skull prevented her from doing so.

Dabayl descended, throwing her bow to the ground to assist Noakh. Hilzen and Halftal, who did not seem to believe what they were witnessing, also landed.

It was Dabayl who turned Noakh over, laying him face up on a now even redder snow. Hilzen looked gravely at Dabayl after inspecting the wound, unable to believe that Noakh had actually been hit in the heart.

"I know!" Hilzen indicated. He lunged for Distra and pressed the hilt into Noakh's hand, tightening his grip and exerting force to prevent

Noakh from letting go. Then, he brought his own palm to the sword's blade and deliberately ran it along the sharp edge. The Aquo's blood stained the sacred weapon. "Don't worry, Dabayl, it takes a while, get the bow ready."

Dabayl listened to him. Her bow ready as he had instructed, not knowing quite what to expect. However, nothing happened.

"Hilzen..." Halftal began, trying to make him stop in his attempts.

The Aquo was not listening. He desperately cut his hand again, then his face, then his forearms, his neck.... "Why don't you take control, you stupid sword!" He demanded in a piercing cry of madness.

The ground shook. Hilzen and Dabayl turned around. Gurandel had just landed beside them.

"*His presence, it has almost completely disappeared.*"

"You mean he has...?" Hilzen was not even able to finish the sentence. His mouth twisted into a grimace of terror at the thought of such a fate.

Gurandel watched the boy's limp body. "Every *instant what little presence is left in him is vanishing. Shortly he will have left this world.*"

"Isn't there... isn't there anything we can do?" Halftal asked, trying not to lose the last glimmer of hope.

Gurandel stared at Noakh's limp body. Without moving one inch.

"*Seek shelter, far away.*" She finally instructed them.

Hilzen and Dabayl looked at each other, quizzical. Then they seemed to understand that it was better to do as he said, starting to walk away followed by Halftal.

Gurandel waited until their presence was far enough away. She couldn't help but wonder; what her kin would think of what she was about to do. Surely, they would not understand, she assumed. That boy had released her from an eternal prison, simply because he had considered it wrong for her to remain locked up.

After killing so many soldiers intent on reclaiming the sword, she had not felt better. She had merely fed her growing rage and desire to kill. She hated to admit it, but Noakhail was right, she had been locked up for so long that she didn't know how to live in freedom, she had turned the custody of the sword into her new prison. The world had become cold and inhospitable, a place where she felt out of place, devoid of purpose. Except for one thing. She gazed at Noakhail's limp body, the very being who had shown her the goodness in humanity.

The dragoness opened her maw. Her mouth glowed with the orange light that emanated flowing from her insides. The blazing fire impacted

Noakh. The flames began to consume his body completely, relentlessly, endlessly.

54. Unthinkable

Noakh woke up. Looking from side to side, he held his hands to his heart, where the throwing axe had struck him. Had it been a dream? *No, it had been very real,* he decided as he saw the frozen mountains in the distance.

He looked at the ground, there was no longer snow at his feet, the earth had turned black, devoid of any vegetation, only his two swords were on the ground. At that moment he realized, his body was completely naked and, in spite of that, he was not cold.

It was a peculiar sensation. He should be dead; instead, he was perfectly fine, without the slightest pain accusing his body. He turned around, slamming his face against the dragon's face. Motionless, empty.

"Gurandel!" He yelled, rising as best he could.

The dragoness had lost her purple appearance, her scales and skin now had an ashen hue. Her eyes were devoid of pupils. She had left this world.

My return to life, her death... he reflected, thinking he understood what had happened. Something told him that, in some way that a mere human like him could not discern, the dragoness had sacrificed herself to save his life.

"Thank you, Gurandel." He said, resting his head on the dragoness's cool scales.

He wondered what he should do. Leaving her body there, at the mercy of the beasts that might inhabit that place, did not seem to him an end worthy of the dragon queen. He struck the citrine in his right hand, Distra took off from the ground heading towards him, Noakh raised his arm, catching it on the fly. He clenched the hilt with both hands and summoned the full power of the sacred weapon. Gurandel's body was engulfed in flames.

"Rest free, Gurandel, you've earned it."

It was unfathomable. The dragoness had sacrificed herself for him, to save his life at the cost of her own. He felt upset, sad, and happy at the same time.

Just at that moment, his three friends glided into view. Hilzen hastened to offer him his cloak to shield his friend's nudity.

"Are you all right, Noakh?" asked Halftal.

"We saw it all." Hilzen told him. "Everything burst into a sea of flames. It's as if Gurandel had expelled all her fire on you."

Noakh nodded. They would probably never know exactly what had happened; perhaps it was a spell, the power of a dragon, or it would simply have to do with the presence Gurandel was able to sense in beings. In any case, it was obvious that Gurandel had sacrificed herself for him and that was all that mattered to him.

"I'm sorry that because of the sword we almost lost you." Dabayl lamented, moving in for a hug.

"It's nothing, I'm fine," He answered her, then pointed to Tizai, "there you have it, Dabayl, it's all yours."

Instinctively the Aertian took a step and reached out to grasp it. However, just as her fingers were about to caress its pommel, she stopped.

"No, I don't want it anymore, Noakh. My wish nearly cost us our lives. We should have heeded the wise words of that man and turned back."

"But we are not going to leave the sword here, are we? I wouldn't want to unleash Shiana's fury..." replied Hilzen looking fearfully towards the mountains.

Noakh reached over and grasped the hilt of Tizai. He pulled lightly; the blade came off the stone with ease.

"This game is not over yet. We owe it to Gurandel and all the innocents who fell for going in search of this sword." Noakh said seriously. "King Lieri gave us a mission, and we must uphold our part of the agreement. They played with us, just as they took pleasure in the lives of all their people. Now, it's our turn to play."

55. An impossible scenario

Graglia sat in a chair within the command tent, gathering her thoughts. Thanks to Crystaline's healing powers, she was practically unharmed. However, she felt the pain of such an unexpected betrayal.

She had asked her sisters and Galonais to leave her alone, to reflect on all that she had been informed of. Only Vienne remained, seated in a tent corner, sipping a hot drink with her newfound pet, allowing her mother a moment of reflection.

Gelegen had died, so had the vast majority of members of the Congregation of the Church... and, as if such acts were not enough to ensure that her daughter Katienne would never reach the sea, she had also allied herself with Wulkan.

Such atrocities committed by one of my own daughters. Blood of my own blood.

As much as she knew all those accusations to be true, her mind seemed to insist that it was not possible. How had her own daughter gone so far as to commit such disloyalty against her family and her reign? And in her infamy, she had dragged Gant, House Delorange and the Congregation of the Church, how could such an atrocity have occurred behind her back?

In a way, she couldn't help thinking that it was her own fault. She had allowed that stalk of betrayal to sprout instead of pulling it out by the roots. She thought that introducing some competition for Vienne might invigorate her and help build her character. And, although it seemed to have been so, she would never have believed that it would be at the cost of paying such a high price.

Oh, Gelegen, to think that I will never hear your inappropriate comments again, she lamented. A lump rose in her throat. She had not lost a soldier, but an invaluable friend whom she would deeply miss.

The queen glanced at Vienne.

Her daughter sat with her elbows on the small table, blowing on her hot rabbit broth. Zyrah, perched on her lap, pawed at the princess, hoping for a taste of the soup.

The Queendom fell into utter chaos during my absence: deaths, betrayals... and it was all resolved solely because of her. She pondered, still in disbelief. *So different from me, so inadequate in my eyes, and yet so capable of dealing with such an exceptional situation.*

At that moment, the princess left the bowl on the table. She approached her mother, unhooking the sacred sword from her belt along the way and stopped in front of her.

"I believe this belongs to you, mother." She said holding out her arm, offering Crystaline to her.

The queen bowed her head and looked at her daughter. Vienne's gaze was fixed on her, no longer elusive as before. She still had a certain look of a skinny little girl, but something about her appearance made her look more grown up.

"No," Graglia replied shaking her head, "you have more than proven yourself worthy to possess the sword. Keep it with you, there is still much to fight for."

"The war isn't over then?" asked Vienne, furrowing her brow.

Graglia grimaced at her daughter's innocent disbelief. "By no means has this war come to an end. I know King Wulkan too well to even consider that that bastard has called the battle over. I'm sure he merely ordered a retreat to contemplate your words and the embarrassment of one of his swords extinguishing."

And he has much to reflect on... Graglia considered. Vienne's strange words to Wulkan had troubled the Fireo monarch. Furthermore, the sacred sword's extinguishing upon contact with rainwater was a significant event. Vienne had told her everything, and after calming her anger over the almost unforgivable fact that they let the boy who possessed one of the sacred swords of fire escape, she was astonished.

Her daughter had insisted on the young man's kindness. Even more boldly, she proposed the possibility of a future alliance between the two peoples. An alliance between Fireos and Aquos? The mere consideration of it caused her to grimace in disbelief. Yet, for some strange reason, she knew that if anyone was capable of achieving such an unlikely coalition, it was Vienne.

Graglia cleared her throat. "You've done a good job, Vienne. You didn't just unleash the sword's power; you also took control of the situation and dealt with your sister. I congratulate you on that."

Her daughter's cheeks reddened to unsuspected limits. "Tha... thank you, mother." She managed to say. After those words, a smirk appeared on her face.

Vienne looked elated. Reflecting on it, she realized she had never seen her daughter so pleased in her presence. Had she been hard on her? Certainly. Did she deserve to have been treated so harshly? There was not the slightest doubt in her mind. Living proof of this was that, by resorting to such uncompromising measures, Vienne finally seemed to resemble someone worthy of reigning in the rather near future.

At that moment, she heard the sound of a spear strike twice against the canvas of the command tent.

"Come in," she urged them.

Two soldiers of the Royal Guard appeared, escorting Alvia.

At first, she expected her sister to make some jocular comment as soon their gazes met. How, if it hadn't been for their appearance, she would be dead now or some similar impertinence. Alvia's face, on the other hand, showed a serious countenance, not a trace of her usual carefree smile. *Has the trip to Tirhan Lands not only forged Vienne's character but also corrected my sister's irritating jovial nature? No, that would be asking too much of the Aqua Deus.*

"Your Majesty, the Knight of Water Alvia wishes to speak with you." One of the soldiers informed her. "She insists it is important."

The queen nodded. The two soldiers stood in the doorway, their spear shafts resting on the earthy carpet. Since the news of treason, the queen's security had been increased, at the suggestion of Counselor Galonais.

Alvia stood facing her with her arms crossed, then cast a glance towards the back of the tent.

"Vienne, why don't you take a walk with Zyrah? I'm sure my sister the queen would not like this one wetting the royal carpets in the command tent."

"All right." Replied Vienne, "Come on, Zyrah, they want to talk in private."

Acknowledging the soldiers with a nod, the princess exited, her loyal canine companion trailing behind.

Graglia and Alvia were silent for a moment. While the queen observed her sister, the latter seemed to wait, eyes on the ground, perhaps ensuring Vienne was at a distance.

"I have a lot of things to take care of, Alvia," she admonished her, "may I know what it is you want?"

"I don't see your eyes reddened in the least." She accused her, raising her head, her eyes looking at her with a fury she had never seen in her before.

Graglia frowned, "what do you mean?"

Alvia gritted her teeth, then moved swiftly toward Graglia, delivering a resounding slap to the queen.

"Halt!" One of the soldiers ordered. The two spearheads positioned a short distance from the Knight of Water's back. At such a threat Alvia made two daggers appear in her hands.

Their throats will be slit before they even begin their attack.

Graglia raised her hand, urging the soldiers to stop. She had to make a great effort not to bring her hand to her burning cheek. "I thank you for your protection, soldiers, but I am sure the Knight of Water is acting as my sister and does not intend to offend the queen or the queendom."

Alvia made her daggers disappear, nodding, "it's just big sister teaching a lesson to the stupid, selfish, self-centered sister who thinks she can do whatever she wants just because she sits her ass on the throne."

"Leave us alone," the queen ordered them, ignoring Alvia's accusations. The soldiers hesitated before lowering their weapons. Yet, a nod from the queen prompted them to offer the Aquo reverence and depart.

As they were left alone her furious eyes returned to Alvia. Rising to her feet, she pointed an accusatory finger at her sister. "If you ever touch me or speak to me like that again in front of my subjects, I swear by the Aqua Deus I will have you thrown from the Tower of Hymal and feed your remains to the pigs!" She threatened her angrily.

"Did you think I wouldn't notice?" Alvia reprimanded her, as if she hadn't heard her threats, "Vienne's little toes are cocked, exactly the same as Gelegen's!"

The queen raised her eyebrows in understanding. *So that's what it's all about.*

"You know perfectly well that as queen I have that right, I don't understand what all the indignation is about." She replied, certain that her sister, though silent on the matter, was well-acquainted with the Lege Rictum.

That law, known as *Legacy Law* in the common tongue, dictated that the priority of the queendom was to secure the birth of the next Lacrima. To this end, the queen had both the right and the duty to sleep with the men she deemed appropriate, so that she would be more likely to beget the next princess capable of invoking the powers of Crystaline. Such an imposition allowed the monarch to share a bed with whomever she pleased, regardless of whether the man was married, engaged or even willing.

"Bring the stupid crown back into this and I promise you, you won't have a head to hold it on!" Alvia's eyes watered, a sight her sister had only seen once before, when they were brats. "Of all the men in the queendom, you had to take the only one I loved, didn't you?" she said, between sobs.

"Oh, sister," Graglia continued, not before rolling her eyes, "it just happened. It's not my problem that you were more interested in your training than in his company." She reminded her. "In any case, that's water under the bridge."

"Water under the bridge, eh?" she repeated angrily, "Well, I hope it at least pains you to know that Vienne witnessed it all, not knowing that the one she was watching beheaded was none other than her father."

379

56. Royal Favor

They rode at a slow pace along the muddy road, surrounded by lush pink-fruited trees. They must be close to the place where they would meet the kings, hand over the sacred sword, and claim the Royal Favor.

"What a mundane place to gather." Hilzen complained. His horse snorted, as if backing up his words, "something tells me we won't be having a gratitude ceremony."

Noakh smiled at such a comment. They had followed King Lieri's instructions: to congregate in the middle of that road, right at the location of the only tree with a yellow crown and gray bark like ash. It was a discreet and remote place; it certainly did not seem the ideal location to be honored for recovering the sacred sword.

It made sense that the kings Lieri and Zarta chose such a secluded spot for their rendezvous. He had no doubt that if Tizai had been recovered by any citizen of Aere Tine that citizen would have been greeted with celebration and praise, thus becoming an illustrious figure about whom a thousand and one songs would be written. Yet, the kings of Aere Tine likely deemed it unacceptable for a Fireo like him to get credit for the dragon's defeat.

"Look, the golden-crowned tree." Halftal remarked, seated behind Dabayl on their shared steed.

They stopped. His horse Acorns flapped his ears, seemingly content with the idea of taking a break. Noakh turned to Dabayl. Her jaw was tense, she hadn't said a word since they had set off down that road.

Hold on a little longer, friend, thought Noakh, *it's time for you to find out the truth.*

They didn't wait long. Three horses approached from the opposite direction, trotting steadily. Surely, they were trying to look calm, despite the obvious urgency he had no doubt they would have in checking that they had indeed recovered the sword.

381

As they neared, he spotted King Lieri on one side. On the other stood a young woman with a half-crown, presumably Queen Zarta, positioned opposite her brother. The faces of both were very similar, even from a distance it could be seen that her pose seemed as haughty as that of her brother. It only remained to be seen who the third companion was, that dark-skinned man in white and gold who rode in the middle.

Noakh descended from his horse just as the monarchs and their companion stood before them. He could feel the eyes of those three inspecting him with more nervousness than their calm faces tried to pretend. King Lieri waved his hand.

"I am glad to see you all safe and sound. Before you stand Queen Zarta, the Master of Ceremonies of the Wind Council Zumdao, and yours truly." He introduced them.

The master of ceremonies gave a slight nod in greeting.

"Do you bring the sword?" said Queen Zarta, not being able to wait any longer.

"That's right," Noakh revealed to them.

Despite your damned army of soldiers and prisoners, he would have liked to add.

He then turned to Hilzen, nodding to him. The Aquo pulled Tizai from one of his horse's saddlebags, grasping it by the hilt and with the other hand by the blade as Noakh had previously instructed him to do. That way, the monarchs would be able to verify at a glance that the sword was pristine and avoid any startle.

Hilzen walked and stood beside Noakh, taking precisely the position they had rehearsed. He rested his right knee on the ground and extended both arms slightly upward, presenting the coveted Tizai.

The three Aertian representatives gazed at the sword, unable to hide their enthusiasm. Noakh could understand such rapture, aware that he would feel equally overwhelmed if someone returned Distra to him.

"Hand it over to us," Queen Zarta requested. From closer, Noakh perceived that her face was much sterner and coarser than her brother's. The monarch leaned forward on her horse and extended her arm.

The master of ceremonies frowned, "my dear queen, remember that we are to perform the procedure properly." He pleaded in a very clear and careful voice.

"Forgive our haste, Master," interceded King Lieri, addressing Zumdao, "surely you can understand our eagerness to retrieve the weapon that protects our people. However, that does not exempt us from having to adhere to due protocol." He turned to Noakh and his companions, "you have kept your word." He conceded to them, giving a slight bow of his head, then turned to the master of ceremonies again, "proceed."

Zumdao dismounted and approached Hilzen. The master of ceremonies advanced with both hands behind his back; the long, wide sleeves of his robes swaying in the wind. He stood in front of Hilzen and lightly raised hands full of pink jeweled rings.

"May I?" he requested, his affable face showing a cordial smile. His face exuded trustworthiness, but Noakh had learned to stay alert regardless of outward appearances.

Hilzen handed him the sword. The master of ceremonies inspected the blade closely, then the pommel.

"Looks like Tizai," he asserted, nodding toward the kings. Then he tilted his head, placing his right ear to the blunt part of the blade. "And it also emits its presence." He revealed, not hiding his joy, "I can assure you with utmost confidence that we have been presented with the true reaper of Aere Tine." He indicated, walking with the sword back towards both kings. On his way he cast a furtive glance towards Noakh's belt.

He has sensed Distra's presence as well, the young Fireo noticed.

It was Queen Zarta who quickly grabbed the sword. Then Zumdao returned, positioning himself in front of the four brave warriors who had recovered the precious sacred weapon.

"By the power vested in me by Queen Zarta, monarch of Aere Tine South, King Lieri, monarch of Aere Tine North, and as a representative of the Wind Council I congratulate you on your triumph. You accomplished what no other participant could.

Your triumph means everything to the nation which I faithfully serve and represent. That is why, in the presence of the kings, before the Lady of the Bell and Shiana herself, I declare you rightful claimants of the Royal Favor. We have no doubt that the Lady of the Bell will keep a special place in her boat for those who have helped her people so immeasurably," as he said these words, the master hesitated slightly, his eyes shifting from Noakh to Hilzen. He probably realized that his speech didn't quite fit the peculiar winners, but he continued, "as thanks for your immeasurable contribution to our people by retrieving the sacred sword, freeing Tizai from the merciless clutches of such a ferocious dragon, it is my honor to offer you your due retribution. May

383

our humble offering be able to repay the priceless act you have performed on behalf of the crown." He performed a bow, "well, what will be the Royal Favor you will decide to choose as your reward?" he concluded, clasping his hands together looking at Noakh.

The young Fireo turned around.

"Dabayl?"

She nodded. Taking several steps forward, she stood in front of the Master of Ceremonies.

"You can't bring my brother Loredan back to life, can you?" she finally said.

"I'm afraid not," the man smiled, trying to sound complacent, "of the many favors I am in a position to grant you, snatching someone from the embrace of death is not among them, I'm sorry."

Dabayl nodded, "then I will have to settle for this." The young woman raised her head, looking towards both kings, "my brother Loredan was a troubadour, he died under strange circumstances and we only received a letter signed with the royal seal telling us that he had passed away. I wish to know how my brother really died."

The kings stirred in their chairs.

They know, Noakh sensed, caught off guard. He had assumed that they should find out, that they would need to open some kind of investigation that would allow them to clarify what had happened to Dabayl's brother; but he was absolutely sure, the surprised looks of both kings made him not have the slightest doubt about it.

Zumdao nodded, "that is a request I can indeed grant you," he turned back to the kings, "perhaps my gracious monarchs will be able to offer an answer to your request and thereby grant this group of tenacious warriors their deserved Royal Favor?" he said affably.

"I have no idea who this Loredan is," King Lieri hastened. The latter made a fleeting glance towards his sister, who returned the gesture, visibly uncomfortable.

"Master of Ceremonies," interceded Noakh, "I know it's an unlikely scenario, but what would happen if they lied?"

"Oh, that is not possible," Zumdao replied with a snort, "the Royal Favor constitutes a request offered by the kings on behalf of Shiana herself, to fail in the request of one who has justly earned it would cause the Lady of the Bell to severely punish those who dared to fail to speak and act on her behalf."

"Why don't you ask for something else?" Lieri requested indignantly, "gold, land... why be so stupid as to anchor yourselves to the past and waste..."

"Brother," Queen Zarta stopped him. Once she controlled Lieri's temper, her gaze shifted to Dabayl, "I remember your brother Loredan and I know what his fate was. I killed him after hearing him perform the musical composition Lieri had sent me. It is the way my brother and I communicate; we send each other sheet music with a coded message, and end the lives of their interpreters so that the pattern hidden in them will not be discovered."

Dabayl opened her mouth, her gaze lost, her lower lip trembling. The living face of shock. Hilzen and Halftal were not far behind; their faces equally discomposed.

They are not lying; they are telling the truth. Noakh wanted to think that Queen Zarta was lying, that Loredan had not died from the mere sinister play of two siblings.

"Well, there you have it," King Lieri spoke, ending that awkward silence. "The confession you so desired, a splendid way to waste the Royal Favor if you ask me. And now, it is time to leave here, hurry, Zumdao, my sister and I have kingdoms to rule."

The master of ceremonies returned to his horse, until now he had been watching Dabayl, as if he was able to share her pain.

"They are leaving?" Hilzen spat indignantly. "They intend to leave just like that?"

"Wait." Noakh said before they turned around with their steeds. He glanced towards Dabayl, she was in complete shock, attended by Halftal, who was grabbing her arm to try to bring her back to her senses. "Aren't you even going to apologize for ending her brother's life?" He questioned, noticeably annoyed.

King Lieri gave a laugh, "are you so stupid as to think that my sister owes anything to a mere citizen of Aere Tine?"

Noakh had had enough.

"What I am is stupid enough to assure you that either you apologize right now, or I assure you that you will apologize once the edge of my sword is at your throat."

Queen Zarta was scandalized. "You dare threaten the kings of Aere Tine?"

Noakh nodded. He was going to wipe the irritating smirks of superiority off their faces. And he knew exactly how to do it.

"King Lieri, you said you did not believe I was capable of standing up to Burum Babar, I invite you to face me and witness with your eyes that it is true. In addition, Queen Zarta will be able to understand a hint of the pain that our friend Dabayl suffered when she learned of her brother's death."

"You are insolent, boy," said King Lieri with a scowl, "guards!"

"We agreed that you would come alone." Noakh reminded him.

"And what are you going to do about it?" Queen Zarta provoked him.

"Halftal?" Noakh merely said.

Halftal tilted her head slightly. "Two in the trees on the left, one in the back." She indicated, pointing to the locations of their hidden enemies.

Dabayl shot two arrows, Hilzen fired the remaining bolt. The birds ran in disarray at the uproar; the bodies of the soldiers infiltrating the trees fell to the ground, lifeless.

"You want a duel then?" indicated King Lieri as he saw his soldiers dejected, "you shall have it, there is nothing better than recovering our sword and being able to make use of its power to give a deserved lesson to a braggart. Follow me, let us go to a place where I can execute you without having to fear for these innocent trees."

* * *

They had moved a considerable distance away from the rest. Standing in a plain of green leaves and small plants with white-petaled flowers. In the distance, in an elevated area, stood their companions, who would witness who would emerge as the victor.

"I take it for granted that you are unfamiliar with Aertian-style duels." King Lieri began once they were in the middle of that plain. "Back to back, four steps in the opposite direction and let the combat begin." He instructed him.

Noakh nodded, tossing his cloak slightly to one side so he could walk better. They stood, back to back. King Lieri walked with his right hand glued to his leg, ready to draw weapons as quickly as possible.

"Let's get started." The monarch pointed out.

One, two, three steps.

King Lieri turned around prematurely, drew swiftly, launching a quick thrust that caught Noakh completely off guard, only giving him time to turn around.

386

The wind attack hit Noakh. He dropped his swords from the force of the blow and flew through the air, soaring into the skies relentlessly.

I knew it. That boy was nothing but a common fraud, Lieri thought with satisfaction as he watched with delight as Noakh flew through the air unchecked.

A smile of superiority flooded his face. It had been easy.

He turned back to where his audience stood. He bowed forward, performing a majestic and somewhat theatrical curtsy. It had been a brief but very intense performance.

It was time to revel in the various reactions of his audience. His sister offered a graceful applause from atop her horse, Zumdao remained oblivious to the fray, displaying the cordial neutrality one would expect from the representative of the Wind Council.

He had resorted to this technique with the sacred sword on previous occasions, which allowed him to anticipate what was going to happen: Noakh would continue to rise in the skies without being able to do anything to avoid it, then he would be slightly suspended in the air for an instant, a brief moment just before he began his inevitable descent. Then he would quickly plunge towards the ground, until his body would impact against the earth, leaving behind an explosion of brains, entrails and blood.

He had saved the best reactions for last, he turned, expecting to witness the broken faces of Noakh's companions, distraught faces filled with pain, anguish and weeping. He frowned. They didn't seem to show any of those emotions, they just kept looking up at the sky.

Deluded, he thought, the *harder the blow will be when you realize the harsh reality.*

By his calculations, Noakh must have been about to hit the ground and die on the spot. It was time to turn around and witness the final act of their combat.

He turned, a smirk of superiority on his face, one eyebrow raised.

Thud!

Noakh hit the ground hard.

Lieri's prediction had come true.

However, the monarch's smile had completely disappeared. Instead, his face had changed to one of utter stupefaction.

Noakh had landed on his feet, unscratched and ready to claim revenge.

* * *

His stomach burned from the hard impact he had suffered, he felt an irrepressible urge to put his hands to his belly, to lean forward to soothe, even slightly, the intense pain. But he was not going to give King Lieri such a pleasure. If it hadn't been for Dabayl's cloak and flying lessons, he would now be crushed to the ground like a mere insect.

He had to be alert; he did not know what power he was facing. His opponent had made a movement with his sword and that had been enough to be hit roughly by a current of air, an impact as hard as if he had received the onslaught of a battering ram in the stomach. And, most disconcerting of all, it had been an invisible attack. Wind with overwhelming power.

My turn.

He struck two blows with his middle finger to each of the citrines. The swords flew off the ground towards him, he grabbed them on the fly. Distra was engulfed in flames. Ready to do battle.

He made a lunge towards Lieri. The flames emanated from the blade heading towards his opponent, then he took advantage of the distraction to advance while his opponent was busy making the flames disappear with a swing of his sword.

Facing attacks I can't see, Noakh thought, weighing the difficulty of his situation.

He ran towards King Lieri, he wanted to fight him hand to hand. To feel the reflection of Distra's fire in his yellow pupils until that insolent smile of superiority was erased from his face.

It seemed that Lieri was not so willing to come face to face, he made several thrusts in his direction. Noakh tried to move out of the way, however, he felt the impacts before he moved. A cut on his cheeks, another on his thigh, two on his arm, his clothes cut and soaking with his own blood. That wind was harshly sharp. He sensed a slight difference from his initial attack, those fast-cutting attacks were slightly perceptible, as a slight whitish color probably due to the speed with which they were performed.

Blood from his wounds trickled down. Noakh realized something at that moment. *A sword guarded in a tower, a power divided between two kings and, worst of all, two brothers used to having others act for them.*

This realization led him to a conclusion. It was a mere hunch, but he had to test it, it was the perfect way to humiliate King Lieri. He extinguished Distra's fire and continued walking towards him, without

388

making any attack. He wanted to embarrass his opponent as much as it was in his power.

He simply walked in a straight line, presenting himself as an easy target. King Lieri launched an attack again from a distance.

This attack had no flash, Noakh noticed, just an instant before he was thrown backwards as if he had been rammed by an enraged wounk.

His swords came loose from his hands again, his whole torso ached, he felt the lack of air from the blow to his lungs. But it wasn't enough to stop him. He stood up again, dusted himself off and grabbed the swords in flight once more, resuming his march towards his opponent.

"Enough of this charade!" King Lieri complained, performing several thrusts in the air.

In an instant, cuts appeared on his legs, his hands, on his eyebrow. He felt the blood fall in abundance, as he felt the beating of his heart in each and every one of his wounds.

But Noakh kept walking.

"Why? Why won't you halt your advance?" Lieri said, making more cutting attacks.

The ground was soaked by his blood; a whole trail that announced the path he had traveled, he was already very close, so close that he could feel Lieri's fear. And, despite this, Noakh did not make the slightest pretense of attacking, he simply continued to advance.

His skin kept opening up, he felt his blood running down his torso, arms and legs, but that didn't stop him from continuing to walk, as if nothing had happened. As if those wind attacks were not enough to stop him.

"You say I'm a fraud..." Noakh managed to enunciate just before an onslaught of wind threw him violently to the ground again. His bones were aching, his common sense urging him to fight the hell out of it, but he ignored his impulses. He simply called his swords through his citrines and continued to approach King Lieri once more.

"Fall down already, you stupid fraud!" he shouted angrily, throwing thrusts as if he had been plunged into madness. King Lieri had lost control, his attacks lacking even the slightest uniformity, a desperate act of trying to get Noakh to fall to the ground dead once and for all.

The Fireo advanced; the slashing attacks making their way into his already severed flesh. Despite all the pain his wounds caused him, the tremendous stinging he felt in each and every limb of his body, the only thing he could feel was the absolute joy, the pure pleasure of witnessing how King Lieri watched in terror as he could do nothing to stop his march.

"Enough!" demanded King Lieri. This time his sword was not pointed at Noakh, but instead he launched three strikes towards where Hilzen and the others were standing.

Cowardly bastard, Noakh hastened to ignite Distra and launch a flame. He summoned all his power and let the flames sweep across the battlefield. With a quick flick of his wrist, he created a wall of fire, deflecting the wind attacks of King Lieri. His fire was so intense that his opponent's attacks simply caused a few flashes amidst the dancing flames.

"You wanted to see how I was able to stand up to Burum Babar." He said to King Lieri, who stood with his mouth hanging open after witnessing how he had stopped his attacks. "There you have it."

Noakh fixed his cold gaze on the now terrified monarch. The tip of the flaming Distra pointed now to where Queen Zarta and the Master of Ceremonies stood.

"No!" The king implored.

But Noakh had not had enough. Flames emanated from the tip of his sword, without his eyes straying one inch from the monarch's awestruck gaze.

King Lieri hastened to make a thrust. Then another and a third, trying to stop the advance of that flame. But his feeble wind attacks were mere nuisances in a voracious flame that advanced impassively toward its prey. Noakh did not need to avert his gaze to know that his fiery attack was about to consume his target, the terrified face of his pathetic rival was all he needed to see.

"Fine, I am sorry!" He shouted at the top of his lungs.

Noakh allowed himself a second more, enjoying with all his being the sweet taste of those words of clemency. Then he raised the tip of the sword, a gesture that caused the course of the flame to veer toward the heavens, where it continued its advance until it faded away.

It was not over. Noakh approached with his swords ready towards King Lieri. He attacked first with his steel weapon and then with Distra. His opponent parried, moving his sword to defend himself as best he could. Then he made a feint, then attacked hard with Distra. The blades of both sacred swords met at last, Noakh felt the frenzy of his weapon, eager to taste blood. With a flick of his wrist, he quickly disarmed Lieri. Tizai flew through the air until it landed humiliatingly on the ground, far from its bearer.

As he suspected, King Lieri was not overly skilled in close combat. Nor had he been able to summon all the powers of the wind sword. It made perfect sense, those two kings did not resort to their own deeds, but used others to do their dirty work. They had placed that sword at the top of a tower, where it had lain solitary. Untrained, unlearned to use it skillfully. They had been condemned by their own doctrine of life.

Noakh had no doubt that the lowly and cowardly attitude of those siblings was the reason why they had not been able to take full advantage of a weapon as lethal as Tizai seemed to be. A sacred weapon capable of attacking imperceptibly, it was certainly a power to be feared in the hands of a worthy wielder. Fortunately for him, fate decreed that Aere Tine's sacred sword would choose those two louts.

His opponent had given up, he had said he was sorry, but that fight had never been about asking for forgiveness. His only goal was to make Queen Zarta understand the pain of losing a brother. Noakh knew what his task was, he made his lunge, ready to deliver justice.

The edge of his steel sword went deep into the entrails of King Lieri, who only made a mute scream as he felt the weapon pierce his flesh.

Noakh then delivered a resounding kick to the monarch's face. A nasty *crack* announced that his nose had been broken. He placed his boot on the chest of the hitherto impertinent monarch, who now looked pathetic and weak. Noakh's fiery sword was positioned near King Lieri's neck as he turned into the distance and bowed his head, urging their audience to come closer.

As they headed towards them, Noakh fixed his gaze on the coward's eyes, in the pupils of which danced the flames of a sword eager to consume him in its intense fire.

"I think it has become quite clear which of us here is a fraud."

It was Queen Zarta who approached first. Her face looked troubled, with tears that had reddened her eyes.

"Please, don't kill him." She begged, her voice had lost its authority, she now sounded like a mere child making a prayer. "Take what you will, we will stop using bards as messengers, but, don't do anything to my brother, I beg you with all my heart."

"You decide, Dabayl." Noakh indicated, turning to his friend. The latter still looked clenched-jawed.

Dabayl remained thoughtful for a moment. As if considering whether it was worth getting her hands dirty for those despicable beings.

King Lieri and his sister Zarta were the living image that the gods did not always choose their representatives wisely.

"All right, let them go, Noakh." She decided contentedly. This time she looked different, proud, as if a huge weight had been lifted off her shoulders, as if she could finally be free.

Noakh withdrew the sword away from King Lieri's neck, proud of Dabayl's decision. The monarch got up as best he could, helped by his sister while an embarrassed Zumdao had rushed to pick up the sacred sword from the ground.

"You will allow us to leave Aere Tine without any trickery," Noakh demanded, "you will treat us like kings until we leave your domain. And you will issue an official report where you will explain to Dabayl's family the shameful reasons why you ended Loredan's life."

Kings Zarta and Lieri nodded like mere puppets. They had been defeated in their game, completely humiliated, proving to them that on their own they were not capable of achieving anything.

"Oh, could we arrange for a carriage as well?" proposed Hilzen.

57. Lacrima

She walked as if on a cloud, her happiness rendering her oblivious to her surroundings. Zyrah, aware of Vienne's happiness, rested her front paws on the princess's pants momentarily and then circled around her, trying to be part of her bliss while raising a tremendous cloud of sand.

Her mother had acknowledged to her that she had done a good job, and it had not been mere words. She had been able to feel that, for the first time since she had been conscious, the queen had spoken to her with genuine recognition and respect. It might seem silly, but to Vienne, that show of consideration meant the world.

I wish you had been there to see it, Gelegen, she thought wistfully. Had it not been for him, for the gentleness and thoughtfulness of his manner, she would surely not have been able to fight on.

There was someone who should hear such news. She waded into the waters, reaching into her trouser pocket, from where she pulled out the sapphire and slipped it into the water, resting it in the palm of her hand. Distracted for a moment, she contemplated the seagulls flying in the clear skies of the beautiful beach of Ghandya.

Without any expectation, she looked down. Suddenly, she gasped as she pulled the glowing bluish stone from the water. The sapphire was glowing! She hurried to place it to her ear to hear the message. She smiled, as the waves crashed on her legs. Noakh apologized for his delay in responding and blamed Hilzen for it, then told her about their journey, how they had gone into Aere Tine and little else... the voice coming from the sapphire had ended abruptly. Noakh probably did not know very well how communication through such stones worked, and had been telling her about his journey without knowing that she would never hear him. Imagining that scene made her chuckle, even though she regretted not having been able to hear the whole message.

Now it was her turn. She placed the stone back in the sea and, once it glowed, she brought it close to her lips. She told Noakh about the fall of Gelegen, about the victory against her sister, and her mistake, telling Wulkan about his existence, Noakh's, that he was after him. And she used the last moments to briefly remind him how a sapphire worked.

I hope that telling Wulkan that you are eager for revenge won't get you in trouble, Noakh, she wished.

Extracting the sapphire from the water, she headed toward the shore. There stood Otine, stroking Zyrah's belly, who was lying on the sand receiving cuddles with pleasure.

As Vienne approached, Otine performed the Aquo reverence, "you must come to your tent, Princess Vienne, you won't believe it."

"What happened?" she replied in fright, bringing her hand to the hilt of her sword, "are we under attack?"

Otine shook her head. "You'd better see for yourself." She added smiling.

They headed to the tents housing the key officials, each enclosed by a high palisade and vigilantly guarded at every corner. This time, Vienne had been assigned a large tent, situated right next to where the queen was staying.

The princess frowned. "What's going on?" She blurted out, unable to believe what she was witnessing. From that high ground she could see her tent and the surrounding tents perfectly. At the main entrance to the tents, there was a huge queue of soldiers that stretched to the horizon.

"They are awaiting the blessing of the Lacrima; they would all like to be in your presence and receive the sacred water of Crystaline before returning to the front again." Otine revealed to her.

Vienne approached, the soldiers were talking agitatedly, oblivious to the fact that the Lacrima was before them. One was complaining about the pain in his knee after having been hit by an arrow, two soldiers were trying to decide who had executed the most enemy soldiers. On the other hand, when her presence was perceived, there was absolute silence, and in an instant the word spread.

All the soldiers knelt almost in unison.

The princess swallowed hard, walking before the countless head-bowed and motionless soldiers. She stood at the front of the line, followed by Zyrah who sat next to her, arching her head uncomprehendingly as to what was going on. Otine took her place at her rear; her cousin Erin appeared from the line, placing herself next to Otine in order to protect the princess's back as well.

The first of the soldiers, a short-haired woman whose left side was badly burned, glanced up furtively.

"Come closer," Vienne instructed her. The princess did not quite know what she should do, much less what to say. However, after weighing it for a brief moment, she supposed that whatever act she performed would be well received by those who were willing to kneel in her presence.

The soldier approached her, then knelt and raised both hands to the level of her bowed head. Vienne understood and drew her sword. As she did, several heads rose, not wanting to miss the solemn act that was about to take place.

"Crystaline, grant me your power, please."

The soaked blade of her sword left the soldiers at the front of the line astonished and surprised as she displayed its power.

"Receive this gift from the Aqua Deus, so that its waters may protect you against your enemies." She recited; it was a speech she had probably heard in some church, which she had modified slightly for the occasion. "Here is your offering."

She flicked her wrist, allowing a drop from the tip of the sword to fall into the void and wet the soldier's palms. After this, the soldier stood up, looked at her with teary eyes and nodded mumbling a thank you that was never heard. She stepped back from the line, another soldier taking her place.

The princess performed the same act, over and over again. She was tired, both from resorting to the powers of the sword and from holding the weapon for so long, feeling her forearm stiffen tremendously. However, how could she stop this kind of ritual when there were still soldiers who hoped that this offering would protect them in the future battles in which they would take part?

She continued in her ritual, without rest. Despite the fatigue, the pain and the desire to sleep. None of those brave soldiers should be left without their offering, it would not be fair.

"I have been doubly blessed, the Dragon Slayer has also given me her blessing!" boasted one soldier, as he received not only the drop of water but also a lick from Zyrah.

Not so long ago, Vienne had thought it unthinkable that her presence would command the slightest respect. That afternoon, an entire army had gathered at her feet, watching with absolute devotion and fervor the young woman who had emerged from the seas; healing their wounds and driving back the enemy.

58. Legend

The grand carriage of immaculate white wood, pulled by majestic steeds as black as night stopped in front of the tavern. Bystanders on the bustling street watched with keen interest, eager to know which wealthy family was going to honor them with their presence. The door opened, and a young man with black hair and brown eyes quickly descended from it, followed by an Aquo, a unickey carrying a lute and an Aertian with very short hair.

"Here you are." The coachwoman said, putting her hand in her pocket and then handing Noakh twenty gold coins.

"Excellent, we will squander it in honor of King Lieri and his sister Queen Zarta."

The coachwoman was about to correct him on the impropriety of such a remark. However, before she could utter a word, Hilzen had put his arm around Noakh's neck, urging him to invite the entire tavern.

They sat at the forefront, enjoying the concert that a bard was giving in that tavern located near the borders of Aere Tine with Firia. The musician was singing a well-known ballad about a wandering mermaid, thus captivating almost all of his audience.

Noakh savored the tranquil moment, delighting in seeing his friends lost in the mesmerizing musical performance. He stopped his gaze on Dabayl, observing how his Aertian friend moved her lips unconsciously, as if she was singing the lyrics to herself. He smiled, it was the first time Dabayl was paying attention to the music, enjoying it. He took a gulp, satisfied that the wound in his friend's heart had finally healed as she had finally discovered the truth about her brother Loredan and repaid Queen Zarta in kind.

"It doesn't say that," Hilzen complained sulking at the inaccuracy of the lyrics, "we say she fell down the waterfall, not that she went down a river, that's stupid! Why would a mermaid swim down a river?"

Dabayl scoffed, "If an Aertian bard says it was by a river it was by a river. You seem to forget that most of the songs you have heard in your beloved queendom have been composed in Aere Tine, isn't it, Emisai?"

Halftal merely nodded, deeply amused by Hilzen's exalted indignation.

"Grimm Jala!" Dabayl toasted.

The four crystal glasses raised the sky, clinking in the center of the table.

"Grimm Jo Ne!" they celebrated in unison.

Then they both spread their fingers apart, allowing all those little glasses to plunge into their respective cups. In any other realm, such a group of people would have attracted all eyes and raised eyebrows. However, the Aertian inhabitants seemed quite indifferent to the fact that a group of people with such a variety of eye and hair colors were engaged in a busy celebration.

"How are you feeling, Noakh?" Hilzen asked him, jabbing him in the ribs with his elbow in a friendly manner. "It must be a most strange feeling for you."

It was true, he felt strange, he had defeated King Lieri. He had taught that pompous pedant a lesson he hoped he would never forget. And, if that wasn't enough, they could leave across the border to Firia without having to resort to any kind of ruse. Just walking along knowing that the Aertian troops would do nothing to stop them from leaving. They were going into Firia, the place where he was born, where he would finally face King Wulkan.

He noticed that Dabayl was deep in thought.

"What's the matter, Dabayl, are you sorry to leave your home again?"

She snapped back to reality, "uh, no, I was thinking precisely about leaving. And I think it's not a good idea to cross the border to Firia, no matter how much King Lieri promised us that his troops wouldn't arrest us."

Hilzen frowned, "But why not, for once things go easy on us..."

"Do you think King Lieri will not keep his word?" inquired Halftal.

"It's not going outside the Aertian borders where the problem lies, but rather entering the Fireo ones."

"Oh." Noakh said, understanding.

Hilzen and Halftal also seemed to equally get her point. They had heard the rumors. With the fall of the Tower of Concord the security of the realm had been heightened. There would be Aertian troops on the border with Firia, but that would not be a problem, as King Lieri would probably keep his word and allow them to pass without the slightest harm. However, one did not have to be an expert in military strategy to expect that likewise Wulkan would have answered in the same way.

"That bastard King Lieri," Noakh cursed, realizing the trap. Halftal frowned, not understanding what his discomfort was about. "Aere Tine's troops will allow us to cross to Firia without resistance, only to witness us being handed over to a Fireo army that will see no problem in skewering us with arrows."

Hilzen grimaced, pursing his lower lip and nodding in acknowledgment, "A smart move on King Lieri's part, indeed."

"But do we even have a choice?" Halftal pointed out.

"There is one," Dabayl revealed, her gaze distant on the horizon, "but you're not going to like it." She said turning slowly towards them. She even looked a little pale. "We can try to get to Firia through the Void."

Noakh's hair stood on end just thinking about it. Hilzen shook his head again and again.

"There has to be another alternative, entering into the Void..."

"Is it that you are afraid, Hilzen?"

"Of course I'm afraid!"

"Going through the Void sounds like a great option, Dabayl," Noakh said enthusiastically.

It certainly sounded like a route equally fraught with danger, not to mention the sinister legends that accompanied that secluded place, but the dwarf had informed him that to delve deeper into the mystery of the word *Akhulum* it must be in that place, and he wasn't about to turn his eyes elsewhere.

* * *

The night grew long. Dabayl had retired to her quarters to sleep, and Noakh, after having a bit more to drink, did the same. Only Hilzen and Halftal remained, enjoying the pleasant music filling the room, provided by a young woman with a braid of reddish hair so long it touched the floor, who played a harp emitting a melancholy sound.

"My daughter Lynea would have loved this tune," Hilzen said wistfully.

Halftal just smiled at him and grabbed his forearm, pleased that the charming music made him think of his loved ones. She just listened to

399

the song with great interest, she loved watching other musicians play, it was a source of inspiration as stimulating as it was exciting.

"All that remains now is to reach the Kingdom of Fire," said Hilzen resting his head on his arm while with his other hand he fiddled with the cup tracing circles with it on the damp wooden table.

"That's right, I didn't ask you, I'm sure you have a most exciting plan for Noakh to claim the throne." Said Halftal with curiosity.

Hilzen laughed, "Plan? Far from it. We're not much for making plans, but so far, we've been doing well... well, sort of." He replied, draining his drink.

"But if no one knows of Noakh's existence in Firia, how do you intend for him to claim the crown?" Halftal asked grimly, "with no one to support him, it will be especially difficult for the Fireo people to accept Noakh as king, no matter how much the sword has chosen him."

"I haven't really considered something like this," Hilzen replied with a shrug, "and I'd say Noakh even less so. After all, I don't think either of us thought this day would come."

Halftal shook her head. Noakh would not be known in Firia; he would appear as nothing more than a stranger attempting to usurp King Wulkan's throne, a monarch who, from what she had heard, enjoyed the affection and devotion of the Fireo people. How could the Fireos support someone they knew nothing about? They would scoff at hearing Noakh say that he was the rightful heir, even if he showed his fire of his sword, they would probably argue that it was some quibble?

"Emisai Lilac, is Emisai here?" A voice said.

Halftal and Hilzen turned, two soldiers in white uniforms stood in the doorway, scanning the tavern with their eyes. She raised her hand, confused, who could be looking for her?

One of the soldiers approached, the other stood in the doorway without moving an inch. The first handed her a document, the other hand near his sword.

"It's a message from the Cloister of Music." Halftal said with a frown. Then she read it cautiously under Hilzen's watchful eye. "I am informed that," she said aloud, with some difficulty, "after much consideration, they have decided to make an exception and allow my *Unfinished Ode* to be included in the Sempiternal Archive, the members of the Cloister stating that, despite the time that has elapsed since my performance, they have not yet managed to forget my song and look forward to learning how beautiful it will be once it is finished."

"But, that's fantastic!" celebrated Hilzen getting up to give Halftal a hug, however, he stopped midway when he saw that the latter was biting her lower lip. "Is something wrong, Halftal? You don't seem happy, does the message say anything else?"

Halftal shook her head, her eyes beginning to water, "I have never been happier, Hilzen."

"So?"

"If I allow the Cloister to archive my song, it will not be heard by the people without queen Zarta and king Lieri hearing it first, it may be months, even years before that happens if they want to save it for a special occasion. I can't do that. Every time I remember Noakh's face of disappointment when he found out that we had tricked him, that it had all been a ruse of Garland's to steal the emeralds... I don't want to see that face ever, Hilzen, I don't want to see him that sad ever."

"Why would Noakh be sad?"

"It is not the soldiers nor is it Wulkan who will ultimately be a problem for Noakh to take the throne, but the people. If they do not accept him as king, his crusade will have been in vain. However, all that would change if they knew the truth, if they were to be partakers of all that Noakh has been through, that he is the rightful heir to the Kingdom of Fire, the Ascendant Phoenix himself."

"But that's something we'll have to worry about later," Hilzen reassured her, "why worry now about something beyond our control?"

"*Music knows no walls, no cells, no borders.*" She recited, "So momoi used to tell me. Create a song that will win the appreciation of the people and you will have an army of minstrels at your feet eager to sing it to get their fair share of coin. "

"Won't that stop you from fulfilling your dream?" reminded Hilzen, seeming to understand, "according to what you said, only the Cloister can hear your song, you haven't even wanted to sing it to us privately."

"My dream wouldn't be possible if it wasn't thanks to Noakh, how selfish would it be if I didn't help him?"

"I don't know," Hilzen said contritely, "I'm sure when Noakh finds out he won't let you do it, I'm sure he'll say we'll find another way and..."

"I know," Halftal cut him off, "that's why you have to promise me you'll never tell him I gave up my dream for him."

"But..."

Halftal was not listening to him anymore. She began to walk towards the stage and climbed onto the weathered platform, as she had done on countless occasions. The tavern was packed, it was the perfect time to

401

sing a song. She lightly lightened her voice, her fingers placed firmly on the strings of her lute. This time she was not afraid.

The beautiful music pierced through the tavern's bustling noise, the promising chords made their way through the heated discussions bathed in alcohol, gradually silencing them. As Halftal intoned the first note with her prodigious voice, not a single customer dared to open their mouth.

It was a peculiar situation. All those present were immobile to the point that they did not seem to blink, as if something inside them was urging them not to miss an inch of the majestic piece of music they were having the honor of listening to.

Halftal looked straight ahead, not focusing on anyone in particular, a trick she had learned to avoid getting nervous when performing her music. In the beginning, she used to close her eyes; however, she had soon discovered that this method was risky, not only did it distance you from your audience by not having eye contact with them, it also prevented her from being alert in case her performance was met with some flying object that would serve as a form of unconstructive criticism.

Her melody continued, growing more epic, narrating an adventure accompanied by the most beautiful music ever composed. The faces of those present were a vivid reflection of their thoughts, they wanted to know more, to find out how the story continued.

This time, her performance was longer than the version she offered before the Cloister, narrating the adventures of its protagonist in Aertian territory, but again ending abruptly. A slight inclination of her head was enough to make the audience go from absolute silence to the most sickening clamor ever seen in that tavern. Coins began to rain down incessantly at her feet. Meanwhile, the musicians in the room eagerly approached Emisai, wanting to know more about her song.

That night the Unfinished Ode collected the largest number of coins ever witnessed in a tavern. The proprietor offered the performer room, food, and drink for life in exchange for her exclusive performances at his venue. Twenty-seven musicians rushed to learn the tune to be the first to play it in other establishments in the city, earning the distinction of being the first composition to be performed by the largest number of artists simultaneously. Fifteen other bards left for other cities, in the hope of being the first to play it in those places and thus obtain great benefit and applause. Forty patrons offered Emisai payment to learn how the song concluded, while another thirty offered her gold and jewels in exchange for revealing to them who the masterpiece was about.

That night, the legend about the young man wielding a fiery sword, journeying through the four kingdoms to reclaim what was rightfully his started to spread.

Fly, song; fly to the rhythm of the wind, make Noakh a legend.

- END OF BOOK 3 -

Thank you for reading the third book of The Sword's Choice series!

I hope you enjoyed *The Citrine Earthquake*, there is only one book left to conclude the series!

Now, it's time to **ask you a small favor**. I want to know what you thought of my story: if you liked it, if you didn't... if you recommend it.

Anything. So, **could you please write your review on Amazon?** It is very helpful to me, and I also love to know your opinions.

Leaving a review is very simple. You just have to search for my book on Amazon, go to where the customer reviews are and click on the *Write my review* button. If you have decided to leave your opinion, I truly appreciate it!

Also, if you want to be among the first to know when the next book in the series will be released, you can follow me on Amazon. Just look for the "Follow" button next to my author's name, and you'll be notified as soon as it's published.

Or, if you prefer, you can follow me on Instagram, TikTok, YouTube (@imredwrightauthor) or subscribe to the newsletter on my website (imredwright.com).

The Sword's Choice Characters

The world of Alomenta is a place full of characters, so here's a little reminder of people who have appeared in the story and have some relevance:

Aquadom – Queendom of Water

- **Aqua Deus:** Aquo deity that dwells at the bottom of the sea, where he will receive his faithful servants once they die.
- **Crystaline:** Sacred sword of the Queendom of Water. In possession of Vienne.
- **Vienne Dajalam:** Penultimate princess of the Queendom of Water according to birth, chosen by Crystaline as heir to the throne, thus making her the Lacrima.
- **Graglia Dajalam:** Queen of Aquadom and High Priestess of Water (therefore representative of the Congregation of the Church).
- **Aienne Dajalam:** Younger sister of the princesses, worker in the research workshop run by Lampen.
- **Katienne Dajalam:** Eldest sister of all the princesses, betrothed to Filier Delorange and supported by him and by the Congregation of the Church to assume the regency of the Queendom of Water.
- Other princesses of the Dajalam family: Lorienne, Candenne, Urulenne, Dalienne, Mimienne, Zurienne, Dambalarienne, Sendarienne, Pondarienne, Bolenne.

- Alvia Dajalam: Sister of Queen Graglia and Knight of Water. Known for her good sense of humor, lethality and impressive speed.
- Gelegen Hurehall: Veteran soldier known by many as The Fifth Knight of Water. He solves mysteries for the queendom, he accompanied Vienne on her journey to Tir Torrent and is the master of Zyrah.
- Zyrah: White Maltese dog (breed originating from Maltesia) already a little old but full of vitality, faithful to her master Gelegen and great friend of Princess Vienne.
- Hilzen: Devout Aquo who lost his wife and daughter. He decided to accompany Noakh on his journey under a blood debt.
- Marne: Hilzen's deceased wife.
- Lynea: Hilzen's deceased daughter.
- Dabayl: Also known as *Dabayl on the Spot* because of her impressive archery skills. A woman with blonde hair and yellow eyes, she hates music and wears provocative clothing. She met Noakh and Hilzen during the tournament in the city of Miere, where one of her arrows saved Noakh from certain death at the hands of Vileblood.
- Dleheim: Elder who helped Noakh and Hilzen. He gave a shield of the Criven de le Dos family to Hilzen, while to Noakh he gave a word of which he was to discover its meaning.
- Rivetien: One of the four guild leaders who ran the Golden Tower. He fled, enlisting the services of Noakh, Hilzen and Dabayl to escort him safely to the Kingdom of Earth. He perished in Tir Torrent as a result of the vile actions of the White Raven.
- Menest Casaniev: Leader of the Knights of Water.
- Gant: Knight of Water who was entrusted by the queen with the mission of capturing Rivetien, leading to his confrontation against Noakh in the Valley of the Fallen. After this combat he has burns on his face and chest.
- Tarkos: Knight of Water. It is said that he cut off his tongue to never contradict the queen. His face always hidden under a cloth, not much is known about him.

- **Filier Delorange:** Nobleman, heir to the powerful and wealthy House Delorange, betrothed to Katienne.
- **Dorniaseus (Dornias) Delorange:** Nobleman, ally of Aienne.
- **Porleas:** faithful steward of the Delorange family.
- **Gorigus Emsier:** Nobleman, ally of Aienne.
- **Laenise Naudine:** Noblewoman, ally of Aienne.
- **Arilai Rosswode:** Brown-eyed noblewoman, ally of Aienne. Also known as the noble unickey.
- **Erin Saboil:** Soldier of the Sea Guard, helmswoman, entrusted with the mission of sailing to the Tower of Concord.
- **Otine Saboil:** Soldier of the Sea Guard, navigator, entrusted with the mission of sailing to the Tower of Concord.
- **Lampen:** Research Counselor.
- **Galonais:** Defense Counselor, controls the three Guards (Sea, River and City Guards).
- **Meredian:** Tribute Counselor and Crown's Favourite after the Queen's departure to the front to fight against the Fireo army.
- **Ovilier:** Priest, oldest member of the Congregation of the Church. Katienne's ally.
- **Marune:** Member of the Congregation of the Church, she is missing an arm as a result of an incident with vulcanite, previously a member of the Divine Protection (elite soldiers of the church).
- **Stear:** Member of the Congregation of the Church.
- **Leeren:** Member of the Congregation of the Church.
- **Oben:** Son of the Church, entrusted with the mission to destroy the Tower of Concord.
- **Baise:** Son of the Church, entrusted with the mission of destroying the Tower of Concord.
- **Jerhen the Taisee:** Soldier of the Divine Protection. A taisee.
- **Ores:** Soldier of the Divine Protection.
- **Merrybelle:** Ship believed to be haunted due to the speed with which it ploughs the waters, used by Vienne to sail to Tir Torrent as quickly as possible.

- Finistia: Waterfall believed to end the world at the northern latitude.
- Dajalam: also known as the Lady of the Mountain, first in the dynasty of the royal family. She who received the gift of the Aqua Deus.

Tir Torrent – Kingdom of Earth

- Dai: Tirhan Deity, in common language this word would be translated as *God.*
- Modai Tir: Also known as Mother Earth, subdeity that protects with her mantle the Queendom of the Moon.
- Fodai Na: Also known as Father Nature, subdeity that protects with its mantle the Kingdom of the Sun.
- Maenawa: Sword with the power over nature. In possession of the Daikan Arbilla.
- Maetiwa: Sword with power over the earth. In possession of the Daikan Arbilla.
- Burum Babar: Daikan who succumbed to a disease that prevented him from controlling his body and caused him insufferable pain. Wise, noble and great king of Tir Torrent (Kingdom of the Sun). He died at the age of over three hundred years, at the hands of his granddaughter, after an epic confrontation against Noakh.
- Arbilla: Granddaughter of Burum Babar, current Daikan (Queendom of the Moon).
- Gurandel: Queen of dragons, locked in a cave and freed by Noakh after he cut off her tail.
- Laon: Protector of Daikan, loyal friend and defender of Arbilla. Belongs to the Bear caste.
- Halftal: Her nickname comes from *Half Talented,* being her real name Emisai Lilac.
- Garland: Leader of the Tirhan in charge of freeing the unickey in exchange for charging them what he considers a reasonable reward for doing so. Incredibly tongue-tied. Belongs to the Wolf caste.
- Gond Iphodel: Warrior of the Bear caste, Garland's henchman.

410

- Juray: Soldier in the service of the Daikan. Belonging to the Wolf caste.
- Mahesen The Grey Crow: Faithful advisor to the Daikan.
- Winay and Yunea: Unickey siblings proud flag bearers of the unickey army led by Noakh.
- Pothai: Potions that confer regenerative power and incredible abilities to those who consume them (incredible strength or superhuman speed), after a time of consumption they render the consumer immobile.
- Lakai Ma: Tirhan sacred tree, known as the Maker of Daikans.
- Forest of Mist: Mystical place that ends the world at the western latitude.

Firia - Kingdom of Fire

- Incandescent: Fireo deity imbued with eternal fire.
- Distra: Twin sword of fire, wielded with the right hand. During the reign of Wulkan it has always been used to perform the ritual when the sky is red. Currently in possession of Noakh.
- Sinistra: Twin sword of fire, wielded with the left hand. Possessed by Wulkan.
- Noakhail: Usually known as Noakh. Ascendant Phoenix, legitimate heir to the throne. His name has the meaning *No surrender*, composed of the word *Akhail* (Surrender in Fireo) and the negation in the common tongue *No*. He was chosen by the fire sword Distra when he was just a baby, raised in the Queendom of Water by the soldier Lumio, who taught him to fight and revealed to him his true identity once he was a teenager.
- Wulkan: King of the Fireos, Descendant Phoenix.
- Joher: Wise advisor to King Wulkan.
- Minkert: Wulkan's grandson, knowledgeable of all his grandfather's plots, physically very similar to his grandfather.
- Lumio: Noakhail's stepfather. Soldier in Firia's service who saved Noakh from certain death during the ritual. He fled to Aquadom taking Distra and the baby with him to ensure that

411

the Ascendant Phoenix would live, leaving his wife and daughters behind.

- Flarelle: Lumio's wife.
- Cosmille: Lumio's eldest daughter.
- Aenze: Lumio's little daughter.

Aere Tine – Kingdom of Air.

- Shiana: Deity of the Kingdom of Air, this word would be translated into the common language as *She*, since really very few are able to hear in the wind the true name of their goddess.
- The Lady of the Bell: Subdeity in charge of guiding the Aertian dead to reach a place filled with music.
- Tizai: Sacred Aertian sword.
- Zarta: Queen of Aere Tine South.
- Lieri: King of Aere Tine North.
- Tower of Concord: Sacred place that symbolized the union of the two Aertian kingdoms (north and south), at its highest point was levitating the sword Tizai. Destroyed by one of the Sons of the Church.
- Wind council: Entity in charge of overseeing all matters related to divine decisions within Aertian lands.
- Cloister of Music: Organization in charge of watching over the music, responsible for choosing which songs are worthy of being listened to by kings and queens and also preserving them for eternity.

This adventure still has a lot to say, how will the story end? Find it out in...

Want to be notified when it's published so you can read it as soon as possible? Then subscribe to the newsletter on my website (imredwright.com) and follow me on Instagram (imredwrightauthor) so you won't miss any news about my books.

Made in the USA
Las Vegas, NV
11 January 2024

84209638R00246